"A deftly woven tale, *Darkness Calls the Tiger* examines the China-Burma-India theater of WWII. While Tromp doesn't shy away from the grit of war, she focuses on the light that can be found—even in the darkest spaces. With lyrical prose and vivid settings, this story delivers a poignant view of Asia while emphasizing the value of home."

—Julie Cantrell, *New York Times* and *USA Today* best-selling author of *Perennials*

"An important and unique new addition to the body of WWII novels set in the underrepresented reaches of the Pacific theater. Evocative and transportive, filled with nuance and spiked with the violence of war, *Darkness Calls the Tiger* is a story of redemption in the midst of hope-lessness."

—Tosca Lee, *New York Times* best-selling author

"Janyre Tromp stuns in this new release that highlights the long-forgotten region of Burma during the Second World War. Readers will be well re-warded for pushing this chilling, heart-aching tale to the top of their TBR pile. And may we never forget the sacrifices made on the Pacific front of this bitter period in the history of mankind."

—Jaime Jo Wright, author of Christy Award–winning novel *The House on Foster Hill* and best-selling novel *The Lost Boys of Barlowe Theater*

"It's rare for a novel to so capture me from the very first page and keep me riveted all throughout. Janyre Tromp's *Darkness Calls the Tiger* is such a story. Intense, passionate, and heartrending, Tromp's is a retell-ing of a little-known piece of history. The reader will be changed after experiencing this story."

—Susie Finkbeiner, best-selling author of *The All-American*

DARKNESS CALLS THE

TIGER

A NOVEL OF WORLD WAR II BURMA

JANYRE TROMP

KREGEL
PUBLICATIONS

Darkness Calls the Tiger: A Novel of World War II Burma
© 2024 by Janyre Tromp

Published by Kregel Publications, a division of Kregel Inc., 2450 Oak Industrial Dr. NE, Grand Rapids, MI 49505. www.kregel.com.

Published in association with William K. Jensen Literary Agency, 119 Bampton Court, Eugene, OR 97404.

The persons and events portrayed in this work are the creations of the author, and any resemblance to persons living or dead is purely coincidental.

"Amazing Grace" and "It Is Well with My Soul" are public domain.

Scripture quotations are from the King James Version.

Cover design by Faceout Studio, Jeff Miller.

The map on page 6 is the author's own creation.

Library of Congress Cataloging-in-Publication Data
Name: Tromp, Janyre, author.
Title: Darkness calls the tiger: a novel of World War II Burma / Janyre Tromp.
Description: First edition. | Grand Rapids, MI: Kregel Publications, 2024.
Identifiers: LCCN 2023048507 (print) | LCCN 2023048508 (ebook)
Subjects: LCGFT: Christian fiction. | Novels.
Classification: LCC PS3620.R668 D37 2024 (print) | LCC PS3620.R668 (ebook) | DDC 813/.6—dc23/eng/20231025
LC record available at https://lccn.loc.gov/2023048507
LC ebook record available at https://lccn.loc.gov/2023048508

ISBN 978-0-8254-4850-8, print
ISBN 978-0-8254-7165-0, epub
ISBN 978-0-8254-7164-3, Kindle

Printed in the United States of America
24 25 26 27 28 29 30 31 32 33 / 5 4 3 2 1

To my beloved girl,
you are the very definition of strong and courageous.
I am in awe of you. May you choose to continue to trust and,
in doing so, find the peace no one can take from you.

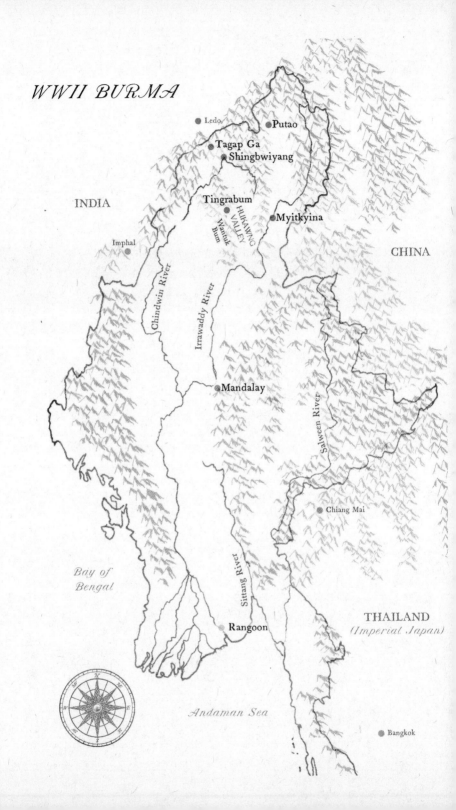

PART ONE

Now I lay me down to sleep,
I pray the Lord my soul to keep;
If I should die before I wake,
I pray the Lord my soul to take.
—TRADITIONAL CHILDREN'S PRAYER

Chapter One

1933
The Village of Tingrabum
Kachin State, in the Himalayas of North Burma

THE BEATING OF ANCESTRAL DRUMS throbbed across the mountain, tangling with the rhythm of my thudding heart. Faster and faster, the pounding echoed between the jungle and the solid peak of Nojie Bum, reaching for freedom in the heavens only to collapse in on itself in a helpless chaos.

Despite the roaring fire in front of me, my bare toes were stiff with cold. My back ached from sitting tall on a log—I would rather have squatted with the other girls and joined in their whispers and camaraderie. But that would have been nearly impossible in the American skirt Mama insisted I wear to my ninth spring festival.

My days spent playing in the jungle had slipped through my fingers and trickled into the past. Already Papa expected me to read and write in both English and Latin. And Mama, despite the fact she couldn't even speak Latin, agreed.

Why I must look and act like an American was beyond me. I would never leave my mountain—the place that held me safe like Aunt Nang Lu's arms.

I studied Mama, sitting next to me ramrod straight like a mountain queen, despite her belly full with another baby.

Across the fire a neighbor woman stared at me. Baw Ni's mouth was coerced into a perpetual sneer by a ropy scar, and I swore it moved in silent incantation. Shivering, I wondered what curse she was calling down on me today.

Another animal scream ripped through the jungle, and an answering gasp slipped from my lips.

The *jaiwa* swiveled toward me, as if my movement had called his attention. Fresh blood trailed down the wrinkled face of the traveling storyteller, and I cringed into Mama's side. The black-and-white striped feathers of the old man's headdress lifted, fluttering in the breeze—a bird frantic to escape a snare. Throwing his head back, the jaiwa cackled at the starless sky.

I traced my knuckles with a finger, concentrating on the steady motion.

The stench of burned flesh and hide shrouded me, and I swallowed the sting of dinner rising in my throat. I wished we could simply dance and listen to the stories of Aunt Nang Lu's people without witnessing an angry old man burn food in sacrifice to the *nats*.

Papa sat on the distant side of the circle, just inside the ring of light. His white skin glowed against the darker sea of the others I considered family. He saw me and tilted his head in question.

I smiled, knowing the answer. *The nats have no power here.*

I started to tuck a strand of dark hair behind an ear but dropped my hand. Mama ignored my squirms and watched the jaiwa in stony silence. But Papa's shoulders were relaxed, sympathy for the storyteller playing on the edges of a small smile. Squaring my shoulders, I watched the drummers play, their wild beating trembling in the flickering firelight.

With one last thud, the drums stopped, and the jaiwa lifted his hands. Aided by the flames, his shadow danced across the village path, alive in its own right.

"Ah." The jaiwa leered at me. "The tiger-eyed one. A story, perhaps for you, Moran Kai?" The points of his yellow teeth shimmered in the firelight.

"It is okay, little tiger. He cannot hurt you." Mama's hand gripped my fingers, but though a smile hovered on her lips, her fingers shook against mine. The jaiwa was no friend of the foreign missionaries or their daughter.

A vicious snicker gurgled low in his throat, and he swayed on his feet.

A log cracked, falling from the fiery heap in front of me, sacrificed to the huge appetite of the fire. Sparks leaped in celebration of their victory. My mother's adopted sister, Nang Lu, hunkered next to me on the log. Another woman to defy the jaiwa. Mimicking my *amoi*, I fixed my stare on the fire, chin lifted. I would not allow my courage to flee with the setting sun.

The jaiwa frowned at Aunt Nang Lu and wheeled to his audience, gathered from the surrounding villages.

"The legend of the *sharaw*." His nasally voice penetrated to the edges of the village. The story of the tiger-people. I clenched my fists as the crowd shifted, no doubt watching my amber eyes glow in the firelight. Let them be afraid, then. I summoned anger and lifted my chin higher.

The jaiwa flung his hands out into the darkness, his lilting words summoning the imagination of the people.

"In the darkest night of the jungle,
    When the sun turns his back and swallows the moon,
    When the sky collapses and the great mountain gasps in
        terror,
    Sharaw—the tiger—will come.

"She is tiger's youngest sister, born of fire,
    Birthed of midnight and brilliant flame.
    Man and beast bound together,
    Darkness and Light tormented forever.

"Screaming silence on footed paws she stalks,
    Anger and fear twisted, prowling revenge for our people.

Slashing through the jungle she roars for justice;
Destruction seethes behind her.

"Consuming herself, she rages;
Ashes cover the jungle, clinging, choking, dying.
When there is no more,
Broken and alone she collapses.

"And there is no more.
No more."

As the last echo ran into the jungle, the jaiwa glared at me, daring me to challenge his prediction. That, somehow, I would become the twisted beast of darkness.

The circle of girls stared at me, leaning away, as if I might slash out at them. Mama stood, bowing to Papa and the leaders of the gathered villages.

"Thank you for the entertaining story. We bid you good night." Mama's fingers tightened on mine as we strode to the mission *basha*, my home.

She swung my arm back and forth, and I wished Papa were on the other side, the two together lifting my whole body between them—my toes reaching to the starlit sky, our happy chatter erasing the images in my mind. But Papa had stayed, smiling at me as we left. He stayed so they would know we were not afraid.

≈

Inside my room, fingers of light from the main fire pit reached my woven bamboo pallet.

Mama groaned as she leaned over me, her hand pressing into her belly, before kissing my forehead.

"My little tiger, do not listen to that old man or Baw Ni. They cling to the old ways and fear the coming of a new, more true, more powerful way. The sharaw is merely a dream, a flimsy shadow vulnerable to the light of the moon."

She held her red prayer bag against her as if she were pressing her prayer for me into it. "Sleep well." She turned and shut my door. I squeezed my eyes closed against the darkness and the murmuring of the village.

There is nothing there. Sharaw is not real.

No matter how many times I repeated Mama's words, my belly still twisted.

That night I knew the tiger would visit my dreams and repeat the whispers of the villagers, luring me into the fire, where I would join with him and become a strange blend between a tiger and a human—a sharaw.

I tucked my knees in.

"There is no darkness in me. I am a worshiper of *Karai Kasang.* The supreme God will protect me. You have no power over me. No power over me."

Heat flicked across my back, flames licking at my heels. A taste of my foretold future as destruction seethed behind me, consuming both me and my jungle.

A scream ripped through the basha, and I bolted upright, the fibers of the woven bamboo floor digging into my clenched fingers. The sting of my cry lingered in my throat, the echo of laughter ringing in my ears.

When no one raced to my aid, I knew the others were still at the celebration, and the sounds of joy were theirs. I prayed no one had heard me. Baw Ni would hold up my fears as proof that Papa's God wasn't real.

I stole out the door and down the ladder. Papa would know how to destroy the fear creeping inside of me.

At the center of the village, the shadows of my adopted family bent and flickered. Papa sat at the edge of the circle, talking to Mama, his body leaning into hers. I paced toward them, but then the dark silhouette of the jaiwa danced between us, the shape of hands becoming jaws, swallowing. I shrank away. Perhaps I would be safer at the basha.

My stomach complained, and I rubbed my middle. The only food in the house was hard beans soaking in the cooking room. But a few days ago I had found a handful of red berries on the mountain. Perhaps more had ripened since.

During the day, the jungle was as much my home as the village, but at night . . . I faltered, thinking of the bears, the snakes, the tigers.

My cramping stomach made my decision. Surely my mountain, Nojie Bum, would protect me. I clambered up the ladder and snatched the cooking room lantern along with the bow and arrow Papa had made me and then trotted into the waiting arms of the mountain.

On the far side of the rice paddy field, the darkness embraced me. With the feeble beam barely lighting my feet, I followed the path more from memory than actual sight until the towering mass of elephant grass gave way to an enormous rock overlooking the village—my sanctuary.

Tiny people wavered in the light of the bonfire. But distance swallowed the sound of the celebration so that all I heard were the gentle chirps that formed the language of the jungle.

My bare feet slid silently across tiny rocks, my legs brushing against fingerlike ferns. The maple tree towered ahead, and the berry bushes should be off to the right—above a little opening in the jungle.

A snuffing came from my left.

I stopped, my fingers tripping across the bow strapped to my chest. It sounded almost like a muntjac deer barking. Almost.

I lifted the lantern, willing the light to cast farther into the darkness.

The jungle went quiet, and I eased back, searching for the disturbance. A twig snapped, and I spun.

The lines of trees shifted, and a scream ripped through my throat. I dropped my lantern and flung myself into the nearest tree, scrambling into the limbs. Light from my lantern flickered at the base of the tree.

Sharaw is not real.

The huffing again. Closer this time. Amber eyes reflected the shifting flames—a hunter come for me.

I unslung the bow, my fingers shaking as I nocked an arrow, the tip soaked in the poison from the *upas* tree. My only hope against a tiger.

A shape stalked in the jungle undergrowth, and I released the arrow. *Please run true.*

The animal roared with rage and stumbled into the light—the rippling of orange and black stripes stealing the last bit of hope from my heart. It was the largest tiger I had ever seen.

My tiny arrow stuck out from his shoulder and bounced with his loose-limbed march around my tree.

My arrows would never be enough. Even Papa's rifle might not be enough.

I huddled in the protection of the leaves, biting my lip. *Be one with the leaves. One with the leaves.*

He snuffled at the lantern and knocked it over with his paw. The glass shattered, and the flame sputtered before catching in the grasses.

A shout came from the village. Papa. Lantern light sped up the mountain.

Papa. Please hurry.

But the hope rising inside me fell when the tiger lifted his head and leaped into my tree. The enormous trunk shivered with the impact, the ancient rigid strength no match for the tiger.

A limb the size of my arm poked the tiger, and he lashed out, his jaws snapping the branch like a twig. He lifted his head, grinning at me, enjoying the chase. A warm wetness spread from between my legs, and I whimpered.

His roar snatching my mind back, I released another arrow. The creature shrieked as the arrowhead pierced his eye. A huge paw slashed at the tree, nearly dislodging me from my perch. I matched the creature's scream and scrambled to a higher limb.

Please, Karai Kasang. Please.

The tiger shook himself and climbed higher, its claws shredding the flesh of the tree. It groaned under his slowing attack.

I fumbled for another arrow, my quiver tipping, the arrows raining useless to the ground, consumed in the growing fire below.

A sob strangled me, and I eased higher, the branch bending hard against my weight. I launched my bow at the creature, and the tiger's growl vibrated through the tree and into my very bones.

A cry rose from the village, the lights weaving up the path.

They would not make it in time.

"Papa!" My voice cracked under the strength of my fear.

The tiger was so close, I could smell the dead sourness of his breath, see the roundness of his remaining amber eye as it rolled, trying to focus.

Hurry, Papa.

Papa would not fail. Could not fail. I scooted backward along the branch, my legs wrapped under me, whimpering, heaving air in snatches, trying not to look at the tiger but knowing he would attack if I glanced away.

Lights bounced at the base of the hill, shouts echoing around the clearing. The tiger swung his head back and slipped, cracking its lower jaw on the branch. I clung to the limb as the tiger shook his head, slid, fell, crashing to the ground, the poison finally working its deadly task.

Papa burst into the clearing, clutching a lantern in one hand and a shotgun in the other. "Kailyn?" The light landed on the tiger. "Dear Lord. Kailyn."

≈

Somehow the villagers smothered the fire licking the dry grasses, and Papa eased my hands, legs, body off the branch, tucking me in his arms. His heart beat slow and steady against my cheek, not quite drowning out the whispers of the villagers.

Over Papa's shoulder, I watched a group dragging the dead tiger down the mountain. They would skin it and give me the pelt—a reminder of conquering the beast. Of defeating the king of the jungle—a tiger.

Papa sat me in front of our home's chief fire pit, a blanket over my shoulders. Mama set a bowl of water in front of me and wiped away the tiny streams of blood covering my body. I stared at my reflection in the bowl, my teardrops battering the water's surface. Everyone knew the only animal who could face a tiger and survive was another tiger.

I touched the surface of the water, shattering my image.

Mama had promised there was no truth in the legend of the sharaw. But I'd stood against the tiger and won.

Perhaps the jaiwa had been right. I shivered under the heavy blanket.

"You are safe, little tiger," Mama whispered into my hair. "There is no great darkness in you or this world."

I laid my ear against Mama's giant belly, her dark hair tangling in my own. Her stomach tightened, and Mama groaned, bending against the obvious pain.

It had been the first and last time Mama was wrong.

Chapter Two

February 1942
Tingrabum

I SAT HUNCHED IN THE shade of the enormous teak tree at the edge of the village. The sun stretched high, the sky as blank as the slate on my knees. It was the beginning of dry season, and the air trembled from the heat. The spicy scent of Aunt Nang Lu's curry simmering next door mixed with the heavy aroma of the jungle plants. There was no better smell.

Down the mountain, the boys played some sort of game with the new missionary, Ryan McDonough. They hit a knot of fabric with a stick and ran in circles, shouting to one another as the others ran to catch the knot.

The tall, narrow basket behind my back pressed on my shoulders and reminded me of my duties. A woman's basket was unbearably ungainly in the forest. But I dared not take it off and lose anything in it, least of all my books.

Little Tu Lum caught the makeshift ball, and Ryan's loud American guffaw burst across the forest. All the boys called to Tu Lum, patting him on the back—all but Baw Gun. He threw the stick on the ground and stalked into the jungle.

Far older than the others at the school, Baw Gun might even have surpassed my own eighteen years. Old enough to take a wife and be responsible for his own home instead of playing with schoolboys. But that was Baw Gun. Never one to do as he should. Rumor said he planned to join the Burmese army in the south—trading his heritage for money. Though his mother, Baw Ni, and most of the villagers would be upset, his leaving would be no true loss.

Ryan clapped, signaling the end of the game. The students jumped and ran to the open-sided porch of the mission school, no doubt expecting harsh words and perhaps the sting of a switch if they dawdled. Papa had trained the students well. Ducking under the thatched roof that hung like the long hair of a wild dog, Ryan chuckled, the gentle sound floating into the sudden silence. He never carried a switch.

I dragged my attention back to the Latin book I'd abandoned in the dust and sighed. Latin held no appeal, despite Papa's vigorous determination to convince me otherwise. I traced the thin scabs beaten into the soft palms of my hands, a reminder of how much he had changed since Mama had left us for Karai Kasang.

Papa would ask Ryan if I had done my work, and the new missionary would never lie, even for me, even when my schooling seemed pointless. Who needed Latin to either keep my father's house or be sent to America to marry and do the same for some stranger? Not a single other girl in the village had been subjected to school.

Still, Ryan would test me this afternoon, but as the boys quieted for more learning, I doodled sketches of monkeys and leaves instead of conjugating verbs. Latin was nearly as useless as I was.

At some point Papa would tire of thrashing me and fulfill his threat to send me to my grandparents in America.

And Mama wasn't here to stop him.

I ran my thumb over Mama's woven red pouch hanging from my neck. It bulged with the secret of a white stone from the river. Fear roiled in my belly, and I rubbed the stone again, pushing my fear into its surface.

Please, Karai Kasang. Don't let Papa send me away. Don't make me leave home.

The John Moran who had snuggled his daughter after a tiger attack had died with Mama, burned in her funeral pyre. I knew only the papa who raged with the angry, powerful God throwing sinners into the pit of hell's fire. I had memorized the verses saying Karai Kasang loved me, but it was Papa's angry eyes I saw when I imagined God on heaven's throne.

The rock in my hand warmed, but no answering rumble from heaven interrupted the chirping jungle insects. No sign that Karai Kasang listened or cared at all. I dropped the rock into the pouch around my neck and wiped the sketch of a tree monkey from my slate. I needed to concentrate, prove to Papa I was helpful to the mission, that maybe I could put my schooling to work and teach.

From the school, Ryan's instructions rose and fell, stumbling over Kachin phrases and teetering on the edge of horrific offense.

The missionary had been here since the beginning of last rainy season, almost a year, but he was still a bumbling bear in a tiger's lair. Papa said Ryan would never learn, never be able to run the mission if we kept intervening when he failed. But somehow the man with a sloppy grin had won everyone's goodwill. Something I could not seem to do.

The boys bent over their work, and Ryan peered into the jungle before trotting to the village center, little Tu Lum shadowing the missionary. Dust from the road puffed from under Ryan's feet and coated his trousers.

I sighed, flipped the worn pages of my Latin book to the assigned page, and wrote the first verb on my slate, reciting the conjugations under my breath.

A movement caught my eye just before Baw Gun stepped into the path on the opposite side of the village from the mission. His dark skin, the color of polished teak, smoothed across high cheekbones. He studied the school, scowling, watching Ryan. The muscles in his arms flexed, straining against his dirt-streaked shirt. A magnificent jaguar prowling.

Baw Gun slipped into the nearest basha and came out moments later, arms loaded with a basket, obviously heavy—likely with things that did not belong to him.

I swallowed, shrinking behind the edges of a palm leaf. Time to disappear. I'd finish my Latin later.

A shout made Baw Gun turn.

Little Tu Lum shot out from under a nearby palm tree. "I saw you take that food. Put it back!"

Baw Gun sneered and pounced on Tu Lum, twisting his skinny arm. "Or what, little mongrel? Who would believe an abandoned pup over me?"

My fingers tightened around my slate. *How dare he?*

I jumped to my feet but then hesitated. Ryan might believe Tu Lum and me. Even Papa might. But the villagers? We both were, at best, inconveniences for them. At worst, the epitome of bad luck.

How I wished I had my bow or at least the long *dah* knife Papa made me leave at the mission. I would make Baw Gun do as he ought. But then Papa would lose face. I shifted. *What would Papa want me to do?*

Tu Lum's yelp propelled me forward, a heavy stone in my hand. The boy's wide eyes flitted to mine, pleading with me. Whirling, Baw Gun followed Tu Lum's glance. Baw Gun licked his lips and shoved Tu Lum away.

Baw Gun's face lit in a wicked smirk.

A blush creeped up my neck as I realized I was alone and had drawn attention to myself, inviting a man to notice me. Baw Gun of all people. This was why Papa never allowed me in school with the boys. I spun and scurried toward my hiding spot.

When a dark hand seized my shoulder, I jumped, the rock slipping from my fingers, upsetting my basket before thumping to the dirt.

Baw Gun's body filled my vision. I was trapped between the post of the house and my tormentor. Baw Gun had hunted me for as long as I remembered. His fists were the ones that had given me my first black eye, and his words, joined with his mother's, that led the others in their whispers—tiger-woman, forever cursed.

"Moran Kai. A beautiful tiger lily should never be left to wilt on her own."

My knees shook as his calloused fingers traced my cheek and trailed down my neck. I had no weapons. No one to protect me.

I should run, but my feet had grown roots and my lungs refused to scream.

Baw Gun set down the basket, his grin growing, and yanked me into his chest, trapping my arms.

"Ryan sent me to find you," Tu Lum squeaked.

"Let him come." Baw Gun's whisper, reeking of fish, crept across the hair on my neck. "I will taste the flower before I leave, and what will the fool do about it?"

My shudder drew a low bark.

"You will learn to like it . . . eventually."

When his lips touched my neck, fear surged through my body, and I rammed a knee into his groin. Baw Gun folded across his injury, but his grip tightened. As he struggled to regain his breath, his dark eyes hardened. His nose flared—the panther, angry now, gathered to attack.

Pain burst across my cheek before I even realized he had struck. Again and again, his fists blurring in their attack. I raised my free hand to protect myself and wrenched around, my shoulder protesting, my ears ringing, my tears frozen in shock.

"I am glad you found Kailyn for me." Ryan's voice—low, hard, and unarguably in charge—stopped the barrage.

But Baw Gun still trapped my trembling arm behind me, shoving me between himself and the missionary.

"She needs to run an errand for me." Ryan towered over Baw Gun and fingered the wickedly sharp dah strapped across his chest.

Would Baw Gun attack the bear of a missionary?

I stiffened as Baw Gun leaned into my back. "You will pay for interfering. You and that mongrel boy."

What had I done?

"Do not fear." Baw Gun spun me, his hand tracing my flat chest, narrow hips, and back up my chalk-dusted fingers and scrawny arm. "No one wants a pale-faced tiger-girl. You are almost beautiful . . . almost." He shoved me backward.

I tripped over my basket, sprawling in the dirt, the wide skirt tangling in my legs. The basket spun, scattering dust, wobbling, stopping in the grass.

My cheeks burned in shame, and tears flowed down my battered face as I shoved my belongings into the basket, crushing the cascade of yellow *paduak* blossoms I had gathered, and then skittered into the jungle. Ryan called to me as he stumbled on the path behind me, but I clambered into a tree and disappeared into the embrace of my jungle.

≈

All afternoon Ryan forced himself to concentrate on the boys—encouraging them, allowing them to explore and learn, while still keeping some semblance of order. But he struggled to concentrate. Kai had run into the jungle again. He couldn't blame her.

John wouldn't let her anywhere near the school while the boys were there. But it was a waste not to have her teaching. Capable female teachers had taught in the States for years. Why not at Kachin schools?

Tu Lum's squeals of delight broke through the general noise as one of the other boys dove to make a spectacular catch in the outfield. Ryan clapped and joined in the cheering, calling the teams in for another lesson. Tu Lum grinned and raced to Ryan. The dah hanging across his small chest clattered against a wooden toy gun slung over one shoulder and the hunting knife hanging from his belt. The boy reminded him of a miniature bandit from the dime novels back home—smooth, broad face, and dark straight hair. But the boy was more mischief-maker than marauder, unlike some of the other village boys.

Ryan scanned behind him, wondering if Baw Gun was plotting his revenge. Maybe Kailyn would be better off in America. At least there she wouldn't have the threat of being carried off and made a "wife" without ceremony or permission. He shook the thought from his head. There wasn't anywhere truly safe. He knew that better than most.

The day raced past in a blur of recitations and chatter until Nojie Bum's peak was half covered in the coming night.

Ryan's entire body ached as he wandered up the path to the mission, his mouth watering at the smell of curry wafting from the village. He was nearly home when Tu Lum raced around a corner.

"Have you seen Kai?"

Ryan glanced to the darkening jungle. "She's not home?"

Tu Lum peered over his shoulder, as if hoping she'd materialize on the path. "The Jungle Light is waiting for his dinner."

And John didn't like waiting for anything. "Ask Nang Lu to bring dinner, then you search on her sanctuary." Ryan pointed to the bare overhang. "I'll follow the trail down the mountain."

Surely she wasn't far.

The elephant grass edging the path swayed in the breeze, and the sharp blades dipped, narrowing Ryan's way, increasing the darkness, reaching toward him. He'd been walking long enough that he'd have to turn back soon when a strange scream filtered through the thick jungle canopy. He hesitated. It sounded almost human.

How close was it?

His skin crawling, he searched for the source of the sound.

The jaiwa's stories flitted through his mind—capricious nats tormenting the mortal world—and twisted through whispers of cannibals attacking the village and vengefully slaughtering neighbors for sport. Or was it . . . Baw Gun?

Another scream sent him running, slipping down the trail. He reached out to catch himself on the first tangled bamboo sacrifice pole, but he yanked his fingers back, as if a deadly krait snake were coiled at the top. No salvation would be found there.

He had nearly reached the prayer posts when a person shot out of the jungle and rammed into him, slamming him to the ground. The person slashed razor-sharp claws into Ryan's skin. Ryan snatched one hand and then the other and dragged the stranger to his feet.

"What in heaven's . . ."

The stranger jerked up.

"Kailyn?"

She stilled and threw herself into his arms. A chuckle exploded through Ryan—relief tangled with amusement. He'd never seen her afraid on the mountain before.

"Shush. It's okay. I'm here." He settled her on her feet before she could object to his arms around her, but he still clasped one hand in his, holding her attention. "Are you okay?"

Kai nodded, and Ryan searched her face and bare arms for signs of harm, while she stared at the ground—whether out of fear or respect, Ryan didn't know. A few scratches spread across her cheeks, but she seemed unharmed. What were the screams?

"I've been searching for you for more than an hour."

"I'm sorry. I fell asleep."

And that explained it. Ryan had woken more than once to her unnerving cry in the night. He'd wondered what terrified her, had even asked once. But instead of helping his daughter, John had punished Kailyn for waking the new missionary.

"We need to get home before your father starts looking too."

Her eyes widened before she whipped around and dragged him down the path.

"Slow down, Kai. I'd prefer not to go head over heels."

Kai stopped, but not for him. Above them, the sky stretched enormous, with dark purples etched across a glowing pink. The brilliant color reflected on Kai's skin, and the fear drained from her face. Calm. Something Ryan rarely saw in the missionary's daughter.

He stepped back, letting her take her time. He'd think of some excuse to tell John about their late appearance.

Sometimes it's worth taking a breath. Ma had been right about that.

So much about Kai reminded him of home, and yet she was so different from anyone he'd ever encountered before. Her education, flawless English, and dark-brown waves were decidedly American, and her Italian heritage leaked through in her toasted skin. With her hair wrapped in a scarf, she almost appeared to be part of her adopted home. But the unusual amber color of her eyes gave her an otherworldly aura.

"Maybe you could remember this sky and draw it for me tomorrow. Or maybe you can re-create the monkey you drew on your slate earlier."

Kai drew a breath through her teeth and swung toward him, dropping his hand. "You can't tell Papa."

Ryan took a deep breath. He'd been teasing, like he would have pestered his sister. But he'd forgotten the nature of things.

He had no right to question John. Still, Ryan couldn't understand the man's harshness. His daughter was beyond brilliant. The young woman read ancient Greek poems, Shakespeare, and Augustine with as much ease as she scampered through the jungle. He'd never met anyone like her, and she had no idea how special she was. John had no idea how special she was. The whole situation made no sense.

And yet his job was to be sure she did her schoolwork and not spend all day drawing or traipsing through the jungle.

"We'll let your test scores speak for themselves." He nudged her shoulder. Her secret was safe with him, would always be safe with him. "Trust me?"

Kai rolled her bottom lip between her teeth, obviously debating. But she nodded and lumbered up the path. Slower this time. By the time they reached the village entrance, Tingrabum was empty, everyone inside their homes for the night.

Just as they stepped through the gate, Tu Lum trotted around the corner and threw himself into Kai's arms.

Kai murmured something to the boy, and he wandered off toward Nang Lu's basha. Ryan trailed Kai as she wove through the village and past the pigs under the porch of the mission.

Ryan tripped up the ladder of the mission as Kai burst through the narrow door. Home.

Smoke from the indoor fire pits burned Ryan's lungs, even from the doorway. He squinted, adjusting to the gloom of the windowless room.

"Kailyn Marie Moran, you are late." John stepped around the chief fire pit of the family room, emerging out of the haze like the devil himself. His eyes sparking, the anger there hot enough to start its own fire. "And I don't suppose you finished your Latin . . ."

In two long strides, the missionary stood in front of his daughter. Grasping her chin, he forced her to face him. From across the room,

Ryan could see the dents in her cheeks, could nearly taste the blood in his own mouth.

Ryan's fist tightened on the doorframe, his body trembling against the effort to restrain himself. He wasn't her father. Wasn't her brother. Wasn't her protector.

"Where is that fool Ryan? What has happened?"

Kai gasped, her body weaving a moment before she collapsed to the floor.

Chapter Three

I RUBBED AT GRIT CLINGING to my lashes, reminding me of last night's tears. My own mouth had betrayed me. I had told Papa about Baw Gun. Papa banned Baw Gun from school and told me that this morning he would not only ask the *duwa*, the village leader, to send him away but would also decide what to do with me.

I ran my thumb over Mama's pouch. What good were my prayers against Papa's iron will?

The clunk of firewood in the cooking room made me jump. Papa had already lit the fire for me. After yesterday I knew exactly how Papa would respond to my tardiness.

I scrambled off my pallet. The woven bamboo floor sagged under my feet as I yanked a dress over my head and struggled to button the front with swollen fingers.

When I stumbled into the family room, Papa looked up from his tattered Bible and frowned, as if Satan had entered the room. I leaned over him and accepted his habitual kiss on the hair—a blurry reminder of the father he'd once been.

"I'm sorry I am late, Papa. I'll have breakfast ready soon."

"If you had planned ahead and set the firewood last night, I would not have had to do your work for you."

It didn't matter that I had banked the coals, soaked the beans and rice, and collected dried grass and water before bed. Or that my body ached from yesterday's attack. I swallowed the retort dancing on my lips. I would not dishonor my mother's memory by talking back to her husband. I must trust, as she did. Make myself whatever he needed, as she had. He could not send me away.

"You are more than eighteen summers, a woman. You should know by now."

"Yes, Papa."

I scurried into the cooking room, hands flying. The banging pots and dishes might upset Papa, but I would sacrifice quiet for speed today. I did not wish to feel his walking stick on my legs this morning, and tardiness was far more likely to sever the leash on his self-control.

"Need help?"

I dropped a pan and clenched my teeth at the sting of hot oil on my fingers. Ryan, his blond hair spiked from sleep, popped around the corner.

"No. Thank you. I'm quite capable of doing it myself."

Ryan chuckled. "I never said you weren't capable."

"Why you insist on doing women's work is beyond me."

"But you won't complain either." Ducking his head to clear the doorframe, he hefted the milking buckets before scampering down the back-door ladder.

By the time Ryan returned with the goat's milk, I was flipping rice cakes onto banana leaves. Tu Lum stood at the door, his grimy face lowered and little foot twisting in the dirt. It used to be that the boy would always be with me, offering help in exchange for bits of leftover food—whatever Papa allowed me to give. Now, wherever Ryan went, the little boy followed, like a puppy behind its master.

I peeked into the main room. Papa was occupied with his reading, so I snatched a rice cake off my leaf and pressed it into Tu Lum's hand. I would have more for lunch—he might not. The little boy nodded at me solemnly and then bowed to Ryan. Before I could object, Ryan plucked another rice cake from the pan and handed it to the boy, thanking him for his help. The boy grinned, his two front teeth missing, before scampering down the ladder and skipping away, a thin whistling tune trailing behind him.

"You best not complain about being hungry today. You just gave away the extra cake I made you."

"I shall survive on your delicious and gracious leftovers." Ryan wiggled his eyebrows and plucked a crumb from the pan.

Already my feet hurt, and I sank onto a cushion by Papa while Ryan eased himself to the ground across from me. Head bowed, Ryan prayed, thanking the supreme God for the shining sun, the roof over our heads, and the hands that prepared the meal. I often thought how differently he approached Karai Kasang . . . as if it were a joy to talk to him rather than duty.

Papa grunted an amen and then ate his cakes without comment. Ryan winked at me and sprang into a steady stream of chatter, more befitting a dimple-cheeked child than a full-grown man and scholar.

Papa had told me Ryan was twenty-three summers old—as old as Papa had been when he'd married Mama—but was no more ready to lead a mission than Tu Lum was . . . At least, that was what Papa said.

My fingers tightened in my lap as I counted the times Papa's jaw clenched and unclenched, until his patience burst, shattering Ryan's chatter.

"Kai, you will study with Ryan today. Ryan, you can, perhaps, keep up with my daughter today. Yes? Perhaps you will find how God expects his representatives to comport themselves."

Ryan's gaze skittered over me and then Papa, a muscle in his brow twitching before he stood. "Of course."

Was Ryan angry with me?

"And when you return, you will begin packing. I have made arrangements for your transport to America two weeks from today. To Texas, with your mama's family. They have room for you and a position as a tutor."

"What?" The word slipped from me.

Papa's eye twitched in a single flash of a gathering storm. "It is for your own good. You are finished with your high school curriculum and need to make your way in the world. There is nothing for you here."

And what could I say? The man of God declared leaving was for my own good. Who was I to challenge that?

Despite the fact that my stomach had soured, I forced myself to swallow the rice cakes along with my questions. Good daughters obeyed without debate.

Ryan wrapped the leftover cakes in a banana leaf and dropped them into his knapsack, along with our study materials.

When Papa saw I still sat, he frowned and pointed with his chin at Ryan. I stood and walked through the living room. But my mind rebelled, questions tumbling through my head like an avalanche. Was I to leave so soon? Who would take me? Would I not have time to say goodbye to my jungle? To Nojie Bum?

I remained silent and forced my gaze to the ground. I hadn't been given permission to speak.

Ryan stood in the doorway, blocking my exit, and scowled at Papa. I backed away—a jackrabbit caught between two angry predators. No one ever disagreed with Papa.

"You will keep her safe, and she will have plenty of time to say her goodbyes later." Papa was patronizing, as if explaining life to a toddler.

But his explanation bred more questions. I looked at Ryan for clarification, but his hands clenched against the doorframe, his jaw tight.

Nodding in decision or perhaps resignation, Ryan snatched his guitar and trudged away.

With a glance at Papa, who already returned to reading, I slipped out the door. Following Ryan's broad shoulders up the familiar path gave my mind too much space, and I found myself fidgeting, my imagination carrying me through the jungle to a ship bound for America. Screams echoed from above me, and I jumped, realizing a moment later that it was simply a hawk circling the mountain, carrying away its breakfast—some poor creature caught helpless in its talons.

Ryan's long strides propelled him up the hill, forcing me to scramble to keep pace. My breath rebelled along with my mind, and I stumbled on a root.

Ryan spun and caught me. I gaped, astonished at his speed.

He steadied me on my feet, and I snapped my mouth shut, stiff before him. Fear twisted in me. I could not even trust my own mountain anymore.

My gaze fell. The rocks under my feet blurred, the pattern beautiful, familiar. No. I clenched my fists. Even if I had to disappear into the jungle, no one would take me away from Nojie Bum. No one.

≈

Ryan clasped Kai's shoulders, trying to think of something to say or do. She'd always been as skittish as a captured wild colt, but after last night, her soul seemed to have jumped the fence and run away with her mind in tow. He'd never been good with horses.

"Things will get easier, Kailyn." It was something Pop had always said when Ryan was struggling through advanced math or failing to fix the carburetor in the tractor again. It seemed to help Kai as much as it had helped Ryan . . . not at all.

Kai's body remained as rigid as the stone under their feet. She rarely asked for help. Never seemed to want it. She probably didn't even believe Ryan was capable of doing anything helpful. *Just like her father.* He dropped his hands to his sides.

Ryan's ears still rang with John Moran's torrent of angry questions: Why had Ryan left Kai alone? Why had he allowed Baw Gun to leave school? What had he been thinking? Why was he so inept?

John might as well have asked why the earth rotated around the sun or why Kachins believed in nats.

It hadn't mattered that John had chosen to not allow Kai to be the only female in the classroom as either student or teacher. Or that she was as capable of conjugating verbs by herself as she was surviving in the mountains. Or that Ryan had rescued her and gotten her home in one piece. Ryan cared about Kai as much as his own sister. He wasn't entirely useless.

Then again, maybe he was.

Kai's gaze was fixed on her feet—a sign of respect for Ryan's manhood and his position of leadership—despite her rigid back revealing her barely-held-in anger.

Kai tucked a strand of dark hair behind her ear, and Ryan's mind spun, thinking of ways to show her he didn't see himself as better, stronger, more worthy. He'd be happy with distracting her, even for a moment.

He rotated his feet up the mountain and grinned, an idea coming to him.

"Race you to the top."

Kai's head snapped up, confusion galloping through her golden eyes and loosening her jaw. Ryan winked and tore up the mountain as if an entire army were at his heels. The hard, black guitar case slamming against his back matched the rhythm of his boots striking the path. The book bag he wore across his body lurched from side to side, threatening to spill him down the mountain in an undignified heap.

At first Ryan thought Kai might ignore the challenge, but he heard the whisper of her feet behind him as they turned the last corner before the clearing. Despite his head start, Kai still slapped a bare foot onto the rock ledge a hair's breadth ahead of Ryan's.

Good heavens, she is fast.

"Better luck next time, you big, lumbering bear." There was lightness in her now, and she nudged his shoulder.

Ryan ruffled her hair, and she frowned. He'd miss her when she was gone. The thought sent Ryan's mood plummeting.

At least he'd convinced John to give her a week or two to say goodbye and to send her northwest into India instead of south to a steamer, which was normally the safest, fastest choice. The last time they'd made the long trip to the market, traders from the south had carried rumors that the cries for the British to release Burma from colonial rule had morphed into something more. If the tales could be trusted, the Japanese had attacked Burma, and the Burmese had sided with the enemy against the rest of the people groups in their cobbled-together country. Knowing how brutal Imperial Japan had been in China, Ryan hoped the mountains would keep the remote mission hidden.

Sighing, he forced the tightness in his shoulders down and settled himself on the edge of a huge rock overhang high above the village.

Count your blessings, Ma had always said. *It'll chase away the worst of the darkness.*

And like most things, she was right. The beauty of this place stood in such contrast to the hard life of its people. Rippling down the side of Nojie Bum, the jungle twisted in a crazy patchwork of green. The vast range of Wantuk Bum mountains rose somewhere behind him to the northeast. A distant splinter of the Nambyu River sparkled with a thousand diamonds, cutting the valley from north to south. On the village plain beneath him, the perfect lines of dry rice paddies, so much like the cornfields of home, pointed to the terraced mountains on both sides.

Home. Opening the long black case, Ryan pulled out his mother's battered guitar. He imagined sitting on Ma's worn couch, the brown fabric showing white threads at the edges, the flames dancing in the fireplace, Ma's fingers stroking the strings, her singing rising and falling with the familiar melody. "Amazing grace, how sweet the sound . . ."

She had only been gone a few years, and he already struggled to remember her clearly.

Humming, Ryan let his legs swing free above the sheer drop, partially facing the others. He heard Kai squat behind him, ready to bolt at a moment's notice. When Ryan didn't turn, she removed her basket and nestled into the crook of a rock. She retrieved her books along with the tiny carved wooden tiger she carried everywhere.

John wanted her to study, but Ryan didn't have it in him to force her. Not today. And it wasn't like she lagged behind. She had what amounted to a college-level education and spoke five languages. When he'd been eighteen, Ryan was lucky to get through *Treasure Island* between farm chores and football practice.

He peeked behind him to be sure she was at least staying nearby. But he needn't have worried. Kai stared blankly into the distance. The dark circles under her eyes testified that she'd slept as poorly as he.

Visions of the rumored Japanese soldiers attacking the capital, combined with memories of the assault on Kai, had invaded his sleep, storming into dreams that had kept him awake, swirling with tornado winds, a bloodied bayonet, and haunting laughter.

Ryan watched the elephant grasses at the edge of the jungle twist in the wind.

Was it the wind?

So help him, if Baw Gun had returned, Ryan would kill the young man with his own hands. Setting the guitar aside, he grasped his dah and steadied his foot under him, preparing to throw himself in front of Kai. At times like this, Ryan wished he had a rifle.

A branch snapped, and Kai jumped, feet spread, a knife poised in her hand. A voice hailed them from the path, and little Tu Lum popped into view. Air flooded from Ryan's lungs, and he sank to the ground, grasping the neck of the guitar so hard, it was a wonder it didn't snap.

Tu Lum leaned into Kai, her arm draped across his back. Ryan studied the boy, the question in Tu Lum's face revealing his concern. He knew something was wrong.

No one was quite sure how old Tu Lum was, but Kai had said her father had pulled the boy from his dead mother's womb seven or eight summers ago, a year or two after her mother had passed. Her aunt had taken the boy in and recruited Kai to help care for him as much as John and the duwa would let them.

The boy whispered, reading from a book of poetry, and Kai's teasing response released the tension from Ryan's shoulders. It could be considered studying, and she was teaching the boy too. Probably better than he ever could. Ryan angled back toward the panoramic view and his guitar. Soon he heard Kai slip into her assigned homework, reading from Augustine's *Confessions* . . . as if the week's events had been blotted out of existence.

Ryan cringed as his fingers tripped over another chord, and he snuggled the guitar into the case, careful not to disturb the stack of his mother's letters. Ma had been sure he'd be the next Adoniram Judson—making his home in these very mountains and singing about Jesus to the natives, just like the famous Texas missionary. But she'd never had the chance to see Ryan graduate from seminary, let alone to say good-bye as he left for Burma.

He tossed a stone into the jungle.

At least she'd never see him come home a failure.

Kai struggled through a pronunciation and then mumbled about a theological concept as she scribbled on her slate—a truth Ryan had studied in depth at school but found little use for in the mountains.

The fact was, Ryan was restless. Restless and, as John had again reminded him last night, pretty much useless—he'd not been able to do anything with Baw Gun, couldn't build a basha, and knew next to nothing about growing rice, bartering, hunting, or delivering a baby. Heaven knew he couldn't even answer normal questions about God. The only helpful things he'd brought with him were the medicines, a few books, and Ma's guitar. He would have been better off training in a survival camp . . . and trading his blond-haired, blue-eyed, farmer-boy appearance for something a little more on the swarthy side, like John himself.

As if he'd heard Ryan's thoughts, Tu Lum winked at Ryan.

In reality, Kai was better suited to take over the mission than he was. She knew the people and their traditions—enough that she wasn't a burden on those around her. Ryan stared out at the paddy fields. Most of the village women were beyond the fields, searching for firewood, their enormous white hats looking for all the world like alien birds lighting here and there between the rows.

Normally, a young mountain woman Kai's age would be out with the women, working. He knew Kai always resented that John held her apart, refusing to let her be one of the mountain people. Not that Ryan disagreed. Life on the mountain was hard, especially for women.

And Kai would be a prize for any mountain man. The daughter of an influential foreigner and beautiful.

"What does this mean?"

Kai's question drew Ryan's attention. "What?" He'd heard the anger in her question but had lost track of what she was reading.

Her hands fisted around the book. "Did I do something wrong? Is the supreme one so angry with me that he"—she looked back at the book—"that he threatens me with misery? That he takes everything from me?"

Tu Lum's eyes snapped to Ryan's. But Ryan shrugged, his mind skipping. He had yet to figure out why God took mothers from children or allowed soldiers free rein against innocent people. And he sure didn't want to face it, explore it, even acknowledge it. Those questions just spun a person in dangerous circles.

Tu Lum's face scrunched in confusion.

"Karai Kasang took your mama too. Don't you ever wonder why?" Kai sat back.

Tears collected on the boy's lashes.

"Careful, Kai." Ryan knew she'd meant the question for the orphan boy, but the attack stung Ryan as well.

"I remember so little about Mama." She trailed a finger in the dirt. "Can't remember her face, her touch."

"But that doesn't—"

"God stole her." Kai cut across Ryan. "Now Papa's sending me away. No one . . ." Her voice broke. "No one wants me."

Shock tinged the boy's face, and a single tear escaped his eye—a twin to one sneaking down Kai's cheek.

"Do you think I don't hear them whispering about me being cursed? That I don't see their fear? I didn't ask to be born with these eyes or to be attacked by a tiger." She choked out the words, anger burning the edges. "And then Baw Gun . . ." She rubbed her hands against the enormous stone beneath her. "Did I do something wrong to make Papa send me away?" A tear dropped from her chin. "What did I do?" She stared at the sky, as if demanding an answer to scroll across it. "I don't want to go to America. Why is this happening?"

Ryan found himself examining the clouds as well. Why indeed?

Ryan was supposed to be helping, or learning how to run the mission, or doing *something* worthwhile, but all the seminary answers fell flat.

Tu Lum patted his weeping friend's back. "I don't know. But it's not your fault." The boy eyed Ryan. "Right?"

"Everything'll be all right." Ryan said the words they expected, but how could he know they were true?

Tu Lum frowned at Ryan, shaking his head in obvious disappointment. The little boy grasped Kai's face. "I would hide you if I could." Tu Lum's lips tipped into a cheeky grin. "Then you could make me as many rice cakes as I wished!"

Kai snorted.

"I know I don't count for much, but . . ." The little boy squirmed, staring at his grubby toes, before throwing his arms around her neck. "I want you."

Wanted. It had been a long time since he'd felt that. Ryan threw another rock into the gorge and listened to it trickle down the mountain until it was lost in the jungle below.

Kai's tears dropped into the book, darkening the page.

"You'll come back, Moran Kai," Tu Lum said.

Ryan cringed. John would leave her in America as sure as the sun rose in the morning. Ryan stood, closed his guitar case, and gathered his papers and books.

"Ryan." Tu Lum's voice was quiet, pleading, and Ryan pretended not to hear as he finished packing and trudged away.

"John asked us to come back when we were finished studying."

"Ryan." Tu Lum repeated. "Can we go to the jungle? Please."

Ryan hesitated. He studied the point where the trail to the village disappeared behind an enormous teak tree.

"Please." Tu Lum stood behind him, skinny legs braced wide.

You might learn something. Ma's voice came to him, speaking as she patiently pressed Ryan's fingers into the guitar strings for the millionth time.

Ryan's grip tightened around the handle of the guitar case. But he pivoted and retraced his steps to their stone sanctuary.

"You won't find anything to hunt if I come with you."

"I think we need you today more than we need meat. Even the most experienced hunter cannot survive the jungle alone for long." Tu Lum turned to follow Kai, already making her way up the mountain. "Come, please."

"It's not what we were told to do."

But Tu Lum was already too far away to hear him. Maybe the boy was right. Ryan steeled himself as he plodded to a gnarled tree at the edge of the jungle. Lightning had struck the tree years ago and twisted it, and it writhed in petrified stillness. Ryan could identify.

But the tree was handy. Safe from any rising water, a hole gaped a few feet off the ground, creating a natural storage cabinet for anything Kai wanted safely hidden away. Ryan removed Tu Lum's bow and arrows, Kai's blowgun and pouch of darts. Then he tucked Kai's basket and his guitar case into the protection of the hole.

Trailing the duo, Ryan lumbered across the stone and scrambled through the hillside. Maybe they'd still find a bird or two for the curry stew despite his bearlike presence scaring off the animals. Ryan's stomach grumbled at the thought.

The pair in front of him ducked behind a screen of bamboo. He knew the entrance to the trail they were on. At least he was learning something. Ryan jogged after them. The moment he crossed into the jungle, Kai took her blowgun from him and loped off. But Tu Lum nodded at Ryan and wandered after Kai, leaving Ryan holding the boy's bow. Though Tu Lum had taken great joy in teaching Ryan how to use it, the weapon was Tu Lum's greatest treasure, and Ryan had never been the one to carry it away from their sanctuary. With the boy already disappearing behind a drop in the hill, Ryan shrugged, dropped the bow over his head, and followed.

≈

The trio spent the day in the steady pulse of the jungle. Feet in rhythm with the mountain, Ryan felt the whisper of wind through the narrow bamboo leaves and light dance across the path, his soul steadying despite the empty snares. Little Tu Lum had been right. They needed to remind each other of the good things.

As the sky took on the golden colors of late afternoon, a clutch of birds scuttled across a tiny brook and under the broad leaves of a bush. Kai pointed to Tu Lum, signaling him to the side.

Ryan had watched the two hunt many times in the past. They spent entire days silently anticipating each other's movements, and they rarely came home without something for the pot. Ryan stayed as still as a scarecrow until he saw Tu Lum signaling wildly, slapping his own chest and then pointing at Ryan. Ryan still carried the bow.

Kai scowled, and Ryan couldn't agree more. The mission needed meat more than Ryan needed to be included. But it was too late to move the weapon to reliable hands.

Ryan sank to a knee, then stabbed a few arrows into the ground before fitting one against the bowstring like Tu Lum had taught him. It wasn't much different from shooting the rifle back home. Or that was what he told himself as he made his breath even and sure. If he missed, Kai would hate him forever.

Ryan nodded to Tu Lum, and the boy made a shushing noise, waving his arms at the undergrowth. The bush erupted with terrified partridges. Ryan's aim followed the brown birds, and he let loose a succession of arrows as he heard the short puffing sound of Kai's blowgun.

The last of the birds flew out of range, squawking indignantly at the hunters.

Kai handed her blowgun to Tu Lum and then took off into the jungle, returning with three fat birds—one killed with a dart and two with arrows.

Kai ran her fingers over the smooth feathers. "Thank you for giving your lives to sustain ours."

Tu Lum nodded solemnly and then grinned at Ryan. "You are a great hunter like the bear now."

"Thank you." Ryan couldn't help feeling giddy as a schoolboy at the praise. He yanked the remaining arrows out of the ground and held out the weapon to Tu Lum. But the boy shook his head.

"You have earned the bow, Bear of Burma. I can make another."

"It appears you have another hunting partner already." Kai snatched her blowgun from Tu Lum. "Don't miss me too much when I am gone." She spun and stalked into the jumble of underbrush.

What had he done wrong?

When Ryan started to follow her, to apologize, to bring her back, Tu Lum grabbed Ryan's arm, his face far too grave for his age. "We will not find her if she does not wish to be found. Chasing her will only drive her farther away."

Leaves swirled where Kai had disappeared. The boy was right. Ryan would have to return without Kai and absorb the other missionary's anger again tonight . . . and pray she did not stray too far.

Chapter Four

THE HEAVY NIGHT SKY HAD chased me home despite the strangler fig wrapped around my heart. I'd had a moment where I thought to never return. But I knew better than to think I could survive the jungle on my own. I didn't know of anyone unwise enough to try it who'd actually made it more than a year or two. I didn't want to die in the jungle. But if I returned to the village, Papa would send me away and America would choke out Moran Kai, all while the new missionary replaced me on my mountain. But at least I wouldn't be dead. Perhaps I could reinvent myself in America. Perhaps I was more adaptable than I thought. Could a mountain tiger become something else in the barren desert of Texas?

Outside the mission basha, Aunt Nang Lu squatted by the square outdoor firebox and poked at the logs with a stick before turning her rounded back to the jungle. A huge steaming pot of water sat over the fire, balanced precariously on three flat stones. The lingering smell of the night's curry made my stomach growl. The jungle roots I had scrounged for dinner had been nowhere near enough.

Papa must be inside. Maybe if I waited until he slept to sneak into the basha, I could—

"Come out of the dark, little tiger. Do not linger. You will make this old woman wonder if the nats indeed haunt the jungle. I saved a bowl of vegetable curry for you." My amoi nodded at the bowl by the fire.

I hesitated a moment before I slipped into the ring of light. Aunt Nang Lu grunted as she wove another bamboo strip through the circular form at her feet. She would soon have another basket to trade at the market.

"Our Tu Lum brought birds." Her chin pointed to the three partridges hanging from a branch, their throats slit, with blood pooling in bamboo bowls beneath them. "Where were you?"

"I was with them. One of the birds fell from my dart." I drew a broken *X* into the dirt with my foot. The Hebrew aleph and the first letter in the Hebrew word for *friend*. It was *our* mark, the one Tu Lum and I used to tell each other where we were headed. Tu Lum had left them carved into trees all the way down Nojie Bum, but he'd followed Ryan instead of coming to find me.

That man was stealing everything that was mine.

"Hmm." Aunt Nang Lu shuffled to the pot. "Perhaps you had other things to do that prevented you from coming home. But I think you are able to help now. Yes?"

"Yes, Amoi." I bobbed my head, not wanting my amoi to be alone with the task but dreading preparing the birds nonetheless. I heard the men inside and envied their easy chatter, their ability to choose for themselves. For a moment. Despite the unpleasant task, sitting under the dark sky with Aunt Nang Lu was far better than inside the stuffy basha, discussing politics or theology with the men.

"There's rice for you in the bowl. Food always makes you feel better." My amoi, palms down, pushed her crooked fingers at me. The others might replace me without thought, but Aunt Nang Lu would always hold a place for me.

I unstrung the fowl and carried them to the pot. Holding one in each hand, I repeatedly dunked them into the steaming water until the acrid smell of scalded birds filled the air and the tail feathers slipped out of the carcasses without effort. The birds dripped as I passed them to Aunt Nang Lu, who laid them across a clean stone and began a rhythmic plucking.

Once I'd baptized the last bird, I joined Aunt Nang Lu at the stone, our movements choreographed from years of working together. My fingers tingled with the heat and the pricks of sharp feathers.

"You have enough feathers on your arms to take flight yourself, Mo-ran Kai."

I shook my head and brushed as many of the feathers into the collection basket as possible. We scraped the last of the down off, cleaned the innards out, placing the gizzards, heart, and feet in with the usable meat. We would clean the intestines to use later. Nothing was wasted here.

"Good. I have a pot inside heating. Put the meat in and come back to talk with this old woman."

"Yes, Amoi."

I dropped the birds into the pot over the cooking room fire, made sure to bank the fire well, and doubled back to the door before any of the men could investigate the noises.

But the duwa's words stopped me.

"The women who went to the market came back with disturbing news. They saw smoke and, thinking the jungle was on fire, hurried to help put out the flames. But when they reached the clearing, nothing was left of the village or the market. Survivors said soldiers had burned it." The village leader paused, his coughs heavy and labored.

So the rumors were true. The war had snaked north from the capital, reaching even into the valley just a few days' walk from here. How could I leave not knowing what would happen to the village?

Perhaps Papa's stick for eavesdropping might be worth it if staying banished the demons. Surely things weren't as bad as the women had made them seem.

The duwa recovered his breath and spit into a piece of dark cloth. "I wish to know what we should do."

"No harm will come to us here at the mission. God will protect us." Papa was confident, dismissive.

"But, John—" Ryan's quiet voice was respectful.

Still, I sucked in my breath.

"But nothing." The crack of his hand on the floor sent me cringing farther away. "I am still in charge of this mission. You will do well to listen and learn to trust and obey! God's hand will hide us."

Heat burned my cheeks even though Papa's tirade wasn't aimed at me this time. I pulled a speckled rock from Mama's pouch and rubbed its smooth surface.

Most of the time Papa helped the people, was their Jungle Light. Since they were my adopted people too, I was glad of that. Even if it meant he left me behind for weeks at a time to visit other villages. But this. This blind trust that we were safe was different. The same God who had allowed Mama to die might very well allow the Japanese to find us too. Why did Papa not see it? I rubbed the rock until my sweat made it shine.

The wind outside breathed. And suddenly the creaking of the house and scratching of the chickens underneath made me imagine dark fingers scraping away the bamboo walls to catch me. I scuttled to the door, dark, twisting forms from the cooking fire chasing me—nats emerging from the other side. A flash of light across the metal cross on the doorframe stopped me, and I touched the smooth surface.

There are no nats here.

I lifted my chin. They would not dare enter the home of Pastor John Moran.

Aunt Nang Lu's steady eyes watched me slip out the door.

"Busy hands make good conversation and ease the mind." Aunt Nang Lu patted the ground next to her and pushed a barely started basket in my direction.

I had never seen my amoi's hands still. Her steadiness never failed to tease my thoughts out before I could hold them back.

My hand fluttered to the red pouch and the stones inside.

"Ah. Your mother's prayer bag."

"Tell me about Mama again."

"Your *kanu*, your mama? She was beautiful, a butterfly on the mountain. You look so much like her." Aunt Nang Lu dragged another stack of spiraling bamboo strips closer. "But you know that already. Did I tell you how afraid she was when she first came?"

I nodded but smiled, encouraging Aunt Nang Lu to tell the tale. I loved the story of the dance between my parents and our adopted people. I could close my eyes and have them back the way it had been when life was as Papa had expected.

"I was the first to spot Pastor John on the path and flew into the village, arms flapping, hair standing on end, telling tales of a strange creature on the mountain. Your papa came to us, white skin, enormous beard, strange ways, talking of a God of love stronger than the nats and spirits of the mountains. He was odd to be sure. But your mama was gentle and kind. Her face glowed, and her hair shimmered dark and shot through with fire. She was the one who convinced us to let Pastor John show us the metal tools. There were things I had never seen before, tools we could not find on the mountain or afford even if they were available—shovels, axes . . . He even brought a plow on the back of a buffalo. We had no idea how he convinced the creature to walk the narrow trails."

Aunt Nang Lu paused, staring into the fire as if she saw the events there. "My honorable husband was fascinated by this white ghost with much hair on his face and sat with him that first night while Pastor John used his too-short knife to carve a tiger into a section of teak wood. I hid in the cooking room, fascinated but mostly terrified. When your mama spied me staring, she asked him for the tiger and then gave it to me. I dropped the gift and ran from the basha as if the wooden tiger had morphed into the sharaw and chased me into the darkness. Your mama never gave up though.

"After that night, I always edged out of the room when Pastor John was nearby. But your mama learned how to harvest and cook and did it without complaint. She was no ghost, but another woman. Real as you and me. Your papa built a basha for his home, helped the villagers build water canals and terraces, and told us about Karai Kasang—that he was powerful and cared about us. Most of the villagers were polite, but we had all seen what the nats were capable of and had no evidence of the power of the white ghost's God. Until . . ."

I could have finished the story, word for word, but Aunt Nang Lu was a better storyteller than even the jaiwa. I snuggled in closer to hear the words rumble in my amoi's chest.

"Until the night I died and your papa reached into death and brought me back again.

"Your mama saw me fall from the mountain. I remember the sky fading. While Pastor John prayed, your mama blew life into me, before putting my bones back where they belong.

"As a thank-you for saving me, my husband offered your parents a place in our family. It cost a month's worth of food for the adoption ceremony. But what is the price of life?" Aunt Nang Lu chuckled.

"The duwa, most of the village, and I were all baptized the first day of the celebration. Your papa, his smile was wider than the river. After that our people called him the Jungle Light. I think it was as much for the miracle as for how he radiated the afternoon sun for the most dis-couraged among us."

I closed my eyes, trying to picture Papa's smile reaching all the way to his eyes, but the image was lost behind a veil of years. My amoi cupped her hand on my head and ran it down the short length of my hair, then tapped Mama's pouch.

"Your mama was the strongest person I knew. She held miracles in her hands but knew your papa had a special connection to the supreme one. Pastor John never allowed your mama to have prayer shelves like the rest of us, but her red pouch always reminded her of the power of Karai Kasang. She stuffed her prayers into those stones and then left her fear behind as a reminder of a coming answer."

My amoi began weaving her basket again, her fingers steady and sure. "Pastor John loved your mama too. You came along a few years after I re-awoke to life. You were a sign of blessing. Full of courage and fire. A true little tiger." Her hands stilled. "I do not know why bad things hap-pen, little one."

The crickets and frogs called to one another, a happy chorus of life.

The bamboo strips under my fingers refused to bend through the vertical spokes of the basket. The basket crumbled as Aunt Nang Lu touched my shoulder.

"I know it is hard to not understand. The world is all upside down and inside out right now, but your father will find his way again. And in the meantime, I am here. And your Ryan is here too."

Aunt Nang Lu held up her hand before I even had a chance to protest.

"He is a good man, like your father, and they could both use your help more than your anger."

≈

Ryan sat under the black domed sky, watching the red embers in the outdoor fire pit pulse with the wind. Everyone else was inside, but he'd volunteered to do the nighttime chores, including extinguishing the fire. He often took the chore as an opportunity to pluck a few notes on his guitar and relax. Earlier he had helped Nang Lu gather the firewood and stones to build the makeshift fire pit. She had even asked him to help her carry water to fill the pot she used to scald the partridges. The villagers considered it a woman's task, but Ryan was happy to help. Back home the whole family helped slaughter the chickens for market.

Ryan had offered Nang Lu a seasoned hand to help pluck the birds, but she had shooed him inside, with the other men. The twinkle in her eye had told Ryan he'd done well, while she'd excused him from the horrible job and allowed him to save face with the men. Ryan would relish the bits of meat in his stew tomorrow because of Nang Lu's kindness.

He set his guitar beside him, leaned into the log behind him, and closed his eyes, wishing for the blankness of sleep. His body was tired from trekking in the jungle, but his mind refused to quiet. While John was convinced the mountains were safe from the soldiers, the people had told too many stories for Ryan to be sure.

At least he'd heard Kai climb into her pallet. Safe for now. It had taken every ounce of Ryan's patience to listen to the other men talk of theology, politics, and crops while she was alone on the mountain. Tu Lum had regaled him with tales of Kai's survival—somehow even killing a tiger once. But it wasn't just the mountain animals that concerned Ryan.

When Kai had sneaked into the cooking room, Ryan had wanted to scoop her into his arms and then give her a good lecture about wandering in the jungle alone with Baw Gun and a host of Japanese soldiers looking for trouble. A slight shake from the duwa's head prevented Ryan from embarrassing himself and Kai. The duwa was right. Kai wouldn't want the attention, and Nang Lu would take care of the girl she considered nearly her daughter.

The logs in the fire snapped, and a shower of sparks raced to join the stars. How he wished to fly with them—floating free, above the jungle, unaware, unafraid—until they were snuffed out.

Dark ashes momentarily blotted away the stars before careening back to earth.

What was the point of being strong, being a light, if you couldn't help? If you couldn't protect anyone? What good was trust when you had to trust in things that weren't promised?

The Japanese were coming, and John refused to prepare. Refused to alter his plans to send Kai through what might be a line of enemy soldiers.

Some Adoniram Judson Ryan had turned out to be. He'd never pictured the famous missionary at a loss for words or stumped for the right thing to do. The man had written down their language, helped them farm and build, brought them medicine. Actually done good for the people. Maybe Pop was right. Maybe Ryan should have ignored Ma's dreams for him and stayed home to help on the farm.

Ryan's fingers absently picked out the tune to Ma's favorite song, his lips forming the words. If only a song could bring him through the danger to home.

"A sad tune for such hopeful words." Nang Lu hobbled into the light.

"Maybe I need a little hope." But hope floated somewhere in the darkness.

"You could not sleep?" Nang Lu groaned as she sank onto a log next to Ryan.

"No." Ryan held still as the mother of the village weighed her words, deciding. It was obvious Nang Lu saw the darkness inside him.

"It's a wonder I ever sleep inside your Kachin death traps," Ryan said, then winced at himself. He was evading, but his mind was too dark, too full of broken pieces. He didn't want to answer questions tonight.

Nang Lu pulled on her ear, as if the motion might make Ryan's words more understandable.

"Your indoor fire pits. There's a wood box with a bit of sand in the bottom. That little layer of sand is all that's between you and setting fire to your bamboo floors, walls, and ceilings. It's enough to make a boy from Indiana have nightmares." Ryan winked.

Nang Lu's hand smacked across her mouth in sudden realization.

"It's okay." Ryan patted her knee. "Pastor John says the danger is only in new bashas, before the soot builds up."

"I suppose this world has many dangers that yours does not. Tell me about your home. Your In-dee-ana." Kai's aunt stared at her feet. That blasted sign of respect again.

No one had dared to ask about his past. Until now. Darkness grasped at him, and he wanted to ignore it, push it down. But this was a onetime offer of friendship. He sighed.

"There isn't much to tell. It's a little like here. Most folks are farmers, but our farms are bigger, and we rotate our crops so we can stay in one place for longer. My father's family has been farming on the same land for more than a hundred years." Ryan thought of everyone sitting at the table, chins propped in their hands, while Ma read from the Bible. Every night was the same, except for Sarah springing up taller and Pop's hair turning grayer and his hands becoming more like tree roots rippling above ground.

"We're farther away from other people too. We could go weeks without seeing anybody if we missed church gatherings. But like here, we help each other when there's need.

"There are no mountains, no hills, really, at all. I used to climb on the roof of the barn and watch the sun set over hundreds of miles of farmland. I used to think there wasn't anything worth more than all that land painted gold. I haven't seen it like that since . . ."

Broken boards thrown across the land like Tinkertoys. Trees uprooted. Quiet tears from the neighbor woman.

"A big storm hit a while back and destroyed almost everything. Pop had been downstate buying a new tractor." Ryan realized with a jolt that he was still speaking, that the black memories were pouring out—Ryan arriving home just after his father; Pop's chapped hands sitting idle; finding the cow, bleeding, barely alive under the roof of the barn; draining the floodwater out of the tractor; praying for the farm to be saved; watching the sun finally break through the clouds, a beam of light illuminating the freshly churned earth of the twin graves. One for Ma. One for Sarah. Even the storm cellar hadn't protected them.

"If I would've been home like he'd asked, maybe I would've been able to do something to make it turn out differently." Ryan picked a few notes from the guitar. "I worry about him sometimes. I wonder if I should have stayed. If my leaving made it worse for him, and maybe me too."

Nang Lu nodded, holding the silence with reverence.

Ryan rubbed the length of his face. "Being a leader means being responsible. But I can't *do* anything here. John doesn't think the Japanese will come. He's even planning to visit the villages east again. I can't convince him otherwise."

Nang Lu patted his knee. "I worry for my husband's village. I worry about our crops failing, that we should move farther into the mountains again, and that to move would be more than we could bear. I worry and I wonder how much heaven sees. The Jungle Light often tells me to lift my eyes to the mountains and find my help from Karai Kasang."

DARKNESS CALLS THE TIGER

Ryan rolled his eyes. "He quotes that one to me too."

"It is his favorite, I think." Nang Lu's chuckle held a note of conspiracy.

"'The Lord shall preserve thee from all evil.'" Ryan mimicked the seriousness of Pastor John. "'He shall preserve thy soul. The Lord shall preserve thy going out and thy coming in from this time forth, and even for evermore.' If I'm honest though, I'm not sure I really understand it."

The two fell silent, watching the embers of the fire pulse, the lazy trails of smoke catching in a slight breeze, then reaching to the boundless heavens. For evermore.

Nang Lu prodded the dying flame, dispersing the ashes. Ryan stared at the dark silhouette of mountains, the sharp edges silent.

"For now, my husband and Pastor John must bear the weight of the decisions. You are a good man, Ryan, and your shoulders are broad. You will find your way when the time comes. Both you and Kai."

Chapter Five

THE VILLAGE COWERED, HOLDING ITS breath for a handful of days while we prayed that Karai Kasang would send the monsoon rains to make the village paths impassable before the Japanese could come this far north. Even the immovable trees seemed to shake in fear. Despite his assurance that the Japanese wouldn't attack, Papa kept me close—not sending me away but also refusing to let me set foot in the jungle. Meanwhile, the duwa sent out scouts, and every night the scouts arrived back, trading places with their partners with no word of approaching soldiers.

And then the clouds of war opened and refugees flooded north into the Hukawng Valley and onto our little mountain. The night after a Sunday gathering, a family stumbled into Tingrabum. A British father carrying a little girl, her pale arms flung out, begging the sky for help. The Burmese mother following behind, tripping over invisible ruts in the road, dry streaks of paler skin running down her face, tears forever frozen. The baby strapped to her back so still I wondered if death had stolen it away already.

When Papa heard of their appearance, he and Ryan scrambled to gather water and medical supplies, running to meet them. The duwa sat in front of his basha, coughing heavily into a cloth, and sent his people to gather more food, bracing for those still coming.

As soon as Nang Lu heard that the newborn baby boy was not the woman's own and was an orphan, she arranged round-the-clock care. The first day we all helped collect goat's milk. But he only ate when I was the one dripping liquid into his mouth.

Though honored by his choice, the burden to care for him bent my shoulders down. Fingers shaking, I dipped the rag into the milk and eased it into the boy's mouth. My amoi stood above me, a dreamy smile on her face, as if heaven itself had entered her main room. The baby suckled another moment, until his eyes drifted closed and his tiny pink lips parted in sleep.

"You have a way with the child," Aunt Nang Lu said, as if her words answered the problems of the universe. She lifted the baby out of my arms and nestled him in a lined box in her room before nodding at him. "It is time he had a name." She wiggled her eyebrows at me. "What do you think? What shall we name this little one?"

I shrank back. I had no right to grant the child a name.

Delight creased her face in well-worn paths. "Matthew." Her finger traced the baby's forehead. "Matthew. A gift."

Aunt Nang Lu would only name the child if she thought he would survive. And it seemed he would, if my amoi willed it.

The family slept in my room that night.

Lying by the chief fireplace, I listened to the whispers of the woman and man, and then the silence as they fell asleep. But the girl whimpered all night, fueling my nightmares.

Mama, faceless and pale, blood running down her bare legs and through the bamboo floorboards. And a white-toothed man cackled until a tiger ate him and roared away into the jungle, grasping the tail of the rising sun.

I woke to the roar of the tiger-man. Jumping to my feet, I snatched my dah, searching the darkness, shaking, my breaths coming in hard gasps.

Just a dream. Just a dream.

Knowing I wouldn't find sleep again, I stole outside. It wasn't safe beyond the protection of the village. But the wind called to me as it rushed through the bamboo trees standing as gatekeepers to the mountains. A swirling mist hung low on the jungle floor, trapped between the towering teak trees and the cliffs.

With one last look at the low-burning fire at the center of the village, I arranged a wide-brimmed hat on my head, swung my basket onto my back, hugged my tattered sweater tight around myself, and let the heartbeat of Nojie Bum thrum through me.

Trotting past the paddy fields, I brushed aside the brambles and disappeared into an animal track.

The illumination of a million stars broke through the canopy here and there, making the light hiccup across my body as I jogged up the path away from the claustrophobic mission. Above me the moon haunted the sky, casting her spell on the veiled earth and allowing me to see well enough. As the trail tunneled through the elephant grass, I relished the burn in my lungs, and I dragged my fingers across the grasses. The barbs ripped into my arms and face, cutting the tendrils of chaotic thought, until a drop of blood trickled into my eyes. I stopped. *What are you doing, foolish child?* Papa raged in my mind.

Spinning in a circle, I listened to my heart pound in my ears, fear pushing it faster. The blades of grass stirred, and I jumped.

Just the wind. This is my trail. My home.

I lifted my defiant chin and hiked the last of the incline where the sky opened. The moon hung cold in the sky, her light striking the rock outcropping in stark profile. This was my sanctuary, but under the bleak light, I didn't recognize it. The peace of the rock was gone, swallowed by the darkness.

I had not left home, but it had left me. I stumbled backward. Unsure where to go, I fell to my knees, and my cries echoed into the bamboo.

≈

Ryan had woken to the sound of soft footsteps and the creaking of the front door. He'd yanked on his clothes and tiptoed out the door of the mission, wondering if a refugee needed help.

A shadowy figure had trotted through the village, paused at the foot of one of the mountain paths, and checked behind before disappearing into the brown grasses.

Kai.

Hesitating only a moment, Ryan strapped on his dah before dashing after her.

The missionary's daughter was out of sight when Ryan finally entered the trail to the mountain ledge.

Though he could hear her crashing through the undergrowth, Ryan hadn't caught her until she'd stumbled onto the huge rock of her sanctuary, weaving almost as if she'd drunk too much of the villager's fermented *jaru*. Her clothing was snagged, wicked slashes on her face oozing dark trails of blood.

What was she doing?

Ryan reached out for her, but she released screams that battered the rocks, and the force of them slammed against Ryan, stilling his feet, yanking him back through time.

He clenched his fists against the memory of his family's broken barn. He could still feel the mud leaching through his coveralls, coated in dirty straw. That day he'd cried his tears alone, desperately alone. He had sounded like Kai.

But she would never welcome his compassion. Ryan dug his nails into his palms and forced himself to wait, to trust, a practice Ma had mastered and Ryan was still learning. If only she were here to advise him, to show him. But he'd never hear her voice again. Never overhear her pray for him.

They said that Ma's body had been wrapped around Sarah's at the bottom of the gaping storm cellar hole. Trying to protect his sister against an act of God even in death. Ryan had never gone down those stairs again. If he had, he might never have come out of the earth.

After that, he'd been determined to escape the monotonous fields of Indiana. Ironically he'd gone to the other side of the world and ended up in a place that forever reminded him of all the things he'd lost. Not much of an escape.

Ryan squatted in the shadows, forcing himself to remain where he was. Kai's sobs slowed as she folded herself into the nook of a broken tree and quieted.

Above him, the stars shimmered, and a thousand streaks of light streamed across the sky.

"'Lift up your eyes on high,'" Ryan whispered, "'and behold who hath created these things, that bringeth out their host by number: he calleth them all by names by the greatness of his might, for that he is strong in power; not one faileth.'"

Not one star missing. Not one element out of place. Ryan shook his head.

War was coming. They should prepare, but the older missionary was convinced that God wouldn't allow the mission to fall under Japanese authority. Ryan scrubbed a hand through his hair. It was like living in Tornado Alley and refusing to build a storm shelter at your church on account of your church being a church. He had seen plenty of broken steeples in his day.

It didn't matter what he knew. Absolutely nothing would change Pastor John's mind. Nothing Ryan could do to alter what the Japanese might do in the future or how John would respond to any of it. But Ryan could stand watch over Kai tonight and then protect her as much as possible come morning.

Chapter Six

I WOKE WITH A START to the sun washing the edges of the mountain in color. The skin on my face was tight with drying blood, but my heart was remarkably quiet. I'd dreamed of gentle whispers in the night and warm blankets snuggled close. I brushed my cheek, remembering the quiet touch.

Far down the mountain, the pigs squealed, and I knew the village was awake. Papa would be searching for me and angry again. I studied the jungle, wishing it to take me into its leafy arms. If I had to leave Tingrabum, maybe I should run now and be done with it. Was there somewhere I could go? Another village who wouldn't send the Jungle Light's wayward daughter back?

But even if I could, by some miracle, find someplace to go, Ryan and Aunt Nang Lu and Tu Lum would worry. And Matthew already depended on me to feed him. My amoi's miracle would not die because of me. Sighing, I grasped my dah and hacked at the dry twigs and stumps, collecting the firewood in my basket and completing my first morning chore.

When I arrived home, I found Papa and Ryan gathering medical supplies and emergency food. Papa's head was down, light from the doorway reflecting off the silver in his hair. He hadn't heard me come in, so I cleared my throat.

Papa jumped. "Kai. Oh, you have firewood. Good. Bring it in. More refugees came during the night. I'm heading farther into the mountains. They will be in need, and I hope the other villages will agree to help us make a safe passageway to India for you and the refugees. I need you and Ryan to help coordinate things here until I get back."

Papa hadn't even missed me. He could leave, never return, and not miss me at all. "What about Ryan? Can't he go?"

Papa shook his head while he stuffed a sock full of rice around a jar of medicine.

"Why not?" I would not let him brush me off so easily, not when my belly churned with apprehension.

The lines around his eyes were deeper than I remembered . . . like he hadn't slept well either. "You will be fine. Nang Lu and the duwa are here to help, and that boy will stay in the kitchen to help you."

Ryan smiled at me, one side of his mouth tugged higher than the other. "We'll have plenty of help to hold things together."

Papa grimaced at Ryan. "I rather think that the Japanese would hesitate to attack a village with an American mission. After all, America is not at war with Japan."

"The rumors say otherwise," Ryan mumbled.

"Regardless, the people farther north and west are more familiar with me than you and are in need of supplies. With less access to the market, the arrival of refugees will no doubt strain their villages even more than it does ours."

I clenched my fist. It was always this way with Papa. Everyone else took precedence over me.

"But why leave at all?" The selfish question burst from me before I could curtail its ugly hope. "Those villages have runners to tell them to prepare for the refugees, to tell them why it's impossible for us to continue as normal. The duwa is becoming weaker. If you go, you leave us vulnerable." My voice had snaked higher, my anger choking my good sense.

Papa stalked across the room, hand raised. Ryan stepped in front of me, putting his body between Papa and me.

Papa stumbled to a stop, staring at Ryan. "I have made my decision," Papa said, never really acknowledging me. "And you will obey."

"The village is safe with us." Ryan took my elbow and led me into the cooking room. I jumped when the front door slammed behind us.

Tu Lum clambered up the back ladder, eyes wide in question. Though I pretended to be as peaceful as the mountain stream, my hands shook as I packed dried meat and vegetables into bamboo tubes, plugging them with fabric and wood. If it were not for Ryan . . .

"It'll be okay." Ryan ruffled my hair.

I slapped at his hands.

"I am not a child. It is not the first time I have handled the mission on my own." Though it might be the last. I swallowed the thought.

"At least you don't have to do it alone this time." Ryan's fingers engulfed mine and squeezed.

I stared at his knuckles. Unwilling to meet his eyes, I spun to retrieve my basket of water tubes. But Tu Lum snatched them and chased after Ryan.

I shook my head as Tu Lum's legs churned to keep up with Ryan's long strides. Most boys Tu Lum's age would never agree to fetch water—a woman's job, to be sure. But somehow Ryan had charmed the boy. I was grateful Tu Lum had found a purpose, and though I was loath to admit it, I was glad someone else would care for him when I was gone.

I sank to the ground. What was I going to do now?

≈

Early the next morning, Papa strode across the village, the mule trudging behind him, with me trailing still farther behind. Papa stood straight despite the heavy pack strapped across his body. The dah tapped his long legs with each stride.

Ahead, the duwa leaned heavily against the fence post at the village's entrance. Tu Lum waited behind his patron, holding Matthew. Papa stopped and spoke to the duwa.

Aunt Nang Lu hobbled out past her husband, nodded to Papa, and grasped my shoulders with her bony hands. She smelled of curry and made me think of her warm cooking room and all the meals we had prepared and eaten together. As I eased my head to her shoulder, my amoi patted my back.

"It will be all right," Aunt Nang Lu whispered in my ear, her hot breath tickling the hairs on my neck. "The supreme God has control. He watches all things. Go now. Say goodbye. When you are done, come help your amoi care for baby Matthew and cook meals. I fear we will be forever cooking for the strangers."

As Aunt Nang Lu released me, Tu Lum handed her the refugee baby and then slipped his hand into hers. I smoothed down Matthew's dark hair.

If I didn't know better, I would think the two little boys were relaxing with their mother—a perfect picture of comfort. How I wished I could snuggle into that family and freeze the moment there, never going forward or back.

Baby Matthew woke, fussing weakly, no doubt asking for food. Aunt Nang Lu patted my hair and shuffled away, my imaginary family broken.

I scurried to catch Papa. I had seen Karai Kasang do amazing things, like make Papa and me get stuck behind a flash flood to protect us from Chinese raiders on the path ahead. Or use an arrow launched by a little girl to kill a tiger. But I also knew he let mamas die with babies in their bellies and papas not come back from over the mountain. My stomach twisted in knots, like a wringing cloth.

What would happen if I threaded my fingers through Papa's long ones? Would it be like when I was small—him swinging my arm back and forth until he knocked me off balance? I stared at the trees, listening to a pair of children chattering, chasing each other, their voices tangling together. I had been happy here once.

What would it have been like to have lived in Chicago with Papa's family or Texas with Mama's? Would Papa have been more available? I wouldn't have my Kachin family, but would Mama still be alive? My baby brother?

Papa dropped his heavy arm across my shoulders. "Take care of the villagers for me. Be the Lord's hands and feet while I'm gone. Do not forget your studying or your responsibilities."

He stopped at the edge of the green paddy fields and grasped each of my arms. "Nang Lu will be here to help, and I will be back in two blinks of an eye. You will be a strong, little tiger. Yes?"

I stared into his eyes and nodded, his image wavering in my tears. "The Lord bless you and keep you, Papa," I breathed. "The Lord make his face shine upon you, and be gracious to you." My lip trembled.

Papa lifted my chin. "We've done this a hundred times, and it's always the same, Kailyn. No crying." His fingers bit into my jaw, solid, dependable fingers.

It hurt, but I didn't pull away, not wanting him to stop touching me and leave.

Papa dropped his hand, spun, and strode into the jungle without a backward glance.

"Goodbye, Papa," I whispered as the jungle swallowed him whole, the shifting grass the only sign that a man had been on the path. I swiped at my tears, but one escaped and landed at my feet, darkening a rock as black as midnight and a bit smaller than my palm.

I stared at the rock imprisoned in the red dirt. Squatting, I rubbed its surface until I saw a thousand stars twinkling in the darkness. Like the sky last night.

I pushed my thumb into the mud to free the rock, but the ground refused to release the midnight stone. I swiped the sweat from my forehead, smearing myself with dirt. I jumped to my feet, kicking at the earth, grunting until the soil shifted. I dropped to my knees again and attacked the stubborn ground.

Sweat and the blood from my torn fingernails loosened the dirt. And with one final tug, I broke the rock free.

Aunt Nang Lu would say the stone was fine and would remind me that my fear for Papa rested with God now and I should leave my anxiety there. *Keep Papa safe.*

I sniffed and stood. Straightening my shoulders, I strode through the village, ignoring the stares and the throbbing of my fingertips.

I ducked under the roof of my porch and wove through the chickens and pigs stabled in front of my home. Nudging a piglet away from the ladder, I snorted and dropped the dark stone into my pouch. May this not be another prayer that twisted on its way to heaven. What I wouldn't give to be sent away now, if only I could take my loved ones with me.

Chapter Seven

May 1942
Tingrabum

THE MONSOON RAINS CAME EARLY, the heavens weeping alongside the people until the entire mountainside drowned in heaven's tears. Burma had fallen. Any coordinated troops had joined the flood of refugees in a full-fledged retreat. No one stood between Tingrabum and the enemy now.

The nearly impassable paths, however, stalled the Japanese soldiers. But desperate for the relative safety of India or China, refugees poured over the mountains. Diplomats from the West. Foreign businessmen. Whole families. Children. Even ravaged British and Chinese soldiers. Most hardly able to move. Some, like Matthew, orphaned and arriving with strangers. Their eyes were sunken into deep pits as they stared into the jungle. Their sharp cheekbones sliced through Ryan's hopes that the worst had already passed.

As Ryan organized villagers to build huts for the overflow, the people whispered of entire families dying of dysentery, malaria, and starvation. Their bodies strewn across the jungle in various stages of decay, maggots crawling over the putrefied flesh of infants. And of the relentless Japanese soldiers pursuing them, brutalizing prisoners, killing the wounded, drinking the men's blood. Of them destroying every soldier and every foreigner they found and carrying off the women and children.

Days churned by, and Ryan moved from the mission basha to a men's tent to make room for the refugee women and children in the basha with Kailyn. And still more people came, filling the tents and hastily built bamboo shelters, which flowed into the surrounding jungle. And John did not return.

Weeks passed, and Ryan sent sorties into the jungle to collect more food, more medicine, and more supplies to build yet more shelters. And still John did not return.

Every morning as Ryan lumbered up the mountain, he encountered the duwa standing at the edge of the village, hacking into a dirty cloth clutched in his hands. Every time Ryan passed by the village leader, Ryan measured his decline—his pale skin, the amount of blood in the cloth, how hard he leaned against the fence line. What would they do if they lost him too?

Ryan had lost all track of how long John had been gone. His daily life measured in how many people still needed food, how he could safely get them to India, if India was even still safe, when the Japanese would come.

"Ryan." The duwa's hoarse greeting stopped Ryan's feet from crossing into the village one morning. "Thank you."

"Of course," Ryan said and then waited in respectful silence to be dismissed.

"You think the Japanese will come."

The duwa wasn't asking, but Ryan nodded anyway.

"What should we do? We can't just leave these people."

Ryan faced the collection of huts spreading at the feet of the village. "I'm working on ideas to get them out. But we do have to be ready to leave."

The duwa pursed his lips in thought. "I will make it so."

"And . . ." Ryan hesitated. How far did his authority go? "And I'm concerned about people coming and going . . . even to hunt."

"You think we should not leave the village?" The duwa's voice was even, as if he already suspected the answer and agreed.

"I think we should keep everyone here at night and make sure anyone hunting or gathering food doesn't go alone."

The duwa shifted his attention to Ryan. "They are coming soon, aren't they?"

"Yes. They'll follow the trail of the refugees, and the British soldiers have assured me that the Japanese won't hesitate to kill anyone they find . . . and it's worse for the women."

"Then I will post watchers as well. They will give us warning," the duwa said. "But then my people will need someone to lead them. Moran Kai will help, but she is young, and the villagers, well, they've always liked you, and now they see you lead well."

"But you are—"

"Old. I cannot lead if I cannot keep up." The duwa grasped Ryan's arm. "I have already informed the elders of my decision. Kailyn will need convincing. She will not wish to leave Tingrabum, let alone Burma, without her father."

For the first time, Ryan wished he hadn't talked John into letting Kai stay a few months ago. If John had had his way, Kailyn would be well on her way to America and no longer in the path of the Japanese. What kind of leader was Ryan not to have foreseen what was coming? He'd suspected that the rumors of war were true, and yet he'd let his soft heart dictate what was best.

Of course Kai refused to pack even still. She was as immovable as the mountain itself. But Ryan shut down the ache he felt for her, unpacked her travel trunks, and packed a light basket with clothes—including the tiger pelt and warm leggings—dried meat, and hollow bamboo stalks filled with water and placed it near the back door. Just in case, he'd said, even as he promised he would do everything he could not to leave without John.

Kai's eyes had hardened, and she'd stalked out the door and into the jungle. Every day she hunted in the jungle alone, gathered roots and water by herself. Ryan tried to send Tu Lum, but she rebuffed him. She even slept with her blowgun now, and whispers in the village were that she often sneaked out at night—a direct violation of the duwa's command. Maybe he should have lied and told her that he wouldn't leave without her father.

It was strange to work through an entire day without once sitting with Kai to study or fall asleep to her nighttime murmurs in the next room. Ryan hated the fear growing in his own gut almost as much as he hated the ferocious anger strengthening in her. How far away would she push him? He needed her—her knowledge of customs, of the jungle, of the history of the Kachin villages. He wished he could trust that all things would work out well, but he could not see a way through the coming fight with a brutal, well-equipped army.

≈

The urgent shouts of men just beyond the village woke me with a start, and I bolted to the window. Had the Japanese arrived?

As I peeked through the frayed curtains, I caught the last glimpse of a group of British soldiers marching into the jungle.

I'd heard that Ryan was sending word with the troops to the Allied forces at Fort Hertz, far north in Putao, to establish food and medicine deliveries. How the raggedy Brits would get through the mountains was beyond me. But any hope was worth grasping.

While we waited for help from the Allies, Ryan coordinated work details for the fields, for cooking, and for caring for the sick. Everywhere I looked, I saw him—head down, planning, stanching the flow of crises. And I watched the stooped shoulders of the refugees lift in response to his camp for them, with peaceful lines for food, medicine, and water.

My adopted people were busy planting rice in the fields and scavenging extra food in the forest. If they still had breath in their lungs, the people of Tingrabum would not allow anyone to starve. And so far we had enough, and the fear of the nats and Japanese had yet to take over. Perhaps Papa was right and Karai Kasang had sent a line of angels to keep the enemy out. And perhaps he'd sent Ryan to lead the people.

Both Aunt Nang Lu and the duwa depended on him. Though it took me a week to shake off the anger at Ryan's brazen acknowledgment that my father might never come back, I found myself trusting him as well. After all, he'd been right to be concerned about the war. What else was he right about?

When I trailed into the refugee camp that morning, Ryan grinned and, without saying anything about my thorny absence, assigned me to the cooking room with Aunt Nang Lu. With Matthew strapped to one of us, we constantly prepared food and medicine for the refugees and helped the mothers too weak to care for the children.

It wasn't until the relative quiet of night that my mind had time to spin disastrous tales. Papa captured, tortured, wasting away. The Japanese attacking, swarming, destroying the mountain and devouring her people. My nights ended as the sharaw slipped out of the jungle, striped skin rippling with power, the heat of him enticing, burning the darkness, setting me aflame until I startled awake to gray morning light.

Near the end of May, I sat holding Matthew in my arms in the mission basha, humming "Amazing Grace." I could almost hear the strum of Ryan's guitar accompanying me. The haunting chords steadied my soul. The tune was never far from Ryan's fingers, and it had tunneled into my mind until it was always on my lips, as if the nebulous words of hope and grace and salvation might conjure a surplus of safety and peace.

Lightning streaked through roiling clouds that devoured the sky. Even with the light draining from the world, I could see people milling around the supply tent. A woman and two soldiers had saved the remaining children from an orphanage and brought them here. The others were trying to figure out a plan to get them over the mountains.

How had the world come to this? That an orphaned baby and little children needed protection from soldiers with guns and knives?

I dipped a cloth into a bowl of goat's milk and wrung drops into Matthew's mouth.

Dip. Wring. Drop.

Dip. Wring. Drop.

Alone.

They were all alone. Matthew was all alone, like me.

A rumble of thunder in the distance made one of the other children whimper. Lightning flashed through the woven bamboo walls and etched black slashes across the baby in my lap.

Dip. Wring. Drop.

The sky spewed rain down on my mountain, an angry nat cleansing the world. A steady splash of water trailed through the grass roof and puddled at my feet.

The baby grunted, his face screwed in concentration. He let go an enormous, wet explosion, and I flinched as the filth dribbled out the sides of his nappy, wet, stinking of goat's milk, and dripping down my front. This was the third time since dinner he'd exploded into his diaper like this.

"Aunt Nang Lu may appreciate that you're eating enough to decorate my skirts regularly, but I"—I kissed his forehead—"I'm not so sure."

"You're a tricky little fellow, Matthew."

Ryan's voice made me start.

He stood in the doorway, holding a bowl of steaming rice. "Pretending to be weak and then attacking when she least expected it." He traded the bowl for the baby.

Except for his enormous height, Ryan could, perhaps, have passed for a Kachin now. He'd covered his light hair with a faded red turban. His tired face was clean shaven and tanned dark. Around his waist, trimmed from hunger, he had tied a traditional *longyi*—the tubelike wrap all the Kachin people wore instead of pants. I mirrored the goofy grin he gave the baby. Ryan had truly grown into the powerful Bear of Burma that Tu Lum had dubbed him.

"You go clean up. I'll take care of him."

Ryan laid the baby down, cooing all the while. The child groused and snared Ryan's thick finger. Ryan dug out a new cloth, changed the baby, and dropped the old nappy in a basket.

Was there anything he couldn't or wouldn't do? Leadership *and* women's work. Papa had been wrong. Ryan was a good leader, and I wondered what it would be like to always be with him, to have his strong fingers wrapped through mine. Would I always feel this cared for?

As if he sensed I was watching him, he glanced up. I dropped my gaze to study my dirt-crusted bare feet, horrified at being caught staring, of my own childish thoughts. I opened my mouth with an excuse that I needed to change my clothing but realized that I had nothing to change into. All of my dresses were stained with mud, sweat, and cooking grease. One I had ruined when I'd nearly fallen asleep stirring rice and scorched a hole in it. The only stitch of clothing I had left was the tiger pelt. I couldn't even care for myself, let alone be considered adult enough to think about Ryan in such a way.

Heat climbed into my cheeks, and I was thankful for the dimly lit room.

"You've been doing more work than three people put together." Ryan gestured out the door. "There's a clean longyi and shirt in the cooking room. Nang Lu brought it by, apologizing for burning your dress earlier this week. She couldn't replace your American dress but hoped the longyi would be good enough."

How like Aunt Nang Lu to cover up another's embarrassment. I breathed a thank-you and fled to the cooking room. Draped across a clean pot lay a longyi. Aunt Nang Lu's signature pattern of bright red and blue threaded its way through the material. Underneath was a green wrap shirt that matched the skirt, and I twirled, knowing Nang Lu had picked it to remind me of the jungle canopy. I ran shaking fingers across the mismatched white buttons. I had worn nothing but American shirtdresses since I was young. Papa had always wanted me to have a different life than the mountain women. Mama's Italian heritage had lent both of us ebony hair. While I would never pass as Kachin, British officials and soldiers had left enough by-blows in their wake that I might be able to slide in and out of the market without too much notice if I dressed the part.

Surely Papa would not mind me adopting a Kachin longyi under the circumstances. I wouldn't be traveling over the mountain roads anytime soon, and considering the number of male refugees, I'd be safer blending in with my adopted people. I knew far too well what men were capable of.

I grabbed the clothing and slipped into Ryan and Papa's old room to change. The room smelled of lye soap from the refugee women, but the musky smell of Papa fought underneath.

I took a deep breath and pretended he was still here. He would know the right thing to do. He always did. If only he hadn't left when we needed him most.

I set the rice bowl on the floor, unbuttoned the front of the filthy dress, and allowed it to pool at my feet. I slipped into the shirt, then stepped into the longyi, pulling the wide tube of fabric over my legs, gathering it at the side to make it fit, and tucking the ends against my waist.

Tiptoeing back into the room, I saw Ryan's broad shoulders sheltering Matthew. Ryan was humming quietly, swaying like a tree in the breeze, steady and strong. He must have heard my movement because he turned, baby Matthew tucked into his elbow. He would make a good father someday. When he smiled, the skin around his blue eyes crinkled, and I looked away, shame creeping up my neck. Ryan was certainly not my equal.

"Thank you." I took the baby boy from Ryan's arms. I brushed the dark hair off the boy's forehead as his lids drooped and snapped open before drooping again.

Ryan snuggled a corner of the baby blanket into my arm. His fingers lingered a moment, and the wistful look disappeared. When I met his eyes, he snatched his hand back, as if he'd felt the snap of electricity that ran through me. He hesitated a moment, as if he might say something, but then pivoted to leave.

"How do you know how to do all this?" The question slipped out of my mouth before I thought of how disrespectful it sounded.

Ryan chuckled without turning, and I relaxed. This was Ryan, not Papa.

"I was the oldest, and I had a younger sister that needed tending, not to mention all the neighbor kids. My sister was about your age when I left home for school. Boy, was she ever mad at the added chores. You remind me of her, you know."

The fire in the box sputtered, and I stood motionless, waiting, not wanting him to leave. I knew so little about him.

Ryan touched the doorframe but still didn't turn. "I'll have Tu Lum and a friend fetch the water for you tonight so you can rest. Good night, Kailyn."

"Good night."

He stooped to lift my basket filled with empty bamboo water containers and disappeared out the door. His footsteps faded, overtaken by the constant murmur of the refugee camp, and I was left alone.

I stared at the baby, my hand splayed across his tiny chest. The baby whimpered and pulled my finger into his mouth. Matthew sighed contentedly, his brows scrunched in question. *Are you my family now?*

I knew he hadn't spoken, but my hand shook as I traced his cheek with my thumb. What would Papa think if I adopted him?

My baby brother might have had blue eyes, like Matthew's. Like Papa's. I'd never had a chance to see my brother before his spirit had seeped out of his body and taken Mama with him. Maybe Papa had already joined them and I was the only Moran left in all of Burma.

The baby squawked, and I gathered him to my chest, rocking slowly. "Papa will be back, little one." I echoed Aunt Nang Lu's barren promise. "And in the meantime, Karai Kasang will help Ryan keep us safe."

I hope.

I swayed, humming, forcing myself to stay awake as the baby's lids drooped and then relaxed into sleep. I snuggled him into the cradle I had found underneath a pile of Papa's things. Aunt Nang Lu said Papa had made it for me, but I didn't remember ever seeing it before.

Laying my palm on the worn teak, gray with age, I imagined Mama's hand next to my own and tried to remember Mama's voice and the tune she sang. But my memories were hollow and shapeless. A tear slid down my cheek. So little of my home was left now, and the rest was eroding under the surrounding torrent of rain and refugees. How long until the last of it washed away?

Chapter Eight

Night had fallen, and Ryan stood in the doorway of the mission hut, trying not to laugh as Tu Lum licked the last crumbs of rice from his fingers, then searched his banana leaf for any he'd missed. The boy reminded Ryan of a stray puppy.

Tu Lum sprang to his feet. When he saw Ryan, he dropped the banana leaf and dipped his head. "Thank you, Ryan, for the extra rice. My stomach not speak so much tonight."

"Your English is getting better. You've been practicing."

The words restored the boy's smile. How anyone could resist his charms was beyond Ryan.

"I will go finish work for Nang Lu now."

Ryan could easily imagine a tail wagging in pleasure as the boy trekked to the duwa's home.

Ryan's stomach, however, rumbled, missing its portion of rice.

"Be quiet, you." He rubbed his middle. "You're no longer a growing boy."

It had been a long day, and there was little relief in sight. He prayed John would be safe, wherever he was, and for help to arrive soon. The enormous numbers of refugees were quickly depleting the village's stores. Ryan rolled his shoulders and lumbered to the outdoor fire pit, his guitar tucked in his arm.

The night still carried the day's heat, yet a fire smoldered in the yard of the mission basha. It reminded him of the times he'd spent out in the Indiana forest with his sister. He just needed someone to sing with him and the image would be complete.

He eased himself to the log bench, his knees cracking in protest.

"This war's liable to kill me one way or another," he said to the sky.

"Everyone will think you're crazy if you keep talking to yourself." Kai's quiet statement from the doorway nearly caused Ryan to drop his guitar.

"I thought you were in bed." He swiveled to face her.

"I heard you come out. I . . ." Her finger traced the doorway, the fire highlighting the curve of her cheek. "I wanted to thank you for your help."

"My pleasure."

"I know you gave your dinner to Tu Lum."

"Everyone's sacrificing."

"Not everyone would." Shadowed against the dim light, Kai glided down the steps, a bowl cradled in her hand. "I found plum trees in the mountains. I was saving them for Papa. But . . ."

But she wasn't sure he was coming home. Any other time, Ryan would be confident that John had gotten caught up in his work, but he was afraid of the darker possibilities, the things outside his control.

Kai bent and offered Ryan the bowl. Three dark plums nestled in the bottom.

"You're welcome to stay." He shifted the guitar to make room for her.

She hesitated, one bare foot lifted, an elegant deer poised at the edge of the woods, sensing danger.

What was she afraid of?

Ryan spun to scan the edges of the jungle but saw nothing other than the soft contours of the trees. John would never forgive him if he allowed something to happen to her.

Finally Kai seemed to finish with her measuring—of him?—and accepted his help over the log.

"It feels good to sit." She stretched her long legs out in front of her.

Her toes touched his, and she snapped her foot back, tucking it under her.

Coolness slipped into his body, already missing the warmth her touch had brought, as he leaned his guitar between them and picked up a plum. Spinning it, he tested the firmness of the early fruit before biting into it.

The sweetness surprised him, and he licked his lips to catch every drop of juice.

"It's delicious. Thank you." He passed her one of the dark fruits, but she pushed it back.

"I ate so many yesterday, I made myself sick."

"So that's why you and Tu Lum looked a little green," Ryan teased.

Kai twisted her capable fingers in her lap.

"It's okay." Ryan rested a hand over hers, stilling their relentless movement. "I would have done the same thing."

"No. You wouldn't have." Her enormous eyes peered up at him. "You would have shared with everyone."

Back home there'd been times when Ryan had wished he'd had more food, but it'd never been like this—always the numbing sense of hunger. Ryan shook his head, thinking of all the selfish things he'd done in his life. Most of them far worse than a desire to be full for the first time in months or even years.

"Did I ever tell you about the time my mom bought raisins to make Christmas cinnamon bread? I was about Tu Lum's age when I found the tin a few days before Christmas. It was enormous. I ate the whole thing. I still can't believe I did it. Ma wanted to thrash me good. But I was sick for two days straight. She figured I'd been punished enough. I never ate another raisin again." Ryan chuckled. "It was so bad, my poor sister, who had to help clean up, never ate raisins again either."

Ryan lifted the guitar and strummed a few chords. "Besides . . ." Ryan shrugged. "You shared with me." He nudged her shoulder.

He gazed in wonder at the woman beside him. No matter what she said, she would willingly give all she had and more.

He picked out a few notes of Bach's Minuet in G. The guys in his high school had teased him mercilessly for his interest in the classics, but it had been Ma's favorite. She and his sister had twirled across the living room, their skirts lively flowers during the darkest nights of winter. His spine stiffened, sending his fingers stumbling to a stop. Only then did he hear her sniff.

"Kai?"

"I miss Papa." A tear trickled down her cheek, and she swiped it away.

When another followed, Ryan reached across his instrument and thumbed the moisture away. "I do too."

And as much as it surprised him, he did. Second-guessing someone else's decisions was far easier than making the decisions yourself. And the fact remained that John's absence hurt Kai. Ryan would do anything to ease her hurt, anything to protect her from what came with life and, worse, with war. If he could, he would sweep her into his arms and run. He would carry her away from here, bring her and the entire village to Indiana and let them colonize the farm.

But he knew that was a fanciful dream and might just make everything worse. Her home was here, in Burma. His was now too. His fingers picked a few notes, hoping the music would free his thoughts.

Kai touched a slender finger to the guitar's tuning pegs.

"Would you like to learn?" Ryan shifted so Kai could take the instrument.

She snatched back her hand and tipped her head, the glow of the fire pressing dark pools in the downward curve of her lips. "Learn? Even Papa would understand that you closed the school."

"No. I meant this." Ryan lifted the guitar, placing it between them. "Do you want to learn to play guitar?"

Kai squirmed. "I tried once . . . when you were at the school." She held up her small hand. "My fingers couldn't reach across. It sounded awful, like two old biddies arguing with one another. Papa stormed into the basha, wondering who was causing all the racket. He found me reading and quite confused at the commotion."

Ryan's laughter erupted in the dark space. "Well, aren't you the sneaky one?" He imagined her opening the guitar case and struggling with the instrument. "What else did you explore without me knowing?"

Kai's eyes grew wide, and Ryan laughed even harder, wondering what she would find interesting in his stack of clothing and books.

"I wasn't . . . I didn't . . ." Kai shrank away, obviously making her body a smaller target.

Realization stopped Ryan cold. If her father had caught her, he probably would have beaten her. The man had no idea how to love a child. Love wasn't measured in how well a person followed rules, especially when they were ever-moving lines.

"I'm not angry." Ryan touched her shoulder, gently easing her closer to him. "It's normal for you to be curious."

"It wasn't proper." She coiled her legs under her to spring away. "I . . . I apologize."

"Really." He dropped his hand to his lap. "It's okay."

But the words melted, useless as a diamond in the jungle. How many times had she been punished for her curiosity?

"How about I play? You've earned your rest. Tomorrow you can draw for me. And if you're ever curious about playing guitar, you can always ask. It's what friends do."

Kai unfolded slightly and nodded. "Friends." She tasted the word and seemed to find it satisfactory, because she added a log to the fire and then sat next to him with a shiver.

"You're cold."

"I'm fine." But by wrapping her arms around herself, she betrayed the lie.

"Come here. I promise not to bite." Ryan laughed and coaxed her closer, shifting just a hair so she could nestle into his side. A perfect fit. The thought unlocked the tension he hadn't realized he'd been sheltering behind his rib cage. It had been a long, long time since he'd been able to take a full breath.

A scant few minutes passed before Kai's breathing steadied into sleep. Her arm, draped across the log, dropped around his back, and he leaned into her gentle vibrancy, taking solace in the comfort of her touch. The two of them were well alone in the world.

Despite sleep hounding him, Ryan sat a while longer, picking monotonous notes and humming. He watched the stars move above him, oblivious to the evil stalking the mountains. "What am I supposed to do?" he whispered to the heavens.

Kai was hurting and scared. Pastor John might never return. Things were getting worse, and the duwa seemed to think Ryan was ready and able to take over both the mission and the village. In reality Ryan had no idea what to do. If something didn't change soon . . . That was a thought he didn't care to finish.

He watched Kailyn's eyes jump behind her lids and wondered what she dreamed about. If anything she dreamed would take her far from here. Her hand curled around his shoulder, and she nestled deeper into him. He set the guitar aside and allowed himself to ease his arm around her. He didn't care to think about what would happen when the Japanese came. It was foolish to think he could protect her, but he would find a way.

Careful not to wake Kai, he scooped his arms under her and carried her into the mission basha. Tiptoeing across the bamboo floor, he prayed he wouldn't wake the refugee women asleep in the other room. He eased to his knees, nestling Kai into her pallet and tucking the blanket to her chin. Ryan's breath stirred the wisps of her hair, and she curled toward him, a smile teasing the edges of her lips. He smiled an echo of hers, and he brushed a strand of hair from her jaw. If only she could see the tricks of her own mind.

Maybe tonight's music would ease her through the night, covering any lurking nightmares.

But there was one thing he could do to assure a better night's rest for her. Ryan leaned over the sleeping baby and lifted him to his chest. For days Kai had nearly adopted the baby, refusing to let anyone help care for him. Ryan knew she needed the rest. While he couldn't keep the baby in the men's tent, Nang Lu and little Tu Lum wouldn't mind caring for him. He was, after all, a relatively easy child.

Chapter Nine

IT WAS TU LUM WHO came for Ryan.

The day was just shifting from black to gray when the little boy touched Ryan's arm and woke him. Tu Lum's call was a breath above the sound of rain. "Ryan?"

For a moment Ryan thought he was still dreaming, and he grasped the boy's arms to be sure he was real and wouldn't melt into the refleshed skeletons of his sleep. The mist hung low, winding through the village—the rain clouds pierced through with gray pink, the light battling the dark.

Ryan blinked back his dreams. "What is it?"

"The baby." His voice hiccuped. "Baby Matt. Something is wrong. I couldn't find Nang Lu."

Ryan's head slammed back onto his pallet. The baby had been fine yesterday. Hadn't he? Surely someone else could handle whatever the child needed.

"Ryan?" Tu Lum stood, twisting his hands through the worn longyi. "I don't want to worry Kai. But I . . ." The boy sniffled.

Tu Lum rarely overreacted to anything. Had Ryan missed something? Ryan struggled to his feet, his nightmares dripping in. The jungle never did anything in halves. Like the setting sun, sickness came quickly, darkening what had been light moments before.

Oh God, I would rather have the nightmare. At least it isn't real.

His fingers clumsy, Ryan pulled up a longyi and buttoned a shirt. Tu Lum trailed behind him as Ryan dashed through the village, fear climbing into his throat.

Nang Lu leaned over the huge clay bowl that the women used for milling rice. Seeing her, Tu Lum threw himself into her arms.

"What's wrong, small one?" Concern flitted through her eyes, and she shuffled behind Ryan through the village to her basha.

The stench of human waste caught in his throat, and Ryan covered his mouth. Nang Lu swallowed, cringing back before straightening her shoulders and striding to the bassinet in the main room.

Squatting, Nang Lu lifted the limp baby, whispering to him as she stroked his tiny head, his lips already turning blue.

Ryan lit a lantern and held it out. The flame trembled against the darkness as waste trickled down the baby's leg, dripping off his heel.

Please.

The words stuck in his throat. Everyone depended on Ryan, and he had nothing more to give.

Tu Lum fanned the baby with a palm frond to shoo away the flies and keep him as cool as possible. The boy's movements were filled with purpose. He would save the baby with his fan if he could.

As Ryan watched the rhythm of the boy's hands, he wondered how Tu Lum endured his vigil. How had it all come to a little boy who cared in such a place as this?

Nang Lu leaned back on her heels, glancing at Ryan over her shoulder. Questions filled her eyes, then resolve as she leaned over Matthew.

"The Lord bless you and keep you," Nang Lu whispered to the tiny form as he shuddered and inhaled. "You will not be forgotten, little one. Go to God with peace."

The bundle stirred, a desperate breath followed by a long rasp. And then, silence.

As if the whole world inhaled, gasping.

Tears cascaded down Ryan's cheeks and joined those of Nang Lu's, falling, lost through the cracks in the bamboo floor.

Tu Lum jumped to his feet. "He is not gone. God would not take baby Matt from us."

Ryan touched Matthew's smooth neck, still warm, feeling for . . . praying for a pulse, for movement.

Ryan felt his own heart beating against his fingertips, but there was no answering thud in the baby.

Oh Lord. Please no.

"He's . . . He's . . ." The words wrapped themselves around Ryan's throat and refused to come out.

"You must save him." Tu Lum shook as he pleaded with Ryan. "You must use your magic medicines and pray to the supreme God."

"I am sorry. I truly am." Ryan's voice cracked, and he prayed his knees would keep him upright.

The palm leaf fan dropped from Tu Lum's fist, twisting once, twice before falling to the floor. The boy frowned at the leaf, as if it had betrayed him, and fled from the basha, the door straining to fly away with him.

The door then swung partially closed and cut off Ryan's view of Tu Lum's retreating form. Ryan scavenged for a hint of light outside. But he forced his feet to remain in the darkness.

"It is not your fault, Ryan." Nang Lu touched Ryan's shoulder.

Tearing his eyes from the sliver of sunlight, Ryan nodded.

"Tu Lum will be all right. But we have work to do." Nang Lu gestured to the bundle in her arms. "And we should work quickly. We cannot let the sickness spread, and it will not help the others to see him so."

Ryan eased the bundle away from Nang Lu, the tiny burden weighing him down, making him wonder if he could make the trek to the far side of the village. He'd been sure the baby would survive. That letting Kai care for him would help. Now . . . now . . .

They had no time or space to honor every person who had died in the last few weeks. The British soldiers, some young men barely old enough to carry a rifle. The older government workers, the wives . . . the children. The earth swallowed them without complaint, without regard to class or age. The refugees had long since ceased normal ways of saying goodbye. Even the villagers were too drained of energy for ceremonies. We could manage no more dances, no long days of mourning, no laying out, no funerals, not even individual graves. The men had dug a series of pits in anticipation of the day's burial needs. There were too many bodies. The living simply couldn't keep up.

Ryan followed Nang Lu. He trained his eyes on the yellowed shirt of the old woman in front and refused to look at the villagers, the sky, the mountain.

What was the point?

Ryan plodded on, his vision dimming, his steps swaying. Nang Lu stopped in front of a pit the men had hastily dug specifically for the child. Ryan stumbled, nearly dropping the bundle.

Using a bamboo rope, Ryan eased Matthew into a yawning hole until the body rested in the mud swirling at the bottom.

Ryan watched in horror as the water tugged at the blanket shroud, sucked away the covering. Everything inside Ryan wanted to run, but a sudden spark of light from the sky lit the baby's face. The boy's eyes were closed, quiet, and something more.

Peaceful. He was at peace. Somewhere in heaven, snuggled into his mother's arms. Maybe Ma and Sarah would be there to help take care of him. Ryan clung to the image, white knuckled in his attempt to keep moving.

"Ashes to ashes. Dust to dust."

Matthew was no longer here.

Ryan pushed a shovelful of dirt into the pit, and the weight pushed Matthew's body beneath the waters.

He was gone. Free of pain, fear.

Sunlight shimmered on the surface of the water, marred only by Ryan's reflection.

Another shovel of dirt rained into the water, shattering his image and sending ripples of light to the darkest corners of the pit.

Ryan took a deep breath and clutched the shovel as he finished burying the child.

≈

Just inside the doorway to Kailyn's room, Ryan stood, the wall holding him upright. Dirt and mud from burying Matthew clung to him as unwanted reminders. The list of things to be done was longer than the mountain was high, but he needed the quiet for a moment and a reminder of one of the few things making the struggle forward worth the effort.

Most days Kai would be awake, doing chores already. But the late hour proved she was beyond exhausted, and Ryan didn't have it in himself to wake her yet. Matthew had found his way into her heart. Telling her would destroy her . . . again. He'd have to do it, but it could wait while she rested.

In the meantime, Ryan would continue to find the strength to take another step and another. Most days he found a solid place under his feet, but Kai . . . It was no secret she was struggling.

She curled into the wall, a blanket tangled in her legs, her lashes dark against her smooth cheek. In sleep she was quiet, calm—a drastic contrast to the pinched, stressed look she wore most days. Maybe he was selfish, but he hated to wake her to the reality of life without Matthew, hated the idea of being the one to watch her crumple, hated that he could do nothing more than put off the inevitable.

A fly, lazy in the morning chill, buzzed around her head, and she swatted at it in her sleep.

Because she lived deep in the mountains, Kai would normally have been someone's wife by now, have a child of her own. If a mountain man would have a foreigner as his wife. The capable young woman, a half-wanted property of another man. The thought churned Ryan's stomach, but the thought of her being forced to leave the mountain didn't sit well either.

A tap sounded before Nang Lu slipped through the front doorway of the mission basha. Rain ran through her hair and dripped to the floor. Ryan stared into the darkened bedroom and felt Nang Lu's careful steps cross the room behind him, bouncing on the drooping rush floor.

"She's so peaceful now."

Ryan barely heard the woman over the steady sound of rain on the roof.

"I found Tu Lum. He is sleeping in my basha now. The women there will tell me when he wakes. He is a good boy. You and your Kailyn have done well with him."

Ryan nodded and turned, the contented feeling slipping at the sight of the monsoon mold creeping up in the corners of the basha and the pile of unwashed clothes in the corner. His mind swam with the details of feeding and caring for the hundreds of refugees and moving them on, let alone dealing with responsibilities of the mission.

First things first. Ma's admonition pushed down the panic.

"I'll start breakfast." Ryan's stomach growled, complaining of another breakfast of bland rice. What he wouldn't do for just one day back home. One day of no responsibility and maybe a serving of Ma's fluffy pancakes.

Ryan poked at the fire before scooping leftover rice into a small pot. Nang Lu's host of women, minus Kai, had likely started cooking for the refugees already, but Nang Lu didn't need to worry about feeding him or Kai. Dropping in a few shriveled vegetables Kai had gathered yesterday, Ryan poured water in and sprinkled curry across the mixture. He banked the coals so the food would warm but not burn before Kai was likely to wake.

Ryan trudged back to the main room to gather the dirty laundry. He'd at least lug it outside and start the fire for Kai.

But Ryan stopped when he saw Nang Lu still leaning against the doorframe of Kai's room.

"She's strong. She'll be okay. Won't she?" he said.

Nang Lu shook her head, a wild deer shaking off her captors. "My husband. He grows worse every day." Nang Lu eased down in front of the chief fireplace. "She is like a daughter to me."

Ryan realized that Nang Lu was speaking English. When the woman squinted down at her mud-soaked feet, Ryan grasped the doorway to steady himself. With Kai sleeping and the refugees out searching for food, he was the only person who would understand the conversation.

"I fear for her."

To be honest, Ryan was afraid too, and not just for Kai. He knew from Pop's stories about the Great War that war wasn't like football, where everyone played by the rules and you made a game plan based on the opposing team. It was unpredictable, and Ryan didn't know what he was expected to do. He had no response for the storm brewing in the village mother.

"I don't think Pastor John will come home, and I cannot send her to India alone." Nang Lu's knobby fingers twined together and then released. "I need to know someone will take care of her."

Ryan's mind scrambled. He didn't like the direction of this conversation, didn't like what it might mean for the village.

"She is American. Like you. The Americans will listen to you. You could—"

"*We* will take care of her—you and I—until Pastor John comes back and figures out what to do. I won't abandon you." *I won't lose anyone else. Kai can't lose anyone else.*

"Ryan, that may not—"

"No." Ryan's contradiction echoed loudly in his own ears. "No. We will do it together."

"Together." Nang Lu nodded.

But calculated disagreement radiated in the pinch of her mouth, and as he answered the call of another refugee with another concern, Ryan couldn't help but wonder what the mother of the village had seen.

≈

I rubbed my nose and rolled on my pallet. I stretched, toes reaching for opposite sides of my room.

Someone needed to take the pot off the fire—it was burning. I yawned and squinted at the bright light.

Suddenly the smell of scorched food punctured through the fog of sleep, and I jumped up, dashing through the basha, tripping over pallets, toys, laundry, into the cooking room. I snatched the pot off the fire and dowsed it in water.

Ugly black residue of burned rice caked the pot. I sank to the floor, my breath coming in quick gasps.

I didn't know how to keep going. At least with Papa I had a solid routine, someone to tell me what to do and when.

Now. Now, the world was draining through my fingers like water, and I couldn't hold it long enough to figure out what to do with anything.

Scooping out the top layer of browned rice and vegetables, I dropped the grains onto a plate. Taking a few bites, I left the rest for Ryan, knowing he had likely put it on the stove. It would be like him to start something for me and then forget about it in the midst of helping someone else.

I licked my fingers clean, my stomach grumbling at the meager breakfast. Perhaps today the jungle would produce extra food for us.

I blinked into the sunlight coming in from the window. Realization at the late time slammed into me. Why hadn't baby Matthew awoken yet?

Fear climbed my throat, threatening to spew my meager breakfast. I spun, running back to my room. A note from Ryan lay at the bottom of the cradle. He'd brought Matthew to sleep at Nang Lu's last night and asked me to come find him the moment I woke. Relief warred with frustration. Why did Ryan think I needed help? More than a few women my age were caring for their children. Had I not proven myself worthy?

Ducking out the front door, I grabbed the milking bucket and called to the nanny goat. I'd at least bring milk to Nang Lu, saving her that chore. "Come, Lily. Let's have your milk then."

The goat waddled up, more than willing to endure her milking, both for the relief and the expected treat afterward. The steady rhythm of the milk hitting the bucket soothed my bruised pride.

Children ran by screeching, and the goat jumped, stomping on my bare foot. Gasping, I leaped to my feet and knocked into the bucket, sending milk flying across the yard. I sank to the ground, inhaling, foot throbbing. I fought the sobs. We needed that milk. Matthew needed that milk.

I clucked at the goat, soothing until Lily stood silent and content again. I leaned my forehead into her side. The burden of caring for a child pressed down on me. As usual Ryan had known what I needed even before I did myself. How did others parent alone? I sighed, thinking of Papa. The sound of his crying hidden in the empty pallet he'd shared with Mama must sound so much like my own.

The mission felt empty without him. Maybe Ryan would move back in. Perhaps having someone familiar nearby would make it feel less empty. More like home.

And he could help me with the baby. A perfect solution.

"Kai? Are you well?" My neighbor, Baw Ni, peeked over the fence, her wrinkled, round face the perfect picture of concern. Even her scar seemed to tip down in feigned pity.

"Of course." I choked back a biting remark. This woman only brought trouble, especially since the duwa had sent Baw Gun away as payment for his actions.

I leaned back into my milking. "What is it you need?" I forced my voice to remain light, treating her how I imagined Ryan might.

When Baw Ni didn't answer or leave, my rhythmic pulling stopped. Her grin exposed betel nut–blackened teeth, a cemetery full of broken tombstones. "What do you know?" My words were low and hard.

"I—"

"I have had enough of your poison." I sprang to my feet. "What news do you bring? More bad news for little Moran Kai, the tiger-eyed orphan? Or are you gaining information for your gossip circles?" My words rose in pitch as I stood towering over the bent old woman. "What is it you know?"

Tears gathered in the corner of Baw Ni's eyes, but a smirk still crept onto her lips, giving away her delight in holding power over me.

"Oh, Moran Kai, I thought your friends had told you. Baby Matthew . . . they buried him hours ago. I am . . ."

The air around me thickened. I couldn't take it in. I was choking, heaving. I had to get out. I stumbled past the old woman and through the gate and ran into the open arms of my jungle. Perhaps I'd be better off dying at the hands of the Japanese than continuing to lose the people I loved.

Chapter Ten

SITTING UNDER A PATCHED-TOGETHER command tent, Ryan squinted at the list of refugees capable of walking to India. The trickle of people searching for shelter had finally slowed, which either meant that the survivors had all gotten out or that the Japanese had caught up with the trail and cut them off.

Ryan made a note to double the number of scouts on the mountain trails and went back to his list of names, ages, and medical issues. Some were even willing to carry the less critically sick out on stretchers. Ryan had recruited guides for this group, but there was not enough food to get them through the mountains to India. He didn't even know which fair-weather trails the rains had flooded, let alone which paths might lead straight into a Japanese unit. The Kachin guides were fierce men but armed with only bows and arrows.

And what about those who couldn't handle the trails?

He dropped his head into his hands. Nothing had come of the British soldiers who had promised to send help. Tingrabum was alone, with the Japanese circling in for the kill . . . if the dysentery didn't kill them all first.

Ryan shook his head. They needed a miracle. The village and surrounding mountains simply did not have enough food, let alone protection.

For a moment, Ryan sat listening to the rain patter against the tent walls. Worst of all, he still had to tell Kai about Matthew.

Ryan stared at the tent ceiling, wishing the flooding rain, the deaths, the responsibility—everything—would stop for just a minute. That he could hide long enough that someone else would tell Kai, that someone else would find a way to protect all these people. He wasn't sure how much more he could take. The shadow of branches danced across the canvas, the trees bowing against a gale. It was a wonder they didn't snap with the force.

Outside, footsteps splashed closer to the tent, and he braced himself for more news.

Lord, help me bend and not break.

A scout burst through the door, pointing behind him. "Ryan. A growling bird flew low over the mountains and dropped eggs with wings on the fields."

Ryan stood, confused, until the scout's words converged into a mental picture. "An airplane," he whispered. "A plane. Please let it be what I think it is."

Ryan ran out of the tent and skidded across the waterlogged path to the fields. Three enormous bags and two crates sat partially submerged in the ground, their sodden parachutes rolling in the breeze.

He swung back to the Kachin scout, who stood shifting his weight.

"It's food." Ryan did a little hop of joy. "Food!"

The two men each hoisted a bag of rice on each shoulder and staggered into the village. Unable to hold the weight and open the door, Ryan kicked the support poles of Nang Lu's cooking hut.

"What fool is pounding at my house?" Nang Lu flung the door open, scowling into the half light. "Ryan. What in heaven's name?"

"Rice. And there's more. They've found us."

"Bring it in, child. Put it by the fire." Her voice was smooth, unaffected.

Ryan shook his head. She'd expected help to come. How did she never waver?

As soon as Ryan stacked his bag, she pulled him into a fierce hug

90

and patted his cheek. "Praise Karai Kasang. You have done well, Ryan. Your kanu would be proud."

Ryan twirled the old woman in a circle, her feet leaving the floor, their hopeful happiness ringing out.

Other villagers raced to the field and helped carry the supplies— additional medicine along with signal flags, instructions on building an airfield, and the Allied plans for the village.

The Americans were going to land light aircraft to fly out the injured. Giddiness lightened Ryan's steps as he dashed to the field to direct the last of the boxes across the path. Tu Lum brought up the rear, sloshing up the path with the bag of flags slung across his slender back. Ryan matched the boy's grin, as wide as the Cheshire cat's.

They ducked under the flaps of the medical tent, and Ryan's lungs deflated as his eyes swept across the space. So many still wouldn't make it, hadn't made it.

In his mind, Ryan could still see Kai holding Matthew and whispering to him. The villagers would clean his cradle and burn the bedding. But no one could clean out the ruin in Ryan's heart.

He stared at the boxes stacked in the corner. He needed to stop avoiding Kai. At least he had good news to tell her too.

Sighing, Ryan dragged himself across the village and knocked on the door of Kai's basha. When no one answered, Ryan opened the door a crack.

"Kailyn?" Ryan called out as he burst in. The steady drip of rain and the smell of charred rice hung heavy in the air. Ryan shivered against the chill on his wet skin.

Why was the fire out?

Kai was not with Nang Lu, so she should be here, still sleeping. But the door to Kailyn's room stood open. If she was awake, why hadn't she come to find him as he'd asked?

"Kailyn?" Ryan called again as he darted through the basha and into the kitchen. His ears strained for sound, any movement underneath the rasping of his own rapid breathing.

He wheeled a circle before bolting out the door.

Tu Lum stood at the base of the ladder. "Perhaps next door?"

Ryan dashed to the neighbor's house and knocked on the door.

The door opened, and Baw Ni emerged, hair tangled, shirt rumpled and stained dark with betel nut juice. "What is it you want?" She spit a stream of juice, just missing his foot.

Ryan shrank back, his words tangled in his brain. Though she didn't even reach his shoulder, something about this woman cowed Ryan. "I am looking for Moran Kai. Is she here?"

"Does it appear that she is here? Is it my job to watch for her and do my laundry duties as well? You've banished my son and now thrust all this on me. I'm an old woman. You will kill me with all these demands."

Ryan peered around the older woman, hoping Kai would spring out and surprise him. If she had found out about Matthew and sought refuge in the jungle . . . Ryan fought images of her washed away in the flood, injured in the jungle, or worse.

"You don't know where she is?"

"Do you think I would continue in this way if I did?" Baw Ni huffed.

"I'm sorry, Baw Ni. If you see her . . ." Ryan's words rushed out of him, his mind trying to plan even though panic bubbled underneath. He would find her. He had to.

≈

Mud sucked at Ryan's feet as he raced to the command tent. He burst through the flaps, startling the men who had gathered, excited to hear from their leader about the strange bird in the sky.

Their excitement soured as Ryan barked orders to scour the mountains for Kai. None of the neighbors had seen her leave. Had she missed Ryan's note? No, the note had been in the cradle. She had to have seen it. Why hadn't she come to see him? She wouldn't leave alone. Not with how close the Japanese were.

It wasn't unheard of for men to kidnap a wife for themselves. But most men in Tingrabum avoided Kai, afraid of her tiger eyes and the wrath of the supreme one. All save one.

Baw Gun. Had he come back for her? Ryan grasped the hilt of his dah.

As the search party dispersed, Nang Lu shuffled into the tent. She shifted out of the flow of men and dropped the banana leaf she'd been using as an umbrella.

"What else has happened?"

"Kai's missing." Ryan set his shaking palms on the table in front of him, willing himself into calm.

"Missing?" Nang Lu stiffened but remained calm. "What did she say when you told her of Matthew?"

Ryan's stomach dropped.

"You did not tell her?" Nang Lu's thunderous exclamation cracked as she closed her eyes and sucked in a deep breath. "Come. I will help you look."

Kai was in danger all because he'd been too afraid to tell her the truth. When would he get it through his thick skull that telling the truth was always the right choice?

≈

I placed another stone over the freshly mounded dirt. Blood dripped across my knuckles, testimony to the number of rocks I had pried from the stream bed. My longyi was heavy with mud from the countless times I had slid on the monsoon-soaked hill. Pushing my hair out of my face, I stood. Raindrops pelted Matthew's grave.

Another brother stolen from me. A sob erupted from my soul, and I crumpled to the ground, fresh mud seeping into my skirts and the cold stealing my breath.

Why? Why, Lord?

My fingers snaked around the red pouch at my neck. The tiger inside snuggled into the white and black stones I carried. The reminders of my mother, my failed prayers for Papa, my broken desire to belong.

"Are you even listening? Or maybe this is your idea of a joke. Give me hope, but then steal him away. Let me stay home, but destroy it while I watch."

My words hardened in my chest as the rain beat against me, trying to wash me away with the mountain. I opened the pouch and took out the white stone, pushing my fingers against the surface. "Please."

Thunder roared, hollowing my hearing, even as the answering lightning blinded me.

A hand on my shoulder made me scream and spin. My feet slipped out from under me, and I knocked into the pillar of stones, scattering them into the mud.

Aunt Nang Lu squatted next to me, her wet hair clinging to her cheeks. But Ryan towered above, his face a storm of fury.

"Where have you been?" Ryan's rage drowned out the rumble of thunder. "You take off without telling anyone, abandon your responsibilities."

I bristled, my own anger roaring. "I am saying goodbye." The rock in my hand cut into my fingers. Ryan, at least, should understand.

"Anything could have happened to you. I—"

"I'm doing the best I can." I stood, shaking, stretching to my fullest height. "I'm not perfect like you—able to talk to these strangers, make friends, act like I've got it all under control."

"I'm *not* perfect, and I didn't say—"

"I want my home back." I threw the rock to the ground, and mud exploded against my legs before slopping back into a slow-moving sludge.

I whirled, intending to bolt away, but Aunt Nang Lu snatched me, her aging hands strong and firm as she held me against her. I stood stiffly, wanting her to both stay and leave in equal amounts. I was no longer a girl who could sink into my amoi. As surely as the jungle had swallowed Papa, I could not see how any of us could escape the same fate as Matthew.

"It is okay, little tiger. We both feared for you. I am sorry for your hurt, but your Ryan also has good news." Nang Lu signaled to Ryan and spun me to face him.

Ryan forced a hand through his rain-darkened hair. Streaks of dirt ran across his cheeks onto his drenched shirt, but it was the dark circles under his eyes and the lines of worry between his brows that silenced my billowing tirade. Regret for the fear I'd caused skittered through my chest.

"The Americans found us." Ryan watched a group of men carrying a few dirty bundles into the village. "They dropped medicine, food, and directions on how to make a landing strip."

"Food?" My stomach growled in response.

Ryan smiled and bent to retrieve my stone. "Food." He placed the white stone in my hands. "And a way to get all these people out of the country. They'll fly out anyone who can't walk."

I sank to the ground. Rescue had been so close. If we'd had the food, the medicine a week ago, maybe we could have saved Matthew. Rain streamed from the sky as if Karai Kasang himself wept. But why should he weep? Yes, I had failed, but he had not done enough either.

Ryan knelt next to me, his forehead against mine and his arms around my shoulders, sheltering me from the rain.

"I'm sorry, Kailyn. For everything. I wish . . ."

I leaned into him. What I wanted wasn't possible anymore. But the death of my desires wasn't Ryan's fault. He'd done everything he could to save us. My arms flung around his middle, and I was suddenly tired.

He smoothed a hand down my hair, then groaned to his feet. "Let's get you inside, and we'll figure out how to set up this airfield." He held out his hand to help me find my feet, and I tucked my hand into his, our arms nudging each other as we walked toward the village.

Maybe this would be the end of the war for us.

Chapter Eleven

NONE OF US KNEW MUCH about airplanes, runways, or army signals, but we learned quickly. We had to. The planes were returning in less than a week. And they needed a landing strip.

Ryan pressed every able-bodied person into hacking at the jungle, moving rocks, and hauling timber away from a fairly flat piece of ground outside the village.

Late in the afternoon the day before the plane was scheduled to arrive, Ryan, Tu Lum, and I stood admiring our handiwork. The sky drizzled sullenly, but the torrential rains had paused long enough for us to finish.

Ryan, the only one in the village who had even seen an airfield, declared ours small but usable for a light plane. And the ragtag Allied military men agreed.

Pride welled in me. Ryan had done it. Our village had done it. We had outwitted the enemy.

By the next day, most of the refugees would start their trek to India and the planes would begin taking the handful who couldn't get out any other way.

I unrolled the pack containing the enormous signal panels and scrambled to collect them as the wind unfurled the fabric and sent them snapping under my fingers. One escaped my grasp and sped toward the jungle, a maniacal ghost twirling and spinning, showing its twin sides in turn. Yellow, then white, and back again.

The small cry that escaped my lips sent Tu Lum and Ryan scurrying after the panel, slipping in the mud, shouting at each other until they leaped at the same moment and crashed to the ground in a pile tangled inside the muddy fabric.

The jungle tripped into silence for a moment, and I gasped at the still forms. "Are you all right?" I struggled to constrain my bundle even as I ran toward them.

Ryan's laugh guffawed across the mountain, and I released my breath only to stumble over the edge of a panel and land sprawling on top of the two friends.

Tu Lum snorted and burst out laughing, his little body bent over the moment, cradling it to his belly. I tried to stand, but my legs were tangled, and I fell in an ungraceful heap onto Ryan's chest, my forearms forcing his breath out in a whoosh.

He winked at me, his blue eyes twinkling. "I see you've fallen for me, fair maiden."

At the implication, my mouth opened and closed like a fish in a basket, and I pushed away from him. "And where's the knight who's to rescue me?"

"Your wish is my command." Ryan snatched my hand and tugged me against him. The corner of his mouth lifted as he gathered himself to stand. But his foot slipped in the mud, and he fell again, sending a spray of mud into my mouth. I latched on to his shirt, giggling and spitting the mud.

Tu Lum stood, glancing between me and Ryan, a strange expression flitting through his eyes.

I scooped a handful of mud and dropped it on Ryan's head before pirouetting and launching a mass at Tu Lum, his accomplice.

Pushing myself to my feet, I grinned as the others sputtered in surprise. But the sweetness of my revenge lasted a single breath before they turned on me with handfuls of red mud.

With a yelp I spun and ran to the shelter of the forest. I caught a low branch and swung into the tree, hauling myself up—a monkey with a bear at her heels. Ryan caught my leg before I clambered out of his reach. Grinning, he yanked me from the tree, and I crumpled to the ground moments before he pelted me with a mud ball, followed by Tu Lum's contribution.

Mud dripped from my hair into my eyes. I swiped at the mess, squirming under Ryan's scrutiny, my stomach aching from the joy. "I'm sorry. I'm sorry." I held my hands in surrender.

Ryan released me, and I plucked a piece of grass from his shirt.

He nudged my shoulder. "I've missed a good snowball fight. This is a little messier, but it works."

I couldn't remember the last time I had laughed like this, and it was as glorious as if the sun had shone in the sky. Ryan hoisted Tu Lum to his shoulders and linked his arm through mine. Pinned to his side, we backtracked to the field, as close to a family as we could get. We needn't run through the jungle for the signal panels. The mud had plastered them to the ground for us.

The three of us manhandled the panels into an arrow signaling safe landing, nailing them to the ground with the metal spikes. In the morning, our first load of hospital-bound refugees would fly to safety. Soon we would be free.

≈

During the next few days, the Allied planes flew back and forth from India to our tiny gap in the jungle. They collected injured and sick refugees, along with any remaining British and Indian children, until the only people left were villagers and one last group preparing to walk. I saw little of Ryan during the day. But every night he sat with me, strumming his guitar while I drew pictures of the village, the airplanes, the life I dreamed of in the mountains. The night before, Ryan had moved back into the mission, as had Tu Lum and a gaggle of Kachin, Shan, and

Chin orphans. The mission would care for the people of Burma as our own until we could find better places for them. My world was smoothing out, and my unconscious mind led my fingers to draw its whispered desire—a giant of a man sitting side by side with a tiger-eyed woman. The man's arm rested lightly across her shoulders while he contemplated the rice paddy fields in front of them—content in his dreaming. But she stared at me, daring me to hope, to imagine the weight of his arm around me, the whisper of his lips across mine.

Heat scorched my cheeks, and I crumpled the page and dropped it into the fire, where the fanciful dreams of a child belonged. I was just the other missionary's daughter, another responsibility for the Bear of Burma to carry.

The next morning I sat stirring the day's stew and watching Ryan talk quietly with a British businessman whose wife had died in the night. The man's shoulders shook, and even with him across the path in another tent, I heard him weeping. One man in a line of weeping men. I couldn't summon the sadness anymore. But Ryan's head leaned toward the man, and I saw him sigh, shouldering the man's pain.

In the distance someone yelled my name, but I continued stirring, watching, waiting. There was always an emergency. If they really needed me, they would find me.

"Kai?" Closer. "Kailyn!"

Ryan's head jerked up. "Tu Lum?"

I jumped to my feet as the little boy stumbled into the mess tent. Suddenly Ryan stood at my side, his hand on my spine, holding me upright.

Tu Lum dripped with rain. "Your amoi. She needs your help."

"Aunt Nang Lu?" I dropped the spoon into the pot, splattering precious food onto my longyi.

Ryan's hand tightened on my arm. "Go, Kai. I'll take care of it."

Tu Lum and I careened through the village, scattering chickens as well as people until we stumbled to a stop in front of the duwa's yard.

Aunt Nang Lu stood in front of the basha, bent over her belly, gasping for air. Rain sparkled in the grays of her head and the spilled basket at her feet.

As I reached out to steady her, a moan ground through her body. I wrapped my arm around this woman who had given me a seat at her fireplace, but froze when Aunt Nang Lu doubled over, diarrhea flowing onto the step and dripping into the dirt of the porch.

"Nang Lu?" The duwa appeared in the doorway, leaning heavily against the bamboo frame. But for a slight clench of his jaw, the duwa was calm, as if he'd long expected this.

He reached a shaky hand to ease his wife up the stairs.

At the top of the stairs, the duwa hesitated. "Moran Kai." Tears glimmered in his eyes until he wiped them away.

"I will take care of it." The diarrhea dripped onto the white stones at the foot of the ladder, and I stood watching it slow to a stop. She had the same sickness that had taken Matthew and many others.

"Nang Lu will need fresh broth," I said to Tu Lum without removing my eyes from the empty doorway. "Please have one of the women slaughter a chicken while I get water."

Tu Lum shifted, unsure of my directions.

"It is what Ryan has done for this." I reinforced my recommendation with confidence for Tu Lum's sake but stood helpless until a moan sagged through the basha, shaking me into motion. Snagging the water poles, I sprinted through the pigs and cattle and broke into the rain-streaked village.

I darted down the path and tripped over the tiny tree roots, the branches slapping me, before skidding to a stop at the edge of the stream. I squatted next to the diversion device and collection jug Papa had built, and I mechanically opened and closed the lever to fill each pole.

I slowed my breathing, like Aunt Nang Lu had taught me. Thousands of people survived sickness. Others had survived this one, especially with the American medicine.

Nothing would happen this time.

Nothing would happen.

I rocked beside the running water. Surely the supreme God couldn't be so angry, so cruel. Had he not promised good things for his people? Aunt Nang Lu's death could never be good.

But Karai Kasang had taken Mama and then, with barely a whimper, my newborn baby brother. I remembered Papa's tear-streaked face as he'd prayed.

Papa's spirit was still in his body after the village burned Mama's body, but it didn't want to be there anymore. If it hadn't been for the duwa and Aunt Nang Lu, I would have been utterly alone.

No. Karai Kasang couldn't take Aunt Nang Lu. I stood and stacked the last of the water-filled poles back into my basket.

He wouldn't.

Chapter Twelve

EACH TINY DROPLET FALLING FROM the sky had massed together, gathering in great torrents, transforming my stone sanctuary above the village into a river rushing toward the cliff, frothing in its eagerness to plunge over the edge. I sat amid the chaos, my legs hanging over the rock outcropping. The water dragged on my longyi, and I watched the bright-red fabric tangle and leap into the empty air, only to be snapped against the cold rock.

The water tugged at me, easing me forward, begging me to let go and fly with it.

For a moment, I almost listened.

At the last moment, I flung one hand behind me, anchoring myself to the massive rock. The water wrenched at me, and the rock sliced into my fingers. Numbness dulled the pain but threatened to pry my fingers open.

Below me, a single pillar of smoke, protected by a grass roof, danced and sputtered, battered by the rain but still racing to the sky.

The villagers surrounded a massive pile of wood. It had been only a handful of days since I'd urged Aunt Nang Lu to sip at the broth I'd made. But now she was gone. Her body lay on the pyre. A trick of the wind lifted her skirts, and I reached out, a tiger's scream sounding from inside me—hollow echoes repeating until the sound of the rain swallowed the reverberations. The monsoon roared across the mountains, once again master.

Flames caught the edge of Aunt Nang Lu's skirt, and it lay flat in obedience. The men began a slow hopping dance, arms linked, encircling the pyre. The duwa stood stiff but weaving, a mighty oak cracking under the onslaught. The feathers of his headdress flew on the wind, defying the rain, reaching toward heaven. Ryan stood wedged between the duwa and Tu Lum, watching the people say goodbye to the mother of the village.

I'd left word with Tu Lum that I was going to the sanctuary and would be back. I was close enough to the edge of the village that Ryan and the duwa wouldn't quibble and yet far enough to allow me space to hide.

The dark smell of smoke reached me, and the memory of Papa's voice tangled through the grasses. *Mama's in a better place now.*

I whipped around, searching for him. But I was alone on the great rock.

"Always alone," the jungle whispered, the grasses mocking.

Below me, flames charred Aunt Nang Lu black, crackling as they touched the skin of my amoi. The smell sickeningly sweet.

The duwa started to lift his hands to the sky but fell to his knees instead, dragging Ryan down with him. I let out a gasp and scrabbled backward, away, my hands and feet fighting the flooding rivers. I would not watch the fires take more of those I loved. Stumbling over the familiar rocks, I fell, tearing holes in my longyi, my knees. I flew into the jungle, willing the darkness and rain to drown the lament of the funeral dance in the village, crying at the sky to still the ghosts.

Spent, I huddled in a rotting tree, listening to the far-off sounds of the village and the strange screaming bark of the muntjac deer.

I cradled my knees against my chest. I had no idea where my basket was, but I wished I had my sweater or at least a dry shirt. I thought of my home, the warmth, but I wasn't sure I could face anyone. These days I only seemed capable of causing problems.

As the saffron-yellow sky faded into blackness, I knew that somewhere behind the clouds, a thousand stars sparkled. Earlier that day, Tu Lum had said that my amoi would enjoy her first night with Karai Kasang. That all the stars would shine especially for her.

But I would miss it. The supreme one couldn't even see fit to let me see Aunt Nang Lu's stars.

My legs grew numb, tucked under me, and I shivered, teeth clattering.

I closed my mind against the whisper to allow myself to fall asleep, to succumb to the cold. There were people who needed me. Tu Lum. And Ryan. He had shouldered enough even before Nang Lu got sick. Now he needed me more than ever. I could not add to his burden. Standing, I brushed off bits of wood and dirt, stood, and trekked down to the village.

≈

Ryan sat on a mound in the paddy field, waiting for Kai. For the past few days, she had avoided him, the wretched mixture of her anger and misery nearly drowning him in its intensity.

Before the whole village stopped to remember the mother of the village, Ryan had seen Kai steal up the mountain path, a spirit escaping the sadness. He had thought their nights around the fire had been as healing to her as they had him. But her absence, her shutting him out, proved he'd been wrong. The wild colt had bolted and kicked him in the gut on the way out.

Even though Kai would want him to, Ryan couldn't leave her be. While her sanctuary was safe enough, the jungle, even in the best of circumstances, was a dangerous place—even for someone who had lived here her whole life. And these were certainly not the best of circumstances.

Ryan hugged the oiled cloth tighter around him and scanned the jungle trails again. Foolish woman.

The Japanese soldiers were close, scouting north through the Hukawng Valley, maybe even at the foot of their mountain. While Kai was a capable and proficient hunter, she certainly couldn't overcome a company of well-armed Japanese. The thought of the missionary's daughter at the mercy of the soldiers made his whole body sweat.

That was why he and the duwa had planned an escape route. Every villager had an emergency basket packed and ready to be taken north for refuge. They had specific leaders, meeting places, and a final destination at the village of Zau Tu—Nang Lu's brother. They were as ready as possible. Still, Ryan wished John were here. He knew the mountains and people far better than Ryan or even Kailyn and always seemed to have a ready answer for any problem they'd encountered.

Ryan picked up the bamboo pole at his feet and twirled it in his fingers. *Keeping your hands busy keeps your mind still.* Nang Lu's voice echoed in his mind. He would miss the older woman. She was rarely, if ever, wrong.

Ryan sank his dah into the top of the bamboo pole and tapped it down the length, creating a thin strip. Laying the strip next to him, he started on another length. He would take the strips and weave them together to make string to fix his dirt-encrusted boots, which were held together with bits of string and fabric made of twisted bamboo. Now a split on the top of the toe threatened to burst the entire boot to pieces.

Ryan snorted. *Rather like my life.*

He set his work aside as the storm-filled sky boiled. Ryan's hands hung useless by his sides. He'd spent the last two years choosing bravery, choosing joy, choosing trust. And where had that led him? To a mission in the middle of nowhere, unable to prevent brutal deaths, pummeled by a land of constant rain, and officiating the funeral of a woman who'd cared for him like a mother.

"Why?" A tear escaped and tangled with the rain on his cheek. Thunder rumbled, echoing the roar inside him, and a sheet of rain descended higher on the mountain. The rain ran in rivulets down the hills, through the grass, and into the paddy field in front of him.

Nothing.

"Please don't leave me, God."

As a flash of lightning sizzled across the night sky, Ryan jumped. He'd long ago talked his brain into a logical, stoic reaction to the sound of thunder, but his hands knew the salty smell of a coming storm and shook in defiance of his determination.

"I don't know if I can survive losing anyone again."

Ryan swallowed as memories attacked. Red barnwood flung across broken cornfields. Limbs from the enormous oak tree thrust into the ground. The cords of the laundry line woven through the broken door of the storm cellar. His little sister's favorite blue dress torn from the line and caught in the leafless maple tree, empty of Sarah.

"I came here to be *your* missionary," he screamed at the sky. "To tell people about *your* great love for them, even when—"

The wind roared through the valley, gathered the bamboo bits he had stripped, and whipped them into his legs before scattering them across the field.

"Everywhere I turn, all I see is hate and evil. Everything is falling apart, and I don't even have a bit of bamboo string left to tie it back together."

Ryan raised his dah and hacked it into the ground with a thud. The crevice filled with rainwater, and he watched the blade of his knife disappear in the mud. He yanked it out of the mire and smashed it down again. And again, driving it deeper into the earth, mud splashing onto his legs. And again, again, and . . . Without warning, the knife hit a stone and snapped back, nicking his leg.

Ryan's head dropped between his knees, and he watched as the gash gaped a moment before blood ran down his leg and mixed with the mud.

"You know what? I quit. I'm done."

He threw the dah into the water. Lightning ripped through the sky, and a huge roll of thunder rumbled over his quiet sobs.

Rain dripped from his nose, and he heard the quiet squish of footsteps in the paddy field. Was it futile to hope that whoever was coming wouldn't see him?

The footsteps stopped, hesitated. The feet were half-buried in the mud, which stained the edge of a red and blue longyi—Nang Lu's signature colors.

Kai. How much had she heard?

An arm tucked around Ryan, easing his head to her shoulder, her breath light on his cheek.

"Kai. I . . ." He swiped at his face, sitting up. He needed to be strong to . . .

Kai's gentle touch on his cheek stopped his swirling thoughts.

"Ryan, please. I'm sorry."

He nodded into her neck and took a shaky breath as she wove her fingers through his. Together. Together they would move the village. Together they would survive.

Chapter Thirteen

NEARLY TEN DAYS LATER, I rolled from my pallet to my knees, my prayers stuck in my throat even as the night's smoke still lingered in the air. But I could no longer deny what I'd always known to be true. Ryan could not save us alone. Tu Lum, Ryan, the duwa, me—we needed each other. While the village was as prepared as we could be to run, fate had stood with us thus far, making us feel that we were safe to stay in our home. After all, Tingrabum was an obscure cleft in a rock, covered by the hand of the familiar jungle. What better place to hide than here?

So we continued on as normal. We'd already planted the fields. As the sun stretched her arms over our sky, we would begin weeding the paddy field, giving the tiny plants room to flourish. I quietly corralled the orphans outside, bribing them each with a handful of leftover rice to go about their chores without complaint. Ryan was finally sleeping, and I didn't want to wake him. He had worked hard yesterday doing his chores and leading the church meeting but had still cried out in his sleep, had still stumbled from his room, gasping for reality or . . . perhaps wishing to forget. Whatever had haunted him in the night, he'd returned in the dark and dropped into the sleep of the besieged.

Outside, the morning mist hugged the ground tight and silent. Women emerged from their bashas like ghosts appearing and disappearing on whim. The distant trees hovered over the mountain, giant nats imposing their judgment on the villagers. I swallowed, determined to set an example of faith for the others.

I trotted to a row, kicked off my sandals, and squished into the field. The cold water made me wince as it nipped halfway up my calves. Bending, I plucked weeds, dropping them into the basket tied to my waist.

All around me, the women sang, giving us a rhythm to work by. Slowly the mist around me took on a pink hue as the sun started its journey across the mountains. Our bodies shimmered with sweat, and diamonds of water from the flooded paddy fields clung to our hems. Terraces climbed the side of the mountain, strips of rock and bamboo walls holding the rains for the slender blades of the rice plants.

Tu Lum and the other children flitted between us, emptying our baskets into theirs, then running to dump them in a compost pile.

A breeze blew from the south, bearing heavy clouds away from the mountain. The wind lifted my hair and dried the sweat on my back. I re-buttoned my sweater against the chill. Papa would not be pleased at the skin peeking between my waistband and shirt. Unfortunately, I had no other options, and I doubted anyone noticed anyway. Blowing my bangs off my forehead again, I resumed my work.

A strange growl rumbled. Frowning, I searched the sky for an answer. No airdrop was scheduled for today. Perhaps rain was closer than I thought. But the few white clouds above me floated lazily through the sky.

I peered into the jungle. The sound was too constant to be an animal.

A troop of gibbons streaked through the jungle canopy. The whites of their bodies disappeared as the trees twisted in their wake, and their screams echoed across the field.

A single gunshot sounded below. I recoiled as if the bullet were intended for me. My basket fell to my feet, the weeds scattering across the water.

"Run," I croaked, but the women ignored me, studying the jungle instead, as if it might define the sharp sound.

"Run!" I screamed, yanking on the arms of the woman next to me and trampling the rice plants. "Run!"

The women turned to me, looking for answers.

"The Japanese are coming." My own voice cracked, so shrill it was unrecognizable to me.

A woman dropped her basket and darted into the village, screaming for her children. And the dam broke. The field exploded with feet and baskets.

I ran, stumbling over the trampled rice plants, toward the village, dragging Tu Lum behind me. I found Ryan in the command tent, throwing medicines and first-aid kits into a basket.

"Kai. You heard?"

I stood gasping air and nodding.

Ryan shoved the basket at me. "They were probably after the lookouts."

"Do you think—"

"We have time. Get everyone out. We'll meet in Zau Tu's village as planned."

I shook my head, my thoughts crashing together.

"If they catch you . . ." Tu Lum said the words my throat swallowed. Please . . .

Ryan knelt and grasped the boy's shoulders but focused on me. "They won't catch me. No one would dare hurt the Bear of Burma."

With a grin and small shove, he pushed the boy into my arms and out of the tent. No. No. No.

"Now go. I need you to take care of Moran Kai."

Ryan strapped on his bow, the one Tu Lum had given him. Why had I not prepared more, said more?

"Ryan." I reached for his arm.

"They are counting on you, Kailyn." Ryan framed my cheeks with his able hands, the slow movement of his thumb on my jaw anchoring my mind in the swirling chaos. "I am counting on you."

I stood paralyzed as he strode out the other side, barking orders.

Tu Lum's hand slipping into mine woke me from my impotent stupor, and I scrambled into our basha, snatched the basket Ryan had packed for me, and stuffed it with food. My hands tripped over the cross

Papa had carved, the scrap of fabric I'd hung across the cooking room wall, the pot with leftover rice clinging to its rim, my precious books. All things that I couldn't carry. My fingers fell on a lesson plan Papa had left behind for me, and I traced the loops in Papa's words.

The walls creaked, and I started. For a moment I was sure nats crept in through the gaps in the bamboo.

Throwing Papa's old sweater, my sketchbook, and a blanket on top, I yanked on the basket and retreated out the door.

There were no such things as nats.

Outside, the villagers were already making their way to the next ridge. The trip would take us two days if the older ones and small ones moved quickly enough and could walk with little rest.

Controlling my wish to force everyone to sprint up the mountain, I trudged—one foot slapped down in front of the other—until the sun rose overhead. It would take us a week at this rate. Tu Lum followed in my wake, his lips pursed while he fingered the hunting knife strapped to his waist. Little good a knife would do against a soldier's gun.

I stopped, squinting behind me, watching for signs of Ryan hiding and the duwa joining the flight from Tingrabum as planned. Baw Ni grunted at me when I failed to move out of her way. Heat rose to my cheeks as I mumbled an apology.

She spit at my feet. I had no right to be in charge. I was one of the young ones and a foreigner as well. The others knew the way.

Tu Lum laced his fingers in mine. He, at least, wanted me here.

"Thank you." I squeezed his hand. "Run ahead with the others. I'll be along soon."

The boy jogged a few paces ahead and bent over, digging in the dirt. Running back to me, he pressed a midnight stone into my hands.

"Your supreme God sees us, Kai. You can trust him." He dashed away, the leaves closing around him.

My supreme God.

He seemed anything but in control.

The last villager passed me, and still I stared at the quiet village, rubbing the midnight stone. A potbelly pig, tiny at this distance, snuffled around the nearest basha. The growing wind tussled the palm leaves, each basha waving goodbye. Maybe we'd been wrong. Maybe the sound was something other than a gunshot.

A movement on the trail below the village made my stomach lurch. We hadn't been wrong. A jeep chugged up the mountain, leading a group of several dozen soldiers on bicycles.

I searched again for signs of Ryan and saw a strip of red streak into the jungle north of the village. Ryan hadn't changed his shirt. The Japanese would easily find him. I swallowed hard, thinking of the stories the refugees had told. Nightmares of blood and screams.

Ryan cut down, blood seeping from his mouth like a hunted deer.

Chapter Fourteen

RYAN DUCKED INTO THE JUNGLE, his heart racing in time with his scrambling feet. Just as he rounded a bend into hiding, the soldiers burst into the village, yelling, their voices tangling and garbled by distance. Until one rose above. "You won't be hurt." The soldier spoke Kachin with no trace of accent—like a native.

Understanding crashed into Ryan, knocking his feet from under him, sending him slamming into a tree.

There was a traitor to the mountain.

Ryan dug his fingers into the tree bark. The soldier might very well know the trails, or at least the signs. Ryan whipped around, inspecting the village. Animals in the pens, squealing and squawking, were the only welcoming party for the invading force. No enemy sneaked up the hidden trails. All was as it should be.

Japanese officers yelled, pointing toward the terraces, the trail to the river. Foot soldiers broke off into search groups. They would find the village empty and the visible trails abandoned.

And if the enemy stumbled onto the carefully hidden trail or if the villagers needed more time to disappear into the mountainside, the duwa and Kai had set a few tricks to mislead and distract the Japanese hunters. As a last resort, Ryan had brought along, and now clenched, a bright-red shirt in his fist to call attention away from the villagers. His own safety was something he was willing to sacrifice. He hadn't asked for anyone's input on the decision.

They were as safe as they could be. Ryan dropped his basket at the base of the enormous trunk, found a foothold in the craggy bark, and climbed high into the branches.

Glancing into the mountain, Ryan searched for sign of the villagers. With a few hours' head start on the steep mountain trails unfamiliar to the Japanese, Kai should have no trouble bringing the villagers to safety. They had disappeared into the jungle like ghosts.

In Tingrabum the soldiers cleared out the bashas. As a pile of food and equipment mounded, the officer in charge grew visibly more agitated. Suddenly the officer launched a tirade at an empty-handed soldier, slapping the man and sending him spinning to the dirt. The other soldiers barreled through the village, setting fire to the homes. The elephant grass roofs ignited, crackling, black smoke tangling into the blue sky. A groan scraped at the silent village as the bamboo support beam of the school warped, pausing a moment before the roof caved, sending a crash reverberating against the rock outcroppings.

Ryan relaxed into the tree trunk. The Japanese could burn all they wanted. The Kachin people would survive to replant and rebuild. They could come back, pretend the *Mauhte wa* of their legends had come again and burned the village. Then the villagers would drive the imaginary crazy old man responsible for fire into the jungle.

Difficult? Yes. But no one would be hurt today.

≈

I plucked ferns growing from the side of the oak trees and tucked them into my hair, my fingers shaking as I wove branches through the chains of my necklaces in a makeshift camouflage. Ryan had promised to leave, but he hadn't. He was still there, still in the village, and if the Japanese found him . . . I squelched the thought. I would save him.

A crack sounded, and I stilled like a deer sniffing danger. The shuffles of a small creature moved past, and I sighed. Probably a partridge. I would need to be more steady if I hoped to save us.

I eased onto the trail. I was one with the mountain, a tiger stalking her prey. Even with my stealth, it only took me until the sun touched the top of the mountain to reach my sanctuary.

A glance up the mountain satisfied me that the mountain hid my people. *Good.*

I was nearly at the tree where I'd stashed my weapons when I heard a man's shout. A scream followed closely behind, ricocheting around the mountain.

Please. Let it be one of the village pigs.

When the anguished cry came again, long, stretching into eternity and rising in pitch, I broke into a run. We had left someone behind.

I slowed at the rock jutting from the jungle and crawled on my belly to the edge. A man stood on the edge of the jungle, hands clasped behind his back as if he were surveying a pleasant scene. I squinted, unsure as I picked apart his stance, his movements. The man came around the corner, and I gasped. Baw Gun. He knew the location of the other villages, the trails. No one would be safe.

A shout from the far side of the village drew Baw Gun's attention and mine. Two soldiers dragged the duwa like a rag doll. They had bound his arms behind him, and his gray head rolled limply. Baw Gun's coarse laughter ate into the rock under my feet, my world tilting. He'd traded us for favor with the enemy.

The traitor moved to relieve one soldier of his burden, and their bodies rippled behind the waves of heat moments before disappearing behind a flaming basha. I scooted farther around the rock, my mind flying. *How had I missed the duwa? Why had he stayed?*

The men dropped the duwa in an undignified heap in front of a knot of soldiers. One, obviously the officer in charge, gestured to another officer dressed in white, who was on his knees struggling with something. I squinted, attempting to uncover what the younger officer and his men were holding.

A cry strangled in my throat.

Tu Lum.

The noises that had pursued me in the jungle had been no partridge. Tu Lum had followed me. I leaped to my feet, panic rupturing thought as I threw myself down the trail.

Two Japanese soldiers pinned the boy's tiny arms and legs to the ground while his naked body writhed, pulling against captors four times his size. My feet slapped, pounding down the hill, slipping on the rubble, my soles shredding as I stumbled to my knees. I would never make it in time.

Ryan. Where are you?

The officer stood above the boy's pinned feet and withdrew his bayonet. The ring of metal whispered on the wind. A beam of sunlight caught the bayonet, and I shut my eyes against the burning light. The metallic taste of blood filled my mouth, and the world pitched, spinning, falling into the gaping maw of hell.

A soldier mocked the boy's tiny mews of pain as he traced the blade across Tu Lum's ribs, flaying the skin.

My body arched with Tu Lum's, arms rising, instinctively avoiding the pain. The boy twisted toward the mountains, his screams slamming into my body.

Oh God, I killed Tu Lum.

≈

Ryan's fingers dug into the branch as he desperately tried to hold himself together. They'd set no traps in the village itself. No way to help Ryan's little sidekick or the duwa. Tu Lum writhed against his captors, and Ryan's mind spun. His bow was useless, because if he showed himself here, the Japanese would find the trail. The others. His fist pulled against the branch until it snapped under his fingers.

Another cry pierced the jungle, echoing long. The flame of screams caught by another across the mountain.

Someone from the village had come back. Ryan jumped from the tree, shaking. He saw a streak of movement on the stone sanctuary.

Kai?

Go back. Go back!

If Kai attacked or if he attacked, the Japanese would torture them for where the others were and kill them all. He shouldn't go. Couldn't.

Tu Lum screamed again, attacking Ryan's ears, accusing his inaction.

Ryan grasped the bow, surprised it did not snap under the force. He had left his mother and Sarah to die. God might be able to stand by and watch it happen again, but Ryan could not.

Unslinging his bow, Ryan fought through the thorns to higher ground. The brambles slashed at him, the physical pain muting the chasm that had ripped through him. Another whimper drew his attention back to the village. Tu Lum. Precious little boy, his quiet contentment, thrilled to help with anything.

Oh God. Tu Lum.

A growl erupted from the jungle. The Japanese soldiers scattered, searching the brush as they reached for their weapons. The one holding the duwa pointed at the trail. Sure of himself. Cocky. He wasn't dressed like the others.

Ryan's stomach lurched. Baw Gun. Ryan had never killed before, but this man. This man deserved to die.

A disturbance flitted around a bamboo stand, and an arrow struck the dirt, quivering at the feet of the officers. Kailyn. She'd lost the element of surprise. Ryan let an arrow fly. It fell far out of reach of the men, but it distracted them from Kai's location.

With the soldiers distracted, Tu Lum freed a hand and tore at the uniform of one of the men holding him. The young officer flinched.

Come on . . .

The chief officer frowned at the junior officer. "*Chui* Utagawa." The officer's shout made his displeasure with Lieutenant Utagawa clear.

Baw Gun dropped the duwa and pounced on Tu Lum, pinning him to the ground. Tears slipped down Ryan's face. Tu Lum was an innocent boy. If he had a rifle, he would kill Baw Gun and send as many others as he could into the pit of hell with the traitor.

Utagawa secured the boy but cringed away from the horror. Following the senior officer's pointing finger, several soldiers rushed to the edges of the jungle after Kai, and another pointed his pistol at the duwa. A second arrow streaked out of the jungle, piercing Baw Gun's chest. Ryan dropped his head. Now they knew where she hid.

The chief officer raised his arm above Tu Lum, and a flash of metal streaked down. Tu Lum's screams nearly drowned the sound of gunshots ringing through the mountain.

The duwa crumpled to the ground, and a grunt of pain came from the nearby jungle before silence shuddered across the mountain, nature's shock echoing loud. Surely the ground would rise up and swallow them.

The world was gutted and raw. Ryan fell against a tree, his hands splayed on the trunk, grasping for a steady place, his gasps for air harsh in the quiet.

They were both gone. And he'd done nothing.

Laughter burst from the village, and Ryan spun, heaving his breakfast on the other side of the elephant path. The bitter dregs of horror burned his throat.

Ryan wiped his mouth and reeled back to the tree, clutching the ridged trunk. He willed the nausea down, even as he watched as the Japanese threw Baw Gun's body into a blazing basha and then hunted the perimeter of the village for signs of the Kachin people.

Clutching his basket, Ryan sneaked farther up the mountain, hoping to find a better vantage. Kai could still be alive. If she was, she would likely need help.

From within the relative safety of the tangled undergrowth, Ryan searched the grass on the far side of the village for Kai. As if the villagers might have hidden in the water, the soldiers dug up the rice paddy fields, their glee ringing across the terraces. How someone could find joy in such destruction was unfathomable. How had the world devolved to this? Ryan used the chaos to crawl closer to where she might have hidden after letting her arrows fly.

But she was nowhere to be found. Perhaps she'd made her way back to the villagers' trail. Ryan sat back on his heels, surveying the blackened village as the mass of soldiers kicked at crippled ashes and gnawed on remains of food, their humanity leached away from the acid of hate.

Finally the soldiers tethered the livestock to the jeep and bicycles, to be led away, and then trundled to get in line behind the vehicle. They'd failed to discover either the path in the elephant grass or Kai. Ryan eased into the jungle. Kai must have gotten free somehow, and they would never find her on her mountain. Ryan was tempted to follow the villagers, but he knew enough about the Japanese to be cautious. So he clambered into a tree, waiting, watching to ensure no scouts were left behind.

A shout from the chief officer lured Ryan's attention to the center of the village. One of the men pulled out his knife and knelt at the head of the duwa's body. Ryan recoiled when he realized what the man intended, but he couldn't look away from the flash of the blade as the nameless soldier decapitated the once proud duwa.

Ryan bit into his fist, choking on the building roar of anguish.

The man blithely jammed the head onto a pike at the village entrance. A warning to anyone unlucky enough to stumble upon the village.

As if anyone would willingly come back to this desecration.

Chapter Fifteen

RYAN HUNKERED IN THE TREE for hours until the last of the Japanese threaded back into the valley. At dusk, their fires flickered far to the northwest.

In the red dusk, Ryan watched the sky darken, the moon competing with the light of the fires.

Slowly he slid down the tree, floundering over his basket at the bottom. A roll of gauze trickled out of the upturned basket and unrolled in the dust. Worthless now.

He left the basket and picked his way down the trail. The smell of smoke grew stronger as Ryan made his way to the haunted remains of Tingrabum. Pausing in the cover of the great oak tree, Ryan listened to the night sounds for anything that didn't belong. The frogs trilled happily in the water-filled terraces. An owl's low hoot sounded from higher on the ridge.

He bent and crept into the clearing. A rustle sounded from the paddy fields.

Ryan spun and peered into the darkness. The coals from the fires sent trembling fingers of light ahead of him. Was the movement a person or a trick of the light?

Ryan swallowed. He would much rather retrieve the bodies during daylight, but the Japanese had no doubt noted the Western military tents pitched in the village. They would send patrols to watch for escaping troops, which meant this was his one chance to retrieve the bodies. He owed Tu Lum and the duwa a proper burial. Somehow.

Tiptoeing around the back side of the village, Ryan kept the hulking remains of the duwa's basha between himself and the noise. Ahead, through the center of the village, the lifeless forms sprawled on the dirt path. Ryan paused every few moments to listen and watch.

The wind rushed through the village, howling, threatening. Dust billowed—the breath of an angry mountain. Keeping low, Ryan crept through the village.

It was slow going, but he could not risk capture. The soldiers would assume he knew where the Allies were as well as where the villagers had gone. Ryan slid his dah from its scabbard. The slight swishing sound of metal against leather rang loudly in his ears.

Ryan stopped midstep. The jungle had gone quiet.

He eased out of the moonlight. A figure stole between the ravaged bashas. Ryan's hand tightened on his dah. He'd never used it for anything other than hacking through the tangle of jungle plants on a path. And even those feeble attempts had made Kai giggle. Who was he fooling? Ryan stuffed the knife back into the scabbard. He would only hurt himself.

The figure darted between the next set of buildings. The man had a longyi wrapped around his waist and an errant palm branch dragging in his hair—he belonged on the mountain. Ryan had heard rumors of scavengers following behind the soldiers, preying on the devastated.

Squatting, he rummaged in the underbrush until he found a large rock. Ryan hefted it in his hand and tested the weight. About the heft of a baseball. He may not be handy with the jungle knife, but Ryan had some talents honed by years in an Indiana baseball diamond.

The man slipped through the village, his silhouette fluttering, stalking like a tiger in the shaded light of the embers. On the opposite side of the village path, Ryan tracked the man, shifting around and through. He would not allow any more destruction this night.

≈

Smoke twisted dark above the flickering bits of flame, nightmarish fingers playing shadow puppets. I swallowed, pushing away the scratching story of the jaiwa. *Born of fire; birthed of midnight and brilliant flame.*

I refused to let my nightmares of amber tiger eyes take flight into reality. The jaiwa's tale was not real. The sharaw did not lurk here. In fact, I hadn't seen anyone since the Japanese had withdrawn. I struggled to listen past the sound of the crackle of the dying fires. I'd seen another arrow fly and knew Ryan had released it, distracting them long enough for me to flee. But where was he now? The Japanese had not dragged him from the jungle. I thought of his gentle hands holding baby Matthew, his quiet voice singing me to sleep, the tears in his eyes when he realized he couldn't save us. No, the bear of our village would not abandon us. Had he gone back to rejoin the villagers somehow? Was he dead somewhere in the trees?

The traitorous thought hardened my stomach to stone. I would not borrow that trouble unless forced to.

In the center of the village, the duwa's calloused feet stuck out from his longyi, one foot drooped to the side, the other curled like it might try to carry him away from the carnage. Standing just outside the ring of light, I could almost imagine that he was N-Tang, the village drunk, sleeping off a night of drinking too much fermented *jaru*. Almost.

A sob caught in my throat. It was the pastor's job to bury. Where was Papa? Ryan?

How am I supposed to do this?

I shook my blanket out and draped it across the duwa's body. "The Lord bless you and keep you." I swallowed the burning bile and the rest of the saying. Where was God in this? Where was his blessing? If this was what it meant to be held in his hand, who could survive?

My nails dug into my palms as I bent over Tu Lum. My knees buckled at the sight of my little friend, and I collapsed to the dusty ground.

Tu Lum's mouth twisted open in an unearthly silent scream, his fist thrown out, as if begging me to deliver him from death's clutches. A tear rolled down my cheek. He would never again run the paths. Never beg me to fish with him. Never steal my pencils. Never follow Ryan to the stream to collect water.

If only I hadn't assumed he'd listen to me and stay with the others. I bit my lip. "I'm so sorry."

I reached down and rubbed Tu Lum's muddy arms. He was so cold.

Thunder rumbled in the distance, and I tilted my face to the sky, the tears of heaven pattering down. Too late. Far, far too late.

"Sleep well." The cold of the rain bit into my bare arms, and I welcomed numbing pain.

I dug Papa's enormous sweater out of my basket and draped it over the little boy. Perhaps Papa cradled him in heaven as his sweater held the body.

As I smoothed the material across his torso, a shimmer of light flashed from inside Tu Lum's palm. I leaned over and pried open his fingers, revealing a scrap of fabric with a brass button attached. Tu Lum must have ripped it off the man who had held him down. *Chui Utagawa.* I would find out what that meant and find the soldier who had so little pity for a child. My fingers strangled the scrap, as if crushing the fabric could destroy the nightmare.

The hairs on my head prickled, my body alerting me to what my mind had missed. The jungle had gone silent. I hummed quietly as I scanned the village. I heard whispered movement, but whenever I stopped humming, the footsteps continued, echoing . . . Or were there two sets? Only ghosts, the nats, and the Japanese would walk so brazenly through the village. I swallowed. Or a tiger.

The shuffling hesitated and stopped. I reached for my dah and shifted my feet to attack.

When the footsteps sounded again, I flew to my feet and brought the knife around with a flash. The man jumped back.

Chapter Sixteen

"KAI. IT'S ME." RYAN STUMBLED backward, holding his hands in surrender.

Kai's dah twisted, flashing in the eerie light.

At her snarl, Ryan's arms dropped to his side. "Kai?" He resisted the urge to shrink farther away. She was possessed, wild eyes wide, nose flared with anger.

"Where were you? You told me to go, so I left. And look"—Kai pointed the knife at the lifeless bodies before thrusting the weapon at him—"look what happened."

"Kai, I didn't know they were still here. I would have never—"

"You sent me to herd everyone up the mountain, and you missed Tu Lum coming back."

"I didn't—"

"*And* you were supposed to send the duwa out. How could you have missed them both?"

Part of him wished she would use her knife to cut out his guilt. But she dropped the dah to her side.

"And I . . . I couldn't get back in time." Tears welled in her eyes, and she collapsed to her knees. "How could I have missed them?"

"Kai. This isn't your fault."

She'd been right the first time. Ryan should have seen them, should have known. He knelt and cupped a hand around her small shoulders, the curve of them engulfed under his hand. She twisted, hesitated a moment, and then threw herself into him, pounding and screaming, calling down curses on the Japanese, God, him. And she was right. Where was God in all of this? Why had God sent Ryan if this was the result?

His body absorbed the abuse, and Ryan let it wash over him, desperate to dislodge the guilt that choked him. He had trusted in his preparations, his knowledge of the hills, the God he served. But there was nothing, nothing but evil lurking in the jungle this night.

The fires around him fought the rain beating down, but the water consumed the light, and by the time Kai went still in his arms, darkness had spread across the village plain.

≈

The mountains glowed with dawn's first golden rays when Ryan finished covering the bodies. Alone and without a proper shovel, Ryan scratched shallow graves into the root-tangled earth above the village. He'd covered the mounds in river stones they'd hauled up the mountain. At least the animals wouldn't be able to disturb the graves. Muscles in his back ached, and his hands throbbed, testimony to the effort even that small amount required. Ryan longed to place markers remembering the two friends, but he dared not take the time. The location of the stand of bamboo and the broken X carved into the nearby teak tree would serve as memory enough.

Kai had helped cover the graves. But when she slipped on the hill, dropping a cascade of rocks and tumbling down the trail, Ryan had tucked her in front of a small fire with a pot of rice to tend and extracted a promise that she wouldn't leave without him.

Ryan stood alone at the graves.

He could hear his childhood minister intoning the funeral rites over the graves of his mother and sister. *We commend into thy hands the souls of these, your servants. Ashes to ashes. Dust to dust.*

Ryan opened his mouth to say the words, to send his friends into eternity with at least a scrap of tradition, but tears choked his intentions.

Ryan dropped the last rock on the smallest mound. *Lord, have mercy.*

Sweat dripping from his face, Ryan trudged to the village and dropped next to Kai. The bowl of rice sat untouched in front of her, and she stared into the jungle, rubbing a brass military button between her fingers. Soot covered her face, but the tearstains were old, and Ryan was sure she hadn't moved in the last few hours.

"Kai, first things first. You need to eat if you are going to have enough energy to help me find Zau Tu's village." He knew he sounded frantic, but he couldn't lose her too. "Kai?"

She wavered and then shifted closer to Ryan, a sleepwalker waking from a drugged sleep.

"I can't do it without you." He wouldn't even know where to begin.

The button twirled in her fingers as she stared into the darkness.

"Kai, I need you. Please eat." Ryan plucked the button out of Kai's hand and placed the bowl into her grip instead.

Her head snapped up, and he snatched his hand back, seared by the look she gave him.

"They're right here." Ryan dropped the button and the scrap of fabric bearing the name Utagawa into her mother's bag and laid it next to her. Then he scooped the last of the rice out of the mess kit and made a show of putting the food into his mouth. Ryan cringed at the burned taste and forced himself to swallow. Ma always said the brain worked better with food in the belly, and he sure did need wisdom right about now.

Slowly she picked up a ball of rice, placed it in her mouth, and chewed.

"Good," he said. "Now tell me how we're going to find the village. We need someplace safe to go." Fear clamped down on Ryan's throat. He knew the sketchy outline of the road to India. But he had no idea where the new village was, and he couldn't in good conscience leave without checking on them. "Kai, if the Japanese are using local guides, they could track the others. Your people need you . . . I need you to protect them."

Her eyes flashed and shifted back to the jungle, then the bamboo stand.

Kai had made it plain that she wouldn't leave the mountains, and the war hadn't changed that. But no matter what she thought of him, Ryan would not allow her to fend for herself. No matter how fierce she might be, the jungle wasn't safe to travel alone in. She was the closest thing to family he had left on this side of the globe, and he was hers.

"The Japanese will be back, and you know it." He tucked a strand of hair behind her ear and tried to catch her eye.

"Just leave me here."

"They'll kill you."

"And?"

"What good would your death do? Is dying at the hands of the Japanese paying some kind of penance?"

Her nose flared, and her fingers toyed with the hilt of her dah.

Fear crawled in the pit of his stomach.

"Would Tu Lum want you to die like this?" Ryan cringed at his desperation. But her eyes flicked to him, considering. "Would the duwa? Nang Lu?"

Ryan barely had time to swallow his last bite and load his backpack before Kai had scrambled to her feet and disappeared into the mountain trail. At least she was slashing at the vegetation rather than him.

Chapter Seventeen

THE SUN RACED TO THE western horizon, casting flat shadows that reached out to devour Ryan's feet in darkness. When they'd first started walking, he'd asked Kai where they were and where they were going, but she'd shushed him every time without breaking step. After they'd walked all night, and then through the heat of the following day, he'd given up trying to figure anything out. All he could do was plod along the twisting path.

His mind was numb, and his blistered hands ached from shoveling hard-packed dirt. Two graves added to the overwhelming list of others.

A scrabbling came from ahead, and Kai slipped, falling hard, again. The fifth time in as many minutes. Ryan wasn't surprised that he, the clumsy bear, was sliding in the mud. But Kai . . . Kai was a different story.

Even though blood soaked her hands, she didn't cry out or even wipe away the blood when she stood. The Japanese might not have killed her, but she'd left her soul back in the village. To be honest, he wasn't sure exactly where his was either. He felt untethered and his faith buried under the questions. Why would a God who could have stopped all this withhold his hand of mercy?

He rubbed his fingers through his dripping hair. It was time to stop. Spotting a hollowed-out tree, he caught Kai's arm. "Let's rest for a bit."

She nodded and floated away from the trail, as if she were a bit of ash caught in a gentle breeze. Not the reaction Ryan had expected.

Ryan nudged her shoulder and eased her hands into his. He cringed when he saw the raw cuts slashing her palms. Kai stared into the dusk, shivering underneath her thin sweater. With the sun disappearing, the mountain was cooling.

What would Nang Lu have done? Ryan scrambled around the clearing, dropping sticks into a pile. He could at least cobble together a decent fire under the protection of a brace of undergrowth.

When the flames crackled merrily, he stepped back.

While light danced across Kai's face, she remained expressionless as she sank to the ground.

Helplessness snaked up Ryan's throat.

"Where will we go now?" Kai said, so quietly Ryan nearly missed her words.

Ryan eased down next to her, her shoulder warming his. "What?"

"I know you want to join the others. But they'll never let us be part of the village."

"Of course they will." *Wouldn't they?*

"They never accepted me before, and now . . ." She lifted a shoulder.

"After all you've done. They'll—"

"You, maybe . . . but not me. I was supposed to lead them to safety. The old women will whisper that the tiger-eyed one called the Japanese to the mountain. Or that the Japanese came for the Americans in the village."

"That's ridiculous."

Kai shrugged. "Without Aunt Nang Lu and the duwa, Baw Ni is the eldest now. She will have already convinced half of them, and time will convince the other half."

Ryan knew the villagers teetered between faith in the supreme God and fear of all the evil life brings. A tension he well understood. And trauma did strange things to people, and neither he nor Kai held the respect of the people like Nang Lu or Pastor John had. Despite the fact that Baw Ni's son was the one to betray the village, the others might very well choose her over the foreigners. Especially given that he and Kai were the only ones to witness what had really happened with Baw Gun's betrayal.

Firelight flickered across Kailyn's face, scratched and covered in ash. Ryan eased an arm around her.

"Then we'll go to India or Fort Hertz or—"

Kai shook her head, a strangled cry bursting from her cracked lips. "I'm a woman with no family, no prospects. I've never had a passport. I don't know that the American government even knows I exist. There is no place for me in your world either. At least on the mountain, I know what to expect."

"You don't have to be alone, Kai."

Hope leaped in her eyes, and Ryan pushed on. "The mission agency will protect you."

"You're staying with me though, aren't you?"

"The Allies will need soldiers that know the mountain and the people. If I do nothing, the Japanese win."

Kai stiffened, a cold darkness crushing the momentary warmth. "The Japanese will just take you too."

"I don't think the army will give me a choice."

She jerked away from him. "There is always a choice."

Warmth trickled from his body. But what could he do? *Please, God. What could he do?*

Ryan banked the fire and draped his blanket over Kai. Nestling against a tree trunk, he cradled the bow and arrow. For now he would stand guard, fighting anyone attempting to enter their camp, and in the morning, they'd figure it out.

≈

Light crept into the clearing, cold and ornery like a cranky toddler waking from a fitful night. Ryan's body ached from unfamiliar exertion and awkward sleep, and he twisted and groaned, trying to ease away the discomfort.

Jungle animals scurried about under the cover of heavy leaves, fleeing the awakening bear.

"So much for staying awake," Ryan groused at himself, but they were safe, and that was enough. Now to convince Kai to walk to India—which would take a miracle, plain and simple.

Ryan pushed himself to his feet, intending to have Kai help him make breakfast—Ma had been right that a full belly made everything easier—but she wasn't where he'd left her.

Scrambling across a log, Ryan found the indentation where she'd slept, where her basket had stood. He spun a loping circle, bizarrely wondering if he'd been mistaken, if she'd actually slept on the other side of the clearing.

He leaped back over the log, slipping on the mossy surface, and that was when he noticed it. A white stone snuggled against the wood where they'd sat the night before. Kai's sooty fingerprint emblazoned against the white. It was her prayer stone. Her hope for a home . . . and she'd left it behind.

He picked up the rock, cradling it in his palm. When she came back, she would want it again. Surely she had just gone to relieve herself, to find food. She wouldn't leave without him. Would she?

He turned again, more slowly this time, stopping when he caught sight of a fresh-cut wound weeping in the bark of a tree. Their broken X scarred the tree, but there was no arrow, like they usually added. No sign of which way she'd gone.

He pressed his hand against the wounded tree, the stone slipping from his fingers. Her message was clear as the unblemished sky. God had forgotten them both.

PART TWO

I more fear what is within me than
what comes from without.
—Martin Luther

Chapter Eighteen

November 1943
Foothills of the Himalayas, North Burma

As HE SAT ON THE edge of a wide rock overhang high above a Kachin village, Captain Ryan McDonough's fingers itched for his mother's guitar. But he had traded it for a rifle and pack long ago. Instead he rubbed the small white rock in his pocket and hummed quietly, letting his legs swing free above the massive drop. It seemed a lifetime ago that he'd sat in a similar place, listening to Tu Lum and Kai work through their homework. But it hadn't even been two years.

Ryan retrieved the stone from his pocket and turned it in his hand, studying it as if Kai's prayer rock could conjure the woman herself. She'd be about twenty now . . . if she was still alive.

Almost eighteen months ago, after the villagers refused to help him find Kai, he went to India, hoping to enlist the help of the Americans. He'd known he'd be drafted, which the US Office of Strategic Services had done. But he'd hoped the OSS would care enough about an innocent woman that they'd at least promise to keep an eye out for her. But they hadn't. Not really. They'd merely sent him as an army officer to recruit the mountain people, translate, and help lead hit-and-run attacks behind enemy lines. Through it all, he'd searched long and hard for Kailyn Moran, even calling in favors from his military contacts, but he hadn't heard anything since the night she'd left.

Until two days ago.

While passing through a village, Ryan heard a rumor about an orphaned boy of unknown origin, code name Sharaw. The rumor had led him to a series of reports. Basically, no one knew anything other than the fact that the boy had helped a series of Allied troops—acting as guide, decoy, and brutally effective sniper. Nothing unusual in that, except that the boy was light-skinned and spoke impeccable English—as well as Latin and Greek. He also had a talent for slipping like smoke through the dark jungle. And some also said he had tiger eyes and was the fabled sharaw come to take revenge on the dark horde. Ryan hadn't forgotten the legend or Kai's feelings about it.

His gut said this "boy" was Kai. And if it was her, she was in trouble. Sharaw had become a symbol of the Kachin fight in this little corner of the world. A symbol the Japanese were systematically and vocally hunting down. Sharaw's capture was worth a full year's wages.

The fact that Ryan couldn't strike off into the jungle after a rumor hadn't stopped him from reawakening his search for Kai. He'd had to do it quietly though. If this warrior was Kai, the answer would place her and the remnants of Tingrabum in danger—as in most wars, enemy soldiers were exceptionally brutal to the native women and comfortable torturing friends and family to demoralize enemy combatants. And of course, she'd likely go underground again before he tracked her down. She'd already made it clear she didn't want to be found.

All of which meant Ryan also couldn't let his commanding officer, Major Trace Hogan, know he suspected Kailyn and Sharaw were one and the same. While Trace was a friend, he was an officer first. He might stretch the mission objectives to protect Ryan, but Ryan would be foolish to think that lifeline extended to others.

Ryan tucked the rock into his pocket. Even if Kai wanted nothing to do with him, he wasn't about to let the Japanese catch her. He'd just have to find a way to track her down and follow orders at the same time.

A few days before, his Kachin Ranger team had blown a Japanese railroad and encampment sky high, narrowly preventing an enemy regiment from making their way over the mountains. Then they'd disappeared into the jungle like legendary Kachin spirit-men. While the Kachins who reported to him had been sent to rest, Ryan and his CO had orders to recruit and enlist new Kachin Rangers from the villages and bring them to the rendezvous in Tagap Ga for training. Those orders were easy.

Ryan and Trace were then to turn south and sneak into Japanese-held territory to meet a Japanese officer before heading back to Tagap Ga themselves. None other than Lieutenant "Peach Boy" Utagawa. The grotesque evisceration of Tu Lum, who looked far too much like his own dead brother, was what had convinced the man to betray his country.

Ryan wasn't sure how he was going to work with one of the men responsible for the death of Tu Lum and the duwa, regardless of the man's repentance. He'd have to figure it out though, because Peach Boy was willing to feed them current troop information to help the Allies retake the Hukawng Valley and then the Kachin state capital of Myitkyina, home to a much-needed airport inside Burma. The Allies could certainly use a break like this if they hoped to prevent the Land of the Rising Sun from conquering all of mainland Asia.

Through the babble of people on the path to the village ridge, Ryan heard the distinct southern twang of Trace's voice rising and falling. That man could walk into any village and, despite knowing only a smidgen of Kachin, use a mirror or stick of gum to entice everyone to adopt him into the village by the time the sun set. No one would ever expect this southern gentleman, with his swarthy good looks and ready charm, to be the brains behind a massive number of brutal guerrilla attacks and destroyed munitions depots and railroads. Must have been his training in the hills of Georgia. Of course, Ryan had heard enough of Trace's exploits with debutantes to know the wealthy doctor's son had spent as much time in a ballroom as in the forest.

Ryan rubbed his shaggy beard. They made a good team. Trace plotting destruction and Ryan keeping them alive for another day. Not bad for a Yank.

Over his shoulder Ryan watched Trace blow out a cloud of cigarette smoke before magically making a coin appear from a young girl's ear. She squealed and ran to the older boy with her and hid behind his frayed longyi. The brother's laughter echoed around the clearing.

Tu Lum would be his age if he had lived.

Ryan shook off the thought and sauntered to Trace. "You've got a great magician act. You should take it on the road."

Trace flicked the coin at Ryan, pelting him in the arm.

"Yeah, well, you got something better?" Trace took a lazy drag on his cigarette, studying Ryan. "With that hat and your singin', you're a regular Roy Rogers. Come on, cowboy—sing for the girl." Trace flicked the brim of Ryan's Aussie-style ranger hat, and it lifted in the breeze, fluttering to the ground inches from the cliff.

Bending to one knee, Ryan scooped up his sweat-stained hat and swept it out to the side, a grand gesture to include the entire group. Then belted out the first few lines of "You Are My Sunshine"—complete with western twang.

"That's Gene Autry." Trace sighed dramatically, no doubt imitating his mother when some hired musician chose the wrong sonata for the opening of dinner. "You, sir, are stuck in the Stone Ages. I suppose we'll have to do without dinner entertainment."

The little girl giggled and clapped. *"Pai kalaw-mu. Pai!"*

"Ah, but the audience disagrees." Ryan hooked his thumbs through imaginary suspenders in triumph. "She's asking me for more."

Ryan faced the child again. "What song would you like?"

The girl squinted and then closed her eyes. In an innocent soprano, she sang in her native tongue, "When peace like a river attendeth my way, when sorrows like sea billows roll."

Ryan's deep voice joined hers in harmony, the habit sneaking out without his thinking.

"Whatever my lot, thou hast taught me to say, it is well, it is well with my soul."

The last note hung quiet in the air.

Ryan breathed deep, filling himself with the vision of beauty and goodness. He missed singing with these people, helping them in ways that didn't involve guns and bombs.

Trace cleared his throat, snapping Ryan out of his reverie. "I don't suppose she could entertain us. Unlike you, *she* can sing."

The girl frowned at Trace's tone, and he shrugged in feigned innocence. "At least the fare will be exquisite. I smell curry."

Ryan nodded. Duty called. "The duwa will have heard the jungle gossip and might confirm exactly where Peach Boy's unit is."

And the village leader might know where Sharaw was as well. The jungle gossip was faster than any official means of communication.

Trace tipped his ranger hat and drawled, like any good boy from the south, "Well now. We best not keep the gentleman waiting." He winked at the little girl. "Nor the ladies."

"Lead the way, Lone Ranger." Ryan gave the major a sloppy salute.

Trace stopped and spun. "Well, if that don't beat all. I like that. That makes you Tonto."

Ryan guffawed, and the girl giggled at the crazy foreign men. When Ryan pointed up the path, she ran ahead, bare feet leaving tiny footprints in the mud of a well-worn trail.

Chapter Nineteen

November 1943
Foothills of the Himalayas

STANDING SILENT AS THE MASSIVE teak trees around me, I breathed in rhythm with the jungle. In with the rippling breeze. Out with the wings of the butterfly.

Late-season storm clouds ran from the mountains, and the sun blazed high above me. But the tree canopy stole the warmth before the light reached the top of my head. Despite the chill in the air, a river of sweat ran from under my ranger hat down between my shoulder blades, tempting me to break the stillness.

On the other side of a screen of bamboo and down the slope, I heard the quiet babble of Japanese soldiers. Since I could see movement, I knew these were not the ghosts of my dreams but flesh-and-blood men.

These soldiers were close enough to a Kachin village and the downed Allied plane I hunted. The American military would want information about them and where they seemed to be headed. But the Americans had also warned me that the Japanese were hunting Sharaw—the deceptively small soldier with amber eyes who pounced on the invaders and their Burmese traitors.

My fingers tightened on the ancient flintlock rifle slung across my body.

Normally I'd deal with the Japanese in my own way. For these I'd set a series of bamboo spikes in the jungle and then stand on the other side, letting the Japanese imagine they could catch me. As a rule, they were exceedingly overconfident and would run themselves right through. Then I'd simply complete my original mission task and make it to Camp Knothead in the south, Fort Hertz in the north, or any rendezvous point with little trouble. But the American area commander had made his orders clear—rescue the airmen; do not engage the Japanese.

I drummed my thumb against Mama's bag. I could feel the bulges of a dark stone, my tiger, and one military button. Tokens of the girl I used to be. Reminders of the dangers around me and the path I must take to extinguish these nightmares on my mountain. Nightmares Papa's God had failed to remove.

The plane should be a few miles on the other side of the Japanese camp. My mind raced across the American's orders. I had two days to make the next rendezvous before the Allied team moved on again.

If I obeyed orders, and if I crossed the path without being seen, I should get to the plane before the sun had been sleeping long, if the clouds didn't erase the light from the moon. Then if the survivors were able, and if we walked the rest of the night tonight and tomorrow, we might be able to reach the rendezvous in Tagap Ga by last mealtime tomorrow or, if I stopped to make sure we weren't followed, by the time the first morning breeze blew the following day.

Too many questions, possibilities.

Technically I wasn't required to obey the Americans. I was smart enough to know how to become an indispensable guide and informant without subjecting myself to the inconvenient requirements of enlisting. Their rules would not allow a female in their midst—especially considering the danger posed to me and to any team who would be sentimental enough to try to rescue me—but I only allowed them to see the mountain boy named Sharaw. Quiet, smart, and equal parts submissive and deadly.

What they didn't know would not hurt them. A tiger had no need for their rules of engagement. I hunted when and where I pleased.

Still, I didn't like to make my allies angry—or give them an excuse to look too closely at the boy in their midst.

"Chui," one of the men called, again. "Chui."

I shifted toward the sound. The word *lieutenant* was one of the few Japanese words burned into my memory. It hadn't been difficult to parse out the words I'd heard the last time I'd been in Tingrabum, to uncover a name attached to the military button. I found the ridges of the button in my bag. That settled it. I had to see the camp, to see if it was the man who owned the button, the one who had held Tu Lum— Lieutenant Utagawa.

The smell of rice cooking made my mouth water. With dinner in their pots, the men would stay the night and should be busy enough setting up camp they wouldn't watch well. I could move closer.

Bare feet skimming the soft jungle floor, I glided to the main elephant path. Light flickered across my body. My tanned legs and gray longyi blended into the jungle, and my movements echoed the sway of the trees until I was smoke in the shadows.

Just as the camp came into clear view, my stomach growled loud enough to make the jungle hiccup in alarm. I sucked in a breath and stilled with the animals, but the twenty or so men continued their duties without hesitation. They would be easy prey.

A voice lifted closer to my position, and I scoured the area for what must be another man. I slowed my breathing, listening. The obvious sounds of the man relieving himself narrowed my search. Behind a tree no more than a few yards away, the leaves flickered.

I reached for the hunting knife strapped at my waist and calculated my chance of slicing the man's throat without alerting his companions.

The Japanese soldier turned, and through the leaves I saw a single gold star lying on two red stripes. The man was the lieutenant.

My fingers tightened around the knife, and my other hand closed around the pouch at my neck. The lieutenant pivoted, searching the jungle before trudging to the camp. I released the knife. He wasn't the man I hunted, and the Allied fliers were counting on me. This lieutenant need not be afraid of me today.

I returned to my scan of the temporary encampment, counting weapons and recounting the men, searching for odd equipment that might signal their purpose. The OSS group in Burma was as much about gathering intelligence as executing guerrilla strikes against high-value targets.

A mule brayed, and I watched the men unload a heavy pack from its withers. The shape suggested artillery of some sort. Across the clearing a man flicked a wire into a tree, and I frowned as he connected the lead wire to a metal box. They were well equipped and had a radio. This was not a ragtag group of soldiers, so the Americans needed to know this group had penetrated the mountains.

As the Japanese sat to eat their meal, I stole up the hillside to keep watch.

A monkey troop chattered at me from the trees. I waved, acknowledging the challenge. The largest monkey showed his teeth and made faces at me. Giggling to myself, I leaned against the tree. The monkey reminded me of the small boys in Tingrabum threatening one another with loud boasts of the prolonged torture they would pour out on the other.

The monkey's impertinence would have made Tu Lum run for his bow, his short legs flying as he clambered into a tree. He'd beg me to find my blowgun and help him kill the crazy monkey for Aunt Nang Lu's pot. But the show was always to make me laugh. I swallowed the sudden emotion choking me and squared my shoulders. Wishing for times with the little boy could not make them happen.

But the blood of Japanese soldiers would make it right. It had to.

≈

The little girl ran in and out of the sunlight ahead of them. Ryan stifled his amusement as she stomped back again to urge the two Americans to move faster. Behind them, the boy who'd been relegated to rear guard trudged along, grumbling.

Along the path stood the rotting sacrifice poles, dark splashes of blood dotting the surfaces. Reports said that the duwa of this village had one foot in the old ways and another in the ways of the missionaries who had lived here in the last century. The seeming contradiction was what made him such a powerful ally. He knew and loved his people as well as the Western Allies.

In typical Kachin style, the duwa, along with all the women of the village, ambled between the heron-like posts of village homes to greet the Americans and had the guests quickly situated in the front room of the duwa's home, a fire warming their water-soaked feet. Ryan's toes tingled, coming back to life. If he couldn't still smell the ash of Tingrabum, he might have believed he was at the mission.

Clouds overtook the sun, and the winds intensified, creeping down the mountain, chilling the edges of the forest before descending into the heart of the mountain.

But the village glowed warm and bright. Ryan's mind bobbed into a half sleep, his list of items to discuss slipping beneath the surface as he let the familiar rise and fall of conversation soothe him. In the past week, they'd been successful according to military objectives, but the screeching metal of the resupply train, mixed with the screams of the men trapped and dying in the wreckage, still ravaged his ears. Was this what he was supposed to be doing?

Of course, on the battlefield it was kill or be killed.

The bamboo floor underneath Ryan swayed, and he jumped, drew his pistol, and spun to face his attacker.

A young Kachin woman stood placid in the narrow doorway. She slunk around the fire, stopping in front of Ryan. Her mouth quirked in humor before she reached out and laid her smooth hand across his fist, gripping the gun. His arm dropped. He'd nearly shot her.

"It all right." Her soft pardon purred in broken English. "You eat?"

She edged between the Americans, a bowl of rice on her lap. Her long fingers dipped into the bowl, alternately feeding the two men. The touch of her fingertip on Ryan's lips made his mouth go dry, and he struggled to swallow without choking like a fool.

As if she read his thoughts, she leaned across Ryan's body, offering a canteen of water. She traced Ryan's jaw line with a confident finger. Her dark eyes held his. The high cheekbones sharpened by firelight, and smooth dark hair brushing, tantalizing against his shoulder echoed into the past. Kailyn.

Ryan jumped at the snippet of memory, catching the woman's hand as it traveled down his chest. He gently captured her hand and shook his head.

Her lips, full and tempting, pouted, and her long lashes splayed on her cheeks. Heat crept up his neck. So much like Kai, but not. Ryan thought of the brave young woman, the one who threw herself in front of danger to protect those she loved. Nang Lu had called Kai a little tiger for a reason.

"Ah. Come on, Tonto. You're too much of a preacher boy." Trace let the challenge hang.

Ryan swallowed down a defense. Arguing would only make things worse. Trace didn't really want Ryan to compromise, but he also resented that Ryan wouldn't. Ever since India—when Ryan had been assigned to Trace as his radio operator, translator, cultural attaché, bodyguard, and, apparently, conscience—that had been the way of things.

Fact was, Trace was a whole bag of contradictions. As an effective commander who didn't mind sacrificing the individual for the benefit of the whole or shooting anyone who might be an informant without compunction, Trace was army through and through. But there were cracks in the facade, times when the real Trace sneaked out. And Ryan was one of the few who saw that the flippant humor and callous bravado was layered over a desperate need not to lose anything Trace cared about—which meant he rarely let anyone close.

The fear was something Ryan understood. He'd do anything to go back and protect Kailyn, his mom, his sister. But there was no way to change the history already written. The only hope was to not make the same mistake again.

Trace lifted the woman's other hand and kissed her palm.

A slow smile spread across the woman's face, and she let Trace ease her to her feet. Just before they stepped outside the back door, the woman swung around and wiggled her fingers at Ryan, and Trace grinned like he'd won the war. And there it was again—Ryan and Trace standing on opposite sides of a sticky question. And Trace, desperate to quiet the rumbling in his soul, pretending like the rules didn't apply to him and hoping Ryan would ignore it.

"It is as I have heard." The duwa hobbled into the room, watching the now empty doorway. "You have wisdom and patience. What is it you seek?"

Ryan stood and dipped his head in respect, thankful in more than one way that he'd refused the woman. "Only your wisdom and friendship," he responded in Kachin.

"And you know our ways." The old duwa leaned heavy on a cane as he sank to the floor. "I had heard you lived in the mountains before the war, Bear of Burma."

Ryan sucked in a breath. Though he'd adopted the call sign Bear, the last person to call him his full nickname was Tu Lum.

"The effects of your mission are wide in these mountains." The duwa nodded, like Ryan had passed some kind of test. "We have already sent more men to Tagap Ga." The older man groaned to a seat, adding, "Thanks to your Sharaw" almost as an afterthought. Almost.

Ryan sank, his mind churning even as he tried to wipe his face of emotion. *His Sharaw?* When Ryan didn't respond, the man lifted his eyebrows. Did this man suspect Kailyn was Sharaw? And if he suspected she was Sharaw, who else did? Ryan would have to find a more direct way to find her without tipping anyone off to the fact that Sharaw might be Kailyn Moran, and he'd start at tonight's radio call.

≈

I clambered into a gnarled oak until the path to the Japanese camp opened clearly in front of me. Oblivious to the enemy in the trees, they moved about yammering, still making their meal.

I wedged myself into a V of the tree. Hidden under the broad leaves of the canopy, I counted their weapons and watched to see if they would give away their objective. Opening my pack, I dug past one last box of nearly inedible K rations and a collection of jungle vegetables and pulled out a D-ration chocolate bar and my tiger-fur cloak. I had left the jungle heat only a few days ago, and nights in the higher mountains were cold.

I nibbled on the gooey chocolate and winced.

It had been a year and a half since the first growling plane dropped food stores in Tingrabum. I had clapped and done a twirling dance when I'd realized chocolate hid in the boxes tied to the white tents. When I was small, Papa had raved about the American sweet, making me dream of it.

But reality was nothing like the dream. I forced myself to swallow the mass.

Papa had more than stretched the truth. The chocolate we'd been sent was edible . . . barely. But the stuff was as bitter as betel nut, and chewing the sticky bar threatened to yank every tooth from my mouth.

I tucked the wrapper into my pack and lifted the small bag off my neck and onto my lap. The bright-red pouch was dangerous to wear when sneaking through the trees, but I refused to go anywhere without it. It was all I had left of my Kachin family.

My fingers trailed the swirling pattern, rising over and dropping down to the contents. I unearthed the midnight-colored stone and rubbed it until the thousand stars shone in the fading sunlight.

If Papa hadn't left, we'd all be safe with the villagers. He would have protected me and Ryan against their accusations.

But I'd heard rumors that the Japanese had captured the great missionary John Moran. Just because he'd abandoned me didn't mean I wanted him with the Japanese. I knew what they were capable of.

Keep Papa safe, wherever he is.

The thought of his safety escaped into the air and floated away like a winged padauk seed. I nestled the rock into the pouch. Safe.

Until my fingers brushed the brass military button, and my prayers cascaded to the ground.

The cold metal faithfully reminded me that prayers failed, men who murdered children still stalked the jungle, and I was alone and vulnerable.

I shivered and slipped the bag over my head before tucking the tiger skin tighter around my shoulders. The distant flicker of movement in the camp lulled me, hypnotizing, and my body relaxed into the tree. I should get the strips of bamboo out of my bag and weave a rope or leave or . . .

My eyes blinked shut and snapped open. *Can't fall asleep.* But lack of sleep and the high elevation conspired.

Wind breathed in my ear, and the distant sound of camaraderie cradled me, delivering me back to Tingrabum, my village, home.

Tu Lum and I leaned against the mission basha's poles. Wind ruffled the edges of the grass roof and kissed my cheeks with promise. Tu Lum dug his small toes into the red soil, releasing the smell of coming rain—metallic and rich.

Two children streaked past, weaving in and out of the slender legs of their families' bashas. The little boy hid under the draping edge of the thatched roof. But his skinny brown legs gave him away, and his sister tackled him to the ground.

Tu Lum laughed as the boy wailed and ran down the market trail. The boy trilled like a bird.

The girl broke off her chase and came screaming up the trail in retreat. She toppled over a tree root and fell, sprawled in the mud, her hair now twisted and matted with dirt. She scrambled to her feet, mouth open in silent screams, but the village was gone. Smoldering heaps. Tu Lum's limp arm, streaked in blood, stretched out from the tangle of underbrush, begging for help. No one could survive the jungle alone.

I jerked awake and caught the branch beneath me, barely preventing my fall, but my pack loosened and crashed through the trees, exploding on the ground.

Stupid. Stupid. Stupid.

I scrambled down, snagged my pack, and raced into a neighboring tree. Unless the Japanese were completely useless, they would investigate. I could only hope the jungle floor would not reveal signs of my passing.

Shapes floated along the trail.

I should have killed them when I had the chance.

The lieutenant stopped near where he had earlier relieved himself and contemplated the forest. I held my breath as his eyes raked the ground and then studied the trees. He pointed to the slope where I hid, and four of the men scrambled to obey. The lieutenant followed slowly, scanning the treetops with his bayonet fixed.

Pressing the pouch to my chest, I concentrated on disappearing behind a screen of leaves. The lieutenant stopped a few paces from my tree. In another life I might have thought he looked kind.

A group of brown monkeys raced across the trees, screeching at the invasion of their territory. Suddenly, rotten fruit exploded on the Japanese soldiers, and the men scattered in an attempt to escape the monkeys' counterattack. The lieutenant hesitated, taking one last glance. A bomb of what must have been monkey excrement streaked past me and splattered across the man's back. The lieutenant staggered at the impact, and surprise flickered across his face before he squared his shoulders and abandoned the forest.

I breathed a thank-you, then caught myself. The nats my Kachin family believed in weren't real, and Papa's God, if he was there, wasn't listening.

Thank you, little monkeys. They, at least, were as real as the tree camouflaging me.

With the Japanese on alert, I would wait until the sun was almost resting for the night before crossing the track. And now I was far too awake to fall asleep again. And these Japanese seemed to be an advance party of scouts, searching for signs of enemy contingents. They posed no immediate threat to any of the major Allied outposts. I would follow my original mission: go to the plane and help any surviving fliers. I dug out the thin strips of bamboo I kept in the bottom of my pack. I clenched one end in my mouth to pull the strips tight and deftly wove the strips of bamboo into more rope. I coiled it into my pack as I went along. I never knew when I'd need a length of rope for scaling the mountain or tying together a litter. It always paid to be prepared in the mountains.

To me weaving was easy, soothing. But Ryan? The first dozen times he'd tried, the rope had disintegrated into a pile of random bits when he released the twist. But he persisted. It was the same with all the ways of the jungle. He fought and struggled until somehow he lived in the mountains nearly as well as any who had been born here.

My fingers moved without thought, and my mind drifted, wondering where Ryan was and if he was safe . . . if he still searched for me. I didn't dare search for word of him. It could only lead him to me. And I knew he would convince the Americans to ship me out of the country. As if being safe would make me whole again.

I shoved the last of the rope into my pack and forced myself to focus on my current mission, processing timing, possible delays, and counteractions.

A few stripes of light remained in the sky when I shinnied down the tree and stole to the edge of the elephant path. The Japanese fire glowed in the distance. Surely they had a guard. But where?

I blinked in the growing darkness until I could once again see detail in the trees. Opening my eyes wide, I searched for the small broken X I'd used to mark the trail I often followed.

Just as I sneaked into the path, a body emerged from the undergrowth, lunging toward me, kindness nowhere to be found. Light reflecting from a slashing sword sent me diving sideways, rolling as I yanked my knife from my waist and slashed his Achilles. His body collapsed with a scream, and in one movement I twisted to my knees, silenced him, and was diving into the hidden path—the sound of my passing just a jungle breath.

The jungle listened for a heartbeat . . . two. And then the night erupted in frantic human noise. Shouts, wild shots. They were hunting me.

≈

After dinner and a frustratingly limited discussion with the duwa, Ryan was exhausted. There were only so many careful conversations a man could have and only so many days he could push himself without sleep . . . especially when climbing into higher elevations. And yet here he was, doing just that—hiking while beyond exhausted. The combination of mental and physical exhaustion was additionally dangerous considering how close he and Trace were to where the duwa had said a large contingent of Japanese had recently been spotted. In the state they were in, the last thing they needed was to stumble across a Japanese division.

But.

Something called him to keep pushing forward. The duwa had known who he was. Had seemed concerned about him and about Sharaw. Had even suggested Ryan had known Sharaw in his time as a missionary. The hint was enough confirmation that Ryan was nearly certain Kailyn Moran had taken on the legend of the tiger-man. Ryan had been desperate for more time with the duwa, for better answers, but Trace had sauntered back, smiling, overly content, a cigarette dangling from his mouth. And the duwa clammed up. As well he should. Trace was unknown to the mountain people.

At least the duwa had given Ryan a list of the usual rendezvous points for the tiger-eyed one and her American handlers. The best news was her probable next destination was the same as his own—the training camp at Tagap Ga. He might have to catch her there.

Ryan suppressed the urge to hurry Trace as he stopped to suck in additional air before resuming his trek up the incline. Other than a lack of mountain lungs, Trace reminded Ryan of a young American version of Tingrabum's old duwa. Small, solid but nimble, dark haired, and comfortable enough with his authority that he earned respect without being harsh. He also trusted Ryan.

"Gonna make it?"

Trace grimaced. "I don't know how y'all trot around these mountains like you were on vacation."

"You look as out of place as I'd be at your debutante balls. But you'll get used to it." Ryan paused, amusement tugging at his lips. "After a few more years."

"Useless training." Trace slipped on a root and plunked to the ground. "What idiot Yank thought the Appalachians could pass for the Himalayas?"

Ryan stifled a laugh and scouted the hill for signs of other humans.

The irony of being the army's trusted mountain man wasn't lost on Ryan. When he'd first come to Burma, he was worse off than Trace.

It wasn't until the hunting trip where he'd earned Tu Lum's bow killing the partridges that Ryan had started to feel the mountain, the animals, the rhythms in this world and its people.

Ryan sighed. But his epiphany had come too late. He'd temporarily earned the people's respect but lost the people themselves—and failed Kai in almost every way imaginable.

He eased down toward Trace, letting his legs absorb the impact rather than his knees and toes. "We should cross the elephant trail in about an hour. Then we'll cut across it and head north. It should take us two days or so to make the next village."

Trace unbent himself, his breath back to normal. "And you're sure there'll be mountain people there who will help us?"

"They've been one of the most reliable lines of getting our flyers out, and they have protected missionaries and noncombatants for years. They earned their status as spirit-men, and I think they'll help."

"Wish HQ would have just dropped us in there."

"Kachins are afraid of the roaring birds and their flaming eggs." Ryan pantomimed a plane with a lethal bomb. "But the duwa in the last village says Sharaw told him they'll help."

"You know best. If it were up to me, I'd make a hash of relations for sure. Still, I wish we knew where that Sharaw fella was. If any of the stories are right about him, we could use him for more than recruiting."

Trace raised his brows. "The duwa didn't, by chance, tell you where we could find him, did he?"

Ryan grunted noncommittedly. Even if he did know where Kai was, Ryan couldn't let his CO rope Kai into helping more. He already hated how much danger she was in. Yes, she was also recruiting soldiers, gathering intelligence, and leading hit-and-run attacks, but she was also generally throwing herself into the most perilous situations. No matter how skilled a hunter she was, being alone in the jungle was asking for trouble for anyone.

But what Trace was planning was even more dangerous than all of that. Even Ryan didn't like the idea of trusting Utagawa. Kai would be apoplectic. And Kai's temper notoriously blew her reason and self-preservation instincts to smithereens. She could very well put them all in danger by flying off the handle. And if Ryan delivered her right into the heart of the enemy, they'd torture her until she was nothing but shreds.

Of course Ryan could tell Trace that Sharaw was the daughter of the other missionary, but that would only lead to two reactions. Either Trace would still recruit her—and Ryan would have to deal with an out-of-control Kai bent on destroying herself—or Trace would reveal who she was, and the army would strip her of her status as Sharaw.

The latter might be the worse outcome since that would leave her abandoned in the jungle by herself, without even the slim protection she held while attached to the US military. It would only be a matter of time before the Japanese figured out Sharaw was a woman. He'd seen what they did to village women. He didn't even want to think about what they would do to a woman who'd defied them.

Ryan would have to be beyond precise to find Kai and send her packing before Trace figured out who she really was. Ryan would go AWOL to make it happen.

Trace tumbled over another half-buried log and cursed. "I don't suppose we could use the elephant path to save time."

Barely controlling his amusement, Ryan shook his head. "The Japanese use that track regularly. But you're right that we're behind schedule."

Ryan scrubbed his jaw. "At dusk we have to stop to radio in, but with the full moon, we could skip another night's rest and get ahead of the Japanese contingent that the duwa told us about."

He hoped Trace would trust him enough not to push for the real reason why.

Trace studied his friend and then the jungle ahead of them. "Well, I reckon we'll have to make do with K rations on the go tonight."

With any luck, they could catch up to Kai before the Japanese did.

Chapter Twenty

I CREPT LOW ALONG THE animal track, across the rocks, and up into a dense canopy where I could run along the thick tree limbs. From the sounds of chaos, the Japanese had not discovered which way I had gone, but I did not slow. I had no time to lay a trap for them, and I was outnumbered and outgunned. I leaped across a gap between trees, teetering as the tree limb bent under my weight, swinging my arms to right myself. Just a bit farther and I would—

A tiger growl erupted, and I stumbled to a stop. A roar consumed the jungle once again, and I breathed out relief. He was far enough down the mountains that he didn't pose a threat but close enough to distract the soldiers and send them careening away from the unrivaled king of the jungle.

Heart thudding wildly, I dropped to the ground and plodded up another steep incline and down the back side only to climb once more.

At the top of the next ridge, I could see that the wingtip of an enormous C-46 transport plane pierced the jungle at the top of a monstrous gash through the mountain. It had been closer than I'd guessed. The timing of the tiger couldn't have been better. There would have been no way I could protect the aviators and dispatch enemy scouts at the same time. I would have had to choose what to sacrifice.

By the time I reached the wing, a light sheen of sweat covered me, and I had shed the tiger-skin cape. The broken appendage was planted in a grove of evergreen trees. A neat row ran from the wing, down the mountain as if a giant farmer had tilled the ground. Nothing good would be harvested from this field though.

I wiped drops of mist off my lashes and glared at the sky. Wisps of clouds, the front edge of a billowing mass, covered the moon. My luck was running out.

Keeping to one side of the furrow, I padded down the path. I saw no sign of bodies, supplies, or predators, but no signal panels either. I would be performing a funeral rather than a rescue.

≈

I sat under the makeshift roof of my lean-to as rain pinged off the stub of wing above me. The jungle winds made me pull on my boots, coat, and fur cloak. Rain clouds obscured the moon, morphing the jungle into opaque black I did not dare penetrate with my torch or a fire.

I twined the airmen's dog tags through my fingers, metal clinking against metal. I would be dry inside the plane. But four ruined bodies were entombed in the wreckage, and I did not relish sitting with their twisted forms. One moment, four men flew above the Himalayas, bound for China with much-needed supplies. The next, the plane betrayed them, smashed across the mountain, leaving behind four grieving families and a huge loss of equipment. Supply plane crashes were an unfortunate regular occurrence, and it left me wondering if we could win. If we could fight back the Japanese. If my home would ever revert to normal.

I shoved away the vision of Tu Lum's blank eyes as Ryan threw dirt onto his body. The hollow pound of mud against an empty shell. I tucked the dog tags inside my pack and yanked the string tight.

The predator inside me roared, and I covered my ears against his scream for vengeance.

When I'd first set out on my own, the legend of the sharaw had flickered in my memory, promising power and control. I'd had no real plan and no real training. But I had the promise of the jaiwa of what I could do.

For months I had controlled the whispers, the anger and fear, by stalking small Japanese forces across the Hukawng Valley. I obstructed paths, mimicked the sound of tigers, diverted streams, and generally herded the enemy into pits or impaled them with swinging bamboo spikes and left the bodies for other predators before disappearing like mist. Alone and with no training, it was a miracle that I had not been captured and killed.

When I had rescued a group of six American OSS agents from starvation, they saw the potential under my little mountain-boy facade and trained me. They'd adopted my family's nickname for me and teasingly called me "little tiger." They could not know that Sharaw's anger nibbled at my control. In their presence I was simply a helpful abandoned boy, but I took my new knowledge and weapons into the jungle, and the legend grew. In some tellings I was a lost British child, others a cast-off orphan, and others still the spawn of the devil. Perhaps I was some of each.

Eventually the Americans had stumbled on a survivor of one of my traps and figured out who was responsible. Then the nickname was no longer a joke. After that, any American group I attached to was glad, if a bit hesitant, to have a boy named for a legend.

I didn't mind their hesitance, their askance glances. Let them assume I was the devil himself. If it helped them push the Japanese into the sea, I would do what was necessary, even if I was consumed by the darkness. There wasn't much left of me anyway.

In daylight I relished the fear in the cries of my enemies and smelled their terror as I stalked them. But at night my mind was torn with nightmares and my arms were somehow gnawed bloody.

I shook my head, dislodging the tendrils of fear snaking into my mind.

I was Sharaw—the man-tiger—come to life.

Tigers are never afraid.

I tugged the tiger pelt and blanket tighter under my chattering jaw. I closed my eyes and feigned sleep, never quite letting my mind drift into my dreams, where I could no longer control the tiger inside me.

Chapter Twenty-One

December 1943

AS THE SKY STRETCHED AWAKE, I unwrapped my cocoon of blankets and rubbed life into my stiff muscles. I packed up camp and headed into the trees. The four metal dog tags clanked cold against my chest until I clamped a hand over them, dampening the call of the ghosts.

The sun had rotated through the sky one more time before I slipped below the nearby village, close enough that the watchman could hear my call . . . if I hailed him. I was to meet the Americans a dozen miles beyond—otherwise I would much prefer to continue avoiding this place. The displaced people of Tingrabum would not welcome me.

With the altitude I had gained, the jungle had given way to the temperate forests of oak, teak, and pine. But under my pelt cape, I was perspiring. I skirted the prayer-post-lined path and hacked through the forest instead.

The two-note call of a cuckoo drifted from the jungle. My head snapped around, and I backed behind a tree. Cuckoos only called in spring.

A young girl poked her head out of the underbrush.

"American?" Her harsh whisper carried across the forest. The girl trotted past a fallen oak and peered into the jungle.

"American?" Enjoying her hunt, she proceeded to try to entice me with a description of the curry and local women.

I slithered farther into the shelter of underbrush.

Leaves behind me crunched, and I knew I'd been flanked while the girl had distracted me. For all I knew, a soldier stood behind me with a rifle pointed at my head. Letting out a sigh, I clutched my fur wrap tighter around me and emerged—a proud warrior robed in a striped tiger skin.

The little girl screeched and scrambled away. Her terrified screams pierced me, and I steadied myself against the tree. I must be Sharaw or risk recognition and rejection by my old friends. I must.

An older woman emerged behind me. The one who had sprung the trap. I ducked my head, heart pounding. If anyone would recognize me, it would be one of the women. There were not many with tiger eyes.

"You are not like other Americans I have seen," she said in broken English.

The girl's scream echoed again, and the woman chuckled. "She thinks she sees a tiger."

I jerked upright and answered in Kachin. "Perhaps she did."

I could have outrun this pair, but not without raising the suspicion of the village—who would avoid a friendly village to resupply? They would not let me continue without confirming I was neither traitor nor spy. Besides, something in me wanted to secretly taunt them with what I had become. They no longer had the ability to hurt me. They had been right all along to be afraid.

Stalking up the path, I did not pause to see if the woman came too.

"We were sent to watch for you."

I jolted at the nearness of the woman's voice and heard her shuffle to a stop behind me. I had not heard her follow me, and I cursed myself for letting my agitation override my senses.

I nodded without facing her.

"You are coming to the village then?"

"You give me little choice." My growl earned a chuckle from the woman.

"Well, I, for one, am glad. I have long wanted to meet Sharaw." She said it as if the dangerous legend was a storybook princess.

Ignoring her, I adjusted my pack and ducked under the twisted branches that formed the village gate.

The girl's screams had brought the village men to meet me, bristling with bows, knives, and an occasional flintlock. I had not seen these people since we had left Tingrabum.

Opening my hands, palms up, I dipped my head in respect and swallowed the onslaught of emotions. I could not afford to let them sense anything in my greeting. *"Kaja-ee?"* Sweat collected under my armpits, and I gagged on the bitter smell of my fear.

An older man, bent with age, pushed in front of the few men. He must be the new duwa. He lifted an eyebrow, shifting the puckered scar that wrapped from forehead to cheek.

"Kaja, Sharaw."

I released a quiet breath. He had answered my greeting politely and called me the name of the tiger-man. I remained undiscovered.

"We have been awaiting you. Your Americans asked us to care for you tonight. They said another group is coming to join you." At the slight flick of the duwa's hand, the line of men broke apart, many of them whispering and casting me a wary eye. The duwa signaled for me to follow.

I bent to dig in my pack, allowing the others to follow the duwa first. With the ease of many years' practice, I wove a cloth into a turban on my head and dragged it low on my ears before stuffing my ranger hat over the whole affair and tugging the brim over my eyes. The hat gave me more place to hide, but the turban would be allowed inside, where the hat might not. I needed as much disguise as I could manage. If these people revealed who I was, I would be vulnerable again. Not only did they hate Kailyn Moran, no one was afraid of a woman. No doubt I would find myself facing jungle justice. And if I somehow managed to escape after that, they would still inform the Americans of my true identity. And if the Americans discovered I was female, they would not continue to let me help the OSS team. I knew enough of their prejudice to know that.

A boy who could have been Tu Lum's younger brother stood huddled under the porch of the large basha on the first hill. He watched me as if I might attack at any moment. I swallowed, uneasy with the ghosts lingering in the village.

The remnants of Tingrabum, these people, were among the few who might recognize me as John Moran's daughter. I had no desire to test the accuracy of their memory or the greatness of their forgiveness.

Torn between hiding and acting like the legend of my assumed name, I squared my shoulders and strode after the woman who had trapped me in the forest. I would simply move on as quickly as possible. I had no other choice.

The duwa lumbered under the thatched porch, his white head disappearing through the dark rectangle doorway, followed by the woman. With one last glance over my shoulder, I ducked into the welcomed darkness.

Inside, the duwa hunkered on the far side of the cold fireplace box as the woman drifted into the main room, carrying sticks and a flint. I watched the familiar movements from the corner of my eye, mesmerized by the woman's ease. What would it be like to be safe? To feel at home?

The duwa cleared his throat, and I realized he was speaking to me in my native tongue.

"Sharaw, you grace us with your coming. I am sorry that the Americans are not here yet."

I dipped my head.

"And you? You will not stay long." This from one of the other men was more statement than question.

My hand snaked to the knife at my side. Was he threatening me or merely making an assumption?

"Be at ease." The duwa inclined his head. "I am Zau Tu, originally of Tingrabum."

I dropped my hands into my lap. My ears echoed, pulsing with blood. As Aunt Nang Lu's favorite among her many brothers, Zau Tu had stayed with us on his many trips to the market in the plains. Last I knew, a friend. Now wrinkled and grayed beyond recognition, Zau Tu sat grinning, the twinkle in his eye the only sign of the man I'd known.

"I thank you for your hospitality. But why were you searching for me?"

"The other Americans moved on after hearing of a Japanese hunting party. They asked me to tell you to meet them at the next checkpoint. Perhaps it will not be safe for you here long, but for tonight I will protect you."

Zau Tu frowned, the twinkle gone.

"An American has called our radio. He searches for a woman with amber eyes. Perhaps you know of her?" He tilted his head, touching the small cross hanging around his neck and nodded.

"I will not tell the rest," Zau Tu whispered in flawless English. "They would not understand."

I forced my expression to remain unmoved, but my head swam. Zau Tu knew me, and others were looking. Who and why? Was it Papa?

My aunt's people respected and feared Sharaw as a warrior, but if they knew I was merely John Moran's daughter, would their respect evaporate and leave distrust behind? They may very well punish a woman with such airs. Did they still blame me for the attacks on Tingrabum? The smell of smoke choked me, and I squared my shoulders.

Tigers are never afraid.

I would not allow these villagers to ruin me.

The other man leaned, whispering in the duwa's ear. The duwa swatted at him, a pesky fly buzzing his ear.

"We are catching up on family business." The duwa switched to Kachin to respond.

"Family business?"

Zau Tu stood abruptly. "Enough questions. We will eat dinner, and in the morning, Sharaw will leave to find his friends."

I stood, shaking my head.

"You will stay here with me. We will show the Americans they and their friends are safe here." Zau Tu spoke kindly, but his tone did not leave room for argument.

I bristled. The sleeping arrangements would be awkward at best. Worse, the longer I stayed, the greater the possibility someone would recognize me. A short haircut and military garb wouldn't protect me long. I opened my mouth to argue.

But the duwa settled back on the floor mat, and his wide eyes signaled me to sit with him again.

When I sank into a crouch, Zau Tu grinned. The older woman limped into the room and presented Zau Tu a cup and a small pile of rice on a banana leaf. She bent and whispered in his ear. He grunted assent before shifting his attention back to me.

"The time for our daily radio contact is nearly here. You will eat, and then we will go."

HQ would expect me to check in since I'd arrived somewhere with a radio, but my mind scrambled. If Papa was the caller, did I dare answer? I would have to disappear before Zau Tu forced me into the call. The duwa lifted the cup toward me.

"To Sharaw. May he live long and devour many Japanese."

I swallowed hard, staring into the flame. Part of me wished for familiar village life, but I would find no safety here. No family. They would never accept me as either Kailyn Moran or Sharaw. The jungle called to me. The rolling trees and underbrush were the only home I still had. I shoveled rice into my mouth and swallowed without chewing. My stomach pleaded noisily for more, but the villagers had given more than they could spare already.

I made a show of stretching lazily, then grabbed my pack and swung to my feet like I wasn't half-panicked as I headed toward the back door.

Zau Tu frowned and gathered himself to stand.

I smiled, hoping my grimace was convincing. "I will be back. Unless you'd prefer me to foul myself."

The other man choked at my brazenness, but I kept the plastered grin securely in place, and Zau Tu shooed me out.

I sauntered out the door. I wished for darkness to hide me, but the sun still stood in the sky. Rotating, I searched for the most likely place to relieve myself that was still in the direction of the path northeast.

There. A crop of thick underbrush bristled in the right direction. The spot was even at the back side of a hummock. When I could no longer see the bashas, I squatted to relieve myself.

My ruse would give me a few minutes to sneak into the jungle before the duwa and the others would know of my departure.

The soft murmur of a loving mother talking with her child made my fingers tingle in memory. I clenched my fist closed over the emptiness. Wishing for something could not make it be. I stood and turned away from the village. Just as I emerged from the underbrush, a hand clamped on my arm.

"Where are you going?"

I snatched my knife and swung around in one movement, the blade halting a moment before it connected with a woman's neck.

She lifted her chin, eyebrows lifting in challenge. What could I say to convince her to let me go? I would not fight her and risk her harm . . . or the unwanted attention of the village.

When I sheathed the knife across my chest, she stepped closer, studying me. I stiffened, resisting the urge to retreat. Still, I snuggled the ranger hat lower on my forehead, not daring to reciprocate the scrutiny.

"You. You are . . ." Her hands dropped.

Fear skittered through me, and I shrank back. "I am leaving." My words tumbled from my mouth. "I wasn't planning on . . ."

The woman watched me, compassion swimming in her face. "Moran Kai?" She reached to touch me, as if not quite believing I was real.

I clenched my jaw, refusing to show emotion.

Tigers are not afraid.

"You can't go out there alone." Her voice so soft I barely heard her words. "It's Baw Ni. I—"

I yanked away, my fingers snapping to my knife. "You are not my people." My words trembled against their restraints. This woman and her son had stolen everything.

"Zau Tu has shown me how good you and your Ryan were to me. I was—"

164

"You turned your back on him. Why should I trust you?" I dared study her now, the scar across her cheek, and hate blazed in my gut. "You would have let us die in the jungle."

"Yes. I would have. And I was wrong. I wish that I had helped. That I had helped Ryan search for you then. There are so many things . . ."

A tear slipped out of my eye at the mention of the other missionary, and I slapped it away. Compassion, love . . . they were weaknesses.

"I did not realize my son—"

"Led the Japanese to us?"

"I did not know he had—"

"Sold us to the devils? Allowed them to slaughter Tu Lum?" His screams echoed in my mind. My knees shook, threatening to give way. His blood forever would be on me.

"Karai Kasang brought you back to us. You do not have to be alone, Moran Kai." Her gentle hand burned the skin of my arm. "Stay with me. I will convince the others to accept you."

I wrenched my arm away. "My staying will help no one."

"Moran Kai." Baw Ni nudged my chin with a finger. "What happened . . . it is not your fault."

I shook my head and edged away. "I am Sharaw. Moran Kai died a long time ago."

"You are in danger. I cannot—"

"We are all in danger. Unlike others, I will not stand idly by to let the Japanese take more."

The older woman sighed. "I will hide your leaving as long as I can. The Bear has been searching for you. He plans to come here. What do I tell him?"

The Bear of Burma. Ryan. Ryan was looking for me. He was still in the mountains. I thought of his quiet urging me to eat, to take one more step, his hand engulfing mine, coaxing me to trust him, sloughing off the hard shell. He had kept the name Tu Lum and I had given him.

I shoved away the memories. He was too late. He had planned to abandon me, and now the girl he knew, the girl he had tried to save, was gone.

I pulled a paper and pencil from my pack and scribbled the broken *X* across it with his name underneath and jotted a quick note. I pressed the note into her hand. "If he comes, give this to him. He cannot continue. Others will make the connection too easily."

"Karai Kasang protect you. Go in peace." She ducked into the grasses.

As if belief in the supreme one could bring me peace. I clenched my jaw against the ache of hope. Karai Kasang had long ago turned his back on us. I would gain justice for Tu Lum, for the duwa, and then, once Utagawa's blood bathed the ground, I could lie down and let the Sharaw take me. I watched Baw Ni round the corner of the basha, her steps long and sure. How I longed to go back. But there was nothing left for me here. My family had turned their backs on me. My home was ash. I shifted my pack and slipped into the jungle before they came for me or I could change my mind.

Chapter Twenty-Two

A CLUTCH OF BIRDS BURST from the underbrush, startling Ryan out of his trance. Dusk had sneaked over the mountain and was crashing into night. He cursed himself for being so distracted. Soon he'd barely be able to make out the underbrush he hacked at, let alone any dangers curled inside it. He signaled a stop. It was time for their scheduled check-in with the headquarters stationed in Nazira, India. Colonel Eifler and his OSS staff would want a report about the contingent of Japanese in the area, and Ryan also wanted to know if anyone had a response about his inquiries into Kailyn.

He was getting desperate. It was just a matter of time before the Japanese tracked her down. And while he wanted to fulfill his promise to watch out for her, he also missed her confidence, the brush of her fingers across his arm, her teasing laughter, her unquenchable desire to build a home for those she loved.

Of course, the fact that Trace was unlikely to let Ryan escort Kai to India put Ryan in a fine pickle. But first things first. He had to find her before he could do anything about getting her out of the crosshairs of the Japanese—and that meant checking in. Ryan dropped his pack and fished out the small wooden box with his OSS radio.

The radio was a wonder of gadgetry created by the American OSS agents in India, made of cast-off Signal Corps supplies—C-ration cans, flashlight batteries, and a maze of wires, tubes, and dials were covered by a metal sheet retrieved from a busted C-47 and attached to a hand crank. Its range made it possible for field officers to communicate over hundreds of miles, even with the massive Himalayas in between. It was something regular army grunts never would have thought possible. American ingenuity. Such a beautiful thing.

Ryan opened the box and attached the lead-in wire antennae, which Trace then threw across a bush before manning the crank. Setting the frequency low, Ryan donned his headphones and flipped the switches to designate the wire antennae. He flipped the main power switch, expecting static and instead hearing a silent line.

He flipped off the set, checked his settings, the connections between the crank, antennae, and radio, and spun the dial again. Nothing.

Trace stopped cranking.

Trace and Ryan took apart the radio and reassembled it again and again. Despite their training, they could not make the blasted box transmit. Ingenuity was beautiful . . . until it failed.

Trace merely shrugged, packed it away, and ordered Ryan to push on to the next village. Ryan carefully stowed the radio, resisting the desire to smash it against the ground and then jump on it for good measure. Several hours of labor wasted, and Ryan still had no word of Kai. He had no other option now. He would have to sacrifice discretion for speed and get to the next village radio sooner rather than later.

Barely waiting for Trace, Ryan set out toward a known elephant path in the direction of the next village, which was where the remnants of Tingrabum now lived and one of the few places Ryan might not be welcome. Not that he blamed them. He had failed to protect their village and their leader.

A huge moon rose and highlighted a recent barefoot print and another. The confident use of animal paths and the lack of shoes suggested a native trailblazer and therefore probably friendly. At the connection to the main trail, Ryan stopped so suddenly Trace ran into him.

"Japanese." Ryan pointed to the large collection of telltale narrow footprints dotted with hobnail marks.

"Which way are they headed?"

Ryan unshouldered his carbine and slid into the main path. "It looks like they were originally going north, maybe toward the Brits at Fort Hertz. They set up camp over here."

Mule droppings and prints hugged the jungle—a well-supplied group. Ryan paced to the opposite side, kneeling at the sight of fire-blackened earth. His head snapped up, and he waved Trace into the forest.

"It's still warm," he breathed.

Trace unslung his rifle and retreated into the forest path from where they'd come. Ryan scuttled out of the silver moonlight and scanned the sides of the trail.

The Japanese were cunning fighters. They'd been known to set traps for unsuspecting Allied forces. Body low to the ground, Ryan searched for signs of their native friend and the larger Japanese force.

"Some went through there." He pointed at a few bent blades of elephant grass. "But most of them went south." Ryan pushed through the elephant grass to the base of a hardwood tree and hesitated, listening. To his relief, the jungle pulsed with life. No large group of soldiers hid terribly close by, or the jungle would reveal them. "I think they're gone. Hasn't been long though."

"Good thing the radio held us up."

Trace was right. The radio fiasco had probably saved them from stumbling into a nasty scrap. *There's no such thing as coincidence.* Ma's mantra slipped through Ryan's mind, and he grabbed hold of a tree to steady himself. Tree sap stuck to his fingers, and he grimaced before wiping his hands on his shirt.

The sap bled from several deliberate slashes to the trunk, like a broken *X*. Kai's mark stood white against the dark bark, along with a stylized arrow pointing the opposite direction from her path. Did Kai know he was following her? Why would she advertise her whereabouts in a way he would know? Or was it simply an old mark?

"Seems odd they'd tear down a camp in the middle of the night. Why do you suppose they left?" Trace's voice in his ear made Ryan jump. "And what's that?" Trace pointed to the white marks glowing against the dark bark.

"Just a Kachin trail marker." The half truth slipped out before Ryan could call it back.

A tiger's roar echoed in the distance.

Trace swallowed. "This is where they say Sharaw prowls. Maybe he—"

"The man-tiger? What crazy villager told you that old legend?"

Trace shrugged, the white of his eyes glowing in the moonlight. "I've seen some mighty strange things in the hills. I'll feel better when we get farther into the mountain. Tigers don't live higher up."

Ryan slipped past Trace and searched the brush and trees north of the scorched earth. "What do you think, Major? Do we keep heading north to Tagap Ga or divert to follow the force south?" Ryan's mind raced. He needed his CO to follow the northern path. But Trace would never do anything for personal reasons. Forcing himself to remain still, Ryan looked steadily at his commanding officer.

Trace rubbed his jaw. "We need those Kachins."

Despite the fact his mind raced, Ryan held still. "Yes, sir. And our radio's been attacked by gremlins."

"There'll be a team waiting there."

"And we're low on supplies."

Trace grinned, deceptively lazy and confident. "Come on then, Tonto. Let's ride north."

Relief flooded Ryan. He wouldn't have to convince Trace to change his mind.

"Now if we could just wrangle us some horses, my feet would be ever so grateful."

Ryan straddled an imaginary horse. "Giddyup, Scout."

"You're the *size* of a horse, Bear, but I ain't so sure how helpful that is in the jungle," Trace scoffed.

"No one said size was everything. But there's a reason you called me Bear, and it isn't just because of my size. Remember?" Ryan grinned at the memory. In full view of his training class, Ryan had sneaked up on the OSS training officer and laid him flat before the man even knew what was coming. *"Bears may be big and look dumb as a lump on a log,"* Trace had said, *"but they're quiet and deadly as cobras."* The takedown was one of the many reasons Trace had requested Ryan accompany him.

Ryan stepped back to let Trace step onto the trail and swept his rifle across the clearing one last time. The last thing they needed was to be flanked by a Japanese scout.

Chapter Twenty-Three

As I HIKED NORTH, EVERGREENS overtook the mountain, stretching from the rocks, scraping at the sky. The wind turned bitter, and I sank into my striped fur skin, my body curling into itself. Mama's old woolen leggings under my cotton uniform were better than nothing, but I still wished for a pair or two of woolen military pants to wear on top. I resorted to counting steps to distract myself from the cold nipping through my boots. There was more than one reason I'd rarely traveled to the northern mountains.

How my people adapted to this frozen wasteland was incomprehensible to me.

My people.

I stopped. I had no people.

Even Baw Ni hadn't been sure of how the others would receive me. Would they punish her for letting me go? My feet slowed. Did I truly care? Shaking the tendrils of longing from my head, I reminded myself of why I'd stayed away. The whispering of the man next to Zau Tu had proved the village's distrust. I forced my feet into movement. Baw Ni could care for herself. She had made peace with her son's treachery, if not her own.

The moon peeked from behind the mountains and lent a spotted glimmer to the forest. In another time, I would have climbed a tree and watched the stars swirl their nightly dance. I would not stop, but I was grateful for enough light to trade my careful walk for a fast military clip. The frozen air burned my lungs, and my breath puffed into loops of fog.

Papa had done the same thing the first time I'd been in the high mountains. I was perhaps four or five. Carried by four Kachin guides in a palanquin, Mama and I snuggled under furs and woolen blankets. Papa had brought us to the high mountains and re-created a Chicago Christmas complete with a tree lit by an entire universe of candles.

Mama had knit woolen stockings for us. A deep blue for herself. Red as poppies for me. The snow, reflecting the warm yellow sun, impossibly bright, enticed me. I'd played outside, building snow forts with Papa and throwing snowballs at trees until my fingers were stiff. Then I skipped into the woods, holding Papa's hand, happy. I focused on the sound of him speaking, trying to remember, but the wind tore it away. His image flickering, evaporating, not even hesitating long enough to say goodbye.

Frowning, I concentrated on the Christmas memory, filling in details, grasping hold of the vision. Mama had been strolling behind us, singing, and I turned, desperate to see Mama, but she wasn't there—consumed by the sullen white landscape bearing down on me.

A tree limb snapped under my foot, yanking me from my daydream. The wind blew a cold kiss, and my memory drained of color and drifted away in the swirling snow.

I laid a hand where Mama's pouch bulged under the layers. *Protect Papa.*

I didn't know if the supreme one heard my prayers, but the habit comforted me. Perhaps Mama heard me from beyond the stars.

I sniffed, rubbing moisture from my face. Surely I was the only creature crazy enough to be out. In the stillness, the whisper of a mountain stream trickled to me. *Almost there.*

I trudged toward the sound, tucking away the past. Memories would only slow me down.

My plan was to climb into the crevasse, cross the stream, and then follow it east. Last I knew, another village was a bit north of the eastern slope. Perhaps they'd offer a meal and a warm fireplace. I could use a few hours' sleep before finishing my trek to Tagap Ga.

A quiet shuffle behind me stilled my feet. Holding my breath, I scanned the forest, making out the silhouette of an owl atop a broken tree. He hooted out a warning and then swooped to the forest floor. A mouse squeaked in terror, caught in the talons of the hunter.

I swallowed the impulse to run and continued to watch. Green eyes peered out of the gloom, and I heard the distinct crunching of a deer stripping bark from the undergrowth.

Panicking because of a deer. Keep your head about you.

I listened for the sound of the stream before continuing on, shaking my head at my childish fears.

Skidding down the steep incline, a river of pebbles followed my descent.

Frigid slivers of moonlight rippled on the surface of the stream, and I realized the bottom was obscured in debris and depth. The water ran high for dry season, and the last thing I needed was cold, wet feet. I trudged northeast, searching the banks for a fallen tree to use as a bridge or at least a few large rocks protruding out of the white water.

A dozen strides upstream, the cliff jutted into the river, preventing me from traveling farther east, the way I needed to go. I leaned over the river to find another way around the cliff. But the bare cliff reached as far as I could see.

Between the walls, water frothed against the rocks, separating into shining droplets, flying into freedom, then smashing down before being swallowed whole by the mass. The water at my feet was smooth, and the thin skim of ice revealed the shifting image of a warrior. Papa would never recognize his little girl in the fierce, half-starved, dirty boy.

Underneath the image, a white stone pulsed in the moonlight. It was so like the one I'd prayed over, hoping Papa wouldn't send me away from home. I'd left that stone and last scrap of hope with Ryan. What did it mean that he was searching for me?

The river stone twinkled and shifted under the blue moonlight, and I thrust my hand into the frigid water, scattering my watery reflection into bits of silvery light.

Home.

Old nightmares slammed into me, and I shrank from their force, my feet under my haunches. Raised voices of those who were once friends, angry, accusing. It had been the tiger-eyed one's fault that Mama died, that the crops failed . . . that the Japanese had come, then destroyed the village, murdered Tu Lum, and desecrated the duwa. I pushed against dreamed images—black-winged shadows cursing me, the cold air of night, confusion distorting even the straight tree trunks and liquefying the solid ground, the heat of Sharaw's flames licking my heels and consuming me.

I turned the rock. A tiny sliver of darkness marred the back side of the stone. Dripping through the white like blood.

Ryan had tried to protect me, but even he was inadequate in the face of utter destruction. Even Ryan had planned to abandon me and join the military. And so I left before he could. My fingers tightened on the stone. I had no place in my life for fairy-tale wishes. I heaved the stone into the water.

I will find you, Utagawa. Your blood will make it right.

But first I had to cross the blasted stream. I yanked off my cotton military pants and used them to tie my pack on top of my head. At least I would have something dry on the other side.

I stepped into the freezing water. Sucking air through my teeth, I willed myself to continue through as the water ran across my calves. The river rushed around my knees, my thighs, and I fought to keep my footing while juggling the awkward pack and my rifle.

My teeth chattered, legs numb, and I wasn't even halfway across.

A cascade of rocks scattered down the hill behind me.

I stilled. A man-shaped shadow moved on the ridge downstream.

Cursing under my breath, I dropped into the water, dunking my pack and hat into the water with me until just my eyes and nose showed, hopefully looking very much like a rock. I kept my eyes on the ridge, wishing for a pistol or at least a bow and arrow, anything other than the now wet and useless flintlock and a dismantled blowgun that didn't have the range.

I edged toward the northern side of the river. Another figure emerged, and the two forms slid down the opposite ridge, following my trail. Whispers drifted on the air. Definitely Japanese.

If I'd ignored orders and set a trap to take care of the insolent sons of swine days ago, I wouldn't be freezing in a mountain stream.

Curse the army and their blasted orders.

Crawling now, I felt the rocks bite into my skin. I followed the stream northeast. If I made it around the bend, I could climb the ridge and escape into the forest.

Just as I eased into the darkness, I heard a splash. The men had entered the stream behind me. And then the muffled exclamation of discovery.

I bounded from the water, my entire body shaking. I had seen first-hand what enemy soldiers did to the women they caught. My shirt clung to my chest, and my longyi twisted between my legs. I had no doubt they would quickly see through my disguise.

The moment I touched the bank, I sprang to my feet and leaped to a handhold on the cliff above my head, clambering several feet above me. But my feet slipped on the muddy wall, and I cried out as I lost my grip and smashed into the rocks below.

My leg gave way. Pain radiated from my leg, and it refused to hold my weight. The muffled voices of the men behind me stalked my position. They must have heard me. I hobbled back to the wall, took a breath, and blew it out.

A tiger never panics.

I narrowed my eyes. A tree root twisted out from the rock, inviting me to try again. I grasped the root and dragged myself off the riverbed, scrambling up the ridge. Body shaking, I limped across a clearing. Each step agony in my leg.

A low whistle sounded. The soldiers had discovered where I'd climbed out of the riverbed.

Frantic, I hauled myself into the twisted canopy of an oak and swung across to a white pine. Soft needles cradled me, and I wedged myself into the crook of its limbs.

Grateful for the shelter of the needles, I burrowed in deeper. I clenched my jaw to prevent my teeth from chattering, but my body shook so hard, I was certain my pursuers would see the tree quake.

Even if I could run, would I be able to evade the men and disappear into the forest? Even a toddler could track me in the snow. But if I didn't make it to the village or make a fire soon . . .

My shirt was already stiff. How long would it take for my skin to freeze to the material? Tigers weren't meant for snow and ice.

Ryan's directive echoed in my head. *First things first.* I grimaced, though I was grateful for his calm authority even now.

First. Stabilize the leg.

My hunting knife made quick work of cutting two stout sticks from the tree. Using the rope from the bottom of my pack, I lashed the sticks to my lower leg. My fingers were growing so stiff, I used my teeth to haul the knot tight. I blinked away the tears in my eyes. *Do not panic.*

Next thing. How bad was it? I yanked my pack on and put weight on my leg. Biting back a curse, I sank to my perch. I would never outrun them.

Think, Kai. Think. What would a tiger do if he was being hunted?

An owl trilled her haunting call, and I scanned the treetops. The owl stared at me, unconcerned.

A hunter need not run or hide.

I cocooned myself in the tiger skin, and a grin spread across my lips. I would do what I had done to earn the tiger skin I wore: become the hunter.

I eased to the lower branches of the tree and crouched where I had a clear view of the top of the ridge. I pulled a thin case the length of my forearm from my pack and laid it across my lap.

Another cry echoed from the bottom of the riverbed and then the noise of men rushing up the ridge.

With the case open on my lap, I lifted my blowgun, fit its pieces together, and laid out the poisoned darts across my lap.

The range of my darts was less than a bow, so I would have to be patient to take the shots. Unfortunately, the *upas* tree poison took time to paralyze and kill . . . which would give the Japanese plenty of time to spot and shoot me as I sat in the low branches. So I would also need to quickly shoot and then climb to the relative safety of the treetops. I lifted my gaze to the treetops far above, praying I would find safety there. If nothing else, I could at least take the Japanese with me into the afterlife.

Chapter Twenty-Four

RYAN'S VISION BLURRED WITH FATIGUE, and he blundered into a graying fence post that pierced the vegetation. Finally. The village.

The path wound around a corner out of sight, but Ryan knew it led to the Kachin village with the refugees of Tingrabum. Somewhere he'd have to find the energy to win over the people. Last time he'd been here, Baw Ni had run him out. Other villages had been spared while Tingrabum had been leveled. In Baw Ni's mind, the difference had been the Americans.

Now he was returning armed, towing a strange white man, and asking for troops. Why would things be different this time?

As Ryan rounded another hairpin corner, he heard a rustling and shifted his rifle, wary. A small girl popped out of the undergrowth, hands waving, babbling that it was a good thing they were friends and she'd been expecting them, and the Kachin Rangers had gone days ago, and the tiger-boy had left too, just yesterday, and, sir, was the legend about the boy true?

Ryan chuckled at her antics but then realized what the girl had said. Kai had been here and left. What had happened that made her leave so quickly?

Questions swarmed in Trace's face. Ryan shrugged and followed the girl into the village, hoping Trace would trust Ryan's instincts and not ask too many questions about why he was going in ready to shoot first and ask questions later. Behind him, Ryan heard the soft click of Trace's safety. At least they'd be prepared.

A few men in the crowd emerged to greet the soldiers. Familiar faces peeked from between people he had never seen before. But without exception the people appeared friendly, welcoming. Adrenaline seeped from Ryan, leaving him stumbling through the village even more exhausted than before.

The crowd eased aside, creating a corridor to the duwa's home, and Ryan resisted the urge to search behind him. Kailyn wouldn't be there.

The little girl they'd been following disappeared into the crowd, a mist swallowed by clouds. Ryan stiffened to attention.

Outside the basha, a council of leaders sat together. Their discussion paused, and they frowned at the Americans.

Ryan dipped his head in respect even while his mind swarmed with questions, his chest as tight as his fingers on the rifle stock.

One older man pushed himself to standing. Though bent with age, he carried authority with the others. An ugly scar rippled across his cheek, testimony to some battle fought and won. The head duwa. He motioned for the Americans to join the circle.

"Bear of Burma." The duwa greeted in English. "It is good to have you back in our village. You just missed your Sharaw."

Ryan felt the eyes of the other men on him, and he forced himself to keep a steady, unconcerned gaze on the duwa. Just like the previous duwa, the man knew Ryan's full nickname and even his connection to Kai. How?

"Your Sharaw?" Trace whispered.

"Maybe he means ours . . . as in the army?" Not entirely a lie, yet Ryan's palms sweated, clearly declaring his guilty downward spiral.

The village duwa frowned, his attention sliding to Trace, searching, weighing, strategizing.

"I believe Sharaw could, perhaps, have told you where to find the young woman you once knew," the duwa answered in Kachin.

Ryan's mind scrambled. What did this duwa know about Kai? Or

Sharaw? Ryan searched the man's face for familiarity. If he'd put the two together, he had to know her. Was he a friend? Or an enemy?

The duwa leaned forward. "I am surprised you do not know him."

"I've heard of him, but I don't know anything, really." That he questioned the identity of the legend would remain his own secret . . . for now.

The duwa hesitated a moment before nodding, letting the confusion slip from his face. "We will help you." He swept his arm to include the other men in his assertion. "It did not take Sharaw to convince us. We have sent as many men as we can to the meeting place in the north. We speak now of supplies and travel routes."

"The Japanese are becoming more daring," Ryan warned. "They attacked a village not far from here."

"We are aware. The villagers journeyed here and are now safe. And we have taken precautions. Why do you think you were intercepted outside the village?"

"By a child?" Ryan frowned.

"Kachin children are trained early to hunt, to hide, and to pass silent messages from tree to tree. Silent as spirits, we have our ways. Should the Japanese choose to attack here, they will not find us unaware or unarmed." The duwa paused, switching to English. "Please, in the meantime, if you see Sharaw, convince him there are safer paths than the path of revenge, and that I am sorry I could not protect him this time or before."

Recognition shot through Ryan. Underneath the scars and wrinkles, Ryan thought he saw . . . Yes . . . this was Nang Lu's brother. Zau Tu was a friend, and he confirmed what Ryan had suspected. Kai was in danger, perhaps even from her own people if they found out she was still in the mountains.

Ryan translated the good news about the recruits as well as Sharaw's visit.

"Sharaw is real then?" Trace whispered. "Do they believe the man is the legend?"

Ryan shrugged. "Perhaps. But Sharaw is in danger." Ryan switched to Kachin for the benefit of the others. "If the Japanese discover Sharaw's identity, they'll not only hunt him, they'll hunt down his family and friends too." Ryan stared pointedly at the duwa, who rested a thoughtful chin on his steepled fingers.

A young man leaned in. "He's little more than a boy. He may be smart, but he's more trouble than he's worth."

Ryan's anger flared. Kai put her life in danger to protect this man-child. How dare he disregard her sacrifice.

Trace leaned an elbow on his knee, lighting the cigarette dangling from his mouth. The tip of the cigarette glowed a moment before he exhaled a ring of smoke. He'd no doubt caught the boy's flippant tone and was debating how to deal with him. Ryan took a deep breath and translated the boy's comments.

"We've heard that the Japanese are tracking Sharaw," Trace said. "If he's half as skilled as people say, we should find him. We could use his help even more."

"And he could use ours." The duwa glared at the young man, who leaned back, arms folded across his chest.

Ryan wiped the smirk from his mouth with his hand, covering his movements with a cough.

The council finished discussing supply details and then disbanded, the majority lured away by the smell of dinner in a neighboring basha. Ryan retrieved two banana leaves with rice and sat propped against the leg of the duwa's home, next to Trace.

A woman tiptoed down the back-door ladder and glanced over her shoulder. She was shaking, and he unholstered his sidearm. He'd heard more than one story of a villager attacking British and American officers. But she slowed as she neared, both hands out, holding out a square of paper.

"Sharaw asked that I give you this."

Ryan stared at the folded paper like it might bite. He nodded his thanks and reached for the note. The woman held the paper tight, forcing Ryan to look her in the face. Though older and more weathered,

Ryan would recognize this woman and her scars anywhere. Baw Ni, the traitor's mother.

Ryan stilled. The remembered stench of her son's blood twisted in his stomach.

"Sharaw was here yesterday. She would not stay, though I offered her a place. They are hunting her, and she trusts very few." She peered sidelong at Trace, her message clear. "Godspeed to you." Tears blossomed in her eyes as she bowed and shuffled away.

Ryan clenched his fists against the sting creeping through him. Everything in him wanted to run down Baw Ni, interrogate her about her regret, how she knew Sharaw was Kai, and honestly, somehow make her pay for the damage she had done. But Baw Ni's bent spine told him she shouldered enough regret for her son's betrayal. What was done was done. He tucked the note into his pocket.

Ryan realized Trace was watching him, and he shoved a fistful of the yellow curry-tinged rice into his mouth.

Trace rubbed his hands on his legs, his expression watchful. "What did she say? And aren't you going to read it?"

Ryan didn't want to read it. At least, not in front of anyone. "I already know what it says. Sharaw is telling me to buzz off."

Trace stiffened, and Ryan realized his mistake. He'd admitted to knowing what Sharaw was saying, which meant Ryan knew him. Ryan bit his lip, berating himself for a stupid mistake before digging the scrap of paper out.

"That's the symbol we saw on the trail." Trace pointed to the broken *X* on the outside. "What does it mean?" His question carried the authority of his rank.

"Loosely, it means friendship." Ryan opened it and brushed the letters on the page, the Latin words only he and Kai would understand.

I am well, Bear of Burma. Your pursuit puts me in more danger and perhaps all those in the village. Please let me fulfill my promise. It is too late for anything more. There is nothing else for me but that.

He wanted to shred the paper and pitch it into the fire. Kai had been here the day before. So close. Worse, now that she knew he was searching for her, would she disappear like the morning mist?

Trace stared after Baw Ni for a moment before picking a bit of elephant grass from the ground. Twirling it in his hands, he blew out a deep breath.

"So you do know Sharaw. The person, I mean. Not the legend."

Ryan watched the fickle firelight chase patches of dark across the outer walls of the basha, fear twisting through his body.

"I'm beginning to think he's someone I knew at the mission." Ryan could nearly hear his mom lecturing him about lying. But he wasn't. Not really. He would like to believe that Trace would listen to his advice about Kailyn, but Ryan just wasn't sure what Trace would do with the information. And the facts were this: the mountains weren't safe for anyone, and if word got out of who Sharaw was or that she was female, she might very well lose the scant protection of the mountain people. Let alone what the Japanese might do to a woman who'd made so many of them run with their tails between their legs.

"Do you think he's capable of what they say?" Trace let the bit of grass drift off in the wind.

"What? Stalking in the night, shape-shifting into a tiger, calling on the spirits to help him eliminate ten or fifteen men?"

"Fair enough." Trace shook his head ruefully. "But there's always a healthy portion of truth in legend. I think we need this Sharaw on our team."

Ryan tried not to choke on his bite of rice. This was a dangerous line to walk. He needed to find Kai, but not on Trace's terms. If Ryan believed that God would safely get Kai out of the country, he might pray for that miracle. But Tingrabum was proof that what God allowed wasn't exactly pretty . . . and certainly wasn't what Ryan would choose.

"That is an order, soldier. I don't care if he's your friend or not." Trace's voice dropped, low and partly joking. But the command was there, and Ryan knew better than to defy his CO directly.

"Don't worry. We'll find him." Ryan cleared his face of emotion and shrugged his shoulders.

Trace studied Ryan's face, then nodded once—a gracious judge letting a prisoner off on probation. "You can keep me in the dark for now, Preacher."

"I appreciate the faith, sir. I'm just not sure enough to say something and cause problems for everyone."

Trace nodded and leaned back with Ryan to study the sky. "Don't go forgetting we're in this together."

"I won't." Ryan wouldn't forget that Trace depended on him, but Kai would always be his first responsibility. Still, Ryan felt like he was bumping around in the dark, rummaging around for the way forward.

And he hated feeling lost in the dark, especially when someone else expected him to be the strong one. Like his sister, who used to beg him to go with her to the barn for evening chores. The creaks in the old wooden rafters spooked them both till they rushed through chores and ran to the house like robbers were chasing them.

There was always something terrifying about that barn in the dark. Pop told Ryan and his sister that the darkness wouldn't hurt them. But Ma used to say, *Ryan, honey, trusting life to be good in the light ain't nothing. But if you have to trust in the dark, well now, that is faith.*

"I have faith in you," Trace said, laying his head on his pack and staring at the stars.

Faith. But Ryan wasn't sure he could scrounge up an ounce of faith that God could work this one out. Because, short of loading Kai onto a mule and leading it out of the country, he couldn't see a way to protect her.

And if he was honest with himself, there was still something terrifying about being in the dark.

Chapter Twenty-Five

LIGHT CREPT AROUND THE TIP of the mountain, stretching its fingers to uncover my hiding place. Branches snagged at my pack as the wind cried through the boughs. Living nightmares of a child trapped. Tu Lum. Blood flecked on his face, seeping into the ground.

The squelch of snow underfoot whispered in the darkness, and I snapped to attention. Rustling uniforms whispered into a forest that now held its breath. They were coming. I lifted the long tubular blowgun and slipped in a poisoned dart, balancing another dart between my fingers and the length of the gun.

I cleared my mind. Forced away the anger, the fear.

Numb. Darkness creeping in. Aunt Nang Lu. The duwa. Tu Lum. Tingrabum would be avenged.

A head popped above the lip of the slope. Careful. Slithering across the ground. How many were there?

A low call.

Another head, two.

A tiger is always patient. I lifted the gun to my lips.

Taking aim at the man on the right, closest to the tree line, I forced my air short and sharp through the bamboo shaft. As the man jumped at the deadly bee sting, I sent the other dart into the second man. His gasp alerted a third soldier, and he swerved to the trees, his companions stumbling in the opposite direction. I heard an anguished cry followed by a crashing that told me the poison crawled through the first man. The soldiers would stop writhing within moments, paralyzed, dying slowly as the poison ravaged their bodies. I was glad I could not see them.

I inserted another dart, my hands shaking. A sound to the left and I sent a dart through the underbrush. A grunt.

I hesitated. Too easy.

A breeze washed through the trees, making the evergreen needles gossip among themselves. Snow trailed down in lazy circles until it landed on my eyelashes, where it melted in great tears. I stuffed down the premonition of tragedy.

The last man either died quietly or was hiding. I inserted another dart, careful not to betray my position.

Adrenaline leaked from my body, the cold stealing my strength. My leg ached, and my mind threatened to spill sideways into oblivion.

Squinting into the darkness, I willed my prey to make a mistake before I did.

A breath underneath my tree. I sent another dart into the bush.

Gunshots burst into the morning stillness. Heat tore through my arm, my body spinning from the impact, the blowgun leaping from my fingers.

I gritted my teeth against the pain, scanning the ground for movement.

There. An arm. I dove from the tree in a last-ditch effort. Flying, momentarily weightless, I crashed onto the man, yanking his head back. His fingers dug into my arm as I ripped my combat knife across his throat. He resisted the blade until his lifeblood burst, flowing across my hands, warming my fingers. He gurgled, went limp. My fingers tangled in his hair, too complicated a knot to unravel. I collapsed. Knees, feet, the world refusing to hold me. Triumph, fear, cold, guilt. Body vibrating, shivering, breaking apart.

≈

I jerked awake, angry muscles stiffening even as pain radiated from shoulder to shin. The sun sat low over the western mountains, caught behind a fog of cold.

I blinked. The world hazed over and then cleared. My hand ached, and I spread my fingers wide. The knife dropped from my clutch, the crust of red cracking around my knuckles. Snow melted down my spine, and a shiver snaked through my limbs. I wanted to close my eyes and never wake, disconnect from this place forever.

But then Utagawa and his ilk would win. I blinked again, my breath ragged and loud in my ears.

The body of the soldier lay inches from my outflung arm. He stared at the sky, frost gathering on his cheeks. Sunlight sparkling and alive in the tiny crystals.

Inhale in. Out. Mist exhaled from me.

I rolled to my side. Nausea spun the world, and I forced my eyes to stay open, to stay awake. Listing badly, I dragged myself to the man's body and struggled to roll him. The body flipped with a muffled thud.

The pack strapped to his back was nearly empty. No food or water, but there was a blanket and extra trousers. As trembling rattled through my body. I flung the blanket over my head and yanked the pants over my leggings. They were big enough for three of me. I sighed, tying the material into a knot over my bony hips. The other men were down the slope, and one of them had been smaller. I squinted through the gray.

They might as well have been on the other side of the mountain.

I jammed my hunting knife into its scabbard opposite my dah and pulled my longyi over the rest. The edges of my vision darkened, pulsing. I would have to risk a fire. Perhaps the needles of the pine tree would dispel the smoke enough that I wouldn't alert the world to my presence.

I crawled away from the man's body to dig into the underbrush for dry leaves and sticks. My fingers refused to cooperate. Hands useless as stumps, I scooped at the debris until I'd gathered a small pile.

Fumbling through my pack, I uncovered the tin with my fire-starting kit. The box slipped between my numb fingers and dropped into the snow. I stared at it a moment before blowing on my fingers, forcing warmth into them until I was able to fight the lid open.

The flint and tinder lay pointless in the box. If I could barely get the kit open, how would I ever use a flint? A sob caught in my throat, and I forced it down.

A tiger never panics.

I would not die in my mountains, not like this.

After fidgeting with the tools, I wedged the flint stone and tinder under my foot, overhanging a stone. I grasped the steel in my fist like an infant holding its mother's fingers.

Please work. Please.

Driving down with what little strength I had, I smashed the steel into the flint repeatedly. Small sparks burst into the tinder.

Please.

A tiny flame leaped and sputtered out.

I pushed back desperation.

A tiger never panics.

I struck the steel again, the force magnified by my frustration, desperation, or both. A spark caught, and I dropped to the ground, protecting the flame from the consuming wind, and blew gently. I sniffed away the tears that threatened to drown the infant life.

I fed the fire offerings of increasing size until heat sizzled against my fingers. The sting of them coming to life again. I sagged against the tree trunk. I would live. Live.

At least for now. I wouldn't last long injured in the snow without help.

Chapter Twenty-Six

RYAN TRUDGED THROUGH YET ANOTHER gray morning. He'd barely slept at Zau Tu's village, as his mind pinged about, trying to find a workable solution to get Kai to safety.

Behind him, Trace yelped and cursed. Ryan snapped out of his drowsing and watched him toboggan down the small hill and land in a skittering, cursing heap that quickly righted itself.

Spell broken, Ryan realized first that he was cold. And then that the forest air was heavy with coming snow. He should have noticed it hours ago. They needed a safe place to make camp to ride out the storm. He spun in a circle, scanning for shelter.

"Hey. You smell that?" Trace's observation cut through Ryan's sluggish mind. Ryan sniffed the air.

"Smoke."

"You think it's friend or foe?" Trace's murmur lifted just enough for Ryan to hear him.

Rifles unslung, the two men slid down an embankment. At the bottom, a half-frozen stream washed by. Trace pointed to a series of rocks breaking through the creek. Ryan nodded and followed Trace.

Ryan's boot skidded on a small rock in the middle, and he faltered, arms swinging for balance, praying he wouldn't be baptized in an icy river. Trace snatched Ryan and righted him, barely keeping upright himself before skipping to the far side.

Ryan lagged for a moment, heaving in air, convincing his rigid body to lumber across the rest of the stones. For Trace's sake. For Kai's too.

On the other side, the two clambered up the bank. Mud burrowed into Ryan's gloves and knees. They'd be a worthlessly stiff mass in no time. As much as he'd come to love this country, he was also beginning to think Burma would chew him up like Ma's meat grinder.

At the lip of the ridge, Trace lay flat, unpacked his binoculars, and peered over the edge.

"It's a forest. Smoke's coming from under a pine. Bodies on the ground. Two. No, three. No movement." He passed the binoculars to Ryan.

Ryan scanned the area. Three bodies lay in the field, dusted in snow.

The clearing closed a little more than fifty yards away in a dark forest. Smoke filtered through the pine branches, dispersing, and from a distance, disguising its location.

"It's someone who knows how to hide."

He shifted his focus back to the motionless forms. Two Japanese caps lay strewn through the snow. "Two are Japanese. Third unknown."

Ryan fixed the binoculars to a white scar on the tree. The broken *X*.

Kai had been here. A bloody handprint writhed across the bottom of the tree in the direction of the smoke. Someone had braced themselves there and then fallen. Kai. It could be Kai's blood. All his military training warred against his instinct to bolt after her.

Hands shaking, Ryan unearthed the scrap of paper from Kai and gave it and the binoculars to Trace. Ryan pointed at the paper and then the duplicate symbol on the tree.

Trace peered through the binoculars. His mouth twisted in thought. "Is it Sharaw?"

Ryan nodded, not trusting himself to speak.

Trace shifted, searching Ryan's face. "Are you telling me everything I need to know right now?"

Ryan kept his gaze steady and nodded.

With Trace leading, the two American soldiers scaled over the lip of the gorge. Staying low, they raced to the tree line.

The two paused in the protection of the forest, listening. The third body wore a Japanese jacket. Hopefully, that meant that all the enemies were dead and the survivor was friendly.

Just above the whisper of the wind through the trees, a low fire shifted. Ryan crept to the edge of the great tree and stooped. Someone had converted the small space under the pine into a tent. Using the tip of his rifle, Ryan parted the branches.

A fire crackled merrily under the boughs, and a small collapsible pot sat on a stone nearby, filled with partly melted snow. On the far side of the fire, a heap of blankets lay piled and empty.

Ryan edged back, skin prickling. Where was the camp occupant? He shook his head. A few gestures from Ryan and the two Americans walked together, sweeping the gray dawn with their rifles.

The trees to their right rustled, and both men stopped. Something clattered to the ground, and a great whooshing closed in on them from the opposite side. Ryan's instincts leaped, and he tackled Trace to the forest floor as a large stone swung into the space where they had stood a moment before.

"Sharaw." Ryan called into the darkness. "It's Captain Ryan McDonough. We mean you no harm."

A figure appeared high in an enormous craggy oak tree. "Ryan?" The warrior shifted, unsure.

"Kaja-ee?" Ryan greeted the warrior. Anticipating a leap from the tree, Ryan stood and scooted back, slinging his gun behind him, signaling Trace to do the same.

In response, the shadow eased out of the oak, using only her arms to aid her descent.

"You're hurt."

The lithe figure emerged from the shelter of the trees. Though Kai was more regal than he expected, her cheeks were smeared in mud and blood.

Ryan's hands clenched. She was in enough pain that she could not help but limp.

Stepping toward her with his hand out, Ryan resisted the urge to sweep her into his arms and wipe away the evidence of the fight.

"Come. The fire is still warm." She brushed past them.

Even in distress she still wouldn't accept his help.

He didn't know why he had hoped.

Chapter Twenty-Seven

I DUCKED UNDER THE DRAPING pine boughs, forcing my movements smooth, catlike. Ryan had already read my pain, but both soldiers must see Sharaw now. There could be no weakness.

Beneath the branches, a fire warmed the space just enough to remove the pain from cold. And I gratefully swathed the blankets on top of my damp clothes while I forced my back straight. I needed help, but how much would it cost? My freedom? My aching need to avenge Tu Lum?

Ryan crawled into my camp and hunched against the tree trunk. His eyes were still the color of a summer sky, but his beard was long and bushy. Despite the fact that his body had thinned out, his shoulders strained the army-green jacket. Army life suited him. I swallowed, reminding myself that even though I had trusted his strength once, his loyalty lay with the OSS and army now.

I sat wooden as he dissected my appearance. The short hair, the bloody clothes, sunken cheeks, hastily splinted leg, back to my face and red pouch around my neck. What did he see?

I lifted my chin. Why did I care? I was a proud warrior, not a little girl desperate for love and attention.

Ryan brushed my cheek where a branch had cut deep. I stiffened. My eyes flicked to the site opening. But his partner's steps led away from my camp.

"Kailyn." Ryan called my attention back.

"Do not call me that." Sharaw's anger snarled, and Ryan reeled back as if I'd bitten him. *Good. Maybe he'd listen this time.*

"You need stitches and some help with that leg. Please let me help." His fist broke open, and inside, on his bare palm, lay the white stone I had left behind.

His presence called like home. I missed having someone who knew me. What would it be like to live in a village? To care again? To hold hope as easily as the stone? I plucked the stone from his hand, relishing his warmth still cradled there.

"You've changed." The edge of Ryan's voice was ragged in a half laugh, and he wrapped me into a crushing hug.

I tugged playfully on his facial hair. "And you look like the Bear of Burma now."

He nudged my arm, and the corner of his mouth quirked up. I couldn't help laughing. Maybe . . .

The crunching footsteps of the other man neared, and I flinched, covering the flare of fear with a lift of my chin. Outside he plodded, circling, careful, quiet. He was an experienced hunter. With the way Ryan's eyes followed the sounds, I knew he could say what he wanted but that the other man made the final decisions. He could ban me from helping the army. Depending on what kind of man he was, he could also send me to prison or kill me where I sat. Either way he could take away everything with a single word.

I could not let Ryan in. It wasn't possible to forget that anyone could be ripped from you at any time when you still carried the hole they'd left behind. It was better to never love, to never lose. I would kill Utagawa, paying one last time for having loved, and be done.

"Kai, I don't know why you are doing this. It's dangerous. Suicidal, even. Please help me understand. Let me help you," Ryan said, longing mixed with . . . mixed with a storm.

I busied myself adding fuel to my modest fire, ignoring the man across from me. Whatever paltry help he offered was not worth the cost of losing my mountain, my mission, my revenge. I'd nearly forgotten.

"You once said if you did nothing, they'd win. You choose to fight. And so do I."

"If I was ever your friend, come with me. I'll get you out. They'll understand. I can't—"

"I will not let him get away with what he's done."

Ryan opened his mouth, but I held up my hand, anger clamoring loud in my mind, drowning out the pleas for my atrophied dreams.

"Kailyn Moran no longer exists. I am Sharaw. You would do well to remember that. I don't need you to protect me."

"You know better than I do that it's dangerous for anyone to be out here alone—especially a woman."

Bile crawled up my throat, and I clenched my fist, hating the reminder of how vulnerable I really was. I'd seen the aftermath of a Japanese invasion. Knew what they did. Knew what even some of the Americans did to both women and children.

"I'm not saying you're not capable." Ryan leaned, elbows on his knees. "I'm saying no one should have to be out here alone."

"I don't need to explain myself to you, and I don't need your permission."

"No. You don't. I'm not suggesting you do. I'm not trying to hold you back. I'm trying to have your back. None of us can see what we can't see. Killing Utagawa won't save you."

I stiffened, hating that name on his lips and the reminder of what I had to do. "I didn't think it would. I expect quite the opposite."

"Then why would you—"

"Because someone needs to pay!" My frustration boomed around the small space, and I hated the reverberating desperation.

"And then what?" Ryan was maddeningly calm. "Who pays for *his* death? Revenge doesn't stop anything, Kai. It just adds fuel to the fire."

"I suppose you'll say God will take care of it all in the end. But you and I both know that tornadoes and armies strike, and we have no say in the outcome."

Ryan sucked in a sharp breath, but the other man paused at the gap in the canopy, stopping Ryan's retort.

"I am Sharaw, Ryan, whether you like it or not. And that is what you will tell him. I will never, never stop fighting." *Not even for you.*

I knew what the legend said about Sharaw, about the destruction I would leave seething in my wake. And so I refused to look at Ryan's face, at the evidence of what I'd done, instead facing the entrance. The other American ducked under the branches and sank down, hovering on the balls of his feet, his hand resting on his sidearm. Dark, small, dangerous. This man had earned his rank and reputation.

Still near enough I felt the heat of his arm, Ryan breathed hard, his entire body a clenched fist.

When I didn't break off studying the major, Ryan sighed. "Sharaw, this is my friend, Major Trace Hogan. I trust him with my life. Trace, this is Sharaw. We've . . . known each other a long time."

I flinched. Ryan hadn't introduced me as a friend or even trust-worthy. Not that I could blame him, really.

"I apologize for the trap. I assumed you were Japanese. I would not have been able to do much by myself without the element of surprise." I gestured to my leg. "And I didn't realize there were friends in the area."

Ryan shrugged. "I remembered the sound of that trap. We set one for the Japanese before . . . before." He cleared his throat and then pulled at his collar, fidgeting. "I almost decapitated Kai while setting one of them. I learned the duck and roll from her."

I stiffened, and Ryan blanched. Though his slip had been accidental, it could destroy everything.

Trace's attention flicked between us in confusion. "Kai. That's the missionary's daughter. Right? Did you travel with them after the village was destroyed? I thought they were alone."

Nodding, I pivoted to lift the pot off the stone. "I'm sorry I don't have provisions to share. But I will have a tea of sorts soon. Aunt Nang Lu would be horrified if I didn't serve you anything."

"I recognize a change of subject when I hear one. I'll leave you two with your secrets, as long as they stay in the past." Trace rummaged in his pack and fished out several ration packets. "We had an airdrop a few days ago. Don't drink the pineapple juice. You'll end up in sick call for sure. But we have rice and rations. And medicine as well. Ryan's one of the best field medics I know."

Ryan jerked as if he'd been stung by the fact he'd not offered yet—his overgrown sense of responsibility kicking in. Fingers flying, he dug out a wrap and pain medicine. "Is it broken?" He pointed at my leg.

I slid it to him.

Ryan eased off my boot and unwrapped my hasty splint. I winced, darkness closing in again. He stopped, his eyes seeking mine. I nodded and forced myself steady. Cold metal scissors skimmed against my skin as he cut away the oversized pant leg stiff with blood—mine or Japanese, I did not know.

Cold nipped my leg and exposed deep-purple bruises exploding up my calf. Perhaps I'd merely bruised it, something my body would heal in a few days' time.

Ryan's warm fingers explored my damaged flesh. I cried out between clenched teeth but held my leg steady. Ryan hesitated, his hands shaking under my calf. Trace scooted to my side. I knew what was coming and dug my fingers into the soft needles under me.

With Trace's hands around my thigh and Ryan's at my ankle, Ryan yanked hard. A scream ripped from me, and the world went black.

≈

Ryan willed his stomach and mind to focus. Taking a breath, he dabbed Kai's leg clean before rewrapping a splint around her broken leg.

Now he had to figure out what to do with her. He'd hoped to be able to convince her to leave with him. But she was neither healthy enough to walk nor in the mood for discussion. If he revealed who she was, given her condition, Trace would no doubt leave her behind. And she wouldn't exactly be safe in the middle of nowhere or even in a village where the town gossip might let it slip that Sharaw had joined their ranks.

He'd have to convince Trace she was a valuable enough asset to waylay their plans long enough for Kai to heal. But by making Kai that valuable, Ryan risked making her indispensable to military objectives.

Once they were on their way to Tagap Ga, he'd figure out a way to force Trace to send her the rest of the way to India . . . or just convince her that Utagawa was in a POW camp in India and take her himself. Nang Lu would smack him upside the head for even contemplating lying, but what else was he supposed to do?

Ryan rubbed his eyes. *One step at a time.* First, check for other injuries.

Ryan fumbled in his pack for a needle and thread. *She's a patient. Nothing more. Nothing less.*

He'd treated other women in the jungle. He knew how to do this.

Ryan stitched the gash in her cheek and then pushed her sleeves and other pant leg up, checking for breaks or deep cuts. A fresh gunshot wound skimmed her slender shoulder, and her arms, winnowed to tight sinew and bone, were covered in abrasions and a crisscrossed web of old scars. How had she lived through the attacks that caused them?

His fingers brushed her jaw, tracing the gentle curve from ears to lips. *Oh, Kailyn. I'm so sorry.*

He'd talked of leaving her when she needed him most. And so she'd run rather than suffer one more loss.

She'd become Sharaw because of him. But he'd seen the old Kai in her desire for a home, a place to belong. He just needed to convince her home was still a possibility.

But she had to survive first.

Next step.

His shaking hands floated above her stomach. Though she passed herself as an abandoned boy of unknown parentage, without the loose clothing, the curve of her body betrayed the fact that she was a woman. His sucked in a sharp breath, his neck heating.

She's a soldier. Beautiful. But just a soldier.

He slipped his hands across her sharp hip bones, stomach, and ribs, feeling for broken bones and hard knots that would signal internal bleeding. At the base of a tight cloth winding around her chest, Ryan's fingers hesitated, his stomach flipping. Now what?

Trace peered over his shoulder. "Broken rib?"

Ryan yanked the shirt over Kai's muscled stomach and shrugged, ears burning as if he'd been caught stealing from Miller's five-and-dime.

"I think he'll be fine." Ryan rubbed a hand across his neck.

"Shouldn't we get him in dry clothes?"

Ryan gaped at the unconscious woman, his mind spinning, scrambling for a logical excuse. But Kai was covered in mud and blood. Even unconscious she was shaking.

"They aren't that wet. And, uh. He'd kill me if we did . . . take his clothes off, I mean. He's kind of private, you know, teased a lot as a kid and all that. Or at least, that's what he was like at the mission." Ryan trailed off. The excuses were stupid. Being a prim boy should never trump taking proper care of a frigid soldier.

At Trace's frown, Ryan tucked Kai's blankets around her shivering form.

"We'll just layer on more blankets."

Trace scrutinized Ryan a moment before shrugging and draping a thick layer of blankets over Kai.

"He seems to be a tough kid. Resourceful too. He'll be fine, I guess."

Basic medical treatment done, the men sat next to each other, sorting out gear and food for dinner.

Trace scrutinized the sleeping figure. "Is that little guy really the legend we've heard so much about?"

"You saw him out there. And all that on a broken leg."

Trace cut shriveled carrots and dropped them in the pot. "If you hadn't pushed me out of the way, that rock could have killed me. Simple but effective."

Ryan tore bits of dried meat, letting Trace process what he'd seen.

"I checked the bodies for anything useful. Sharaw took out two grown men with darts and a third man twice his size with a knife. With that tiger fur, and up in that tree? And his eyes? This boy is the one the Japanese are hunting." Trace went back to chopping. "He's from Tingrabum?"

Ryan grunted, staring into the pot. If Trace caught sight of Ryan's face, there wouldn't be a secret to keep anymore. "Close to the missionary family."

"My father would have loved to have had him on a hunt."

"He always was good in the jungle."

"We'll be in Japanese territory again soon. I want him working for me." Trace paused, letting the command settle before adding, "Provided he won't kill us in our sleep."

"He wouldn't do that." But Ryan still didn't know how much he could trust Kai. "I don't know what he'll do when he finds out about Utagawa. He knows what happened."

"Then we won't tell him until we have to."

And heaven help them when she found out what they were up to.

Ryan monitored the rise and fall of Kai's chest, quietly counting her steady respirations. A grimace flickered across her face, and he wondered how she controlled the nightmares. He knew the danger of waking to your own screams, and he always traveled with a partner to protect him. Kai was out here alone. Ryan blinked away the image of the duwa's head on a pike.

There must be something he could do or somewhere he could take her to prevent the same fate for her. But it didn't matter where he took her if she didn't want to stay there. She'd left once and would do it again. This time she'd be exposed and hunted down.

Ryan smoothed the blanket over Kai's shoulder, his jaw clenching until his teeth hurt. He would not allow God to fail.

Chapter Twenty-Eight

A ROCK DUG INTO MY ribs. I squirmed but only succeeded in jabbing it farther into my spine. I rolled away, determined to curl back into sleep. Something soft brushed my cheek, and I swatted at it. A tiger growl rumbled angry, and the softness hardened—fingers dragged at my body, yanking me under, bits of debris thumping on my body, burying me.

I sat up, gasping. Shaking. Cold. Sweat dripping between my shoulder blades.

The embers of fire lit the underside of a pine tree, my blankets, my pack.

Camp. Bivouacked in the mountains.

I took a deep breath, and the constriction of the wrap around my chest allowed me to breathe again. Ryan had kept my secret, at least for now.

The fire was banked with a tight ring of rocks, and a single mound of blankets lay on the other side.

Where were the others? They'd cut the branches higher. They must plan to stay.

I swallowed hard against the dryness in my mouth. My tin cup nestled into a bed of pine needles. But when I reached for it, the cup shrank away beyond the tips of my fingers. I collapsed onto my pallet. I'd survived this long on my own, and one injury laid me so low I couldn't get my own stupid drink.

I shifted, groaning at the everywhere pain, and reached again, farther this time. My fingers slammed against the cup, spilling the precious water. I swore long and hard.

The mound of blankets across from me erupted, bedding exploding as Ryan burst from underneath, his pistol swinging around the enclosure.

I spread my hands wide, praying he'd wake fully before we both regretted it.

His focus shifted systematically around him until it landed on me. He hesitated, uncoiling himself and forcing his breathing to a regular rhythm.

Once he regained control, he holstered his gun and stood . . . as much as the branches allowed. I'd forgotten how enormous he was. A scar rippled across his bare left arm until it disappeared under his thin white T-shirt, evidence of a previous battle. Even bent, he moved with the controlled power of a hunter now. I rubbed my hands on the blanket to dry the sweat that had sprung up in my palms.

"You're awake." He ducked into a sweater, then knelt by the fire with practiced finesse, poking at the coals until they flared. "How do you feel?"

I shrugged. There was no good answer to encapsulate the thoughts whizzing through my mind. It would help to know who I was dealing with—the soldier or the missionary I once knew. But squinting in the dim light only intensified the ache in my skull. I shut my eyes and let my head snuggle into the pile of needles.

"You were rolling in your sleep a while ago." Ryan's comment echoed hollow and called me from the depths. "I tried to wake you, but when that didn't work, I forced some pain meds down."

That was why I had thought I was choking.

He collected the empty cup. "Water?" He scooped water from the pot and handed it to me.

Water skittered down the outside of the cup and chilled my fingers. "Thank you." My voice croaked, nearly as inhuman as I felt.

I drained the water, the coolness soothing the scratch in my throat. Haze hung heavy on me. I wanted to snuggle into it, warm, comfortable, with Ryan keeping me safe.

He pressed his wrist against my forehead, his face inches from mine. Laugh wrinkles had deepened in the corner of his eyes, but two lines had appeared frowning between his brows. An army-green stocking cap covered his shock of blond hair, but his beard was shot through with gold. His mouth quirked in a half smile.

Shivers ran down my spine, and I licked my lips.

"No more fever. That's good." Ryan's eyes shifted to mine—impossibly blue—then dropped to my lips a moment before he jumped up and bustled about the tiny enclosure, tidying random items, adjusting my propped leg, checking the fire.

I watched his restless movements. "What's wrong?" My question arrested him mid-reach to fiddle with the stew yet again.

"We're nearly out of food." Ryan finally perched on the pallet across from me and buried his frame under a blanket, seeming to will himself to steady himself. "Trace went to see what he could find."

I stiffened. Trace. The major. That was what I'd forgotten.

"You've been asleep for three days. We couldn't move you. And our radio is dead, so we couldn't call for a drop or alert the other teams that we're running late."

He stared into the fire and tugged off his cap to run his hands through his mussed hair. The familiar gesture reminded me of my childish desires, and heat rose in me before I could push it away. Home was merely a myth, one that evaporated under the glare of reality. No physical place could contain home, and people too easily disappeared. I could not allow myself to depend on Ryan again.

"How are you feeling?" He frowned, perhaps realizing he was repeating himself, before chattering on. "Your leg should be fine, as well as the cuts on your arms and shoulder. I didn't see any bruising to indicate internal bleeding, and you seem to be fine."

I bit the inside of my cheek. Why was he nervous?

"I didn't have any extra clothes for you."

My cheeks flamed in realization. "You didn't . . ."

Ryan's mouth flapped open. "Of course not!"

"Then why are you so nervous?" The moment I blurted the words, I wished I had held my tongue. Exasperation had made me neglect caution.

Ryan twisted a bit of his blanket between his fingers as he stared at the gap in the pine boughs. "In addition to recruiting, we're assigned to meet a group of new Kachins and send them to Tagap Ga for training. Ultimately Trace and I are going behind the lines to help the Rangers at Camp Knothead take Myitkyina." Ryan frowned, the light of the fire dancing across his face. "But I can't."

Confused, I pushed myself to my elbows. Why would retaking the capital of the Kachin state be a problem? "You can't what?"

"Trace wants me to ask you to join our team. But I promised Nang Lu I would protect you. The Japanese are hunting you . . . Sharaw, I mean. There's a price on your head, Kai." He scrubbed a hand through his beard. "Because the Japanese aren't searching for a missionary, it's possible to find somewhere safe for you to go."

I clenched my jaw and took great care in straightening my blanket. Already he was leaving me.

"It's probably a suicide mission. I can't pretend to want you to come." He opened his mouth, then closed it, a parent placating a difficult child.

My body coiled, ready to strike in defense. He didn't want me with him. His overgrown sense of responsibility merely obligated him to my safety, to the army, but never to what I wanted.

"But I missed you, Kai."

My mind stumbled. He missed me? I uncurled just enough for the words to sneak around my defenses, just enough that when Ryan covered my fingers with his enormous hand, I didn't yank away. I watched his thumb trace my knuckles, the calluses scratching the back of my hand, the warmth of his hand penetrating my skin. I leaned my forehead into his chest, relishing the freedom, the relief. If only—

"Why did you leave?" Ryan's question was quiet.

Cold scaled my arm, and I wrenched my hand from his. "You were the one planning to enlist. You were leaving *me*."

Ryan blanched, and I nearly regretted the ice in my tone.

"Kai, I—"

"You planned to drop me at the camps without so much as a by-your-leave. You act like you're doing what's best for me, but you're only trying to make it easier for yourself. If you didn't want responsibility for me then, don't start taking it now."

"You think this is easy?" Ryan thrust himself to his feet, pacing a tight circle and muttering to himself.

"No one tells a tiger what to do." I lifted my chin.

Ryan rounded on me, and I flinched despite myself.

"Don't you get it? You're all I have left. I care about you, you headstrong, stubborn woman. I want better for you than this." His arms swung wildly. "And I can't protect you if you're traipsing through the jungle, drawing the attention of the entire Japanese army! Do you realize the amount of money they are offering for proof of your death? Your death! Not even your capture. They want you dead."

Fear exploded through my spine, and I forced myself still. "I'm doing pretty well out here without your help."

"Of all the—"

A branch snapped outside camp, and I clamped a hand on his leg. He stopped, listening with me now. Footsteps crunched in the snow. He snatched his Colt, and I scooted to sit up, searching for a weapon. Where did they hide my knife and blowgun?

I hefted a rock in my hand. It would do.

"It's Trace. None of y'all shoot me now." The man's voice floated behind the pine-needle screen.

I deflated, a sigh escaping my lips.

"Give me a second, Trace." Ryan's nostrils flared, and he leaned over me, grinding out under his breath, "We'll finish this later, but we will finish it."

"Come in," I called. The smile I stretched across my face was as flimsy as the gauze Ryan had used on my shoulder. Ryan would notice, but maybe Trace wouldn't.

The white fur of a rabbit broke through the green screen, followed by Trace's dark head.

"Breakfast?" As any good soldier would, he parsed out the campsite, searching for threats.

He would do for an ally.

Trace brushed the snow off his coat and glanced at Ryan in question. Ryan shook his head—a clear sign he hadn't gotten what he needed yet. But Trace nodded at me anyway. "Sharaw. You're awake. I thought you might be hibernating. Do tigers do that?" He chuckled at his joke and then coughed when Ryan frowned. "Looks like the fever broke. You'll be out chasing Japs and girls again before you know it."

My stomach moaned, and he pointed, self-assured.

"That there's an even better sign. Hungry?"

At my nod, Trace lifted his chin at Ryan. "We did promise you stew, didn't we? There's a little left."

In response, Ryan covered his hands in an old cloth and retrieved a pot from the fire. He scooped me a bowl and handed it to me.

I felt him watching me as I ran my finger around the rim of the bowl. Aunt Nang Lu would have my head for my ungratefulness, but I would not, could not give him anything.

Seeming to surrender, Ryan sank next to me, a stiff, protective wall between Trace and me. I was tempted to scoot away, but the length of his arm warmed my shoulder. Despite myself, I stayed, letting myself feel like we were sitting outside Aunt Nang Lu's, eating pheasant stew. I blinked. The mirage burned away. A trick of the shifting light.

I slurped the soup. Glorious flavor eased across my tongue. Where had they found these amazing herbs?

"It could use some seasoning." I winced. It was an outright lie and obvious needling of Ryan, but I wouldn't apologize.

"I'll let you cook next time," Ryan growled. He pushed to his feet, grabbed the rabbit by the ears, and stomped outside.

Trace watched me for a moment as I ate the soup.

Go away.

"There's something between you and my captain." His observation edged toward boredom as he cleaned his bloody knife with a scrap of cloth.

I took another sip and swallowed, the broth burning my throat. I felt a bit like the rabbit must have as Trace tracked it through the woods. How much did Trace guess? What did I acknowledge? What should I deny?

"I don't need to know what it is necessarily." Trace tucked his knife into its sheath. "Unless it will get in the way of the mission."

Relief made my fingers tingle. "No, sir. We'll work it out."

Trace nodded before standing and pointing to two stout, Y-shaped sticks next to my pallet. "Bear made you crutches. He says to stay off that leg as much as possible. We need you whole and healthy." He pushed through the pine boughs and joined Ryan outside.

My hands shook. Being asked to hunt the Japanese in their own camps meant the Allies were preparing to push the enemy out of my mountains. Wind sneaked through the pine boughs, and the hair on my arms stood. Hunting in Japanese territory was what I'd wanted for eighteen long months. Why was I afraid?

I yanked the crutches upright.

Tigers are never afraid.

Using the crutches for balance, I tucked my right foot underneath me and pushed to stand. Pain ripped through my muscles. The world spun, and gravity threatened to swallow me. My fingers tightened around the crutches, the bite of the wood reminding my body to stay conscious.

I had no time for weakness. Trace would leave me if I slowed him too much. But that couldn't happen. I was too close to be left behind now.

I hobbled around under the branches until my vision cleared and I could move well enough to fool Trace, if not Ryan. It was awkward, but I wedged my bowl between a crutch and my side, intending to wash it and prove I wasn't useless.

As I ducked through the opening, the brightness of the day slammed

into me, and I stood for a moment, disoriented. My bowl slipped from
my side, and I pretended I'd meant to drop it. Ryan stood stiff, watching
me as I awkwardly bent and rubbed the bowl clean with snow. He took
a step forward, but I ignored him. I would earn my place on this team.

It took Ryan and Trace little time to dress the rabbit and throw the
pieces into a boiling pot, along with random things from their packs.
The two worked well together. And even as Trace matched Ryan's ef-
ficiency with the food, he also did it with a well-practiced charm—the
stories of his childhood tumbling out, autumn leaves chasing each
other.

Normally such obvious attempts to win my favor would set my teeth
on edge, but I was fascinated. I loved listening to the major speak, his
words soft around the edges—the dialect from the southern United
States.

The home he described seemed a different world, hot like mine but
full of strange dances of cotillion, starched shirts, fox hunts for sport,
and such an abundance of food that I was sure he exaggerated.

When he told stories, Trace's voice danced with laughter, changing
with each character, his movements broad and loud. It was obvious
why Ryan liked and trusted him in a way neither man would trust me.

But, I reminded myself, they did not need to like me to need me. I
poked at the fire and nearly missed Trace's shift in topic.

"I've heard about you, Sharaw. I don't know if the things people say
you've done are true. But you give people hope."

My head snapped up, hand fluttering to the pouch around my neck.
Hope. Another fairy tale.

Trace watched me. Weighing, processing, sorting.

I shook my head. "Hope leaves you weak, waiting for something
that won't come." If hope was what Major Trace wanted from me, he
wouldn't get it. Both of us would be better off on our own.

"With our military intelligence and your prowess, we can drive the
Japanese into the sea."

"Revenge." I tasted the word, finding it more bitter than expected.

Trace nodded. His answering "absolutely" was far too cheery for the destruction I knew was stalking us.

"No." Ryan's voice thundered around the clearing.

I gaped at him, then turned back to Trace, quenching my anger. "You speak with wisdom. However, I already have—"

"Trace," Ryan interrupted. "I don't think it's a good idea to use him. He's good at what he does, but he's impulsive and undisciplined—"

"You are not my father." I fought to control myself. "While I've done well until now, you yourself told me how vulnerable I am alone. It's a perfect idea. You can keep me under your watch, and I can continue doing what I do best to stop the Japanese horde."

"Please, you don't . . ." Ryan eased down next to me. I shifted away, not wanting his softness to affect me.

"I have made my decision." I sounded like Papa and hated myself for it.

"As have I." Trace stood above Ryan, his spine as straight and tall as the oldest of trees. "He goes with us, and you will get over whatever it is you need to get over. Clear?"

Ryan stood abruptly and crashed through pine boughs, scattering needles and snow into the hidden camp.

≈

Ryan stomped through the woods. Of all the ridiculous situations he'd gotten himself into, this ranked as one of the worst. When he'd been searching for Kai, this was exactly what he'd feared. But he'd never thought she would agree to something so reckless to spite him. She'd finally learned to stand up for herself, but the timing was terrible.

He kicked snow and then a tree and another for good measure.

He couldn't tell his CO why he didn't want the famous Sharaw with them without betraying Kai's identity. And if he did that and Trace cut her out, she'd run on her own again, regardless of those hunting her. And she was right—if she came with them, she would at least have someone watching her back. But they were headed deep into Japanese territory, and with what they were planning . . . Ryan wanted her nowhere near that. Why couldn't she do what was safe?

A huffing noise echoed in the woods ahead of him, and Ryan stopped dead, his senses tight. He'd struck off into the woods without a weapon. Even his knife lay next to the fire, freshly cleaned of rabbit blood.

He eased behind an enormous oak tree. Above him, a squirrel chattered. Ryan squinted against the glare of sun reflecting off the snow. A shape moved between the trees. Snow squelched under boots maneuvering carefully. Ryan surveyed his surroundings, searching for hiding spots or weapons, gauging exit strategies.

Nothing.

The strange whine of a jackal called behind him, from the direction of the camp. Ryan shifted. They were awfully far north for a jackal. The wind picked up snow, flinging it through the air, blurring Ryan's vision.

Soundless shadows drifted on either side of Ryan. He was surrounded.

Stupid. Ryan swallowed. That was what he was. Stupid. He could not afford to be captured, and his footprints in the knee-deep snow led back to Trace and Kai. At the very least, he needed to warn them.

A dah thudded into the deep snow inches from his leg, swaying with the impact. For a moment Ryan thought someone had missed him, until he recognized the hilt of his knife. Another jackal called, and Ryan's hope rose. A face appeared between the branches of a tree, next to the stock of a rifle. Trace. Of course his CO had followed his dunderheaded captain.

Quiet chatter drifted from deeper in the woods, and he snatched the dah, shifting behind the bare tree trunk. It didn't hide him completely, but the sturdy tree would stop deadly shots. He leaned his head against the tree, trying to clear his vision and prepare for close combat. His ears pounded, and fingers tightened around the knife.

Across from Trace, an evergreen tree twitched and a carbine barrel pierced the canopy. Kai. At least she was above the fray.

Keep her safe.

Footsteps crunched through the quiet, snapping Ryan's attention back to the fight. He wiped the sweat from his palms and re-gripped the dah. Whoever was there would have to come through him to get to Kai and Trace. They would discover the power of the Bear of Burma.

Around the bend, a song lifted, and Ryan swung around the tree, a battle cry on his lips as he crashed through the snow.

A haphazard line of mountain men stumbled to a stop, hesitated, then scattered. As the last man ducked into the brush, Ryan's advance stalled. The men were dressed in army fatigues marked with the striped, shield-shaped insignia of the Allied forces in Burma.

"Kaja-ee?" Ryan called.

One brave soul called out in broken English. "We come help."

Reinforcements.

Relief spread through Ryan. No one would die today. Ryan spread his hands wide. "Welcome."

A man eased from the underbrush, head bowed low. "Bear of Burma. Our duwa sent us to search for you. We expected you in Tagap Ga long ago."

"Thank you for coming. An injury slowed us, but our camp is nearby. Come."

While Trace led the new Kachin Rangers to their makeshift camp, Ryan waited for Kai to descend the tree. Relief warred with exasperation as he watched her alternate between hanging from a branch and dropping to the next.

"You're not supposed to walk on that." He winced at his tone. He needed to find a way to make amends.

"A thank-you would suffice." Her snip was as light as her one-footed landing on the ground. She extended him the carbine and his sidearm.

But when he grasped them, she held firm, the vapor from their breath tangling and floating away. How could these imbeciles mistake her for a boy?

She lifted an elegant eyebrow.

"Sorry," he said. "And thank you."

A puff of frozen breath escaped her lips. At least she could laugh about his stupidity. Kai nudged his shoulder and released his weapons.

Whether her forgiveness would survive his continued attempts to send her away remained to be seen. While the Kachins had started calling him Bear because of his size, the US Army had adopted the name in part because he didn't quit easily. But for now Ryan slowed his pace to match Kai's as she struggled to drag the crutches through the snow.

"Ryan." She spoke his name soft, hesitant, and it drew him to stop and face her.

She studied his boots, then tugged off her stocking cap to knead it between her long fingers.

Ryan leaned forward and wrapped her hand in his until she peeked up at him.

"You said you want to protect me. If that's true, right now the best way to keep me safe is to not tell them who I was."

Her wording wasn't lost on him. Who she *was*.

Her eyes flicked to the Kachins. "Please. I'm not a child, and you know a woman is far from safe."

She was no longer a little girl or even the capable young woman he'd come to know in the village. He hated that she was right . . . It meant that Kai was gone forever.

Control burned, slipping through his fingers like ash. Tongue glued to the roof of his mouth, Ryan clenched his fists. How could she not see what her request meant?

"Tell them I'm an orphan of the mountain."

"You're not Kachin."

He saw a flash of moisture in her eyes before she lowered her gaze, lashes dark against cold pinked cheeks. He'd hurt her again.

"Exactly. I'm not anything." She spun.

Her crutch snagged in the snow, and she pitched, stumbling, and Ryan lunged to catch her. Holding fast, he curled her back toward himself, the curve of her fitting perfectly into his arms.

Kai stood wooden against him.

Ryan drew a deep breath. Calm. He needed to be calm. "Kai, you think you can hide. That no one will recognize you. But I've seen the Japanese flyers. Someone somewhere knows what you look like, and those eyes that earned you your tiger-man name have you clearly labeled. Please let me get you out of Burma."

Kai lifted her chin. The rest of Ryan's control blew away in the wind.

"What they are offering in reward is worth more than a year's salary for any of those Kachin Rangers. What makes you think even your friends won't betray you?"

"What makes you think I have friends?"

Ryan blanched at the implication. He'd been a fool to think they might be able to go back, to start over.

Chapter Twenty-Nine

WITHIN AN HOUR, THE RANGERS had a small camp constructed, a stew bubbling inside the ring of tents, and several guards set on the perimeter.

Despite the lure of the familiar language, I avoided the group and slipped under the pine boughs. I was loath to tell Ryan, but my trek had made me as weak as a newborn kitten. If he'd not been there to help me . . . I sneaked one of the pain pills from the American supplies the Rangers had brought and lay down to rest.

I woke a few hours later to the golden light of dusk. Voices and rhythmic tapping outside lured me toward the ring of men. The sky overhead burned yellow, shot through with fingers of pink. The men stood in a circle and passed a *chinlone* ball back and forth, keeping the small rattan ball in the air with knees, head, shoulders, and feet.

On the far side of the circle, Trace caught a wild toss with his toe and flicked it into the circle. The ball traveled around, a crazy orb, slightly out of control, until it flew into Ryan's arm, where it bounced, drifted off course, and dribbled into the snow.

When he bent to retrieve the ball, he saw me and grinned sheepishly, as if to say, "Still as bad as ever."

The men swung around in unison, and their circle dissolved into a mass of chatter. I caught the words *tiger* and *vicious* but also *hero* and *extraordinary*. Stretching myself as tall as my small frame allowed, I fought the urge to hide. If I was to belong to this group, I would have to face them eventually.

Ryan sighed and lumbered to my side, the gentle hand on my arm in stark contrast to the muscles flexing in his jaw. "Best introduce you then. Come on."

"Rangers," Ryan said in Kachin. "This is Sharaw. He will join us on our mission. If anyone has concern about this, you will speak to me, and I will reassign you. If I hear or even suspect that any of you has told anyone outside of this company who or where he is, Major Trace and I will hunt you and slit your throats personally. Am I clear?"

A few men shifted, glancing first at me and then Trace.

"Clear?"

After a chorus of "yes, sir" echoed through the forest, Ryan eased me onto a fallen log stretched in front of the fire, a bench of sorts. I propped my leg in front of me and snatched the blanket Ryan handed me.

"Was that necessary?" I whispered in English. The last thing I needed was for them to fear me so much that they wouldn't accept me as part of their unit. Nature proved those at the edge of the herd were the first sacrificed to the hunter.

Ryan turned to me, his face so close I could see the tiny ice crystals forming on his beard, sharp and hard. "Since you've decided to join our merry crew, you need to understand one thing—I am your commanding officer, and you will do as I say. You will make sure not one of these men gets close enough to you to guess anything. Kachins are proud warriors and don't take kindly to being lied to or led by women."

I flinched as he tightened his grip on my arm. The meek bear I knew was long gone.

"Furthermore, I'm not happy about this, and if you give me a good reason, I will send you packing to India. Clear?"

"Yes, sir." I mock saluted. At the look that crossed his face, I dropped my hand, regretting my flippant tone. Ryan was a powerful man, one I really didn't know any longer, and in a camp of strangers, I couldn't afford to alienate my one ally.

Ryan's mouth snapped shut when Trace emerged from the dusk.

"How are you getting along?" Trace sat next to me with a contented sigh and handed me a bowl of soup and a rifle.

"Fine," I said, refusing to give Ryan any more cause to be angry. If I pushed too hard, caused too many problems, Trace might side with Ryan and cut me out.

Trace's gaze swung from me to Ryan, an eyebrow raised in question. No doubt trying to find out how fine I really was. Ryan shifted, and when Trace bent to sip from his own bowl, I knew Ryan had answered in some way. We had found a fragile truce.

"Apparently HQ got tired of waiting for us and sent recruits with a radio and extra provisions. Including your brand-new rifle. That flintlock's done for." Trace raised his bowl in a toast. "We're dining in style tonight. Eat up, you two. I already called in and got new orders allowing us to hunker here for training. That'll give you time to heal. Then we're off to meet Peach Boy, our little Japanese turncoat."

I stopped the bowl of soup partway to my mouth and tilted my head toward Ryan. "Peach Boy? As in the fabled Japanese boy who conquered demons?"

Ryan flicked his gaze toward Trace, who shook his head slightly.

Were they keeping something from me, or were they just ignorant?

"You do know the Japanese use that story as a metaphor for them obliterating their enemies, right?" My scorn rose, barely contained. "Please tell me you don't trust someone whose nickname is Peach Boy."

Trace shrugged, indifferent. Ryan ignored me, pointedly drinking from his bowl.

"Are you ignoring me?" I clunked my bowl down.

"I don't trust anyone," Trace said firmly. "Besides, I'm not asking you to trust him. I'm asking you to help me talk to him. He has information we need."

As if this traitor would talk to me more than an American officer.

"He might need some . . . persuading. That shouldn't be a problem for the legendary tiger-man. Right?" The major slurped at his dinner, the challenge obvious.

Ryan frowned, and I shook my head. I could handle the major.

I crossed my arms, ready to attack. Fine. If Trace was determined to put himself in danger, he could trust Peach Boy all he wanted. But that didn't mean I would meekly do whatever he asked. I would simply hunt for Utagawa under the guise of meeting with their traitor. No one would be the wiser.

"I've heard the stories, you know." Trace continued, calm, even, a predator luring out his prey. "How you took on dozens of men and left them ravaged. I came upon a contingent of soldiers after you'd gone through, or at least that's what the survivors said. A single man with tiger eyes, everywhere and nowhere at once. It was a bloodbath. The idea of a tiger-man had me shaking in my boots." He grinned at me, one soldier congratulating another. "I still don't know how you did it. You're a legend even this far north."

Trace's grin made the stew in my belly congeal, and my hands strayed to Mama's pouch. Only once had I returned after a kill. The staring eyes of the men. The blood. Vultures, heavy with gorging themselves, struggled to lift off the ground. I never went back again.

"I do what I do for revenge, not glory." My voice was a tight whisper.

The button in my pouch weighed me down. Pulling me under. Dirt falling into the grave. Suffocating. Gone.

Forever. Gone.

"I can never repay the Japanese enough for what they have done." I rose and handed my bowl to Trace. "But I will never forgive myself either." I would follow Trace, come what may. The way of the sharaw demanded no less, but I did not have to like it.

Chapter Thirty

January 1944

WHILE RYAN AND TRACE TRAINED the Kachin men in radios, guns, and tactics for modern warfare, most days Kai sat on a stump close to camp, brooding, sharpening her knives, the heat of her anger singeing any who dared to come near her.

When the Kachins caught sight of her, they whispered of capricious nats and mysterious killings in the mountain passes, the legend of the Sharaw come to life. One man swore he'd seen a tail flick behind her the night before. To be honest, Kai scared Ryan right along with the other men, but not for the same reasons.

Kai was used to ignoring sidelong glances and being excluded, but now she seemed to relish the fear she incited, until night came and her stifled screams woke them both. He was beginning to think Kai might not survive the smoldering fire of Sharaw's curse.

Despite Trace's order to make peace with her, Ryan had no idea how to bridge the raging river that coursed between them. The few times he'd approached her, she'd breezed off her stump and, as if he were nothing but a troubling breeze, wandered into the woods.

Until the day they broke camp, Ryan hoped that Kai would relent and change her mind about being a part of their mission. But when Trace called for the first march, she stood in formation, studiously ignoring

Ryan. It made him want to tie her to a nearby tree until the rest of the team left. Maybe then she'd actually talk to him.

Instead he spent the first few days of the march watching her from a distance as she limped in and out of his vision. The lack of sleep was obvious—the last vestiges of her nightmares pounding their way through.

One particularly rough night, Ryan couldn't listen to her whimpers anymore and sat next to her pallet, rubbing her back and whispering to her. He hadn't thought Kai had heard or noticed him, until that afternoon.

The sun was gaining strength, burning through Ryan's ranger hat, the only relief coming from the downhill terrain. He turned a corner, and she emerged from the jungle in front of him, grinning because she knew she'd caught him off guard.

"Don't worry, Bear. I'm watching out for you." She handed him an elephant-ear leaf, nodding at the red skin on his arms. "Did I ever tell you about the first time I hunted alone?"

Ryan shook his head, shock sealing his lips.

"I was camped on the ridge. The leaves started twitching, and I could already picture Papa's proud face when I brought home deer for dinner." Kai swallowed. "I lined up the shot and released the arrow. The minute it landed, a scream pierced the jungle. I flew through the jungle, sure I had my kill. Instead one of the village boys was cowering behind the bush, stinking of his own urine. I was terrified he'd tell Papa. But he knew he'd be in bigger trouble than I. We were both supposed to be studying, and he'd been caught spying on me. I don't think Papa ever found out."

"Some things never change."

She hesitated, and Ryan feared he'd torched the olive branch she'd extended. But then she bumped his shoulder gently, and the world slid back into place as if nothing had ever changed.

From that day on, Kai marched with him. They sidestepped conversation about the war, their mission, and Kai's nighttime spells—topics that might break the tiny strand connecting them.

Ryan told Kai about Ma's fluffy pancakes, spread thick with butter and dripping with sticky maple syrup. She told about John's secret recipe for a sweet rice pudding. He told her about the stubborn cow who wouldn't let him milk her, and the cats trailing his sister like duck-lings. Ryan waddled dramatically to demonstrate. Kai's laugh was feathery soft and made Ryan long to hear it for the rest of his life.

When night fell, Kai spread her pallet next to Ryan's, their arms nearly touching. There she seemed to relax, the nightmares drained by his pres-ence. But those moments of peace were the few bright spots in otherwise dark days.

Trekking south through the mountains tortured everyone. Blisters, mosquitoes, leeches, little sleep, and reduced rations made tempers short as they picked their way through the treacherous, steep paths. Ryan found himself barely holding in his frustration, grateful for his turn at whacking his dah against the jungle vegetation. But his own discomfort was the least of his concern.

The mountain people were starving, and team morale sank with ev-ery village they passed. Even though the bodies of the children were sharp with protruding bones, they still had enough energy to beg the soldiers for chocolate. Despite Ryan's repeated protests, Trace main-tained orders not to share food. The villagers could forage food in the mountains. His men needed their strength to save the whole country. They couldn't fall behind because of insufficient supplies. Sacrifice the few for the whole was the army way.

As the Rangers reached the warmer climates, where the baking sun had already dried the monsoon rains, it was obvious the people were starving to death, dust their only food.

At the village last night, Ryan's resolve had broken. He'd given a bit of leftover dried meat to a tiny boy. The other villagers had seen and descended on the soldiers, screaming for more food, for it to be evenly distributed. A swarm of villagers trampled the boy and overwhelmed the small Rangers force. Trace had fired his rifle into the air to force the people back.

Instead of spending a relatively comfortable night outside the vil-lage, the unit had to move on. Trace had made it clear in no uncertain terms if anyone else disobeyed his orders, he wouldn't shoot into the air. Ryan had crossed a line. He could voice concern to his OSS commander, but Trace drew the line at outright disobedience.

Ryan sighed. The state of people would just get worse the farther south they traveled. The plains were a land of broken trees where the jungle was whittled down to bone by drought and war. Ryan wondered again why he was still in Burma if he wasn't able to help one little boy . . . or one young woman.

Kai trudged next to him, leaning into a makeshift cane, her usually fluid stride stiff. She'd not used a cane in days.

"I'm sorry." Ryan handed her painkillers from his pack. "I didn't think the villagers would see me feeding that boy. Everything was my fault."

Kai stopped, confusion racing across her face. "You always did think every problem was your fault. I'm not angry with you. I'm glad you tried. It means some things don't change." She walked on, slower this time, kicking at the stones under her feet. The trickle of pebbles tumbled over one another, racing away. "I'm angry I can't help more. Every soldier I kill is replaced with ten others. These thieves come and take everything the people scrape together, until the children starve. And that is still not enough. The demons come back and kill innocent people, old men, and little . . ." She swallowed the tears trapped inside her amber eyes. "I will make them pay."

As if it were all *her* fault or that revenge would bring justice. Ryan touched her shoulder. "Kailyn . . ."

A Kachin man squinted sideways at Kai, and she squared her shoulders, clenched her jaw, and then stalked into the jungle. The thin tether between them, broken. She was Sharaw once again.

≈

At nightfall the Rangers found a somewhat flat stretch. Good enough for an overnight bivouac. They had located no water that day, and no one had the energy to scout for food or string tents. So with the skies clear and warm air whispering through the jungle, they simply built a fire and laid their blankets around it.

Kai limped into the camp a few minutes after the men had made themselves comfortable and threw a pile of broad leaves next to the fire. Ryan stared at her, uncomprehending. But as soon as Kai walked away from the mass of leaves, the Kachins snatched the branches, chewing on the center stem.

Kai handed Trace a branch and then Ryan.

"Plantain. There's water in the stalks. It won't take away your thirst entirely, but it'll help."

"I'd forgotten. Thank you." Ryan dipped his head.

Trace grunted his approval. This hadn't been the first time Kai had proven herself—other times she'd diverted them from an enemy patrol or provided for the team without having to be asked. Though her presence had saved them many times over, Ryan had to admit he was glad to have her with him for selfish reasons too. He enjoyed her company, sometimes even forgetting why they were marching through the mountains.

Kai stood at rigid attention until Trace dismissed her, then collapsed next to Ryan.

Jungle sounds fused with the low murmuring of Rangers' chatter—a natural lullaby that made Ryan droop with fatigue. Trace mingled with the men, setting a night watch with gestures and a smattering of passable Kachin. A few Rangers studied Kai and Ryan, no doubt checking to be sure they didn't morph into nats as the sun set. But soon the conversation petered out, and the Kachins drifted to sleep.

"I don't know what we would do without you," Ryan whispered.

Kai shrugged. "One of them would have figured it out."

Ryan bumped her shoulder with his. "Maybe, but you were the one who remembered."

Folding her body into his side, Kai groaned and stretched her injured leg out straight. Concern crept through Ryan at the rare sign of weakness in her. If anyone saw her snuggled into him, they'd instantly know she wasn't the boy she pretended to be.

He should ease her away, but her head against his shoulder made him desperate to weave his fingers through hers and somehow make her see herself as he did. She deserved to be cherished and given room to heal, not sacrificed for revenge or the expediency of war.

"I'm glad you're here." Kai whispered so quietly that Ryan wondered for a moment if her voice was the wind.

"I'm not going anywhere, Kailyn."

Kai curled down and nestled into her blankets, her feet against his leg, her body relaxing until her breath rose and fell, rhythmic and slow. Ryan's thumb rubbed her leg, mindlessly consoling, wishing he could erase the tension lines in her face, wishing he could find peace with the path he'd chosen.

The fact was that the farther they moved from India, the less likely Ryan would be able to devise a way to get her out of this mission to find Utagawa. It wasn't that she wasn't capable or efficient or that he didn't desperately need her. He glanced at her sleeping form, shoving away the fear choking his throat. He didn't know what he would do if something happened to her.

"He trusts you."

Ryan jumped at Trace's whisper behind him. How much had his CO seen?

"I've known him for as long as I've been in Burma."

"I wouldn't have pegged him as Kachin. But I suppose the Brits left behind more than a few kids in their colonies."

"I know his mother's dead, but his father walked into the jungle and never returned." Ryan lifted a shoulder in feigned confusion. "He called the duwa's wife his aunt. He's adopted, I think." The half truths burned Ryan's tongue. Traveling and fighting behind enemy lines were dangerous enough when you knew your partner had your back. It was deadly when you had reason to question each other. Until Kai, their honesty had always been an unspoken trust between them.

This whole thing dropped him into an impossible position. Ryan was jealous of her peaceful sleep.

While Ryan busied his shaking hands with rolling out a pallet for himself, Trace watched Kai's sleeping form, seemingly content. But he was, Ryan knew, pondering what he'd said. Trace was no fool.

Trace unslung his pack, dropping it in an undignified heap next to Ryan's pallet, and squatted on his heels, eyes level with Ryan.

Ryan felt the heat of the lie, and words burst from him again. "I taught him at school. He was an outcast, and I took him under my wing a bit." He rambled to a stop, snapping his mouth shut.

Everyone will fill the silence if you wait long enough, but only liars overexplain. It was a fact they'd learned in training.

A minute passed while Trace unpacked his pallet and unrolled it, placing it on the other side of Ryan, flicking off an errant leaf, smoothing out the wrinkles. Then he moved on to preparing for bed, running a brush across his teeth, taking off his hat and perching it on the pack.

Ryan knew the interrogation technique and fought the impulse to speak, act, or do something to fill the empty space. He was protecting Kai. Yes, he wasn't telling Trace everything, but that wasn't lying. Was it? And the misdirect wasn't anything pertinent to the mission. Trace already knew that Sharaw had a grudge toward Utagawa. Ryan had nothing to feel guilty about. He focused on the fire and the bits of flames running into the sky.

From here the web of tree branches hid all but a few stars, but he wondered if Ma and Sarah were watching him from heaven now. If Ma would understand why he had allowed himself to be drafted rather than hide out and minister in the jungles. What would she have done with Kai? Probably taken her in like a stray cat.

Ryan's body sagged under the weight of exhaustion, and he drifted toward sleep. The image of Kai in his farmhouse in Indiana flitted through his mind. She was cooking with Ma, white apron tied around her waist, and she sashayed to Ryan, a sunrise in her golden eyes. Peace could never come out of revenge.

"The Kachins should be ready to go to Tagap Ga in a few days."

Ryan jumped as Trace's voice broke into his thoughts. He shook his head, trying to clear the sleep from his mind to focus on planning with Trace. "Then we'll head to our meeting with Peach Boy." Trace eased onto his pallet with a soft groan. "We'll keep Sharaw with us."

"I'm still not sure that's a good idea. Peach Boy . . ." Ryan peered down to be sure Kai was truly asleep. "Lieutenant Utagawa was at Tingrabum, and Sharaw—"

"Tingrabum is what turned Utagawa against his people. We'll show Sharaw that too."

Ryan opened his mouth to respond, but Trace waved him off.

"Utagawa is fully aware that just feeding us information about Japanese positions could get his entire family killed. He'll be jumpy as a bullfrog on a skillet. If necessary, Sharaw will be a good reminder to Utagawa why he can't let his people keep doing what they're doing. And Sharaw will learn to take orders like a good soldier or deal with the consequences."

Ryan heard the order in Trace's words and gulped down his response. Ryan barely trusted the Japanese officer himself. There was no way Kai would. While Kai might be peaceful now, he knew full well the tiger was just sleeping.

Chapter Thirty-One

DARKNESS STILL CLUNG TO THE jungle when Ryan woke with a start. Goose bumps ran up his arms, but he wasn't cold. His training kept his body still as he filtered his senses for whatever had awoken him.

Mosquitoes buzzed in the air. The fire, banked with stones, cast little light but dispelled the chill out of the air. A nearby frog trilled in time with a host of insects, all unconcerned.

On the far side of the camp, the guard swatted at a bug. Rolling to his stomach, Ryan dissected the darkness. A row of men sleeping. The trees, underbrush.

A snap brought Ryan to his feet, sidearm drawn. He reached to touch Kai's foot, to alert someone else in camp, but found her blankets empty.

Ryan jerked around, frantic, searching the darkness. A hiccup in the light. Ryan focused on the spot and snatched his rifle.

As a figure moved into the moonlight, Ryan glimpsed a familiar body, the graceful movements hampered slightly with a limp. Kai.

Relief coupled with concern. Where was she going?

Ryan's foot snapped a branch. The sound echoed and sent the night sounds into hiding. The guard stiffened, then waved to Ryan and returned to duty, but Kai didn't even flinch at the noise. She strode on until she came to a fallen tree, stood for a moment, and then clambered into the tree on all fours.

Hidden behind the brush, Ryan watched the strange scene. Kai sat at the top, head swinging slowly. The jungle breathed, and a tiger's tail flicked. Ryan's breath caught. A vine fluttered in the breeze.

He winced at his gullibility. *Everyone has me believing mountain legends.*

But what was she looking for?

Ryan sectioned the woods in his mind and searched the area with military precision. Nothing but gray stillness.

His pulse ratcheted up, the hairs on his arms prickled, and he looked back to gauge Kai's reaction. But the tree was empty.

Ryan strode to the base of the tree. He found no evidence of her having come or gone. Swinging a circle, he searched for her again.

Nothing.

Perhaps he had dreamed it.

Ryan retraced his footsteps, answered the guard's challenge, and checked Kai's bunk. On her pallet, she'd folded the tiger pelt for a pillow and tucked her pack at one end. Her bunk was empty.

No use waking anyone. Even if they sent out the entire group as a search party, they'd be more likely to end up with injured soldiers and a unicorn than to find her. Ryan burrowed into a tree, grinding his teeth in frustration. One of these days she'd run headlong into something he couldn't save her from, and she didn't seem to care a whit.

≈

Ryan awoke as the sky lightened. Stumbling to his pallet, he shook off the stiffness and cold, fear thumping inside him.

But Kai lay on top of her makeshift bunk, her back to Ryan, a blanket draped over her, boots tucked beside her feet, and a canteen snuggled into the curve of her legs. Ryan tiptoed to her side. She appeared peaceful, so different from the scattered images from last night.

He stood, debating what to do, when he noticed the bloody hunting knife clutched in her hand.

Ryan dropped to his knees. Blood smeared her face and hands. Frantic, he felt for her pulse. It beat strong, steady.

Where had she gone? What had happened?

Ryan retrieved a cloth from his own pack and knelt next to her, hesitating. He needed water. Maybe . . . He lifted her canteen. The weight caught him off guard, and the canteen nearly slipped through his fingers. Where she'd found water, he didn't know, but he was grateful. Ryan poured water over her hands and dabbed at her face.

A bright-red streak came off easily, leaving behind fine scratches across her high cheekbones and slender neck. Kai slept on, the oblivious sleep of an exhausted warrior. Ryan knelt, his hands lingering over her in a silent benediction. The cuts needed immediate attention. The jungle, full of critters and infection, was no place to traipse around with open wounds. But if Kai woke and found him caring for her . . .

He slipped up her sleeve, and the grid work of scars and deep cuts across newly healed skin made him suck in his breath. She'd been cut again.

Who would do this to her? And why? Were the Japanese nearby? Or had one of the men in camp done this, carving her arms to force himself on her?

He scanned the sleeping forms. Everyone was where they should be. Was it something in the jungle? What else could have done this? *But first things first.*

Ryan retrieved his medical bag. He ripped open a packet of sulfa powder and sprinkled it across her arms, wrapping them lightly with bandages before pulling her sleeve down.

He attended to the smaller cuts. Ryan made a paste of water and powder in his hand. Careful not to wake her, he spread it across the web of scratches from the undergrowth and grasses, then sat back on his heels, surveying his work. Blood soaked through the bandages on her arms, but there didn't seem to be blood anywhere else. He dropped his head to his hands, which were spread next to Kai's still form.

What was he going to do? He couldn't help her if she refused to let him.

The guard shifted position, and Ryan squelched the impulse to jump away. He'd only attract notice. But the guard didn't detect Ryan or the odd care he paid the legendary tiger-man.

Ryan untangled a twig from Kai's hair and let it fall to the ground. Lord help him, he would find a way to help this woman or die trying.

Chapter Thirty-Two

THE NEXT DAY DAWNED CHILLY and dry as death itself, but I was happy the snow was far behind. Ryan squatted in the center of the camp, poking at the fire embers, blowing gently. The kindling crackled under his ministrations, and Ryan settled on his heels, confident in his ability, as he shifted a pot over the new flames. The Bear of Burma had come into his own, which left me nothing to do but stretch lazily and burrow into the blankets, momentarily refusing to acknowledge the hazy light around me.

My entire body ached as if I'd endured a hundred lashes, and my mouth was as stale as the dirt. What a luxury to have someone else worry about food and water. And the Allies were scheduled to drop us supplies before the main company split off for Tagap Ga. I rubbed my leg. Perhaps the flyboys would drop more pain reliever. I still had days when I could use it.

I rolled, trying to ignore the pleading of my bladder. With how little I had been drinking, I shouldn't need to relieve myself. I curled my knees into my chest.

Ryan deftly chopped a root of some kind. I studied his calm profile. As we'd traveled, the village women had been enamored with his blond hair and broad shoulders but giggled behind his back about his generous nose. Truth be told, the hard life of an OSS agent agreed with Ryan. He'd always been gentle and kind, and now there was a surety to him, a settledness I couldn't help but notice. He was a catch for sure. For someone who wasn't chasing a vengeance that might just kill them both. I was so very tired, and he was so very tempting. I could just let him take care of me, take me to Indiana to pretend I knew how to be a good little housewife.

He ran his hand through his unruly hair, and I wondered if it was as soft as it looked. The other men often kissed the village women and took them into the jungle, where we all heard their moans. I ran my fingers across my lips, wondering what it would feel like.

I bit my lip, horrified. I could never be what he needed. I'd left too much blood behind me.

But something about the Bear of Burma called me to sink into him. Last night when I'd brought the plantain, he'd almost seemed glad I was with him.

I squirmed, remembering later in the night, when they'd thought I'd been asleep, Ryan had argued hard with Major Trace, almost demanding he send me away. Why would he act glad to see me and then plot to send me away? My fingers tightened around the tiger in Mama's pouch. His tiny feet dug into my palm. Trust only brought pain.

But I couldn't leave. Not yet. I needed Trace, his information, and his access.

I rolled again. We were heading to Peach Boy's last known location, but Trace had been elusive about why he was separating the unit. Although their skittering glances and distance showed their distrust of me, the Kachins knew how to fight. Why would Trace send them away when we were most likely to encounter large groups of Japanese? Something rotted behind his refusal to talk about this Peach Boy, something the major was hiding. Trace was obviously a hunter and a good officer, which meant he wouldn't hesitate to sacrifice himself and Ryan, let alone me, if that was what was best for the Allies.

Sighing, I swung my feet around, shook out my boots to dislodge any deadly critters, and yanked them on. I was thankful for the support they lent, even if it was strange to have something so solid between me and the ground.

Seeing me awake, Ryan smiled and scooped up an assortment of canteens.

"The air transport command gents dropped us food and supplies earlier. They also let us know there's water just ahead. Some of the lads have already brought some back, but we could use more." He checked behind him and then lowered his voice. "If you need an excuse to go off by yourself, you can take some canteens to fill. I'll keep them away."

I took the canteens and nodded.

When the jungle closed between the camp and me, I gave in to the pain and limped to the stream. I sank to the water's edge and stretched out my hands, and stinging pain tore through my arms. I gritted my teeth as I rolled up my sleeves. Blood-soaked bandages wrapped my arms, from my wrists to my biceps.

I sat back on my haunches. Peeling down a corner of the wrap, I winced at the deep slashes crisscrossing my wrist. Again.

How was it possible for this to happen again and me not to know? Not remember?

My fingers trembled as I tucked the edges of the bandage back in. A darkness haunted the corner of my mind, skittering just out of reach so I couldn't quite grab hold. My sight blurred, the world tilting.

While this had happened before, it was the first time someone had bandaged me. Perhaps they knew what demon attacked me. Ryan? If he had helped, he would surely have used the opportunity to tell Trace I was an unfit soldier.

Tempted to rip off the evidence of bandages, I hesitated. The blood would stain my sleeves, proclaiming my injuries more clearly.

Camp sounds rose in pitch. The men were nearly ready to march. I cursed. I had to go back and risk Trace's wrath soon. Without the major, I might never get near enough to the main Japanese force to find Utagawa.

Mechanically, I filled the canteens before trudging back to camp.

When I returned, Ryan had already rolled my blankets and set provisions next to my pack. My rifle leaned against the food and medicine, along with a spare box of ammunition. Across camp, Trace organized the troops. Ryan stood, tying extra supplies onto his pack. Everything normal, calm.

"Ryan?" I heard the quiver in my voice and hated myself for it.

He turned, his calm slipping. His hands cradling my shoulders, a battle raging behind his eyes. "Are you all right?" he whispered.

I cocked my head, trying to appear unconcerned and confused at his question.

"I know, Kai. Who do you think bandaged you?"

It had been Ryan then. At least it hadn't been Trace. "What happened?"

Ryan hesitated, shock and fear slamming across his face before concern softened the edges. "You don't remember?" His hand skimmed down my arm, cold taking its place.

How could I not remember?

I crumpled to the ground, hiding behind an enormous palm tree. My hands reached for the bag around my neck.

Ryan folded himself next to me and gathered my hand into his. "I don't know what happened. I followed you and then you just . . . you disappeared."

The rhythmic circling of his thumb over my palm entranced me.

"You've had a lot to process. Maybe a little too much. Why don't you let me get you somewhere safe?"

My head nodded in time with his movement. Safe. Safe. Safe.

"Let me get you home. I'll find a way to take you."

The wisps of the snuffed fire reached for me, thick smoke, choking, shallow graves gaping, hungry. I shuddered, snapping my hand away, the spell broken. "Sharaw does not have a home." I sprang to my feet, refusing to see the hope and pain I knew were in Ryan's eyes.

"Then let me make Kai a home. Let's go somewhere to breathe and recover and . . ."

My whole being wished to give in, to shake off the weight of Sharaw and curl into Ryan's dream, the dream I'd once pleaded for. But Kai—that girl full of hope—was broken and weak. She would never survive.

"You know Kai doesn't exist anymore." I slung my pack across my shoulders and shoved my way to the front of the line.

≈

I roamed ahead of the Rangers, scouting, each agonizing step reminding me how close I was to cracking. This raging fissure was what Ryan had seen in me. What I couldn't let Trace see. I needed to find Utagawa before I fell completely to pieces.

As ridiculous as the thought was, I wondered if perhaps Peach Boy would know *exactly* where I would find Utagawa. I knew the Japanese army was vast and the possibility slim. Still, my feet slowed as I pictured standing behind Utagawa, knife at his throat, ignoring his pleas. I would be merciful and kill him quickly, a courtesy he'd not given Tu Lum.

Then the memories haunting my nights would end, and I could let Sharaw die. Perhaps there would be enough of me left to scrabble together the pieces, find somewhere to rest. Go home.

Curse him. Ryan had reawakened my desire. But who would ever accept me after all this?

The sun shone relentless above me, and my body throbbed in the heat, making me nearly wish for the lush coldness of the mountains. My palms were damp against my rifle stock and produced a pungent salty smell—the stink of the breathless moments before battle.

At a drop-off, I stopped and peered over the edge. The trail fell away into a gully with a stream at the bottom. Water. And no sign of Japanese troops. I took a long drag on my canteen, knowing that I now had enough halazone tablets to clean any amount of water I could retrieve from the stream. Water cascaded through rocks, and the idea of submerging in the coolness called to me like Homer's sirens.

All down the hill as I ran, Mama's pouch slapped into my chest and arms, and I slammed my hand over the bag to stop the stones and carved bit of wood from ramming my wounds. The bumps under my hand underscored the failed prayers, an absent God, trust gone awry. Ryan might have bandaged me, but he still wanted me gone.

I was the only one who knew what was best for me. Who I could count on.

Behind me and to the east, the other forward scout stopped, whistling low. A bridge spanned the gully. I swallowed hard. An entire regiment of Japanese could have been there and I would have missed it.

Pretending I'd known he'd been there the whole time, I saluted. I pointed to my canteen, as if drinking water had been my objective. The other scout nodded, then pivoted to notify the others.

I sank on an enormous boulder partly submerged in the stream. The crystalline mountain water frothed through the sand and rocks, filtering out the debris and hazards so prevalent in the larger rivers and slower-moving streams.

I untied my boots, hands shaking against the pain that came with removing them. But I had time before the others came, and the water would help heal the blisters. Easing my aching feet and leg into the frigid water, I resisted the urge to strip to my underthings and take a bath. I couldn't risk being caught.

Underneath me the rock radiated warmth, and I sighed at the indulgence. Slowly my feet stopped throbbing, and I stared into the water. Thousands of rocks shimmered in the sunlight.

I ran my hands through the stones, the pebbles tumbling free in the current before gravity lured them into the depths. The curves of the larger stones were smooth from the relentless current—content, peaceful. For a moment I wondered if I could find relief here. Tie myself to the rocks and sink. Just be done.

My hands slid through the stones again, and the sunlight glinted orange. I shifted, digging for the color, and picked out the stone. It was amber, about the size of my palm. One side gray. The other a glowing gem. I held the stone to the light. Inside, a tiny dragonfly hung suspended, trapped. I could feel his wings as if they were my own, frozen, desperate to move, to fly, to escape the golden stone.

"It's beautiful."

I jumped to my feet, cursing, the rifle clattering to the ground. Ryan should never have been able to sneak up on me.

"The stone. It's beautiful." He watched me, one side of his mouth lifted, but held out his hand for the stone.

I hesitated, not wanting to let it go. Afraid he would see what I saw.

I released the dragonfly into his big paw, and he held the golden gem to the sun.

"It's sad though. She had to die to make it. She's well protected." Ryan reached his hand out and lifted my sweating palm. "But I think she was more beautiful alive." He placed the amber into my hand before trudging upstream to the men gathering water and planning.

I blinked at the rock and let it tumble into the water before tugging on my boots and following Ryan to join the others.

$$\approx$$

Ryan forced himself away from Kai. Nothing he said or did would change her mind. He realized that now. To continue layering his pleas on top of her pain only encased her, like the dragonfly, more than she already was. Only she could kill Sharaw and let Kai live.

Trace caught Ryan's attention, and Ryan fell in behind his CO, translating the more complex orders for the Kachins, his finger trailing across the map.

"Ma Shawng." Trace spoke to the man whom he had selected as the leader of the Kachin Rangers. "You are set to lead the others to Tagap Ga?"

Ma Shawng nodded fiercely and stood taller.

"Make note of any Japanese you see, but you are *not* to engage the enemy unless fired upon. Secrecy is our greatest ally at the moment."

Ryan looked each man in the eye as he translated the orders. "Do you agree?"

Ma Shawng bowed. "If I speak not the truth, may the tiger seize me, may the lightning strike me, may Bareng, the river nat, take me when I cross the waters."

Ryan grasped the man's arm. "May the supreme one guide your steps and hide your trail."

"They agree, and I wished them safety on their journey," Ryan said to Trace.

"Good." Trace bowed to Ma Shawng.

The Kachin men bowed once more to their commanding officers and marched away, following the river north and then west toward Tagap Ga.

Pebbles rippled down the ravine behind Ryan, and he knew Kai stood behind him. He forced himself to continue facing away from her.

"Sharaw." Trace glared over Ryan's shoulder. "Even though you are remaining with us, the message bears repeating. Do not engage the enemy unless absolutely necessary."

Kai shifted, and Ryan prayed she would obey.

"You realize they will kill us without thought. That by not killing them, you allow them an opportunity."

Ryan sighed. The vulnerable woman from the river was gone, wrapped again in protective rock.

Trace elbowed around Ryan and glared down at Kai, not a bit of fear showing for the warrior brandishing a loaded rifle. "You could destroy the Allies' chance to regain the mountains if you don't learn to obey orders. Our mission is to rendezvous with Peach Boy. We cannot afford to be distracted."

"Why are you so obsessed with one man? What could finding him possibly do for us?"

Trace studied her for a moment. "I know you're used to being on your own. But y'all are under my command now, and I need you to trust and listen to me, or you can be on your way." His command was low, hard, and placed him firmly in control. "Clear?"

The tiger had met her match. Any other man might have shriveled under Kai's challenging glare, but Trace merely glanced at his watch, dismissing her.

"Ryan, you know where we're headed?"

Ryan's gaze slipped to Kai before he nodded and rambled across the bridge.

Behind him, Kai and Trace followed him southeast across a narrow ridge. They were headed into Japanese territory. Ryan knew the importance of Peach Boy's information, understood the risks and the necessity. He trusted his CO, and yet he would give anything to be going the opposite direction toward India.

Ryan adjusted his rifle across his body. Ningbyen was a few days' march away. He would just have to protect Kai until then. After that, he prayed Kai would never figure out who Peach Boy really was.

Chapter Thirty-Three

Late February 1944
The Plains of North Burma

Despite the soaring daytime temperatures as they trekked into the rocky plains, Kai still wore the tiger pelt across her shoulders. A clear sign she'd wedged herself deeper into her amber cage. Ryan, in his shirtsleeves, was hot just watching her. But she was in another world. Her lithe body slid in and out of the scraggly vegetation, feet never making a sound. He could understand the fear she induced. Even injured, the land was her subject, and she ruled it with impunity. She was terrifying.

But so was what they were walking into. Without understanding the whole picture, Trace couldn't see the problem.

And that was Ryan's own blasted fault, his own decision to shade the truth, thinking he knew better than God himself. Now he was stuck. He couldn't trust what Trace would do if he found out Kai was a woman—he'd just as likely shoot her as to simply leave her stranded and alone in enemy territory. Just for spite.

And he couldn't tell Kai who Peach Boy was for fear of her killing Trace in his sleep.

Perhaps the best thing was to stop meddling and let God work it out as he promised to do.

Trace was, after all, legitimately worried that Utagawa's support of the Allies was wavering. They'd not heard from him in several days and then suddenly received a short transmission with a confirmed meeting place farther north and less ideal than originally planned. It might have been that his unit was moving. Or it might be a trap. The appearance of Sharaw would bolster the man's courage, Trace argued. And he was right. It should. But Ryan knew there was another reason it could be wise to have Kai along. He'd heard rumors . . .

When Utagawa had first made contact with the Allies, he'd sent a message about finding the Jungle Light. Could Utagawa have found John Moran? Ryan knew that if Utagawa felt guilty about Tingrabum *and* knew the missionary, having a relative on hand would strengthen the man's commitment.

But Ryan didn't know what Kai would do if she saw either man.

Ryan's mind burned with broken prayers and plans. How to keep his promise to protect Kai's identity and keep Trace's classified secret from her. All while preventing Kai from endangering herself and others. He was angry with Trace for convincing Kai to come with them. For using her. For forcing Ryan into telling half truths.

God forgive him, Ryan felt the flames of his own guilt.

Ryan glanced at the sky. Near midday. They should cross the last bend of the Tarung River in a matter of minutes. The last major landmark between them and the Japanese Fifty-Sixth Infantry Regiment of the dreaded Eighteenth Division. According to Ryan's research, the sandstone cliffs of the river were often overhung with dried-out vegetation, but the Japanese had cleared a wide swath for a view of their flank. Utagawa had sent word for them to meet him two miles south at a large outcropping of stone sitting on a sandbar near the confluence with the Tanai River. Ryan hoped the meeting place wasn't as boxed in or barren as it appeared on the aerial photos.

Ahead, Kai stopped and unslung her rifle in one smooth motion. Ryan gripped his own weapon and crept to her right. As he neared the desiccated vegetation, he heard the waters of a river rushing in the distance, but the ground in between was a blinding flood of open, sunlit rock.

It was nearly time, and Ryan took a deep breath to clear the adrenaline-sparked spots in his vision. He was no coward, but he wasn't fool enough not to be scared either.

Signaling he was going in for a closer look, Ryan slipped into the clearing. The crystalline-blue sky stretched across the river as it snaked between striated cliffs. A series of enormous rocks jutted from the sand, reaching for the trees in the distance. On any other day, Ryan would say the locale was idyllic.

Kai dragged him under the cover of the trees. Her hand coiled in his shirtfront, holding him against her body as she studied the terrain. "You're meeting the informant there?"

Informant. Traitor. Murderer. Ryan nodded, glancing over his shoulder at the barren country. If he didn't make it out of this, he wanted Kai to run. He needed to know she would survive, find a way to truly live.

Trace edged down the hillside.

The lies pressed in on Ryan. He only had a moment to decide. He untangled her hands, clasping them in his, pleading, begging her to understand. "You should know . . ."

Even though Trace was still a ways up the hill, Ryan saw the shift in his CO's face as he broke into a trot.

"Ryan." His voice raised in a low, fierce call, a father catching his child a moment before disobedience. For a single heartbeat, anger washed into Trace's dark features before he wrangled it into submission. This was not the place for irrational behavior. Trace knew it.

And Ryan knew what he had to do to get them *all* out of this valley in one piece. He sucked in a breath and blew out the panic.

"Ryan, you check and see if our guest is here. Then you and I will talk. Sharaw, make sure no one else tries to join our party. You will stay here unless we signal for your help. If anything goes south, we will meet here." Trace pointed to a mark on the silk map, a series of caves north of the Japanese-held village of Shingbwiyang. "Failing that. Tagap Ga." He pointed to the village even farther northwest through a mountain pass.

"All we're doing is obtaining information. That's it. Capisce? This should be a cakewalk if everyone does their job." Trace stared at Kai. He trusted Ryan to follow orders. But it seemed the major was realizing how much of a wild card Sharaw was.

Ryan's fingers tingled against his rifle. Kai watched him, waiting for him to finish what he'd started saying.

Ryan stared at the rock-strewn ground, anger warring with fear. He couldn't risk letting her read him. It was too late now.

"Be safe, Sharaw."

God protect us all.

≈

Ryan's expression pleaded with me for a moment before his shoulders slumped, and he swung away. I wanted to run after him and promise to be safe, to ask him to be safe as well, but I was too late. He was gone.

Trace half turned toward me. Hard, calculating, distancing me from himself and Ryan. A reminder that I wasn't part of the team. "You will stay hidden unless I call for you."

What was he hiding? What had Ryan been trying to tell me?

I watched the two men navigate to the meeting point. As they disappeared behind an enormous rock for a moment, I shook myself into action, jogging behind them, scanning the trees and the top of the cliffs on the far side.

I waited for my vision to narrow, the feel of the hunt to overcome me. Instead a tingle of unease rippled tight in my shoulders. In the distance, Ryan split off into the open, his blond head focusing on the rocks, searching the woods.

Be safe.

For as long as he'd known me, he'd watched over me. Now it was my job to protect him. Sighting along my rifle, I realized my hands were shaking. Fingers of fear rose in me, peeling away the guise of cold, calculated hunter. Nothing felt right.

Did Ryan notice it too? Was that what he wanted to tell me?

Something moved from the other side of the rocks behind Ryan. A circle of light swung across Ryan's body. My hands tightened, the shape of the rifle's stock imprinted on my palm. Ryan hadn't seen the man.

I imitated the two-note call of a cuckoo bird. Neither man acknowledged the signal or my second, louder call. Cursing under my breath, I leaped from the rocks. Crouched low, head swiveling, I twisted through the trees. Ahead, Trace stood inside the tree line, watching.

Ryan hailed the man coming from behind, signaling for Trace to join them. I stopped, hesitated. *Everything is fine. This must be the man with information. Peach Boy.*

I breathed, letting air flow like the clouds, smooth, calming. Across from the meeting point, a huge teak tree sprawled into the sky. A strangler fig twisted around the trunk, giving me a natural ladder to a higher vantage point. Perfect.

Clambering into the tree, I tested the teak, making sure the wood remained solid under the choking presence of the fig. In a few moments I sat above the three men, scanning the landscape for intruders. Peach Boy was scrawny, gaunt. I nearly felt sorry for him. His bulging eyes flitted around as he constantly glanced over his shoulder and into the forest beneath me. I supposed a traitor should be nervous.

Here and there snippets of conversation were thrown back to me by the curve of the rock and carried on the wind—bits about troop movements and reinforcements.

But when Peach Boy said something about the Jungle Light, Ryan's eyes jerked behind him and caught sight of me in the tree.

Jungle Light? Papa? The expression that crossed Ryan's face reminded me of Tu Lum's when Papa caught him sneaking sugar from the cooking room.

Something definitely wasn't right. I started clambering down the tree, when a movement to my right caught my attention. A cloud of dust. Someone was coming.

Chapter Thirty-Four

I LAUNCHED MYSELF INTO THE midst of the three men.

"Ryan," I hissed, pointing behind me.

Peach Boy scuttled behind Ryan, and Ryan shifted to shield the informant.

Trace turned on me. "I told you to stay out of this." His voice was as icy as the mountain streams.

"For goodness' sake. You are sitting ducks here. We need to move."

Ryan scanned the direction I was pointing. "Trace. Someone's coming."

Trace grunted. "We got what we need for now." He squinted at the man cowering behind Ryan. "You best find a way out of here before they find you."

Peach Boy stepped from behind Ryan, bowing stiffly. "I will do as you say." He spoke in enviably clear English.

I tipped my head, studying him. The stars on his shoulders marked him as a lieutenant. Ryan yanked my arm, spinning me away, but still I watched the Japanese soldier. There was something about him.

"You'll come for him, then?" Peach Boy's question was tinged in desperation.

Him who?

Trace sighed his annoyance at another delay. "Yes, Utagawa. We will."

My head snapped to face the major. "What did you say?" My eyes wrenched back to Peach Boy. Recognition exploded.

"Sharaw." Ryan's hand clamped hard on my shoulder. I tried to shake him off, but the Bear of Burma had his claws in me.

I turned on Ryan, my nails biting into my palms and my fingers going numb. "Tell me it isn't him. Tell me this isn't the man who murdered our people."

"This isn't the time or place," Trace commanded.

I rounded on him, and Ryan yanked me back. Hate leached through me, speckling my vision with white drops of venom. The sound of marching men leaked around the bend in the river, moving closer.

"You. Go," Trace commanded Utagawa.

Utagawa bowed to me. "I am truly sorry," the villain whispered before twisting away.

I whipped around, bit Ryan's hand, and swung my rifle around. Trace lunged at me as I fired, air bursting from my lungs as I hit the ground. The shot echoed between the stone and the forest and back again. A puff of dust erupted above where Utagawa's head had been moments before, but the man continued scrambling down the cliff to the river.

Trace swore as his fist connected with my jaw. I heard the crack but barely felt the impact. Sobs heaved in my chest, and I lashed out at him, scratching his face, his arms. Gathering his blood under my nails.

"You lied to me!"

A rifle report burst from the path. Trace swore again and shoved me down before sprinting into the forest.

My blood pulsed hard through my temples, my ears buzzing an unending lament, and I watched as a lone cloud scudded across the sky. I curled against the dust choking me. My arms wrapped around my middle, trying to hold me together. Maybe this was how it felt to die. I closed my eyes, waiting.

A hand stroking my hair made me jump.

Ryan knelt beside me. "We don't have time for me to explain right now." He flicked a hand at the dust cloud. "I'm so sorry, Kailyn. We need to go. They had to have heard the rifle."

I focused on Ryan's moving lips to decipher his words. He shook his head and leaned forward.

"Hold on, Kailyn." His strong arms shifted beneath me as he lifted me across his shoulder and ran for the woods.

≈

Though Kai weighed little more than a child, Ryan's arms burned with the extra weight as he fought his way through the tangled forest and caught up to a waiting Trace. He heard the occasional shot at what must've been Japanese soldiers jumping at nothing, imagining a Kachin spirit-man hiding behind every tree.

A bruise bloomed on Kai's cheek, and Ryan's temper smoldered. Trace had long ago established his military prowess, but this time he had made a mistake. Every part of this plan had been doomed from the beginning.

Ryan stumbled and barely kept his footing. From the beginning. It'd been doomed from the beginning because of *him*. He had been the one holding half truths.

As the golden hue of evening bent across the sky, Trace stopped, panting. Ryan propped Kai against a tree and forced her to drink.

A single tear escaped and slid down her face. "Why? Why didn't you tell me?" she whispered.

"It wasn't his decision to make," Trace ground out. "If *you* had followed orders, none of this would be happening."

Kai blanched. "Excuse me? You were completely exposed out there."

Ryan glared at Trace, his hands clenching into fists. If he thought he could do it without a court-martial, Ryan would lay the man flat.

"Utagawa had information we needed." Trace scrubbed a hand through his hair. "Information we still need. If there had been another way . . ."

A shout echoed from the hill behind them. Ryan swung his rifle around, dissecting the slanted shadows for signs of attacking men.

The air around them split with the whine of incoming artillery. Ryan twisted and threw himself over Kai. A few hundred yards down the slope, the ground exploded, uprooting trees and sending shards of rock mushrooming out of the ground.

Ears ringing with the explosion, Ryan felt rather than heard the growl erupting in Kai as she pushed him off.

"If all you're going to do is follow his asinine orders, I'm better off alone. Have always been better alone. I don't ever want to see you again. Either of you."

"Kai, don't—"

But Kai leaped over a fallen tree, and the scrub swallowed all evidence that she existed. Fire licked at the twisted trees down the slope— hell's fires breaking through.

Turning to leave, Trace stopped short in front of Ryan, who blocked the trail.

"What?" Exasperated, Trace threw up his hands.

"We can't leave him alone."

"He made his choice, and he can handle himself. I won't jeopardize the rest of the mission for the idiot." The major scrambled up the path.

"Trace, he knows too much."

His CO stopped but didn't relent.

"I won't leave her." Ryan stood, resolute.

Trace stopped. "Her? Did you say . . ."

Ryan had morphed into stone. "She's the missionary's daughter, and I promised to protect her. I . . ." His voice broke. "I understand if you leave or court-martial me or whatever, but I *am* going."

Trace swore under his breath and then loudly for good measure.

A mortar screamed down the wrath of the enemy. Ryan shoved Trace to the ground, rolling behind a tree. Pinned between the trunk and the major, Ryan nearly choked on the burning smell of the mortar combined with the rank stench of their fear.

When the smoke cleared, Trace snatched Ryan's shirt, yanking him to his feet. "Find her," he snapped. "And if we make it out of this alive, I might kill you myself."

Ryan scrambled to his feet and plunged into the forest before Trace could change his mind. Easing each step into the forest floor, Ryan wove his way to the river. He saw no sign of Kai. But several Burmese scouts whispered to the Japanese and pointed frantically to the east.

Just as Ryan moved east, a gunshot and scream pierced the deadly silence, followed by a crash. Ryan hesitated, watching. When two Japanese soldiers dragged Kai onto the road, Trace clamped onto Ryan's arm, preventing him from crashing through the forest.

The soldiers threw her to the ground and kicked her gut, laughing. Her body leaped with the impact, but she didn't wake. A river of blood ran down her cheek, and its twin ran from her shoulder to elbow, pooling in the dirt.

Ryan's hands ached against his rifle, his breathing shallow and rapid. He would kill them.

The officer grabbed Kai's shirt and yanked her to her feet. The buttons on her shirt tore free and revealed her binding. It was obvious what the bandage hid. The two Japanese glanced at each other, surprise crossing their faces.

"American," one soldier shouted. "American. You let girls fight for you? You that desperate? Come save her if you not scared. In the meantime"—he trailed a finger across her broken face—"we entertain her."

Trace held firm to Ryan's shirt, pointing with his head up the path. Shrugging Trace's hand off his shoulder, Ryan unsheathed his dah.

Trace shook his head and placed his lips over Ryan's ear. "We can't save her on our own. We need the others." He paused, studying Ryan. "There's an entire camp of Japanese. They'll just kill us all."

Impotent rage and fear drove spots through Ryan's vision.

"The last thing the army needs is to have to rescue three Americans. We'll get help and come back."

How far would they have to travel to get help? Ryan clenched his fist, calculating the times and locations of rendezvous points.

Too far. Too long.

He closed his eyes against the feel of her hand on his, the moment he should have told her the truth. He flinched away from the vision of the men dragging Kai away.

"They need her alive. They need her to get to us. Ryan, we're trying to free Burma, and if they catch us, they will torture us, and we will tell them everything we know about troops and movements and plans. We can't be captured."

Dread sucked air from Ryan's lungs. Though he was afraid for their lives, death wasn't what scared him most. No, death was eclipsed by the horror of what they would do while she still lived.

Chapter Thirty-Five

MEN MURMURED NEARBY. NOT QUITE distinguishable, yet noisy enough that they niggled at my mind, summoning me from the depths of unconsciousness to the edge of wakefulness. I grimaced against the pain in my skull as I tried to drag my thoughts into line. What had happened? An explosion?

No.

I'd found the American plane. Had the Japanese attacked?

Yes? Maybe?

No, wait. I was with Ryan. We were meeting someone.

Why were we in such a large tent? A voice called in the distance. Why did Ryan sound so strange?

My eyes snapped open. The Japanese. I had been angry, careless, overconfident, and they'd shot me out of the tree like a spider monkey. Panic rippled through my body. I was captured. I jerked away from the realization only to nearly yank my arms out of their sockets. My hands were wrapped around a pole and bound behind me.

The ground beneath me was sticky, and the metallic stench of blood clotted in my nose. My breath took flight like a leaf on the wind, and I desperately snatched it back.

In with the rippling breeze. Out with the wings of the butterfly.

I needed to take stock. Escape.

I tested the ropes, hoping to wedge my thumb between the knots, and when that failed, I stood, twisting my shoulders, levering myself, straining at the pole, trying to dislodge it, then kicking at it like a mule to force it free. But the pole stood firm, my hands tied tight, blood trickling into my palms. My shirt slipped off my shoulder.

Panic stole through my body, my breath racing against time.

Outside, words overlapped, and flickering light warred with man-shaped shadows. I held still. The shadows stopped at the tent flap.

Frantic, I heaved against the pole again. Sweat mingled with my tears. I knew what the Japanese did to the women they captured, and it would be worse for me. I had fought them. Made fools of them.

A triangle of light flashed, and a Japanese officer slipped into the tent. A junior officer stalked in behind him, holding a lantern and guarding the entrance. The first officer leered at me, a predator sizing up his meal. I sniffed and lifted my chin.

Tigers are never afraid. Not even of other predators.

But my hands shook, and my breathing refused to be controlled.

The man nodded at me and sauntered to a table nestled into a dark corner. With a flourish, the senior officer removed a stained cloth. His hands skipped across the objects. He lifted one. The metal blade caught the dim light and sparked fire in the darkness. I swallowed, pushing down the bile rising in my throat.

"You are American. Yes?" His smooth British accent meant he'd spent time training in the West. There would be no feigning ignorance or a language barrier with him. "When my men told me they had captured Sharaw, I thought they were imagining ghosts." He studied the wicked knife, weighing it in his hands. Considering, as if he were choosing a cut of meat.

"Imagine my surprise when I discovered that they were not only correct, but that the warrior making a fool of entire Japanese squadrons was a young woman." He set down the knife, sighing as if it were the instruments that had disappointed him and not the soldiers. "Well, we shall prove that no Imperial Japanese soldier bows to a mere woman."

He nodded at the junior officer, who sauntered to me. If it weren't for the sneer contorting it, his face would be one as ubiquitous as sand.

I squared my shoulders and steeled myself for his attack. The sharaw cackled, mocking my weak courage.

When the officer grasped my arms, I spit in his face. He jumped back, then snarled and ripped the military shirt off my body. I gasped in spite of myself, cold nipping through the thin, sleeveless undershirt.

The officer scowled and waved off Sandman. "I am glad that you have found your resistance again."

Approaching me, he frowned, and then the knife tip dropped toward the ground. He traced his fingers across the grid work of scars and barely healed scabs on my arms, sending shards of fear splintering into my spine. "It seems you either have an affinity for knives or have met with one of my friends in the past. It's a pity that you seem to be immune to the blade. No matter. I have other ways." He ambled to his table, and I let out a sigh of grateful reprieve before catching myself.

Sandman chuckled as he watched his senior officer caress his torture instruments.

Tigers are never afraid.

"You do not know what pain means. Not yet," Sandman whispered, so close his rotten breath tickled the hairs in my ears. "When he is done, it is my turn." His hand trailed down my neck and over my breastbone before he licked his lips and called to the other man, "Let me know when you are finished. I will get the others ready for our games."

I trembled, the courage of the Sharaw fleeing as I sank to the ground. Alone again.

Chapter Thirty-Six

"I'M NOT LEAVING HER, AND I'm not waiting for reinforcements." Ryan dropped his pack on the ground and yanked out anything he wouldn't need for an immediate attack. Ryan had convinced Trace to at least track the Japanese to the edge of their encampment. He'd hoped the camp would be a small affair—one he could easily convince Trace to storm.

"You stubborn, bullheaded idiot." Trace snatched the pack from Ryan.

"She knows too much, Trace. We won't make it to camp and back before they get . . ." Ryan swallowed. "Before they get what they want. We can't leave her."

Trace inhaled. "It would be suicide to go in there, Ryan."

Ryan nodded tightly. He knew. But the panic rising in him was due to more than his promise to Nang Lu.

He loved Kailyn.

He should have found a way to make her go to India, told Trace, risked a court-martial, anything to keep her away from this. Anything.

But even as he thought it, he knew Kai would have found a way back into her country.

"I don't suppose you'd agree to going for backup."

"Too long," Ryan growled.

Trace studied the trail where the Japanese had disappeared. "We'll wait until dark. It's our only hope of actually saving her and not getting ourselves caught in the process."

Ryan opened his mouth to argue but snapped it closed. Trace was right. Darkness and surprise would be their only advantages.

As he paced like a caged animal, Ryan prayed that after Utagawa circled back to the Japanese camp, he would protect Kai until he and Trace could rescue her. *Please, God.*

As the last glimmer of light pulsed on the horizon, a scream ripped across the river, and Ryan spun toward the camp, pebbles slamming down the mountainside, telegraphing their location. He was supposed to wait at least a quarter hour before they'd attempt the rescue. The scream reverberated again, and he snatched his gear, running, tripping to Kai. Trace could shoot him or court-martial him or whatever, but Ryan was going after Kai *now*.

Tree limbs slapped at his face, his clothes. His boots glided across the ground. It took everything in him not to abandon all he knew about stealth as a third scream pierced his ears.

At the bottom of the hill, Ryan pivoted east and wove his way to the curve of the river. A clattering noise sounded in front of him, and he froze. Trotting on the balls of his feet, Ryan bent low to the ground.

Out of the semidarkness, he saw the flicker of lamplight and the shapes of two guards protecting the footbridge across the canyon. He couldn't risk the sound of the rifle to pick them off. Neither could he allow either of them to escape and alert the camp. How he wished for his bow or Kai's blowgun. He gauged the range and unsheathed a short dagger with his right hand and his dah in his left. One blade for each man.

Crouching low, he stalked their movements to the far side of the bridge. The guards were sluggish and tired. Something in his favor at least. One man slunk to the ground and leaned against the support pole. The other grumbled, stomping toward the first. Ryan burst from the underbrush. He threw his knife into the man sitting, then barreled into the other, wrapped his right arm around the soldier's mouth, and dragged the blade of the dah across his throat.

The dah clattered to the ground, and Ryan stood, covered in blood, shaking.

Footsteps pounded behind Ryan, and he spun, wrenching his side-arm from his holster.

Trace skidded to a stop, hands in front of him. "Ryan. It's me." He glanced at the men on the ground and back at Ryan. "Remind me never to get you riled." Trace bent to retrieve Ryan's knives.

Ryan stooped, wiping his hands on the scrubby grass, breathing, willing himself steady. This was something he'd never get used to, no matter the justice of his cause. These men had families, and he'd stolen their lives. When he stood, Trace handed Ryan his two blades.

"I can't let you go in there." Trace nodded his head toward the silent Japanese camp. "Leastways, not alone." Trace lifted his gun. "Tonto can't rescue a damsel in distress without the Lone Ranger, now can he? After you." Trace swept his hand toward the rope bridge spanning the gorge, one southern gentleman inviting a Yank into a party.

Some party.

The bridge was a typical Burmese affair—a collection of three or four ropes woven together for feet and a single strand stretched above for hands. Ryan dropped his rifle strap over his head and swallowed as he edged onto the swaying ropes. He gripped one hand on the upper rope and nestled his rifle into his other. Ryan stared straight across the expanse at the flicker of light in the camp and forced himself to move quickly. His rifle swung on his shoulder, threatening to drag him into the gaping blackness. He snatched the rope with both hands. He'd never gotten used to these things. Never would.

But thoughts of Kai and why the world had suddenly gone quiet spurred him on. With one hand on his rifle again, Ryan scooted across the bridge, then launched himself off the rope onto solid ground. He scanned the empty darkness.

Where were the guards on this side? A grunting drew Ryan's attention to a mass of twisted bushes to the west of the bridge. Underneath, Ryan saw two mounds writhing. The two guards were trussed like a

Thanksgiving turkey. Ryan nearly cheered as he signaled to Trace. Utagawa was helping.

Purposefully pivoting away and toward the camp, Ryan trotted to a small stand of trees and blocked out the sound of the muffled screams and sudden quiet behind him. Ryan could almost hear his CO's command. *Leave no loose ends.*

The blood on Ryan's hands congealed, cracking like drying cement on his knuckles.

At least it wasn't his blood or Kai's. This time.

Ryan rubbed his hands against his trouser legs. What he wouldn't give to be back in the mountains, trekking with Kai, their only danger not finding meat for the pot.

Skirting the darkened tents and avoiding the pools of firelight, Ryan scanned the camp for any signs of Kai. A low cuckoo call sounded behind him. Trace had rejoined his flank.

Ryan felt Trace's hand on his shoulder—two taps and a finger pointing to the right. Ryan would go right.

One tap and a finger to the left. Trace to the left.

A circling flick of the wrist. They'd meet on the other side.

Fingers up and waving. Ryan squinted across the clearing for what Trace was signaling. At the copse of trees.

Ryan nodded and headed toward a long, narrow tent—what appeared to be a command tent.

At the far side of the tent, Ryan heard a low grunt and the scuffle of feet. He squeezed his eyes shut for a moment and then reopened them, squinting into the darkness. A strange hunchback figure emerged, moving toward him, soundless. Ryan slipped sideways into the darkness.

In a few more paces, Ryan realized the hunchback was a man running, bent low, carrying a bundle over his shoulder. A band of firelight stretched into the darkness in front of the man. The man hesitated and then burst through the fingers of light, face averted from the center of the camp.

The bundle shifted, the white of bare skin caught in the firelight, the high cheekbones, dark with bruises. Kai. Ryan laid his rifle against his shoulder.

"Stop," he snarled.

The man skidded to a stop and dropped Kai behind him. Standing between Ryan and the woman at his feet, the man raised his hands and sank into an attack posture.

"Utagawa?"

The Japanese man leaned forward and squinted.

"Bear?" Relief flooded his features. "You must get her away. I heard them capture her, heard them bring her here. I went to her as quickly as possible, but I am afraid I was not soon enough."

Utagawa knelt next to Kai and tucked something into her limp hand. "I am sorry, my sister. For everything." His hand covered her head in an odd benediction. He stood and grasped Ryan's hand. "You know Sharaw is a woman?"

"Yes," Ryan hissed.

Utagawa cringed, hands wringing in front of him. "Then you must know that she may wish we had not saved her. When I got to her, he was . . ."

Ryan gasped for air, wrestling to push his anger underneath logic, control.

"Before I stole her away, I made sure he will not hurt any other." His words tumbled out, the pitch rising as he spoke. "Most of her wounds will keep for now, but she will need medicine." Utagawa warily extended a hand full of medicine packets. He had obviously read the stiffness in Ryan and did not wish to poke an angry bear.

Anger, panic, frustration ran through Ryan's mind, and the last vestiges of control strained, ready to break, even as he labored to find the next step.

Get out. That was it. He needed to meet with Trace and get out. Ryan tucked the medicine into a pouch attached to his belt. "Trace is meeting me at the trees. Tell him to meet me at the rendezvous."

The man nodded curtly but stood rooted to the ground. Ryan hesitated. What was he waiting for?

"And what would you have me do with the Jungle Light?"

Ryan's shoulders drooped. He'd forgotten to figure John into what little plan he'd had. "Can you still get him out?"

Uncertainty flitted across Utagawa's face before he nodded in resignation. "Yes."

Trace wouldn't be able to carry a full-grown man alone, and Ryan could never cross the bridge with Kai in his arms. With the gorge cutting off the route, going south to the closer fort at Knothead wasn't possible.

"Kai and I will meet *all* of you on the trail to Shingbwiyang or in the caves north of there."

"I will do as you say." The Japanese man bowed.

But when he stood wringing his hands rather than retrieving John, fear rippled through Ryan. The last thing he needed was Utagawa to flip-flop.

"I need you all to come, Utagawa. We can't let them keep killing children—and they'll know someone helped them escape."

Tears gathered in Utagawa's eyes. "I know. I am sorry, Bear. I hope that one day you will forgive me." He nodded again, as if to assure himself he'd said all that he wanted, spun, and strode through the camp toward the trees. Hiding in plain sight.

For the first time, Ryan had a clear view of Kai, and his knees buckled. Wrapped in a bloody sheet, Kai's face was raw with cuts, the lobe of her right ear sliced and dangling. Her knees were curled into her chest, one arm devastated with fresh cuts, flung out on the ground.

"Oh, Kailyn." What had they done? His lips brushed her fevered forehead.

Kai's left eye fluttered open, but the other remained stubbornly closed. "Ryan?"

A tear squeezed under her lashes. Ryan brushed the tear away, his own tear replacing hers on her cheek. "I'm here, Kailyn."

"I'm sorry." Her fingers groped at the bag Utagawa had given her. Her mother's pouch filled with stones, her prayers turned anchors.

Ryan eased the bag from her hand, slipping it into his pocket before lifting her body and tucking her into his chest. There was nothing for *her* to be sorry about. His mind tore between wanting to wrap around her until they disappeared and a primal drive to attack the camp and maul every man in it.

A shiver rippled through her body, and his thoughts snapped into focus. *Survive.* The first step was getting her to safety.

With every stride away from the encampment, relief degraded his energy, the strength draining from his arms—but he settled into the easy trot of a Kachin mountain man. From behind him rose shouts sounding the alarm. They had discovered Kai's escape. The clock was ticking.

Ryan kept to the low, hard ground, where his footsteps would be harder to track and the outline of his body harder to see. He wished he were no longer in the open stretch of riverbed and dry valley but in Kai's mountain.

The alarm rose in pitch. Trace. Utagawa. Gunshots echoed hard against an open plain. Ryan forced himself steady, to keep moving. The others could take care of themselves, but Kai depended on him.

From his arms, Kai moaned and twitched in her sleep. Real-life nightmares haunted her this time, and Ryan knew he needed to get her somewhere her body and mind could heal.

He turned northwest. They'd swing around the camp, then strike out across the Hukawng Valley, skirting the main path heading to Tagap Ga. Maybe they'd even find a villager outside Shingbwiyang to send word for help. But then they'd have to wait. Without knowing the extent of her wounds, he couldn't determine how much time Kai would need before she would be able to walk long distances.

Ryan's foot caught on the lip of a rock, and he stumbled, battling to stay upright. He collapsed to a knee, and pain shot through his leg.

Where in this cursed country would she be safe?

He shifted Kai's torso across his shoulder, her easy breath warm on his neck. He pushed himself to stand and staggered up the incline.

The sounds of pursuit grew. Ryan scanned behind him. The glow of daylight filtered through the trees and lit the camp. Too close. The footsteps were too close. Ryan swallowed. There would be no coming darkness to save him. At that moment, the light might not be on his side.

Chapter Thirty-Seven

THE FOREST OPENED INTO A clearing, and Ryan burst through, legs and lungs burning as he pushed faster, farther, fully aware that his exposed back was an easy target.

Ryan ducked into a cluster of trees, careful to stay off ridges, where he would stand out starkly against the blue sky. Hopefully, the ancient trees would shelter him from searchers, even if the hunters used binoculars.

Sounds from the camp had disappeared, and he hadn't seen signs of pursuit in the last hour. Perhaps God hadn't abandoned him after all.

Grateful for the momentary relief of shade, he eased Kai to the ground and sipped from his canteen before dribbling water across Kai's cracked lips. He wished he could give her more, but the only river nearby was inaccessible, at the bottom of a steep incline.

He squatted next to Kai and brushed her hair away from her face. Energy dripped with the sweat off his shoulders, down his legs.

Ryan rubbed his arms and slapped his cheeks. He could not sleep. Not yet. Next to him, Kai breathed steadily. Blood trailed through the tangled white sheet. The evidence stacked against him, heavy on his shoulders. He'd never be able to erase the damage he'd caused.

Footsteps crunched from the other side of the trees. Ryan spun. His knife drawn, he ducked behind a tree, anticipating where the intruder would appear.

A gray-headed white man stumbled from the forest, and then an Asian soldier. They leaned against each other, both walking heavily—tired and probably injured. Ryan dropped his arm.

"Utagawa?"

The younger man's head snapped to attention. Blood streaked from a gash in his head, staining the front of his uniform. His feet stumbled, pulling the old man to his knees.

"Bear of Burma. Thank God."

Ryan stiffened, until he saw the earnestness in Utagawa's face.

The older man's head lolled, a deep cough racking his body, until his glassy eyes focused on Ryan.

"John? Merciful heavens." Ryan swung his rifle behind him, stumbled down the incline, and knelt in front of the older man. He hadn't really believed the missionary was still alive.

Gray wrinkled skin disguised John's strong jawline. The dark hair Ryan remembered was faded gray and sprang sporadically from a spotted scalp.

"Ryan?" John's voice scratched raw.

"It's me." Ryan hefted the missionary, letting Utagawa lead the way up the hill. "How did you get him out?"

"The commander was using him for information about the valley. He has been with us ever since you killed the other informant, Baw Gun. The Jungle Light kept me from ending myself. He's the one who helped me contact your Trace."

Trace. Ryan scanned the faint trail back to the camp, searching for his CO. When he came up empty, Ryan's attention wandered to Utagawa. The man swallowed, his wide nose flaring.

"I am sorry I could not help . . . Trace, he . . ."

Ryan pitched, stumbling, shaking his head, dragging John down with him. Trace couldn't be . . . Ryan could hear Trace's laughter as it echoed in the mountains, see his face as it shifted from charming to serious and planning.

The Lone Ranger didn't die.

"No—"

"He led them the other way. He carried a pack he made to look like the woman. They shot him crossing the bridge."

Ryan's hands shook. His breathing echoed in his own ears. "No." Trace's body twisted, broken at the bottom of the river.

Ryan looked to John. He would refute the story, wouldn't he? Tell Ryan that Utagawa was lying. That Trace would meet them at the caves.

John scrutinized his folded hands, the posture familiar, a minister giving friends and family a moment of silence at the graveside.

"He bought us time. We need to keep moving." Utagawa's observation was gentle but brooked no argument.

"No." Ryan dropped to the dirt, wishing the ground would swallow him and stop the pain.

Utagawa hauled John to his feet. "They will know soon that Trace didn't have her. And they will not stop hunting the legend and a traitor."

Ryan clenched his fist, squeezing away thoughts of Trace's family. His little sisters playing tag with nothing but empty air, his father waiting for a hero who would never come home. Ryan jammed the heels of his hands into his eyes, rubbing away the visions spinning out of control. If Ryan had agreed to wait for help, Trace would be alive.

He felt a hand on his sleeve. Ryan opened his eyes, the dark spots racing away. Utagawa squatted in front of Ryan. "She needs you."

If they had waited, Kai would be dead and possibly Utagawa and John. He'd traded Trace's life for theirs. How dare he make such choices?

"Ryan." Utagawa dragged Ryan from his spiraling thoughts. "With your major gone, you must lead us out. Sharaw needs you, and there's still the mission."

Utagawa stood, giving Ryan the space to come to the same conclusion. Ryan wanted to argue. He hadn't asked to lead, hadn't asked to be their last hope. He'd already failed colossally as a leader more than once—in running the mission, in saving Tingrabum. He hadn't even been able to convince Kai to let Sharaw go. Yet here he was.

Ryan turned to Kai, numb. John's head bowed over her body, swaying to the rhythm of mumbled words. A chant? A prayer? The old missionary was in no shape to lead, even if he had known the checkpoints.

There was no one else. Ryan sucked in a breath and forced himself to his feet before laying a gentle hand on John's fragile shoulder.

The older man tottered, confusion filling his expression as he nodded at the body at his feet. "He said you had a young woman."

Ryan swallowed. The man didn't even recognize his own daughter. Ryan's compassion evaporated. He wanted to scream, rant against the old man for leaving her. For abandoning them. For being so sure and so very, very wrong. If the missionary had listened, they would all be safe in India. Ryan's anger smoldered white hot, and he struggled to contain the volcanic explosion.

"John," Ryan whispered, preemptively closing his eyes against John's reaction. "That is Kai."

John's sob ripped through the expanse, bouncing off the rocks. "Kailyn?" He sank to the ground, his hands hanging limp at his sides. "This is . . . What have I done?"

The older man's heaving breath made Ryan clench his fists in frustration. Ma would want him to have compassion, but he had no compassion left for a man who'd abandoned them. No time for regrets or second-guessing. No space for any of his overdue grief.

"John, I am sorry. We cannot stay here." Utagawa glanced south, as if a contingent of soldiers might materialize on the path.

While Ryan didn't think an attack was imminent, he could see the logic in leaving now. He would be wise to gain as much distance between themselves and the camp before the soldiers redirected their search. It wouldn't take long for trained men to overtake the injured quartet.

"Can you walk?" Ryan peered down at John.

The old man's body shook as he dragged himself to his feet. "I will walk to hell if it will save my daughter."

Utagawa frowned at John and then Ryan, questions filling his face, but he held his tongue. The Japanese man might make a great ally yet.

Stepping around the older man, Ryan knelt and nestled Kai over his aching shoulder.

"Then we will go as fast as we can." And pray that God would hide them from the Japanese.

≈

Twilight was eating at the edge of the world when Ryan realized that the lights low on the horizon were the fires of Shingbwiyang. They were back in the jungle now, and they'd never make it another four miles to the caves tonight. It had taken them more than ten hours to hike the fifteen miles to the large town at the base of the Himalayas, and they'd even risked walking game trails. The town was under Japanese control, but the majority of the Kachin population remained pro-Allies.

Ryan studied the others. Utagawa was a resourceful military man, but he was injured. And even if he weren't, Ryan couldn't possibly trust the man who'd participated in the attack on Tingrabum. The elevation slowed them all, as did the weakened missionary, who leaned against Utagawa. Ryan had to admit that he couldn't continue much farther either. Certainly not navigating the foothills while carrying Kai with one arm and hacking through the jungle with the other.

He halted, sucking in air while he watched the two other men hobble forward. How was he supposed to decide what to do? As much as the anger in Ryan tempted him to kill every enemy he saw, he had to admit that they were not all the same. Utagawa had saved Kai's life—and John's. The lieutenant had risked his life for theirs. He had gone above and beyond being an informant. And he would have more knowledge of the villagers and the Japanese stationed in Shingbwiyang. Perhaps it *was* time to trust him.

Concern tugged Utagawa's thin eyebrows together, making it clear he wondered why they'd stopped but was too schooled in military etiquette to question a higher-ranking officer.

"I think we need to try for help. We have to treat her wounds, and all of us need rest." Ryan swallowed. *Please let this be the right choice.* "What do you think?"

Utagawa held Ryan's gaze, then sighed and surveyed the flickering firelight of the town. "The Japanese are here."

"I can't keep this up much longer."

Utagawa studied Kai, considering, and then John. "They do not control the people here. I think you, perhaps, would find refuge." The Japanese man hesitated, seeming to want to add something.

"And what about you? Would they hide you?"

"Me?" He lifted a narrow shoulder. "I do not know."

Ryan contemplated Kai's still form, then shifted his gaze to Utagawa. The small man stood legs slightly apart, braced for betrayal.

A bit apart from the others, John stood, eyes unfocused, not committing, or perhaps not comprehending.

"We need help." Ryan's statement was firm, his officer's voice. "But I am trusting you to not give us away."

"Yes, sir." Utagawa dipped his head. "And I will trust you not to abandon me."

Ryan bowed in acknowledgment. Mutual trust. It was something the missionary in Ryan easily agreed to. But the soldier in Ryan shied away. But given the circumstances, trust had to be enough.

With one last nod to the rest of the group, Ryan led the way to the far side of the village, where the duwa's long house appeared to be. Kai, with her small stature and dark hair, would have been the only one to easily cross the expanse without detection. But she was blessedly sleeping, giving Ryan hope that her body would recover.

Outside the glow of the village fires, Ryan hesitated. *Please send help.*

When no angel of light materialized to lead them through the village, Ryan studied Utagawa. "Wait here and keep watch over them." Ryan would have to do it himself.

He slipped into the light and then under the grass-roofed porch of the nearest basha.

"Kaja-ee?" Ryan whispered the greeting.

The bamboo floors moaned, and the door creaked open. A small man peered out, taking in Ryan's uniform and the blood on his hands. He blanched and scrambled to shut the door.

Ryan shoved his hand on the closing door. "*Garai hkum sa.*" Ryan pleaded with him to not go.

"You are not safe here," the man answered in rapid Kachin.

"Please. I have a young woman and an old man with me. They are hurt."

"They will find you here and harm my family."

"There's just one other soldier. We have food to exchange for a safe place to sleep. We will leave before dawn."

A small child cried somewhere in the home.

The man's head turned, listening to the child's cry, before focusing back on Ryan. "Food?"

"Rice and dried fish." *Please.*

The man frowned and scanned the village before nodding to Ryan. "Bring the others to the back door."

Ryan bowed. "You will not be sorry."

The man grunted and eased the door closed. As Ryan headed back to the others, he heard the man and a woman comfort the child. The child murmured and then fell quiet, no doubt feeling protected in his father's arms. What Ryan wouldn't do to find that safety. But any security in this world was an illusion.

The trio he'd left behind hunkered together against a rock, Utagawa's rifle up and prepared to protect the other two. Ryan released a breath and whistled the all clear. If Utagawa was going to betray them, he would have done so when Ryan was otherwise occupied and unprepared. Utagawa whistled back and patted John's shoulder, like a father comforting a scared child. Kai's head lay in her father's lap. John's eyes dropped closed, while his fingers absentmindedly traced his daughter's cropped hair.

Ryan ducked under the last bramble and entered the small clearing. "He'll let us stay for the night."

"All of us?" Utagawa shifted.

"Why don't you bring up the rear? Let's get these two in first. It will give me time to explain." If nothing else, he'd leave Kai in the village overnight. Perhaps the Kachin man would know someone who could care for her most intimate wounds. Despite the fact he was a trained medic, some things were better left to others.

Ryan lifted Kai, and his arms trembled under her. Tomorrow, if he hoped to carry her farther, he'd have to make a pallet for her or a sling of some kind. But for now, her soft breath on his neck gave him enough strength.

The boundary of darkness ran ragged at the foot of the hill, bending as light bored into the sanctuary. Toes on the perimeter, Ryan studied the open spaces. Not a soul moved, and he stole to the basha, the others trailing behind. As Ryan reached to knock, the Kachin man threw open the door, then stood aside while John heaved himself up the ladder.

But at the sight of Utagawa and his Japanese uniform, the Kachin thrust his ropy arm across the opening, his whisper harsh and piercing. "Not him."

Utagawa recoiled, his panic obvious in the flight of his hands, the expression on his face.

But Ryan dipped his head in deference to the older man, hoping to appear calmer than he was. "He is one of us. He risked his life to save them both."

The man examined the bundle in Ryan's arms and scoffed. "You lied. You said you and your soldier friend had an old man and a woman. You bring me an old man, a boy, and a Japanese mongrel."

Ryan's ears pounded. He needed to get Kai into the house.

John shuffled forward, his hands suddenly steady and his jaw determined. He leaned across Ryan and laid a hand across the Kachin man's back, whispering in his ear.

The Kachin man's eyes widened. He nodded once and moved into his cooking room. "I will take you in on behalf of Karai Kasang's servant and the food promised."

Ryan had no idea what had changed the man's mind, but Ryan wasn't about to question it. He signaled for Utagawa.

Utagawa dug through his pack and handed Ryan a sock of uncooked rice and several sun-dried fish—half the rations they had left. Hopefully, they could catch more fish in the river or reach Tagap Ga before starving. The sacrifice was worth it to ensure Kai's care, but he still didn't trust the Kachin.

"We're not giving it to you yet." Ryan stretched tall, his head nearly touching the thatched roof as he stared at the Kachin man. "We also need a healer or at least the help of one of the village women to treat the girl."

The man studied John, then the cross hanging above the altar shelf. "For you, jaiwa of Karai Kasang. My daughter will assist you. Your Dr. Seagrave trained her. Even the Japanese leave her alone because of her healing hands, not that we haven't felt the sting of their coming." His scowl strayed pointedly to Utagawa. "Bring the girl here."

Ryan deposited the sock next to three dried fish on the low table and followed the Kachin into the claustrophobic heat of the main part of the house. If the man's daughter had been trained by Doc Seagrave, their luck was improving. Doc had grown up in Burma as a missionary and then was recruited to help the Allies. Fact was, Doc was a miracle worker. And the native nurses he trained were better than some stateside doctors.

The Kachin man brushed through the open door of the front room. Breathy sounds of sleep filled the dark basha and called to Ryan. How he longed to curl into a corner and sleep for a month, a week—he'd even settle for a full night.

Bending low, the man touched the hand of a woman lying behind the smaller form of a child. "Roi Ji," he whispered.

The woman rolled away from the child. The moment she caught sight of Ryan, she bolted, positioning herself between him and the child even as she reached under her pallet. No doubt her hands held a weapon.

Ryan shifted Kai to hold out his weaponless hands and bent his head in respect. This soldier had no desire to fight.

"It is a woman," the man whispered, his hands out, placating her. "The American has medicine and food to trade."

Roi Ji sat up warily. By the light of the small fire, Ryan saw the tissue on the woman's cheek was a twisted, melted mask. Fire had nearly consumed her. What had happened? How had she survived?

Ryan realized he was gaping. "I'm sorr—"

Roi Ji's fingers wandered to her burned skin before she lifted her chin, her gaze scathing. She signaled Ryan to lay his burden on a pallet at the far side of the room. As Ryan knelt and nestled Kai onto the pallet, the nurse stood tall, refusing to bow to Ryan. She would not accept his apologies, but she would help.

Watching the woman collect bandages and salves from a basket in the corner, Ryan couldn't help but wonder if Kai would recover as well as this Kachin woman. If any of them could recover.

Ryan brushed his fingers across the small patch of skin on Kai's shoulder that didn't bear a mark of brutality and clenched his jaw against the emotion climbing his throat. His precious Kailyn.

Roi Ji lifted a haughty eyebrow at Ryan. In answer, Ryan clicked on a small flashlight and handed it to the woman. When the beam captured Kai in its light, Roi Ji gasped, and the flashlight tumbled to the bamboo floor, plunging the room into a distorted darkness. Ryan bent and retrieved the light, handing it back to the nurse.

"Please do what you can. She is a friend."

The woman gaped at Ryan, no doubt because he spoke in her language. Her one good eye searched his face. The other eye wandered, lost in clouded blindness.

"I no medicine here," she answered in halting English.

Ryan answered, again in Kachin. "I have medicine, and I will find water if you need it."

Roi Ji touched Kai's arms with long, smooth fingers. "She must be brave." She traced the scars on Kai's arms, wincing at the slashes there. "And scared."

"We all are."

The woman nodded, her eyes finally meeting his. "Some of us just see the light more clearly than others," she answered, picking up his hand and placing it on Kai's shoulder. "She needs you to find it again, and then, in time, to show it to her."

"How did you—"

She dropped her hand, the spell broken. "There is water in the cooking room. Boil it first. My father will get more. It is not safe for you to come and go. Karai Kasang brought you here. We will hide you as long as we can."

≈

Ryan staggered out of the front room, grateful to leave Kai in capable hands. Scrubbing his fingers down his cheeks, Ryan slapped them once for good measure. He wished he could find as much hope as the Kachin woman had. Kai needed someone to help her through the coming days, and he was obviously not up to the task.

First things first. For now Roi Ji needed the water more than Ryan needed sleep. Though much longer and his decisions might not be entirely rational.

In the cooking room, John slept in the corner, his breathing raspy but steady.

Utagawa squatted next to the fire and carefully lifted a pot off the iron hook with a covered hand. "Bring this while I start more."

"Thank you." Ryan's voice broke.

Utagawa's hands stopped their work. "Everyone looks to you. But you cannot carry everything or everyone all the time. If you try, you will break. And where would that leave those who depend on you? Go rest. I will help. These people will help. The one who conquered death"—he pointed to the cross—"will help too. We are not alone."

Not alone. Studying Utagawa's dark eyes, Ryan realized how much the man had sacrificed for strangers. His job, his pride. And it wasn't just his life at risk. The army would threaten his parents, his siblings, anyone he cared about because he had helped the Allies.

"Thank you, Utagawa."

Utagawa grunted. "My choice came too late for many. I am able to assist you because of your Pastor John." He gestured to John. "He saw the good in me and the sadness at what I had done. He was a light while we both were in a very dark place. He is named well, your Jungle Light."

"But he left his family vulnerable."

"As have I." Utagawa heaved another pot of water over the fire.

"Many who do great things also sacrifice great things. I do not pretend to understand. But I wish. I wish it had been different." His hands paused, and he stared into the fire. "I wish John never had reason to leave home. I wish I never found myself in Burma, let alone your village."

And I wish I'd never let Kai think I'd leave her. The jungle insects chirped, filling the silence.

"I suppose we've all made our mistakes, but you, at least, are doing what you can." Ryan gestured to the pots.

Utagawa handed Ryan the scrap of cloth to protect his hand from the metal pot handle. "If someone had done to my village what I did to yours . . . I do not blame her for her anger. I just pray it will not be too late for her."

Ryan forced a smile, but the twin barbed thorns of fear and anger pierced his core. He shook his head free. She would heal. He had to believe that. And Ryan, too, would find a way to forgive Utagawa for what he'd done.

He took the pot, along with a packet of sulfa antibiotic powder, and lugged them down the hall, the decaying bamboo sinking with each footfall.

His hand poised to knock, he heard Roi Ji's whispers. The Kachin woman squatted next to Kai's still form, rocking to the rhythm of her words, as if she held a babe in her arms, her fingers gliding over Kai's face. The flashlight at her feet gave Roi Ji a luminous, otherworldly look. Her rhythmic words formed a prayer.

"Have mercy on us. Give strength unto thy servant, and save us. Have mercy on us . . ."

Fingers digging into the doorframe, Ryan's lips formed the familiar prayer. *Have mercy on me, your servant. Have mercy on me, your servant.*

Murky waves pulsed in the edges of his vision. "Have mercy."

Roi Ji startled, but when she saw Ryan, she waved him in and went back to stroking Kai's cheek.

Ryan squatted beside the women and placed the water and sulfa packets on the floor. "Use these on the wounds." He touched Kai's arms. There was a peaceful air about Kai now, as if she knew she was guarded. The bloody sheet lay on the floor by the door, and Kai lay under a fresh blanket. It appeared that Roi Ji had even bathed Kai.

"You must rest." Roi Ji shooed him out the door.

"I'll be right outside if you need anything."

"Release your fears. I will care for her."

Ryan nodded and sat, leaning against the woven bamboo wall. But sleep refused to come. In the room, Roi Ji shuffled, a constant, humming lullaby on her lips, the gentle splash of water. Sounds of home.

Ryan tucked his knees under his chin. Why had he ever come to Burma?

Kai was hurt and Trace dead . . . because of him. He had failed as a soldier as surely as he had failed as a missionary. Nothing he did helped the Kachin people. He hadn't been able to stop the attacks on the villages. Or Kai from running. He hadn't even protected her from what had happened since. Everyone who had ever depended on him had paid the price for his inadequacies. And now their little quartet was depending on him. In the middle of enemy territory, with a mission to complete, with sick, injured, and untrained. The responsibility was too much.

God had allowed the Japanese soldiers to destroy Tingrabum. If he chose not to intervene for a village full of innocents, why should Ryan trust him now? But it wasn't God who'd wielded death. It was the Japanese. It was Utagawa. Ryan clenched his fists around the edges of his temper. Yes, Utagawa had held Tu Lum, but he also regretted what he'd done and was trying to make amends. Ryan sucked in a shaking breath, desperately trying to gather his fractured thoughts into line.

A circle of light bounced across Ryan's legs, and soft footsteps approached.

Ryan knew Utagawa stood above him holding a candle. But Ryan refused to acknowledge the other man as he inhaled rapidly, desperate to regain control. The other soldier eased next to Ryan and stared into the sullen flame as it pulsed with the breeze.

Ryan's nose flared. He wanted to curse the man. Throw him out. Destroy him. It would have been easy to blame everything on him.

Easy, but not right. Utagawa was caught as much as Ryan. Evil was winning the fight, and God hadn't shown up. God's seeming failure wasn't Utagawa's fault.

Utagawa leaned his head against the wall and exhaled. "Do you ever wonder why evil doesn't stop?"

How had the man guessed his thoughts?

His surprise must have shown, because Utagawa chuckled. "You think you are the only man to wonder what good faith is?" Utagawa handed Ryan a scrap of worn handkerchief and smiled, the dark circles under his eyes lifting for a moment.

Ryan watched the wax drip off the candle, eaten and destroyed by the flame. *I am poured out like water, and all my bones are out of joint: my heart is like wax; it is melted in the midst of my bowels.* The psalm flickered through Ryan's mind. "But I was there, and I . . . I couldn't do anything. And here I am again, trying to save everyone, and there's still nothing I can do. Evil always wins."

Utagawa nodded, quiet as his finger traced the weave of the floor. "You say you could not do anything. But you think you could do everything? Save everyone?"

Ryan recoiled. "I never said I was God!"

Utagawa shrugged. "It is a heavy load to carry, my friend. Even for one with such broad shoulders." Utagawa laid a hand on Ryan, and Ryan resisted the urge to jerk away. "Only God himself could have saved her."

"And he didn't." Ryan knew he sounded like a crabby child, but he couldn't find the energy to care.

"No," Utagawa whispered. "He didn't. But what has happened isn't your fault. You are a good man, making the best choices you can. That is all Karai Kasang asks of you."

A tear escaped Ryan's eye and left a trail of stiffness on his cheek.

"Sometimes I have wished for God to appear. To hear him speak as you speak to me." Utagawa leaned forward, squinting into the darkness, as if God himself might walk through the door. "I do not know

275

where he is, but I will do what I can because that is all I can do. You will do what you can do because that is what *you* can do. But together we can do more. If you will let me." Utagawa groaned as he pushed himself to his feet and rolled his shoulders. "But if we are to continue, you must rest. Roi Ji and I will care for Sharaw."

"Kai. Her name is Kai."

Utagawa nodded and handed Ryan a blanket from his pack. "Your Kai is safe for now."

Chapter Thirty-Eight

Shingbwiyang
Foothills of the Himalayas

SUNLIGHT WARMED RYAN AND TEASED his eyelids open. The pattern of the woven bamboo floor had branded his cheek, leaving it stiff and oddly numb. He felt like a lazy house cat as his mind struggled to emerge from the fog of deep sleep. Groaning and stretching stiff muscles, he rolled to his back. *House cat indeed.*

Utagawa lay on the far side of the room, facing Ryan, still sleeping soundly. Ryan studied the man, the jagged cut on his cheek neatly stitched. A mended tear stretched across his sleeve, and he'd traded his muddy, torn trousers for a borrowed longyi. All the damage he'd earned in rescuing Kai and John. Who would have thought that a Japanese man—Tu Lum's killer, no less—would become Ryan's closest ally? He shook his head and pushed himself upright.

Harsh whispers floated through the air, and Ryan tried to catch the meaning of the sounds, but they refused to come together into words. Roi Ji and her father were arguing. Another voice entered the fray. John.

A pot slammed. "It is my home. I say they can stay as long as necessary." Roi Ji's whisper rasped harsh with anger.

Ryan rolled his shoulders, stood, and strode down the hallway. It was time he took on the mantle of leadership again.

When Ryan entered the cooking room, the trio stopped talking. Guilt bloomed in the Kachin man's face, and anger fired red in Roi Ji's. John alone was calm.

"We will leave tonight, Roi Ji. I would have left before the sun awoke, but my body betrayed my plans." Humor, he knew, defused most situations. Ryan placed another sock of rice on the floor by the fire in front of the Kachin man, and if humor didn't soothe, kindness might. "I know you risk the soldiers noticing the extra activity. Thank you for what you've already done. I am grateful for a night's rest."

The man touched the sock of rice with hungry reverence before smiling at John. "We cannot take more food from the man who saved my daughter and her child from the fire."

John had rescued Roi Ji? Ryan stole a glance at John, who frowned at his gnarled fingers. That explained why the Kachin man had taken all of them in when John spoke to him last night. That Ryan had knocked on *this* door was a miracle.

Roi Ji cleared her throat and elbowed her father.

"You may stay with my blessing." Her father sighed in resignation. "For as long as you need."

Ryan nudged the rice at Roi Ji. "Assuming we can move Kai, we will leave after nightfall. I don't want you and your family in any more danger."

"I would stand between you and the Japanese, as Pastor John did for us. I owe him my life. We all do."

Pastor John shifted, obviously uncomfortable with the statement, as well he should be. Ryan choked back the retort. Roi Ji didn't deserve punishment for her admiration. But while Pastor John had been out in the jungle saving others, he had left his own daughter vulnerable. Ryan didn't know what he would have done in John's shoes, but he knew he would not ask another man—or in this case, woman—to do what the pastor had done.

John groaned. "Thank you, Roi Ji. But that will not be necessary. We will rest and prepare today, and when the darkness can hide us, we will leave. It's time I took care of my own family."

The statement was the closest thing to an apology Ryan had ever heard from John, but he refused to let that bitter thought leave his mouth.

John laid a brief hand on Ryan's shoulder, transferring authority for the group back to the ranking officer before retreating to the front room.

Ryan pushed a hand through his mop of hair, his fingers snarled in the length. *As tangled as this situation.*

And it was Ryan's job to figure out how to get to Tagap Ga with their heads still on their necks. Chief among his thoughts was how to travel with Kai. They couldn't stay. Not with a Japanese garrison just down the path. Ryan trudged through the basha and tapped on the door of the front bedroom before slipping through the doorway.

Kai lay on the pallet, her shredded arms wrapped in clean cloths. Sunlight flooded into the room through the cracks in the bamboo, highlighting the stitches trailing through Kai's cheek, the broken lip. Though she had no broken bones, nothing to prevent her from walking, bruises stained every part of her body.

It was his fault. All of it. *How am I supposed to do this?*

Invite the blessin' in, Ma had always said.

He snorted at the absurdity, but Ma had rarely been wrong. So he ticked the good things off in his mind. Kai had been cared for by a nurse and dosed with medicine. She was as comfortable as possible. A clean button-up shirt hung to her knees, dwarfing her body. Where the Western-style shirt came from, Ryan had no idea. Likely Roi Ji. Being in this house was a miracle.

Ryan sank next to Kai. Small frown lines slashed the skin between her eyebrows. For as long as Ryan could remember, this woman was always worried about something. He traced the lines across the arch of her forehead. At his touch, she relaxed.

"I'm sorry I didn't protect you." A tear dripped onto Kai's shirt, and Ryan swiped at his cheeks. "Please wake up. Please be okay."

When Kai didn't stir, he took her hand in his and leaned against the wall. He should sleep or at least do something to prepare for the next leg of the journey, but all he wanted to do was sit with her and breathe in the stillness.

He hummed aimlessly, his thoughts drifting to Indiana. His little sister. The funeral. Moving through the empty farmhouse. He had been relatively safe, but life was empty.

Perhaps what he really wanted wasn't to be safe.

He thought of walking in the jungle with Kai, the curve of her mouth when she laughed, the way she tilted her head when she listened to him. They hadn't been safe then. Maybe what he wanted was the freedom to live. For Kai to live. But he'd seen enough to know that might not happen. Not everyone was saved from the lions' den.

He squeezed her small, limp hand.

"Please," he whispered.

$$\approx$$

I groaned. Every part of my body hurt. Even my eyelids were sluggish and stiff.

An enormous white man sat next to me. A bushy beard obscured his square jaw and underscored the dark circles surrounding his closed eyes. The broad shoulders tugged his military shirt tight, and legs stretched long told me he was, perhaps, an athlete. The fingers surrounding mine were rough. He was well accustomed to working with those hands.

All in all, a handsome man. But what was he doing here?

He was humming something I couldn't quite make out. "Amazing Grace"?

I rolled to my side, and fire raced across my ribs. I eased onto my back, gasping and gritting my teeth. The humming stopped as the man opened his eyes, his thumb moving slowly across my wrist.

I stared at him. Such blue eyes, like a happy sky. Kind, I decided.

I did not understand why he held my hand in his. But I did not mind. The thought warmed my cheeks.

The man smiled, one side of his mouth curled higher than the other. He had caught my blush. And oh, his smile. The heat grew, spreading through me.

"Good morning, sleepyhead. I see you've decided to join us." He eased to his knees and lifted my bruised knuckles to his cracked lips. His breath tickled my hands, and his kiss on my skin made me want to wrap myself in him and, for some reason, run away at the same time. I could not remember why. Confusion and unease ricocheted through me.

He seemed to know me, but I did not know him. I forced myself to conceal the fear blooming inside me.

A tiger never panics.

The unbidden thought sneaked through me, and a darkness closed around my heart, pierced only with the eyes of circling predators.

I tried to ease onto my elbows, but pain seared through my ribs, and I crashed back to the pallet.

"It's okay, Kailyn. I'm here." Suddenly serious, the man scanned my face. Examining. Determining. Soothing.

"Where am I?" It was the one question safe to ask.

The man smoothed my hair and handed me a few pain pills. "We're in a little village at the base of the mountains. We need to leave tonight. I don't want to endanger these people anymore. We'll find another safe place."

Safe. The word turned my stomach.

The man seemed to sense my reaction, and he smirked at me. "I know you hate that word, but you need time to heal."

Bruises throbbed across my body, and a sharp, stinging pain radiated from between my legs. I considered my wrapped arms, and my fingers flitted to my smarting cheeks.

"What happened?" The words slipped out before I thought about how the question would sound.

The man's eyes dropped. Shame? Fear? Anger? My hand shot to my chest, my fingers finding the familiar bag there. I sat up, wrapping the blanket tighter across my legs. Flimsy protection, but something more than nothing.

"Kailyn, I . . ."

Another man poked his head around the corner, and I gasped, startled. This man was old and bent. The gray hair on his head grew sparse and in wild shocks, like random patches of elephant grass in the flatlands. The corners of his eyes crinkled as happiness erupted from every part of his body—a terrifying contrast to the churning in my gut. I closed my eyes against the swirling perceptions. A flash of memory. This man tossing me in the air, catching me, happy as he crushed me between himself and a woman. Mama.

"Papa?" I whispered, as if the nats might hear and snatch him away.

The man nodded, tears spilling from his eyes.

I gaped at the bear of a man next to me. Ryan.

Then everything smashed into me—crushing my body, my mind. I wrenched my hand away from Ryan's. Pain ripped through me as the memories flayed my soul, and I flung my body closed, hard, offering only a protective shell to the world.

Life was only death. There was nowhere safe. The darkness had consumed me, and only ashes remained.

Gentle hands gathered me, and I thrashed against them. Flailing, trying to escape into oblivion. But the hands refused to leave, holding me, warm. Unyielding, but soft, gentle.

I gave in. Weeping, beating against the chest, pounding, again and again, until I was drained of strength. No longer able to fight sleep, my sleep claimed me. I only wished it could be my eternal rest.

≈

Ryan cradled Kai's broken body against him, her tears bathing his arms, her fists bruising his chest, but he refused to release her into the grim inferno alone. Finding a rhythm, he hummed, rocking back and forth, guiding her into sleep. Maybe there she would find peace.

Kai's breath hitched a last time as her body relaxed into Ryan's arms, the pain medicine finally kicking in. He brushed a lingering tear from her cheek and laid his cheek against her hair. He'd never been so exhausted. Now he knew what the laundry felt like after Ma had sent it through the wringer. Beaten, broken, drowning.

He had no idea how to help.

Ryan felt John watching as he eased Kai onto the pallet. He wanted to lash out at John's judgment but breathed deeply and lifted his eyes to the older man leaning in the doorway.

Instead of the expected reprisals and anger, John was crying. Ryan gaped. There was a time Ryan had wondered if Kai's father had any feelings at all. What in the world was he supposed to do with this?

"Thank you for caring for my daughter." John's voice cracked. "From what Utagawa tells me, you are a good man, committed and kind, and I misjudged you. I thought I was responsible for the whole world, that if I worked hard enough, I could convince God of what he should do . . . and then I missed what was right in front of me."

Ryan grunted but continued monitoring Kai's steady breathing. Words were easy to say.

John bumped his hand against the doorway, the rasping noise grating on Ryan's ears. "Is it true what Utagawa says about her?" John cradled Kai's hand in his. "Is she Sharaw?"

What could Ryan say? He rubbed at the dirt caught in his knuckles, his jaw clenching around an angry retort.

John's chin trembled. "You don't need to say it." John sank to the ground, dropping his head into his hands. "I thought I was doing the right thing. But I shut her out. Didn't I?"

Murmurs lifted from the other room. Utagawa and Roi Ji, working together to make breakfast. Ryan slumped into the sagging wall. "We both did what we thought was best." And they'd both failed her. John might have left her, but in the name of keeping her safe, Ryan had planned to as well.

"All she ever wanted was to be loved, and I left her. I lost her mother, and now . . ." Sobs convulsed John's shoulders, crushing his body down onto his daughter's arm. "I'm so sorry, Kailyn."

Her eyelids shifted, but her dark lashes remained pressed against her cheeks, barring the world from entry. Too little, too late. A tear trickled down Ryan's cheek, his body and mind drained of much else.

Spent, John leaned back, tracing the raised scars that tangled with the bandages protecting the new wounds. "Did she . . ." John searched Ryan's face. "Did she do the things they say?"

Ryan hesitated and regarded the battered woman. "I never saw it," he said. "But I also don't doubt there's truth to it. I found her hurt in the mountains. Even injured, she nearly killed me and . . . and my CO." Ryan studied his hands again, desperate to steady himself. "I'm sorry. I wish I could tell you something else. But you aren't the only one at fault. After you left, Nang Lu asked me to take her to India, and I didn't. I thought we had time and a good plan. But the Japanese caught us off guard. I wanted her safe." Ryan lifted a tired shoulder, the bamboo scraping at his sore shoulders. "But there's nowhere safe."

"No," John said. "No, there isn't."

Ryan nodded, hating the confirmation. No matter what he did, Kai was in danger, and he had no control. He pushed himself to his feet and trudged from the room, wishing the light would fall so he could lose himself in the mountains. He clenched his jaw and then released it. He needed to keep his emotions together and his mind focused so he could be depended on. He would not run away like John had. Somehow, someway, he needed to get them to Tagap Ga, where Kai might be able to recoup and Utagawa could pass on the information about the Japanese positions.

In the cooking room, Ryan found Utagawa and Roi Ji weaving a mat for a sling. Utagawa lifted his gaze to Ryan, his hands stilling long enough to see Ryan's nod of approval before returning to work.

Utagawa had already seen what needed to happen and worked to do what was necessary. He was a good soldier. And his gentle care of Kai and Roi Ji suggested he truly was a good man. With his help, escape might be possible.

Roi Ji crawled to the small fire in an upright crab walk that reminded Ryan of Nang Lu. How Ryan missed the older woman's wisdom. She would, no doubt, tell him to stop trying to control everything and trust that God was good and would do his job. But Karai Kasang was neither predictable nor safe, and the thought of what could happen made Ryan feel as if he'd stepped off a cliff.

Roi Ji dipped a cup into a simmering pot and held it out to Ryan. "I do not have tea or coffee, but sometimes something warm in my belly is a comfort." Roi Ji nudged Ryan's shoulder, making him look into her face. "You do not need to do all things right now, Bear of Burma. Only take the next step. Drink. Then we will plan."

Ryan obeyed, sipping at the hot water. He could almost hear Nang Lu cackle. Warm drink. Warm heart.

Roi Ji smirked at him, as if she heard the older woman speak too. Ryan took a deep breath and smiled back.

"Now come. Help weave a carrier for your Moran Kai while her father watches her. Her medicine will help her sleep and heal. And here"—she shoved a clean longyi at him—"wear this while I clean your clothes. Your Moran Kai will not be able to wear a longyi in the sling and yours are her best option."

Ryan took the tube of fabric with a bow, thankful for Roi Ji's foresight. After changing and handing his fatigues to Roi Ji, Ryan folded himself next to Utagawa and, using his dah, began hacking bamboo stalks lengthwise into strips. The rhythmic motion lulled his mind, bringing him back to Tingrabum and the first time Nang Lu had taught him how to peel a bamboo pole. Kai had stood off in the distance, rolling her eyes at his ineptitude. She was right—he had been incapable then. But he had learned. It had taken him one painful step at a time, but he had learned. He had finally earned the villagers' respect.

His hands stilled.

He would gladly trade the esteem they had for him for a chance to go back and change what had happened, to tweak the timing, to be less sure of himself.

He couldn't. He knew that. He couldn't have known then what he'd learned since. But that was what terrified him. As the minutes marched toward the time they would leave, his mind circled around one question: What danger was lurking in the night ahead of them?

Chapter Thirty-Nine

JOHN WOVE THE BAMBOO-AND-PALM-LEAF sling with incredible speed while Roi Ji's family collected water for the fleeing group. Utagawa distributed food, ammunition, and other gear into three packs, the heaviest of which he would carry. In addition to a lighter pack and his rifle, Ryan would carry Kai. Pack in front, Kai in back. And John would carry the lightest pack.

Watching the activity of the others, Ryan didn't know whether to pray for a moon or clouds. For a place to hide or light enough to see. He rubbed his hand across his face. He needed a shave.

The random thought snapped his attention back. He was losing focus, which wasn't acceptable. Once they left the protection of the basha, everyone would depend on him. Ryan refocused on his maps, once again scrutinizing the details of the mountain pass.

Utagawa patted the last of the packs and stood. "We are as ready as we can be."

Roi Ji raised her hand above Ryan in a benediction. "We will pray for your safe deliverance. We give you now into the hands of the supreme one."

Ryan nodded and prepared to stand, but Roi Ji didn't move.

"May you be content in knowing his love, and there find the trust you need."

Had she spoken with Utagawa? Ryan studied the Japanese man but read no comprehension of Roi Ji's Kachin words.

"Amen," John whispered into the growing darkness. "We will do what we can."

May it be enough. Ryan stood, wrapped his pack and rifle across his front, and slotted an arm through each sling strap, draping the open sling across his back.

John and Utagawa lifted Kai into the sling. Her legs, dressed in Ryan's rugged military-style pants, hung long, and the men slumped her over Ryan's shoulders while they looped the second set of straps on Ryan's arms. The jostling woke Kai, her head lolling. She slapped at the hands, scratching and snapping at the men. John whispered in her ear, placing a hand on her head, and she quieted. Ryan felt her body quaking against him as she shifted as far from Utagawa as possible.

The Japanese man sighed and scooted from Kai's line of sight.

Ryan's muscles ached as he stood, bearing the additional weight. He would have welts across his shoulders by daybreak.

When everyone was ready, Roi Ji slipped into the gathering darkness. In a moment she was back, waving them out. Ryan eased himself out of the basha first, followed by John and then Utagawa. First Ryan glanced at the glow behind the mountains, and then measured the distance to the darkness of the jungle.

They could make it.

"Thank you." He bowed to Roi Ji.

She nodded. "Now go."

He maneuvered around the outdoor fire pit, taking the impact out of his stride to trot as silently as a jungle animal.

He had nearly reached the edge of the jungle, when a red point flared to his right, revealing a soldier lighting a cigarette. In one motion Ryan spun to face the figure and sighted his rifle. Kai's moan stopped his instinct to shoot without thought.

He didn't know if the man had seen them or not. But he could not risk firing and having the entire Fifty-Sixth Regiment converging on them because of an assumption.

A Japanese soldier called through the darkness behind Ryan, and the smoking soldier answered. Ryan tightened his hands on the rifle.

Help. Please.

"They are coming." Roi Ji's voice was tight. "Go quickly."

Ryan bowed stiffly and ran to the cover of the jungle. John burst through after him, but a cry of alarm from the direction of the enemy soldier rose before Utagawa followed.

Ryan heard the Japanese man hesitate, and Ryan reeled. He caught sight of Utagawa lifting a hand in farewell before he ran south and darted into the jungle, away from the rest of them.

No.

Ryan lurched in Utagawa's direction. But John's hand on Ryan's shoulder spun him in the opposite direction.

"We must go."

Three shots ripped through the night, and though Ryan jumped, John did not release him.

"Do not let his sacrifice be in vain. We cannot risk them following us."

Kai's tears trickled down his neck. Her nails bit into Ryan's neck as she twisted to escape the sling.

John laid a hand on his daughter's arm. "Be still." Quiet but firm. "You are not well enough to run the mountains. Let someone else carry you today."

≈

The night blurred into day and back again as the trio hiked into the mountains, carving into the jungle and avoiding the main path through the mountain pass.

John kept pace remarkably well until the coughing spells ravaged him, collapsing him forward. Ryan would pause, torn between sympathy and the dire need to keep moving.

But Kai was the one who most concerned him. Thanks to Roi Ji, Kai was relatively stable, at least physically. After the first night, he had even relented and let her walk, despite the blood loss and bruised ribs.

Granted, several of her wounds still oozed, and her exhaustion showed in how she stared into the jungle, never once checking the strange sounds or patrolling for enemy soldiers, but Ryan was most disturbed by how far she trailed behind him. It wasn't like her to choose the end of the line. She was a ghost stuck between this world and the next. They needed to get her to Doc Seagrave's hospital at Tagap Ga. Maybe the doctor's medicine and faith could revive her. Ryan had little of either left to offer.

He climbed, breaking the trail until it was so dark he could barely see his feet. He would rather keep putting distance between them and the Japanese, but they all needed rest. Traveling exhausted and in darkness could cause further injuries. Then they would be sitting ducks. And Ryan could not afford to let the Japanese capture them. Of course they wanted Sharaw, but Ryan himself knew far too much. If he were captured, it would only be a question of time before he told them whatever they wanted to know—the path to Tagap Ga, the location of training camps, distribution lines. He would be responsible for the failure of the Allies' attempt to retake Burma.

Just ahead Ryan saw a series of fallen tree branches that created a shelter. He sank to a nearby log and signaled the others to stop as well.

Kai sat next to him and buried her head in her hands. Her silence shook Ryan more than any crying would have.

He settled a hand on Kai's knee, rubbing it with his thumb, wishing he knew of a cure for the aching numbness inside him. He was hollowed out, empty.

John sat in front of Ryan with a groan. From his pack, John fished out a flashlight, its light dimmed with dark cloth, and used it to dig out a banana leaf filled with cooked rice. He took a small fingerful for himself and extended the rest to Ryan.

"You need to eat."

Ryan clenched his jaw. The old man took to bossing again like a fish to water.

"We need you to lead us to wherever it is we are going." John softened, and he offered the food again.

Hesitating, Ryan studied the old man. Had he really changed? The dim light gave him a ghostlike appearance, but the gray pallor was real, and his skin dripped like candle wax, preparing to melt off his cheekbones. But his eyes. Perhaps it was a trick of the flashlight, but John's eyes twinkled with a light Ryan had never seen in the missionary before.

Ryan rose, took the leaf, and leaned forward to pass it to Kai. She blinked at him, taking a moment to focus on his face and then down at the food he offered. Her fist clenched, shaking. He thought she might smash his hand and dump it all on the ground.

Then she licked her lips and reached to take a few grains.

John's face lit up. "Now you, Bear of Burma." He mimicked Nang Lu, pointing at Ryan and mimicked shoving the food toward him. "Food always makes you feel better."

Ryan chuckled. He missed the older woman. "Nang Lu was right about so many things." He nudged Kai's shoulder. *His* Kai was what Nang Lu had said.

Taking a handful of cold rice, Ryan let the nutty flavor coat his mouth. His stomach rumbled in anticipation. He took an enormous mouthful and passed the leaf back to John.

"I can't wait to see her again." John took another handful of rice before thrusting the food at Ryan.

Kai stiffened. The rice became a hard ball in Ryan's throat, and he choked down the food, coughing. John had entered a minefield.

"Be gentle," Ryan whispered to her.

"Gentle, like he was with me?" Kai snarled low and hard. "When he refused to talk about Mama? Pretended she never existed?" Her voice rose, wild, out of control. "Or maybe when he pawned me off on neighbors while he rode around the mountains, savior to the world?" she snapped, turning on John. "You don't know what happened to any of us while you played trail guide to the Japanese. Aunt Nang Lu is dead. She died a horrible death, filth pouring out of her. We tried everything to save her, but Karai Kasang didn't see fit to come help." Kai's hands were fists at her sides. "Just like you weren't there to help me. Ever." Kai sprang to her feet, stumbling and listing before sinking back onto the log, her legs betraying her fatigue. "I think I'll go to sleep now, if you don't mind." Her eyes fixed on her hands clenching and unclenching in her lap.

Ryan ducked his head, laying the bamboo mat that had been her sling under the branches and spreading a blanket over it. Worry niggled in his mind. A cornered tiger was dangerous, especially when injured.

Ryan signaled to Kai, and she crawled to the mat, yanked the blanket over herself, and rolled away from the men. All Ryan wanted to do was lie next to her and ignore the missionary and the anger he raised too. But someone had to keep watch on the jungle, standing between it and everyone else. So he stalked back and planted himself on the log.

John shifted in the darkness and tucked the flashlight into his pack. The darkness was complete for a moment, and Ryan held still until his sight adjusted. He took another bite of food, concentrating on the banana leaf like it contained the answers to life.

John cleared his throat, opened his mouth, then closed it before opening it again. "Utagawa told me about the boy and the duwa. I didn't know Nang Lu had died too. I am sorry I left you both with so much."

A deep sigh escaped Ryan's lips, and he rubbed his knuckles against his longyi. The texture of the weave burned against his fingers.

"You carry a heavy burden," John said.

Ryan lifted his head, bracing for a lecture he didn't have the energy to defend himself against. But John's eyes were soft, understanding.

"None of this is your fault."

"That's what people tell me."

"But you still feel responsible."

Ryan searched the other man's expression for condescension before nodding. "Trace is dead because of me. And I couldn't protect her. No matter how hard I tried, I couldn't . . ."

John chuckled. "If I know my daughter, she did not allow you to do much protecting."

"Well, whose fault is it, then?"

"She wasn't a child, Ryan. She made her own choices."

"Maybe." Ryan scuffed a toe into the dead leaves scattered on the ground.

"What could you have done differently to make any of this better?" John's hands spread wide.

"I could have told the whole truth. I held back information from Trace for her, and I didn't tell Kai what he and I were doing either. I tried to control everything and made everything worse."

John nodded but remained quiet.

"If I had told Trace who Kai was, he would have abandoned her in the jungle with a price on her head. And if I had told her who Utagawa was, she would've taken off after him and potentially hurt the Allies' chances to take Burma. Now . . ." Ryan wiped his hands down his face, trying to wipe away exhaustion, or maybe the guilt. "Now Trace is dead, and Kai . . ." He lunged to his feet, knocking over a canteen of water.

John grabbed Ryan's arm and then righted the canteen. "I learned the hard way that when I attempt everything, I end up not being able to do anything. It's only when I trust—in friends, in God—that I can truly live."

Ryan snorted, his jaw tight. It was easy for John to say that here and now. He wasn't the one forced into a place of responsibility.

"You think I don't know what it's like to be where you are?" Though the words were harsh, John's voice was careful, maddeningly calm. "You don't think I know what it is to feel responsible for the woman you love or the entire village? Do you forget what happened to my wife? I dug deeper into myself for strength and nearly destroyed everyone."

And he was right. John had lived for years with the responsibility Ryan now held. He'd even watched his own wife die.

But how could either of them trust a God who didn't seem to notice, care, or intervene? Would John still trust if it meant he was recaptured? Or if Kai was?

Could Ryan? The answers he'd learned in seminary were as far from reality as Ryan himself was from Indiana.

"Ryan, I know you are struggling. I know the supreme one seems absent. But he is not afraid of your frustration, and neither am I." John wrapped a small portion of rice in the banana leaf and tucked it into his pack before depositing a rifle across his knees. "I will take first watch. You sleep. You need it before the journey ahead."

As if everything in life were that simple—sleep and everything would be fine.

Chapter Forty

Foothills of the Himalayas

A TIGER GROWLED, SLEEK STRIPES flowing into the tent. Deadly. Stalking. I screamed, soundless.

The tiger opened its mouth, panting. White daggers for teeth.

Light flickered through the tent flaps, and the tiger reared back, blood spilling from its flank. The ground rumbled under me, threatening to swallow me, drown me into the darkest depths. The light stood at the edges of the tent, hunting the tiger.

I dropped to my knees, the ground dissolving beneath me.

My eyes snapped open, and I gasped, the humid air refusing to enter my lungs. I bent my head to my knees, forcing my mind to slow, to concentrate on the reality of my world.

Near darkness surrounded me. I touched the ground next to me. Leaves crunched under my fingers, squishing into spongy ground underneath. The canopy above me a tangle of leaves, not tent canvas. The rich smell of decaying leaves.

My rescue hadn't been a dream.

I relaxed into my pallet.

Drifting.

Frayed bits of the bamboo pallet pricked into the skin of my back, and I fought flashes of memory—the sting of leather cracking across my skin, a knife against my throat. The sneering man grunting above me, his sweat dripping onto my bare chest.

I focused on the tree branches, convincing myself that the rustling in the underbrush was merely the breeze kissing my skin. Sweat broke out on my forehead.

It isn't real. Not anymore.

Digging my fingers into the jungle ground next to me, I moored myself in the familiar territory. Dim light trickled through the boughs overhead. Two pallets were strung out next to my own—Ryan's and Papa's. I wished I could see them clearly, be sure they were real.

Ryan slept on my right. The monotonous sound of his steady breaths should have lulled my mind into rest, but I struggled against the raging murkiness, the knowledge that something else hovered just out of my reach.

A hunched shape shifted beyond Ryan, closing off the entrance to our hideaway with a familiar profile. Papa. He was on watch a dozen steps from where I sat. He wouldn't let anyone through. Would he? Or would he leave again when I needed him most?

But how had he found us again? I snared the tail of my unease. My niggling sense of dread wasn't because of something but someone. Another man. A Japanese man. My hands shook.

Utagawa. He had been there.

I grasped the bag with my stones, the button, my anchors. But I remembered the gunshots, and I knew what they meant. Knew Utagawa had sacrificed himself for my freedom. Clutching the button was pointless. How could I burn for revenge when my enemy had laid down his life for mine?

A twig snapped in the darkness. I wrapped my arms around myself, breathing in rhythm with Ryan, trying to summon calm.

Ryan would never sleep if we were in danger. He'd proven that when he came back for me. But he was so tired.

I crawled forward until I felt the corner of the pallet Ryan had made from bamboo stalks. I was desperate to wake him, to talk with him, his arm around me, his beard against my cheek. Maybe then I could put my thoughts in order. I unfurled my hand over the warmth of his stomach. He sighed and rolled toward me.

"Kailyn?" His voice cracked with weariness, followed immediately with the steady breaths of deep sleep.

I hesitated a moment, hand hovering over his solid ribs, and then folded into him, his chest warming my side, his heavy arm draped across my hips, holding me together. I released a breath and sank into sleep.

≈

When I next awoke, pink filtered through the jungle canopy, along with a light rain. The clouds must be fighting with the sun somewhere above the leaves.

I positioned my feet underneath my body to stand and cringed at the debris poking into my soft feet. I'd lost the ability to walk my mountain without leather underneath my feet. The mountain was no longer mine. Sharaw was dying, and Kailyn Moran was gone.

Who was I now?

Colors blurred around me, dark at the edges, and I sank to the ground. A hand on my shoulder made me flinch, but my motions were sluggish.

Ryan squatted next to me, his cold hand pressed against my forehead, then cradled my cheek. My mind slipped sideways, dripping through his fingers. Leaning forward, I rested my burning forehead on his chest.

He was damp from the rain, from sweat. Chill seeped into my skin. But his arms enfolded me, cheek against my hair. Steady. Strong. Deep inside, memory flickered—our contentment, the ease of the time before, my childish longings. Here was the only place I'd felt at home since my mother had died, and I twisted my fingers into his open shirt, forcing myself to respond to the lure, pulling myself into the strength of his body, desperate. Terrified of his closeness. But more afraid of being alone with the haunting darkness, more afraid of not being able to choose for myself. Hating myself for it and yet the roar of power coursed through me, drowning the panic, the fear, and I couldn't stop. Wouldn't stop the raging flow through me.

Ryan's breath caught, and I heard his heart beat faster, my own racing with his, and I knew I was lost.

My trembling hands slipped across his chest, under his shirt. Felt the scars beneath his hair, then the muscles across his back, the folds of his longyi low on his hips. My skin heating.

"Kai." Ryan caught my hands and stilled them, easing me away from him, his eyelids drawn low, dark clouds skidding across his blue eyes.

I dropped my hands to my lap. The heat of shame scorched my cheeks. I had misunderstood.

Jumping to my feet, I mumbled an apology.

Ryan caught my arm. "That isn't what I meant." Exasperation tinged his words. "Kailyn." He curled me into him, his hands tangling in my hair, running the length of my arm. "I can't."

And that was the way of it. As much as I wanted to be, I could never be his. The jungle whispered a cackle, the jaiwa's prophecy fulfilled.

"I understand." And I did. He was an officer, a missionary. And I had rejected him, the remnants of Tingrabum, then bound myself to Sharaw. The legend was coming to pass. Broken and alone, mere ashes in the darkness.

"Kailyn?"

"I'm fine." My throat strangled at the lie. His responsibility for me was more than fulfilled.

Ryan's brows drew together. "I'm not. I mean I—"

"Ryan, I'm fine." The words bit even my own ears, and his hand dropped to his side with a sigh.

"I'm going for firewood. Your father is just on the other side of those trees if you need something."

I lifted a shoulder and dug through my pack for breakfast. A tear dripped onto my hand.

Ryan hesitated a moment before trudging away.

I dropped my pack and slumped against the tree. Ryan's broad back disappeared into the shadows. A last bit of fire ash, cold and dark, floated away after him. I shivered, wishing enough of me remained to follow him too.

≈

Papa returned to camp and dug a ration packet from his bag. He plopped on his pallet and tore off small bites of dried meat and chewed around broken teeth, occasionally swallowing a deep cough with water.

I sat across from him, ignoring the place where Ryan had gone, studying Papa instead. A scraggly beard grew between the scars on his chin. Gray had hijacked what was left of his dark hair. And he was so skinny, his ragged clothes hung off his body, held together with a frayed rope.

Part of me felt sorry for the wretched man. The Japanese were not known for treating prisoners kindly. I should know.

Papa continued to eat, mumbling to himself and laughing at the spitting sky as he chewed. He was slightly unhinged. How long had he been a prisoner? Had he helped Baw Gun lead the Japanese to Tingrabum?

He caught me staring, and his lips curved up.

No. Papa had his faults, but I could not believe he would betray Tingrabum. I dragged a finger through the decaying leaves at my feet. He might not have led the Japanese to us, but that didn't mean it was wise to trust him, considering he'd abandoned me.

Of course now that Papa was here, Ryan had no further duty. I pushed away the thought of Ryan's blue eyes. He was fulfilling an obligation from years ago.

My finger brushed against a stone, and I dug it out.

"Are you still collecting stones?"

I eyed Papa, then rubbed my fingers across the jagged edges. *Was I?*

"Do you still use them for prayer?"

Not when there wasn't anyone to pray to. I nestled the stone back in the leaves.

"Don't they get heavy sometimes? The stones, I mean."

I touched the bag around my neck, empty now save the white stone, the tiger, and the button with the name badge. The reminders of unanswered prayers. Of the debt to be paid.

There was nothing but pain left. I scuffed my foot against a root, the edges digging into my bare sole.

"Kai, are you ever going to speak to me?" His question was devoid of anger.

"I'm going for water." I stood and strode into the jungle, grateful for the distracting sting radiating through my feet. This calm Papa scared me nearly as much as the yawning unknown, and I had no answers for his questions.

I flicked the dah in front of me, clearing the underbrush until I reached a narrow animal track, and then I ran, feet flying until the throbbing of my ribs snatched my flight away. I stumbled into an oak tree, gripping its ragged bark, borrowing its strength as pain trickled through my body.

What was I to do about Papa?

A deep cough bruised the quiet jungle behind me. Obviously, Papa was sick. He needed a doctor as much as I did. I glanced behind me, my fingers tightening around the grip of the long knife, fear and anxiety warring with self-preservation. I did not know this part of the mountain, had no pack, no food, no maps. I could not control Papa's choices, or Ryan's. The ache in my fingers sharpened my mind to that single stinging prick. The only thing I controlled was whether I stayed or left. Would I be my father and abandon my only family?

No.

I would not leave him as he'd left me, but that did not mean he could be part of my life.

≈

Careless footsteps fleeing through the jungle drew Ryan out of his prayers. A spark of color flashed past him, and Ryan sighed. He would recognize that form anywhere.

Surely Kai was searching for food and water. She wouldn't be running away now . . . She must realize the foolishness of striking out on her own now. They were only a few days from Tagap Ga, reinforcements, a hospital, warm water, plenty of supplies.

But all of that might not matter to her. Smacking a tree with his palm, Ryan broke into a trot back to camp. Even given the temptation he had faced, he should not have left her alone again.

What she'd wanted would have hurt her more. Oh, but he had almost lost his white-knuckled grip on propriety. The softness of her chest against his, her lips pressing, pleading. Even now his body warmed at the thought. His lack of control, the roar of his selfish desire, was why he'd stopped her. Why he'd left.

What is wrong with me?

She needed his help, not another man taking advantage of her. But he knew he'd made it seem like he didn't want her. He should have talked to her, made her understand, pleaded with her to let him in.

Through the leaves, he saw John sitting next to his pack. The older man coughed, bent double, and gasped for air. He gagged a moment before spitting red phlegm on the dirt. Another problem. One Ryan couldn't ignore any longer.

He would have to trust Kai to come to her senses and come back, and he'd go talk to John. Ryan sank to the ground across from the older missionary, studying his gray pallor. "How long have you been sick?"

Turning away from Ryan, John rolled his blanket.

Ryan laid his hand on John's shoulder, stopping the older man's movement.

"You need to tell her you're sick."

"She said she was going for water, but something happened. You need to go find her." The edge of anger in John's voice was so slight Ryan wasn't sure if he'd imagined it.

"Will you tell her then?"

"Why?" John shoved an unopened can of K rations into the pack and yanked the zipper shut. "So she can pity her old man, forgive him out of that pity? I abandoned you all when you needed me most."

"A wise man once told me that one person couldn't be responsible for the whole world."

John's hands stilled, his sputter of agreement dissolving into a cough. "Using my words against me?"

"Good advice is worth repeating." Ryan buckled the straps around John's blanket. "How much time do you have?"

John rubbed his hands down his legs.

"I don't even know what's wrong. The Japanese didn't exactly bring the doctor around for weekly visits." He coughed again, the bubbling deep and rattling hard.

Ryan raised a reproving eyebrow.

"I'll tell her once I know what's wrong. Besides, it's worse in the morning. Once I'm up and moving, it will be fine." John slung on his pack and smirked. "We make a good trio, eh? The bear, the tiger, and the boiling teapot."

Ryan shook his head. Like daughter, like father. Unwilling to talk or admit they needed help.

Ryan stood. "I'll go find the tiger. Hopefully, she found water. You finish packing so we can head out."

I studied the plants surrounding me, searching for food or anything that might have collected water. K rations were meant for survival and might be packed with calories, but they lacked flavor and, more importantly, fresh water. I paced to a fallen tree that rose out of the morning mist. The stump stood cracked, with the trunk falling away in a ramp to the ground. The remains of the tree soared well above my head, and I clambered up the trunk, peeking over the edge of the stump.

Water pooled clear inside a basin of bark. I grinned. Despite the fact I had no idea where I was, these were still my mountains. I hauled myself up, allowing my legs to dangle on either side, and peered into the water. Starting, I realized the face reflected in the pool was as unrecognizable as Papa's. A purple bruise was turning green across my right cheek. A stitched cut fell from the corner of my eye across my cheek to the lobe of my ear. Darkness held my eyes prisoner, and my lips were swollen and cracked. A clear handprint stood out purple on my throat. I was as broken as I felt. No wonder Ryan had pushed me away.

Before I made a conscious choice, my hunting knife appeared in my hand, cutting a new trail across my arm. I watched in fascinated horror as the gash opened, gaping a moment before blood oozed from the wound.

Adrenaline surged through my body, fingers tingling, vision narrowing. The power of Sharaw leaped through my body, igniting a dark fire in my heart.

Liquid red dripped from my arm into the pool of water. I watched the familiar stream flow. Dark. The blood fighting the clear water, tingeing it unearthly red. I had seen this before.

The knife slid from my hand, clattering to the base of the tree. I had done this before. This was what had happened all those nights. The dreams I couldn't quite grasp were thrust naked and ugly into the day's light.

Oh God, what have I become?

I rewrapped my arm and watched fresh blood wet the cloth. The urge to feel the power again whispered, calling, promising distraction and control.

The sun burst through the trees, and I stared at my watery reflection, but the brightness only pushed my face deeper into shadow. The light was completely outside of me. I thrust my canteen through my image and watched the picture shatter. It hurt too much to hope in the light.

A monkey cried in the treetops, a strange echo calling behind me, and then silence.

I sucked in a breath, fear boiling in my belly. A man popped out of the jungle, and I brandished my dah, screaming. We'd been followed.

Chapter Forty-One

A BATTLE CRY SHATTERED THE jungle rhythm, and Ryan exploded into the narrow path Kai had made. He ducked under branches and ripped through underbrush until he burst into an animal path.

Drawing his sidearm, Ryan slowed and scanned the jungle.

Dappled sunshine spotted the ground. A monkey peered down at him, his chatter interrupting the quiet, covering any sound of retreat. Ryan held still, and his mind searched the periphery, sensing for movement, sniffing the air for a sign. To his right, a figure stole through the woods.

Ryan gave chase. His footsteps thundered loud and fast, sprinting harder than he ever had around a baseball diamond or even away from a bomb. He wouldn't last long at this speed.

Where was Kai?

His mind refused to follow the what-ifs as he tracked the shape, gaining ground. He would capture the runner.

A wild scream ripped through the trees, and a figure dropped from the canopy, tackling the man.

"Stop." Ryan's voice came out in a harsh rasp.

The tree spirit's arm reached up. A flash of light glinted off metal at the same moment he recognized Kai.

"Stop." The command ripped through Ryan, and he dove for the knife.

Ryan's body slammed into the fight, hand reaching for the weapon poised in the air. A blade bit into his palm, and he grunted as his body slammed into the earth, twisting with the form already grounded. Small fists pummeled his head, and Ryan shackled one hand with his own and then the other. Where was the knife?

"Kai. Ryan." The man on the ground spoke. The man had a bloody hole at his shoulder and scratches slashed across his face.

Ryan swiveled, his eyes wide. "Utagawa? We thought you were—"

"Dead. Yes, so did I. I led the soldiers south, hoping to direct them away. But they quickly realized I was alone and turned north. They are on the trail heading into the mountains. It's a special forces unit. They're moving faster than we can." Utagawa pushed himself to his feet.

"They'll overtake us?" Ryan asked.

Utagawa nodded, his face a grim mask.

"If they find the Allies at Tagap Ga . . ." Ryan's thought trailed off as he filled in implications. The Allies had already suffered one disastrous retreat. It could very well spell a final defeat if they were found before they finished the Ledo Road into China and amassed a large enough penetration force to push through Burma to the Pacific.

Kai writhed against Ryan, her face furrowed in pain, and he released her wrists with a hasty apology. But the moment Ryan released her, she launched herself at Utagawa, fists punctuating her words. "You lie! You led them here. I will send you back where you came from, you demon."

Utagawa shielded himself from Kai's blows but did nothing to stop her. Ryan again gathered her flailing body in his arms. Even with her feet off the ground, Ryan struggled to hold her. The knife cut on his hand pulsed with pain, but he dared not let go.

"Think what you will, Sharaw . . . Kai." Utagawa's stance bled a sad kindness. "The Japanese still come. I cannot atone for my mistakes, but I have done what I can."

"The only way you can make atonement is with your death." Kai spat, her body going limp, energy spent.

"Your wish may yet come to be." He spun to leave.

"Utagawa. Wait." Ryan panted, still struggling with Kai. "We need to trust one another."

Utagawa hesitated, half turning back.

Kai kicked at Ryan and connected with his shins. Gasping, he twisted Kai to face him, his hands engulfed her shoulders. "Stop. Just stop. We *all* have to trust at some point. Utagawa has never lied to me, and there's no reason for him to start now."

Kai stood flexing her fist, no doubt shocked at the heat in his voice. Fear leaped across her face a moment before her mouth snapped shut in anger. Ashamed of his outburst, Ryan wished for a way to ease her fear, show her that anger wasn't the only way to protect herself. She had once loved with a fierceness greater than her anger. She'd been loyal to a father who'd abandoned her. She'd protected a child not her own. She'd started to love him. Or at least he thought she had.

Ryan sighed. One problem at a time. "Utagawa, will you help us stop your countrymen?"

"Of course," the Japanese man said. "I have chosen my path. I will not go back on it now."

Kai's amber eyes, flickering with fire, stared beyond Ryan. Heavens, what was he to do with her?

"He killed Tu Lum. There is no forgiveness for him." She would burn him alive with her anger if she could.

"Kai." Ryan struggled for a way to talk to her, penetrate her protective shell. She understood anger, but was it what she needed? Ryan took a deep breath. Gentle it was. "Kailyn. He saved your life. Twice."

Her unaffected eyes wandered over Ryan's shoulders. "How did he escape?"

That was a good question. He turned to Utagawa.

"Roi Ji," Utagawa said, his low voice cracked. "She followed the soldiers out of the village. I don't know how she ended up between me and them. She just appeared like a ghost, then pushed me into a ravine and followed me down. A deer crashed through at that moment." Utagawa's hand shook as he rubbed it across his face. "The Japanese followed that sound instead of us and then found the trail north." His gaze skittered away.

"I do not know what happened. I believe she escaped." His words were rough with tears. "She risked her life for mine, and I would not waste her sacrifice. So I doubled back and came up the animal tracks. I picked up a trail that I hoped was yours."

He edged toward Kai. "I know you are afraid," Utagawa whispered. "Anyone would be . . . even me."

Ryan nodded. *Even me.*

Utagawa stood, his hands relaxed at his sides, dark eyes peaceful. Despite how culpable Utagawa was, Ryan trusted him. But could he trust his own choices?

Ryan took a deep breath and flattened his voice, hoping his steadiness would reach Kai. "I wish I'd been able to save everyone. If I could go back and make a way, I would. But I can't." Ryan touched her cheek with a gentle hand.

The amber eyes flashed at him, held, and then darted away.

"I know it will be hard to trust him, but can you trust me?"

Kai's nostrils flared, her fists clenching and unclenching. When her head bobbed slightly, Ryan relaxed his grip. She would not go back on her word.

"Once we have taken care of the Japanese in the pass, I will deal with him," Kai growled. "Do not get in my way." She whirled and ran into the jungle, swallowed by the shadows.

≈

Anger roared through my body, a barely contained flame that even monsoon rains would not be able to quench. The fresh wound on my arm ached. Perhaps Sharaw had only been sleeping. When Utagawa's face had emerged from the leaves, the fear that had gripped me evaporated like a creek in a forest fire. But as I limped to camp with the morning mist swirling around me, my soul felt dry and cracked, drained of life. The way of the tiger was consuming me. Of course, Ryan had pointed out another path. One that required me to trust, to hope, to love. A way full of boundless potential for hurt and betrayal. Trust was too much to ask. Wasn't it?

Part of me wanted to settle into the strength of Ryan, but at what cost? He'd made it clear he didn't want me. And circumstances had proven he wasn't able to protect anyone. How dare he ask me to trust him?

But I had just given my word.

The bandage around my arm caught on a thorn bush, dragging the fabric away. I swore under my breath and wrenched my arm free. An angry web of slashes peeked above the cloth.

Evidence. I hadn't been able to protect myself either.

Nothing could stop the flames. Anger would burn until I crumbled into the ashes of the legend. Alone.

Sitting on a fallen tree, I dropped my head into my hands. The green of the jungle vegetation blurred, and my body heaved in a silent downpour of tears.

"Kailyn?" Papa called. He was out searching for me.

I bit my lip, willing Papa to find me yet wishing he wouldn't. I barely heard his unsteady footsteps above the sound of the jungle insects as he limped through the underbrush near me. He would need a miracle to find me hidden among the leaves.

"Kailyn?" He stopped. Turned. And walked in a steady line directly to me, as if someone had pointed me out.

I glimpsed his cracked bare feet through my fingers.

He shuffled around and dropped next to me. "I'm glad I found you."

The scratch of his fingers across the stubble on his chin made me think of the whisker burns he had given me as a small child. We'd been happy, content.

"My little tiger. Are you all right?" He set his hand on my leg. It was bumpy, running with wrinkles and purple veins, a scar rippling across the back. Nothing was like it had been.

"I know you aren't all right. That was a stupid question." He coughed again, hard.

I sat rigid. Willing myself to blend into the jungle.

"I'm sorry about what happened in the years I was gone," Papa said. "I remember the legend of the sharaw. I remember what the villagers said, and I know how it ended—Sharaw broken and alone, destruction and ashes in her wake. The story of the man-tiger, it doesn't have to be you. You don't have to let the darkness call the tiger raging inside you."

"It already is." My fingers tightened into a fist. "That's what you don't understand. You're too late. The best I can hope for is to burn some of them with me." My voice was flat, void of the emotion stirring inside me.

"You are *not* beyond redemption. You do not have to be Sharaw."

"Do you realize I've been fighting almost my entire life? That all I've ever wanted was a place to belong? But I've been alone ever since Mama died. At least as Sharaw, I can do some good before I die."

Papa flinched, as if I'd threatened him with my dah. "Kailyn, I should never have left you." Papa's voice hitched, and he shook his head, as if trying to clear the cobwebs of time. "I know what Utagawa did. He told me."

A tear crept down my cheek, pooling with the other drops on my chin, gravity drawing on them until they fell free, racing to the ground and exploding at my feet.

"I am sorry, Kai." Papa laid a hand on my knee. "If it's anyone's fault, it's mine. I know you never felt like you belonged, but you are never alone. Even if something happens to me."

Never alone. It sounded too good to be true. But I nodded anyway. I was tired. Tired of fear, the emptiness, and maybe even of the anger. None of us could control what was happening.

A cough ripped through Papa, and he bent, gasping.

"Papa?" I jumped to my feet.

Each convulsion threw Papa's head forward, blood spraying red against the pile of leaves. He held his hand up, sucking in air. Desperate. My mind scattered.

"I'm all right," Papa said.

I loomed above him, debating whether to leave him and run for help or stay so he wouldn't be alone.

"Truly." Papa took another rasping breath as I edged toward the path Ryan had disappeared down.

"I heard about the Japanese in the pass."

My attention snapped to Papa.

"Utagawa is truly worthy of trust."

Anger crept into my chest. Forgiving Papa was one thing.

"Kailyn. He stopped the beating that cracked my ribs. He stood between me and the man pummeling me with a club. The other man broke Utagawa's arm for the trouble. He was lucky they didn't kill both of us." Papa wheezed, a cough rattling for a moment. "I've been doing this ever since." He pointed at his chest, and his smile fell into a grimace. "But at least I'm alive."

"Papa. You need a doctor."

"Yes, as much as you."

I flinched at the suggestion to leave the battle. "But Ryan—"

"Is an experienced military man who can handle himself in the jungle. The Bear of Burma has earned a reputation."

Before I could argue, Ryan appeared in the small clearing.

Papa stumbled to his feet, his hand resting on my shoulder. "Kai has decided to take her old man to Tagap Ga so he won't hold you back anymore. You take care of the Japanese in the pass."

I stared at Papa, horrified. I had decided no such thing.

Ryan closed his eyes, nodding. "That's a brilliant idea. We can get you the medical attention you need, John, and Utagawa and I can stop the Japanese from discovering the Allied camp. Thank you for being willing to brave the jungle and the Japanese by yourself, Kai."

"Utagawa has no experience in the mountains or with the ways of your OSS," I snapped, glaring at Papa. How could he put Ryan in this much danger just to save his own skin?

"He has enough," Ryan said. "We'll just encourage the Japanese to search in another direction, even lead them on a wild goose chase for a bit. We won't engage unless absolutely necessary. If we destroy this little unit, we risk the Japanese sending a larger force to search for their missing men."

Ryan made it sound like a game. I stalked around the clearing, rolling my head from shoulder to shoulder to dislodge the tension, the fear.

"A squad of Japanese killers won't be playing checkers with you, Ryan. They will hunt you until you kill them or they kill you."

"Kai, stop and think." Ryan edged toward me. I could almost hear Papa saying, *Think for once, before you act.*

"I *am* thinking. You know you need all the help you can get."

"We don't have time to bring your father to the hospital and cut back across the pass. You have to be the one to go with him. Utagawa doesn't know the way." He lowered his voice. "And I don't think you want your father to die."

"Then let me go with Utagawa and *you* take Papa. This fight is what Sharaw does best. I'm well enough."

Ryan rested a hand on my shoulder. When I yanked away, he sighed and walked around me, forcing me to face him. I stared at his chest, unwilling to let him see the anxiety in me.

"Kailyn." When I still refused to meet his eyes, Ryan tilted my chin with a finger. His eyes shimmered, the paradox of a clear summer day filled with rain. It should never be. Shame wrenched my eyes closed.

"I refuse to ask you to be Sharaw again." Ryan was choosing for me, but his soft touch made it impossible for me to summon anger. "Do you understand?"

"Yes." My own capture. Trace's death. "I put you in danger. Put the team in danger." Ryan could not trust me. There was a time he would never have trusted a traitor more than me. I forced myself to open my eyes to see what I'd done.

"No, Kai. That's not . . . I . . ." He snarled, fists dropping to his side.

A sob escaped my lips as I lurched away, not wanting to see him try to be kind. Ryan caught me, folding me into his chest. I stood compliant, stripped of defense, a child caught in her own guilt.

He cupped his hand around my cheek and tipped my chin up. The question in his expression sent confusion rippling through me. He wasn't angry or disappointed. If he didn't want my confession, what did he want?

His eyes traced my cheek to my lips, and his Adam's apple dipped. His gaze flicked to mine, his raw desire obvious. I swallowed hard, rousing the will to push away, tell him he didn't have to be responsible for me out of duty anymore. But his slow lopsided grin pinned my feet to the ground, and he leaned over me, his breath warm on my ear.

"I love you too much to ask you to be Sharaw," he whispered.

His thumb brushing across my lips shot prickles through my body.

Confusion ripped through me, stealing my breath. Warrior instincts screamed for me to run, but my body rebelled, sinking against his solid presence, my cheek against the warmth of his chest, his arms circling my back. The tickle of his beard on my forehead. The strength in his arms.

A place to belong. Be safe. Be loved.

I sucked in a breath. Loved? My mind latched on to the word. I loved this man. Panic raced through my body, and I finally understood why he might want to send me away.

"Please. Please don't go." If he left me . . . if he died . . .

His lips pressed into my hair, his hands cradling my shoulders. "There is no other way. Help me pack, and then I'll meet you in Tagap Ga."

I wanted to ask for his promise to meet me, but I knew only too well what happened in war. A breeze ruffled Ryan's beard, calling him away. I knew he would leave, and I could not go with him. I had just found a new home, and he was walking to his death.

Numbness trickled through me, cold without his strength pressing in.

Chapter Forty-Two

EVEN AS RYAN'S MIND RACED ahead—shoving away fear with tactics, timetables, consequences, and actions—the walk back to camp felt like a dime-novel march to the gallows. He wove his fingers through Kai's, rubbing his thumb over her calloused knuckles, trying to memorize the feel. Kai's offer echoed in his head. They could have run to the mountains and let the rest of the world take care of itself.

She'd been right. No one would search for them. The army would assume the jungle had swallowed them like hundreds of others. But he also knew how evil invaded the world. If people like him didn't do anything, Burma would be overrun, mainland Asia would fall to the terror of the Japanese, and he would be a coward who refused to protect the people he loved.

Why was it that when he'd finally found what he wanted, he had to leave her behind? Ryan watched Kai. Even injured, her movements still flowed like a tiger's. But the anger in her was gone, replaced with an ash-gray pall. At the edge of the clearing, Ryan stopped. He knew Utagawa was packing while John collected water. Once he stepped into camp, it would be done. The decision final.

Though they both stopped, standing still and silent, the stone continued to trickle through Kai's hand—the white flickering between her fingers.

"I don't want to go." The words burst from Ryan, and Kai's hand stilled.

Please tell me to stay. If she asked him now, his resolve would crumble.

She lifted the stone in her palm, staring at it before tucking it into his hand. The flames in her eyes were flooded with tears.

It was the same stone—the one holding her prayer for home, the one she'd left for him, the one he'd returned. "Kai." Ryan fought to stay steady. If he lost control, he would never find the strength to gain it back.

She closed his fingers against the smooth coldness of the stone—a poor substitute for her warm fingers.

"I can't watch you leave." Kai's words caught. "I know you have to go. I just . . . come find me again . . . if you can."

Ryan wrapped his arms around her and kissed the top of her head.

She leaned into him, shuddering. Palms flat against his chest.

"I love you, Kailyn Moran." The quiet words rumbled between his ribs, threatening to rip him wide.

Kai nodded against him, a single tear staining his camouflaged shirt. "Goodbye, Ryan. Tell Papa I'll meet him on the trail." She retreated, one hand lingering, pleading to stay, before she turned and trotted away.

Ryan's arms hung heavy without Kai in them. The odds were against them to make it back to each other. It was far more likely that one or both of them would become another body by the roadside.

John shuffled up behind him, laying a hand on the younger man's arm, and watched his daughter disappear into the jungle. "We'll get to Tagap Ga and see you there."

"Do you think you can stop her from following us?" Ryan ran his shaking fingers through his hair, never taking his eyes off the twisting palm frond where Kai had departed. He would do anything to ensure her survival, even if it meant his own sacrifice.

John chuckled. "I'll do my best. What she lacks in forethought, she makes up in passion. She may follow you if she thinks I won't die without her. But for now she is convinced of your logic."

"Am I doing the right thing?"

John grunted and shrugged his shoulders. "Only God and the future know for sure, but I'm inclined to say yes. If we don't do something, the Empire of the Rising Sun will more easily devour Burma. If I do not make it, an old man dies and goes home. Morning will come again."

John was right. They were the ones who could protect the security of the Allied position. If Ryan had any chance of overtaking the Japanese, he needed to leave, but he stood still, peering through the jungle, hoping Kai would forgive him for leaving again. Hoping he would be able to forgive himself. That God would see fit to . . . to do what? Quell the fear inside Kai? Protect her? Bring her back? Heaven help him. He didn't want this to have been the last time he held her. He felt the weight of the stone dragging him down. How could he move from here?

Just take the next step.

Ryan turned from Kai's path and strode into the camp.

Utagawa glanced up from brushing away evidence of their presence. Curse him. The man had kept busy, and they could leave immediately.

"Where is your Kai?"

The confusion in his question jarred Ryan. Even Utagawa had thought Kai would never agree to leave.

"We'll meet you in Tagap Ga so I don't slow you down." John blinked at the slow drizzle trickling from the sky. "Especially in this." The twinkle in his eye didn't quite mask his shivers.

Ryan transferred a second blanket from his pack to John's. He was more likely to need it.

John collected his pack and Kai's, and after slinging them onto his back, he bowed to the other men. "Thank you for all you have done. Godspeed to you both. I'll inform the Allied commander of the Japanese squad."

Just in case.

John gripped Ryan's shoulder in farewell and then strode north into the jungle. Roaring thunder hid the noise of the older man's retreat.

Rebelling against his heart, Ryan faced south, away from the mountain pass to Tagap Ga. Away from Kai and her father.

Lord, save us all.

Utagawa lifted a rifle across his body, positioning it over the straps to his pack. "Will you be well?"

Ryan missed a step, throwing out his hand to catch himself on a tree. "Everything is fine." *Please let it be so.*

"Your Kai can take care of herself."

How Ryan wished he believed that. But a warrior knew better than to believe empty promises.

Chapter Forty-Three

RYAN FOLLOWED UTAGAWA'S PATH AS they stole through the barely passable animal track heading south. Utagawa glided through the jungle as if the longyi he wore had transformed him into a mountain man.

Unfortunately for Ryan, both Utagawa and the animals that had pushed through the tangles of underbrush before him were decidedly smaller than he was. And it didn't help that an unexpected rain had transformed the jungle floor into a foul-smelling mire that threatened to suck a man's boots off his feet. Though Ryan had oiled his ranger hat and slicker, they were no match for the downpour. All of which made Ryan, the Bear of Burma, feel like a drowned kitten. At least the rain kept the blasted mosquitoes away, even as it invited the leeches to squirm into his boots.

If he weren't so miserable, it might be funny. Water dripped from his nose, and he swiped at it. The only blessing was that the mud would make the larger Japanese force more noisy, less careful. He could only hope to find them quickly and then catch up to Kai. He hacked at a vine barring his way. At this point he'd be happy if he knew where the sinking sun was.

Utagawa stopped and held his hand up, signaling silence.

Ryan shifted his rifle in the direction of Utagawa's attention and eased off the safety. The cracking of a stick shattered through the patter of rain, and Ryan dropped into a crouch, in unison with Utagawa.

Ahead the ground dropped away to the mountain pass where the Japanese were likely to travel. Chatter floated through the trees in confirmation of the company. Ryan couldn't hear well enough to distinguish words, but one thing was certain—there was more than one soldier.

Utagawa crawled on his belly toward the edge of the slope and peered over. He flashed a full five fingers, closed his hand, and then held up two fingers. Seven. There were seven men.

Despite what he'd said to Kai, Ryan knew he couldn't let this squad out of the mountains. He and Utagawa would follow the Japanese until they made camp, then set traps and feints to draw enemy attention south before pinning the Japanese down and destroying the rest of the unit. Maybe they would be lucky to capture their field radio and use it to feed incorrect information to the Japanese commanders. If not, they could leave a lone survivor to report back about the Kachin spirit-men living in the pass.

Utagawa slithered to Ryan and set to work, creating a swinging screen with bamboo spikes. The Kachin traps were brutal but effective. Tomorrow Ryan's job was to lead the Japanese into their path. Ryan closed his mind against the echoes of the screaming men impaled on other such traps and the blood he was sure dripped from his own hands. He knew all too well that Japanese soldiers were little different from him. Utagawa confirmed that.

But the Japanese had proved to be cruel occupiers. If he wanted a free Burma, a quiet home in the mountains . . .

Ryan lashed a spike to the screen. God forgive him. He would do what was necessary to protect the people of the mountains.

≈

I surged through the underbrush, ignoring the thorns snatching at my clothes. For a moment I wished Sharaw would return and burn the fear climbing my spine.

The crown of a fallen tree reached across the trail, and I ducked between the clawing limbs, twisting like a breeze. I was nearly through when a branch snatched my clunky booted foot, and I fell, skidding across the jungle floor, collecting a year's worth of mud on my face and shoulders. Sludge caked inside my ears, and I blew the filth from my nose. Given the sharp pain in my shoulder, I likely hadn't done my wound there much good either.

So much for a stalking tiger. If Ryan were here, he would tease me, saying now was no time for a mud facial or maybe I was lucky that the rain would wash me clean. Even as he redressed my wounds, he would make me forget myself, uncover a sliver of peace in the middle of this war.

My fingers reached to my mouth. I closed my eyes, recalling the feel of Ryan's thumb against my lips. Desire for more erupted, and my stomach twisted. The Bear of Burma was solid, dependable. Even in Tingrabum, he'd protected us.

I pushed to my hands and knees. Ryan loved me. I loved him. But our love wasn't enough. And if that wasn't enough, what was?

I had been terrified of what would happen when Ryan was gone, and I'd run.

Sharaw was gone—for now. But did that mean there was nothing left for me? No way to survive? Cursing, I slammed a fist into the mud. Pain radiated up my arms, and I frowned down at them. The bandages coiling my limbs were encrusted equally with blood and dirt. Worthy of the rubbish pile and likely to cause infection. I unwound the lengths and tucked them into the pouch around my neck.

"What do I do now?" I asked the heavens.

Take the next step.

I shook my head to dislodge Ryan's voice from my mind. I inspected the world around me, saturated in water. The leaves dark. Every sane, rational creature hid in a hole or nest.

No one had ever accused me of being rational. Still, I needed to find Papa.

And then what? I'd promised Ryan that I would relinquish the fight and let him confront the Japanese without me.

A drop of rain splashed onto an enormous leaf and cascaded down the sloping green until the drop leaped, fell to my arm, and traced a clean line along the length of ravaged skin. Papa's hand had rested there, worried for me. This was the papa I'd always wished for.

No matter how angry I was at him for leaving two years ago, I couldn't abandon Papa now. And I had promised to trust Ryan's decisions. That had to be enough.

Squaring my shoulders, I set off toward camp at a slow trot. While part of me scanned for signs of Papa, the other marveled at the beauty of this untouched jungle. So much of the mountain had been stripped bare by artillery—with only the skeleton of trees piercing the haze. But here, early monsoon rain urged unimaginable green. Ferns even grew from the sides of trees, out of rocks. *This* was my mountain. I inhaled the humid air, listening to the roar of rain against the canopy of leaves.

One minute I hiked on a narrow path and the next I burst into an open meadow. I hesitated in the last of the jungle's safety before easing into the open, surveying the perimeter for signs of another presence. Satisfied nothing was actively hunting me, I studied the curve. Where had I entered?

For a moment, the way eluded me, and I berated myself for not paying closer attention.

Help.

There. On the far side, an abandoned eagle's nest lay half crushed under a fallen tree. The enormous construction of sticks and grass clinging to the branches was familiar. *Thank you.*

As I crept toward the broken tree, a crash startled the jungle. I stilled, my body bent, caught in the process of ducking under branches. It sounded again to the north. Without my pack, my only weapon was my dah. I swallowed, drew the knife out, and shifted farther behind the maze of branches.

A whisper reached my ears of legs brushing against leaves, accompanied by a repetitive sucking sound—footsteps in the mud. Whoever was there followed my trail past the fallen tree. With my fists clenched around the hilt of the dah, my fingertips grew numb, and I wiggled them to banish the pricking. Narrowing my eyes against the rain, I peered into the jungle, hoping for a glimpse of my stalker.

A crash, then quiet laughter made me jerk farther into the trees. Not a four-legged predator then. "Oh Lord, you know I'm too old for this anymore."

Surprised, I stood straight. "Papa?"

The footsteps stopped. "Kailyn? Thank the Lord."

More stumbling and chuckling, and then Papa strode into the clearing. I broke away from the branches and morphed into the gray light.

"Oh! There you are. The jungle agrees with you. It has forgotten me, or perhaps it is I who have forgotten it." Papa jerked a finger in the air, as if he'd discovered something important in his incompetence.

I hesitated, a wary jungle animal. Except for Aunt Nang Lu's stories, I did not remember much of this agreeable, pleasant papa who chose to laugh in the face of adversity.

"The others are on their way to the pass. I promised Ryan I'd find you." He shook his head. "I added 'if the Lord wills' under my breath because I wasn't sure I would find you."

Shuffling to me, he guided my dah into the sling at my side and hooked his arm through mine. "To Tagap Ga, please, if you wouldn't mind." He passed me my pack.

I stood flabbergasted. No lecture about stalking off into the jungle? No self-righteous Bible quotes about anger and revenge? "You've nothing to say?"

Papa's bushy eyebrows drew together. "What do you want me to say? You've every right to be angry. The supreme one has mapped a difficult path for you. If taking a moment to yourself makes you feel better, then perhaps it is worthwhile."

But I didn't feel better. I felt like the dragonfly encased in amber and trapped at the bottom of a rushing river. Churning, dark with debris, out of control.

Papa had his back to me, turning slowly. "So which way to Tagap Ga?"

I studied the sky, taking a bearing from the slight brightness under the clouds that indicated the sun, and pointed north.

Smiling and humming a quiet hymn, Papa trudged off, flicking his dah to clear our path.

"Why are you so happy?" My question was hard, accusing.

Papa's dah stopped midswing. "I tried your way once. I was angry and doing everything my way. When I came to the end of doing everything I could do, I realized how miserable I was. I had two choices—be consumed in my anger and bitterness or . . ." Papa lifted a shoulder. "Or choose forgiveness and trust. At some point I realized that my anger only fed the evil. All this"—he swung his hand—"it isn't your fault. You have no control over what's happening around you. The only thing you can do is make a choice about how you'll respond now. Revenge or love. Anger or trust."

I stiffened. "I trusted Karai Kasang once. It did not turn out well."

"Then you will forever be tied to evil, and it will consume you." Papa's smile was edged in sadness as he attacked the jungle with his dah.

I did not understand Papa. He was so settled now. It was as if he carried home around with him. Ryan's concerned face drifted into my thoughts. Revenge or love. Anger or trust. Was it worth the cost?

I followed behind Papa, his movements slow but sure. I let my mind wander through memories of times Ryan had cared for me, where his kindness was stubborn against my anger. How much he'd sacrificed for me. How he'd found me in the jungle after all that time. But he had no more control over the dangers in the mountains than I.

How could love be stronger than the point of a bullet or an arrow? I shook my head, my thoughts spinning through the air like the driven snows.

Somehow Ryan had become stronger and I weaker. What had he done differently? Had he chosen something so different that he could openly trust enough to love?

If only I had thought to ask Ryan before. But now I walked, one step at a time, farther away from someone who might hold the answers.

I had no idea how far Papa and I journeyed when a racking cough sent Papa to his knees, yanking me from my thoughts. At my running approach, he raised a hand and spit the offending gunk into the dirt.

"Papa?"

He shrugged. "It is just a cough. I will be well once I get some of the medicine the good doctor in Tagap Ga has in abundance."

But we had to *get* to Dr. Seagrave first. What would happen if I lost Papa again? I bit the inside of my cheek. How could love set you free when all it did was fill you with fear?

A crack echoed through the jungle from the east, and the whisper of human voices floated through the rain. The animals held their breath along with me. Papa held a finger to his lips, his eyes following the sound.

My pulse skittered. I wasn't imagining it then. Pointing to my chest and then toward the sound, I signaled I would investigate. A finger at Papa and then a flat hand—stay.

I swung the rifle in front of me, tiger-like instincts propelling me through the trees despite the fear clinging to my shaking body. A Japanese force was preparing to flank Ryan and Utagawa.

Chapter Forty-Four

HIGH ABOVE THE JAPANESE CAMP, Ryan perched in a tree. His borrowed longyi wasn't the best choice for climbing, but it blended perfectly into the canopy as he watched and waited. The Japanese unit had sacrificed stealth for the comfort of a fire, making them easy to track. Even small village children were capable of seeing pillars of smoke this size from miles away.

Or perhaps they were trying to lure out a response and others were hidden in the jungle, watching.

Regardless, Ryan had to stop the incursion. He had no radio to warn the camp farther north or ask for orders. As the senior officer in the field, it fell to him to make the decisions. The army had trained him to trust his instincts. But he couldn't stop his mind from flitting north, past the Japanese camp, praying speed to Kai and John, begging God they'd arrive without incident.

Readjusting the rifle in his hands, Ryan steeled himself for battle. He was the only defense between Kai and the Japanese now.

As black night gave way to gray morning, ghostly fingers of mist crept into the mountain. Ryan whistled the two notes of a cuckoo's song before lifting his rifle. He rested his left arm on a tree branch and aimed at the Japanese lookout. He took three long breaths and, on the last exhale, squeezed the trigger. The gunshot echoed through the mountain pass, and the man slumped to the ground.

A moment later, other men burst from their tents. Ryan counted as he sighted. Six targets. He brushed the trigger. Five.

The others ran for cover, shouting to one another, snaking their way to Ryan's position two hundred yards up the ravine.

Just as he turned to shinny out of the tree, a blur of movement below him caught his eye, and Ryan shot again. A grunt and crash confirmed a hit. Four.

Ryan flitted through the jungle, trying to make enough noise to draw them to his position without being too obvious. A shot rang out farther along the ravine, and Ryan knew Utagawa was firing.

Too early. Something was wrong.

A low scooping moan echoed through the forest, and Ryan stumbled to a halt. It had been a long while since he'd last heard it, but the dark voice was a sound he would never forget.

Tiger.

Rocks tumbled below Ryan, and he knew the Japanese were nearing the narrow plateau where he stood. Slipping into his training, Ryan moved soundlessly through the mud, watching for signs of movement in front of him. Jungle plants tucked around his body might camouflage him from the Japanese, but not from a tiger, and he was trapped between the two.

Light footsteps traced their way toward him. Ryan slipped behind a tree. Relief flooded him—the rhythm suggested human, not tiger. He peeked around the tree and glimpsed a bare foot. A native of the mountains then. That explained the ability to mimic the tiger.

Ryan whistled low, and the feet stopped. Slow, measured. "Ryan?"

Kai.

Ryan leaped at her and dragged her toward Utagawa and safety. "What the devil are you doing here?"

The Japanese scurried through the jungle behind them. Utagawa shot again.

"Utagawa. Hold your fire!" Ryan yelled. A bullet zinged past Ryan, coming from Utagawa's position. Ryan shoved Kai to the ground and covered her with his body. Had everyone lost their minds?

The jungle suddenly went quiet, and Kai bent forward to whisper in Ryan's ear. "There is another Japanese squad. I trailed them to your flank and broke off to warn you. My father is up the hill to cover us."

Ryan dropped his forehead to hers, his mind scrambling. The smoke had been a lure then. Was Utagawa already dead? If so, they were trapped like fish in a barrel. What had he done?

"Please don't be angry. I couldn't let them ambush you without try-ing to warn you . . . and tell you . . ." Her voice shook as she folded her knees underneath her.

Ryan frowned at her, confused. She was nervous. Why? Kai eased a leaf from his beard before licking her lips and lifting her searing gaze to his. Understanding surfaced and nearly stole Ryan's breath. She had come because she loved him. And she was going to die because of it unless he did something.

"It seems you couldn't leave me alone." Ryan smirked and pulled her to her feet. Foxhole humor.

A crashing sound broke through Kai's splutter. A person hurtled through the trees, bearing down on them. Ryan jerked his rifle up and swung Kai neatly behind him.

"Do not shoot." Utagawa burst through the underbrush, caught sight of them, and motioned for them to run.

Kai grabbed Ryan's hand, and the three sprinted up the incline, si-lent mountain rabbits fleeing a predator. At the top, John lay prone, rifle aiming down the hill. With Kai's help, he scrambled to his feet, and the group retreated uphill.

Below them the Japanese were no doubt massing for an attack. But for the moment, the jungle held its breath.

Ryan faced his friends, internally rejecting strategies and counter-measures as quickly as they occurred to him. They were outmanned, outgunned, and nearly surrounded.

"There are three experienced warriors here, Ryan." Utagawa seemed so calm. "We will figure something out."

Ryan shook his head. He wanted Kai away from the battle, not in the midst of it. Leaves crunched below them to the southeast, and the group eased into the shadows. But they needed her right now. Before, they had a choice. Now . . . now their best chance was to stay together. They still needed to stop these soldiers from stumbling on Tagap Ga, and they'd lost the element of surprise. Their backs were literally against a stone wall. Given the pace John would be able to climb the rock face, the Japanese would kill Ryan and Utagawa and then pick off Kai and John. A walk in the park for seasoned soldiers.

Ryan clenched his jaw and sought John's eyes. At his slight nod, Ryan turned to Kai. "There are four coming from the south. How about the others?"

"At least seven from the northeast," Kai said.

"I took these from our original trap." Utagawa dropped a bundle of sharpened bamboo spikes.

"Let's dig those in to protect us from the south. They're going to be wary now." Ryan handed John his collapsible shovel as Utagawa dug his from his pack. "I'll plant mines and drive the soldiers into the spikes when you're ready. Kai, I want you in the trees. You can move between the units and snipe what we can't see from the ground. Hopefully, it will slow them enough for the rest of us to prepare."

Utagawa was already digging small holes, working with John to bury a tight row of deadly spikes in an opening between two massive trees. Anyone fleeing to the north would follow the natural trail and impale themselves. While the steep rock wall behind them prevented an easy escape, it also cut through the jungle north to south and would prevent the Japanese from coming at them from the east.

As Ryan turned to flank the Japanese, Kai grabbed his arm. "Ryan. Be safe."

"I'll be within shouting distance. If you're in trouble, I'll come." He kissed her forehead and then pushed into the jungle, praying they would both survive the next few hours.

Chapter Forty-Five

I DARTED UP A TREE and wedged myself against the trunk before shifting my attention to the narrow ledge beneath me. I'd found the perfect sniper's nest. The canyon walls would cause any shots to echo and disguise my perch.

Below me, Papa grunted as he dug with the trench shovel to plant the sharpened spikes at the bottom of a hill. Then with a swish of underbrush, he disguised the poles with low-lying vegetation. The jungle chorus chirped happily, oblivious to the coming destruction and humans toiling under the canopy.

Movement flashed across the trail as Ryan rigged grenades with trip wires and pulls and even buried a few pencil-thin antipersonnel devices—all of which would make it seem a good-sized force was behind the enemy instead of just one man. Hopefully, the legends of the Kachin spirit-men would do the rest.

I focused deep into the jungle. No movement south. I wiped the perspiration off my palms and swept my attention back north.

Never had I been this unprepared to attack a Japanese force, nor had the stakes been so high. It was my fault Trace wasn't here to help. My fault that Ryan had stopped in the village, which endangered Roi Ji and gave the Japanese cause to wonder where we were headed. I pushed away the urge to run from the weight of my foolish actions. People I loved depended on me.

Papa had told me I didn't have control. But if Karai Kasang had control, why didn't he stop all this? He seemed as capricious as the nats. My fingers tightened on the stock of the rifle.

Papa grunted as he planted the last pole, and Utagawa brushed his hands off against his longyi. We were nearly ready.

A rustling sounded behind me, and I heard the haunting moan of a tiger mimicking its prey. My hands shook as I scanned the hillside, all thoughts of the Japanese fleeing. There was a tiger in these woods.

Silence fell on the jungle.

Then it exploded. Animals scurried out of the path of the great hunter. Papa dropped his shovel and ran to a tree, followed by Utagawa. *Hurry.*

I watched in horror as the underbrush beneath a nearby tree surged with the orange killer. The amber eyes of my namesake flashed between the leaves, somehow calculating and untamed at the same time. Darkness and flames flickering. The animal was impossibly huge, its muscles taut under the rippling stripes.

At this distance my rifle ammunition was no match for the monstrous animal. But I fired into the underbrush anyway, hoping to distract it long enough to give Papa and Utagawa a fighting chance to get into trees of their own.

The triumphant yells of the Japanese echoed off the stone hill behind me, their bullets flying in my direction. They didn't recognize the sound of the tiger. Not yet.

I pivoted, putting the trunk between myself and the soldiers. Out of the corner of my eye, I saw Papa slip from his tree, flail, grasp for leverage. *No!*

Utagawa leaped from his tree and struggled to lift Papa into the branches.

The tiger roared as one of my bullets found its target. A huge paw swiped at a thigh-thick maple, toppling it forward into the jungle, catching Utagawa across the shoulders. Twisting. Falling. Papa sliding.

I screamed, firing again and again into the tiger. The predator roared, its displeasure shaking the very foundations of the mountain. The beast leaped and slashed Papa across the back. Papa arched, hung suspended for a moment, and fell, crashing to the earth, still. Silent. The tiger stood over my papa's broken body, swinging its head, daring any other to approach.

Tears tapped my hands, dripped to my legs as I reloaded and shot again . . . and again.

The Japanese burst through the last screen of trees, a cacophony of triumphant noise until the first man recognized the giant head of the creature, and the motion reversed. Men falling across one another to escape, firing at the new enemy, their screams echoing hollow, somehow far away. The tiger shifted. Annoyance skittered across his face before he bounded away from Papa and into the jungle, the sounds of Japanese gunfire and the rampaging man-eater fading. My ears throbbed in the stillness, shattered briefly with a final distant roar, a predator satiated with his kill. My breath heaved, loud in my ears. Sobs choking.

Anger or trust.

But who could trust anyone who allowed this?

Blood soaked the ground where Papa lay, broken arm extended, reaching for emptiness. He was gone. *Again.* Forever this time. I wished the tiger had taken me too.

≈

The tiger's roar had sent the Japanese in front of Ryan, scattering. Screams and rapid-fire gunshots blasted through the jungle.

Kai.

With the plan already blown to smithereens, he scurried through the jungle.

At the sight of the booby trap, Ryan slowed. Unslinging his rifle, he swept his gaze left to right, shifting his focus between close and distant range. Enormous paw prints marred the muddy hillside. A ragged tree stump pierced the vegetation, the newly fallen limbs forming a tangled screen of leaves.

A keening wail rose from the treetops, and Ryan sighted into the canopy as a body dropped through the branches and landed catlike on its feet. Slender shoulders, bare feet, wild dark hair.

"Kailyn?"

Kai swayed, and he leaped the fallen tree, skidding on his knees to catch her as she sank. Ryan's body collapsed over hers, encasing her. No sound accompanied her tortured sobs . . . soundless screams.

His fingers flew across her body, searching for bullet wounds and signs of an attack. "Are you hurt?"

Kai clung to Ryan's shirt, and she shook her head against him. The rifle next to her was scorching hot from repeated rapid firing. It had been her shooting with so little discipline. Panic slipped into his mind. She was too smart for the barrage he'd heard. What had happened? Where was the tiger? The Japanese?

He snapped his head up, peering around the tree. "Where are the others?"

She heaved a breath, yanking at her hair. Again and again. The rhythmic abuse tearing hair from her scalp.

Oh Lord, no.

Ryan turned, and there, behind him, hidden under the branches, were the mangled bodies of Utagawa and John. It was their blood that stained the air.

Sinking to the ground completely, Ryan faced away from the bodies, blocking them from Kai's view. She beat the ground, seeming to demand it rise up and change the past. The sound thundered in Ryan's head.

The darkness swirled, twisting around him, an enormous python squeezing the air out his lungs. He'd heard the tiger earlier. He shouldn't have assumed the sound was Kai's call. Two more were dead because of him.

Kai drooped into his chest, spent, her shoulders shaking against the onslaught of horror. His Kailyn.

Ryan captured her bloodied hands in his, stilling them. His tears combined with the rain in her hair, and he leaned into a tree. Kai clung to him, her nails digging into his arms, sobs hammering against him.

Ryan desperately sought a foothold, the next step. They couldn't stay. The tiger had likely taken care of the Japanese, but the smell of blood would draw the attention of other predators. The animals had gotten used to cleaning up the left-behind bodies of fleeing refugees and fallen military men. He couldn't risk staying long enough to scratch out a shallow grave the animals would dig up anyway.

But how could he leave them?

Maybe Kai was right to push everyone away. It hurt less.

He slammed the back of his head against the tree. *God, where are you? Why do I keep talking to you when the answers are more of this?*

"Help." The rasping voice made Ryan spin. Kai jumped to her feet, fell over Ryan, scrambling upright, and raced to the moaning. She disappeared in the branches of the downed tree, her small frame easily navigating the twisted maze, where Ryan was unable to follow.

"I am here."

Ryan snapped to attention. Utagawa. "Can you move?"

Utagawa groaned, and the tree shook. "I do not think so."

The leaves shifted, making way for Kai to crawl under the tree's canopy. "His leg is trapped."

"I'll lift. You pull him out." Ryan swatted away the leaves until he found the branch pinning his friend. Utagawa was damp with rain and sweat, his tawny skin torn and laced with blood. "We'll get you out."

Please.

Kai bent to grasp Utagawa's shirt.

Filling his lungs, Ryan lifted, his muscles straining. The tree shifted, but he knew the tiny movement wasn't enough. The base of the tree on the incline wedged the canopy into the ground behind him. Just like the old oak in front of the farm had pierced the earth's crust after the tornado. He recognized the shiver of panic rippling through him and took a deep breath. This was not then. The outcome could be different.

Ryan released the tree. Pa had hired a crane with a pulley to remove that tree from the ground. They didn't have the luxury of a crane here, but maybe . . .

Ryan inspected the trees nearby. A large branch reached long above his head. Perfect.

He found the length of rope in his pack and tied it to the limb on top of Utagawa. He measured the length against the distance to the tree above. Not enough.

Anger ran through him, his fingers and feet tingling, begging for release. He couldn't leave a man behind like this. Curses filled Ryan's mind. How dare God make him choose like this? Hadn't they all been through enough yet?

"Maybe we can roll it?" Kai's voice shook, mirroring his own rising panic.

"John's pack." The breathy response came from the ground.

Of course. John would have more rope. Ryan's stomach rebelled at the thought. He had seen more than his fair share of friends killed by enemy fire, by starvation, but this, this was different. The tiger had torn open his friend—white flecks of broken bone and fat protruded through his blood-saturated shirt. Ryan focused on a green swirl of lichen climbing a tree and pushed down the bile in his throat. They needed the pack.

Ryan knelt and rolled John onto his stomach in one quick motion. A single rip gashed the side of the pack. Ryan eased the straps off his former mentor's arms.

"I'm sorry, my friend," he whispered. Ryan dug out the rope and tied it to the length already attached. Kai took the rope and scaled the teak tree, looped the rope over a branch, and slipped to the ground.

"We'll pull together," Ryan said. "And then I'll hold it while you get him out. On three."

Ryan and Kai heaved on the rope together, a bellow escaping Kai's lips. Bamboo fibers dug into his palm, and the rope bumped a slow rhythm over the tree branch. The fallen tree groaned, and Ryan sneaked a peek. It had lifted slightly. Ryan secured the rope over his shoulder as Kai did the same in front of him.

The mud squelched under his feet, and the fallen tree lifted again, this time higher.

"Go," Ryan commanded, digging his feet into the soft earth for better leverage.

Kai dropped the rope, and extra weight slammed against Ryan's shoulder. A crack thundered from above, and the rope's vibration trembled through him.

"Hurry." The last thing he needed was to trap Kai too.

Grasping Utagawa's arms, Kai leaned back, tugging against the grasp of the tree, grunts punctuating each yank, the world narrowing to each inch she gained and the interminable length she had yet to go.

Ryan's feet slipped, and he staggered to his knees, mud slithering into his trousers. The fallen tree branch shook, leaves cascading from its canopy onto Utagawa as he rolled to his knees and scrambled out, pushing Kai in front of him.

The rope flew through Ryan's burning hands, and the fallen tree crashed, the branches battering the ground until gravity stilled the tree, cradled in its self-created grave.

Ryan lay in the mud, listening to the others panting between his own deep breaths. He scrambled to his knees to see Utagawa alive, awake. A miracle.

Thank you.

≈

The tree limbs had collapsed back into the ground, the sighing death of a giant reaching out its limbs to brush my shoulders. Too close.

Utagawa knelt on the ground next to me, hands on knees, face bleached of color. I'd rescued my enemy, but Papa . . .

Bile burst into my throat, and I stumbled away from the man I'd spent almost two years hunting.

Utagawa had helped Papa. Papa had said the lieutenant was truly worthy of trust.

Papa. I staggered to Papa's body and sprawled across my father as my knees gave way. "I can't . . . I can't see him." An irrational sob caught in my throat.

Ryan gently nudged me back and then levered my father onto his back, crossing his hands across his chest. Papa's face was peaceful, watching the jungle canopy. Maybe he'd seen Mama in his last moments. I brushed the mud from his cheek. Cold. How was he so cold already? A shiver snaked through me. Blood stained his shirt, and I adjusted it straight, the pack laying against his side. Like this, you'd never know a tiger had torn into him.

My breath came fast and shallow, the world closing in. How could I say goodbye? Again. *How much more do you want from me?*

I brushed my fingers through Papa's wiry hair, then traced down his arms, weaving my fingers instinctively into his. The fingers that had held my hand not more than a few hours ago, when we'd decided to come help Ryan instead of journeying on to Tagap Ga. The same fingers that had rubbed away the first layer of hurt. My papa. I'd just found the papa of my memories.

What am I supposed to do now?

The Japanese man regretted what he'd done, and Papa had not only forgiven him but befriended the man. Could I trust my enemy like Papa and Ryan seemed to?

"Kai?" Ryan stood behind me. Solid, steady. His arm around my shoulder sheltering me. Warm. Alive. "Take your time." He released me. His footsteps trailed back to Utagawa, giving me space to grieve.

I knew time was not on our side. We couldn't stay long. *But how do you say goodbye?*

Rain started again, a slow pattern of enormous drops, washing away the fresh blood. I rubbed Papa's hand.

"Goodbye, Papa." I leaned down and kissed the top of his head, my hand holding Mama's pouch close to my chest.

The tiny paws of the carved tiger jabbed my fingers. I reached into the bag and eased the tiger out. The wood was worn smooth under my fingers. The carving was the last piece I had of Papa. My thumb rubbed its rounded belly, the raised teeth. Papa had said I didn't have to let the darkness call the tiger inside me. That I didn't have to be alone. I rolled the tiger in my fingers, kissing the tiny head before tucking it into Papa's bloodied hand.

"Take care of my papa, little tiger." Using my blanket, I shrouded his body. The meager burial was the best I could do. My pitiful sacrifice would have to be enough.

Ryan had untied the ropes and stored Papa's things in his own pack. Utagawa was tying a makeshift splint around his leg, preparing to leave.

I retrieved my pack and rifle as well as Utagawa's and slung them all across my shoulders. Ryan wouldn't be able to carry the extra weight and help Utagawa as well.

While Ryan lifted Utagawa to his feet, I wandered, searching for a likely trail off the ridge. I whistled, catching their attention and waited, picking at the bark of a tree until the others caught up.

Concern pulled Ryan's eyebrows together. I shook my head at the question there. I couldn't afford to feel until we got away. Ryan wove his fingers through mine and bumped my shoulder—almost like we were home in Tingrabum.

If I could go back, I would search until I found Papa, save little Tu Lum, escape to India with Ryan. Do something, anything, different.

But I couldn't. The only way was forward. In the distance a jackal cried, plaintive, warning. Ryan's mouth set in a grim line.

"Once we're up a ways, I'll have you walk." Ryan looped Utagawa's arms around his neck. "For now, let's put some distance between us and this." He lifted the Japanese man onto his back and grunted away the pain.

Neither man would last long. And to be honest, I wouldn't either. Ryan's eyes sought mine, and I nodded. We had no other choice if we hoped to survive.

Chapter Forty-Six

RAIN BATTERED US THE REST of the day, making the side of the mountain one torrential river.

Swirling water nearly swept away Ryan and Utagawa countless times. Ryan had ordered me in front of him, presumably to prevent me from being catapulted down the mountain with them should they fall.

My arm muscles burned from flicking my dah to clear vegetation, and I wished for something to occupy my mind other than repetition of my fears—the enormous trail we'd left behind for animal or human hunters, our waning strength, the loss of my home, and the recitation of my guilt—Tu Lum, Trace, Papa.

My body was beyond cold and had deteriorated into a dangerous numbness. Ryan's face was drained of color, and Utagawa barely shuffled his feet.

Still, we pushed on.

There had been no sign of pursuit from the Japanese, but we weren't far from Tagap Ga. All it would take was for one scout to spy the amassing troops and radio in, and the entire offensive might stall.

At some point, the sky dipped toward darkness, and with the sheer climb and rain, we had to find shelter. At the top of the next rise, three dark openings gaped in the rock.

I turned to Ryan, raising my voice just enough to catch his attention.

"There are mine shafts ahead." It meant shelter—but also the possibility of predators. "It's your call." Ryan was the ranking officer, and I would defer to him.

"We need someplace dry." Ryan squinted at the squared-off holes.

"I will go first," Utagawa said through clenched teeth.

Ryan grasped his arm. "If there is something there, you won't be able to move fast enough."

Utagawa rolled his eyes. "Who else will go? I will not allow you to send Kai, and you are the only one the Allies recognize as one of their number. Without you they will not let either of us near Tagap Ga."

"Why are you so willing to die?" I stood apart from the two men, arms clenched across my middle. "Or is it that you don't think I'm capable?"

"It was not so very long ago that you invited death." Utagawa was maddeningly gentle. "You sought revenge, yes. But perhaps you thought death was a way to stop the pain?"

I made a pretense of searching for scat or prints. I would not allow him to see me as weak or avoiding him, but I could not bring myself to meet his eyes.

"I understand the wish to numb the pain." Utagawa limped closer to me. "I know that I cannot atone for what I have allowed others to do . . . what I have done. I do not wish to die. But I would die happily if I found your forgiveness. I would even accept my death if it simply gave you peace."

A slow peal of thunder rolled across the mountain, so strong it felt as if a rock had slammed into me. I set my jaw and looked into Utagawa's eyes for the first time.

I saw kindness there, and concern. Incomprehensible things from an enemy. But was he an enemy anymore? After all the ways he had helped us?

Was it even possible to forgive the evil this man had done?

I swallowed, thinking of the darkness that had eaten at my soul, the things I had done. If it wasn't possible for this man to be forgiven, was it possible for me? Fear skittered across my mind, and I shook away the thought. No, we were different. I hadn't murdered old men and little boys. But still . . .

"You saved my life and tried to save Papa. Was that because of your guilt or because you desire good things?"

Utagawa dropped his gaze. Rain dripped from the end of his nose as he studied the water rushing across the rocks, bits of gravel breaking free and plummeting away. "When I saw what I had done, I wished to die. That night they brought Pastor John to our camp. They had captured him in the mountains and wished to torture him for information. He spoke of forgiving the soldiers who had captured him, of missing his daughter." Utagawa's chin lowered in respect, but he studied me nonetheless. "Something about him drew me in. An openness perhaps. In the end your father convinced me that somehow I was forgiven. But every morning I wake up and still see the boy. The village. The smell of smoke, of death . . . It makes me sick." A single tear rolled down his cheek.

Despite my teeth clenched tight, tears slipped down my cheek and ran away with the rain. Memory seeped through. Tu Lum's arm reaching for me, the duwa's bloody feet, the smell of sweat, of fear, of mud. And then the screams of the soldiers I had killed ripped through my mind, stealing the air from my lungs and the strength from my legs. My spirit longed to flee where my feet could not carry me. Only Utagawa's hand on my shoulder kept me from collapsing and flying away. I jerked from his burning touch.

Utagawa's hand darted from me to his collar. "I can only do what I think is right. And so, despite the fact that I am afraid of never going home, and of my family paying the price of my treason, I am helping you."

"Forgiveness cannot be earned." The hardness in my throat was thick. At least I did not torture the families of my fallen enemies with pleas for them to forgive me.

"I can never do enough to erase my guilt or make me good. I can't even do enough to earn your forgiveness." Utagawa's words were even, kind.

How was he so calm? The peace was more terrifying than if he came at me shouting and swinging a rifle.

"And yet you ask."

"Yes." Utagawa's voice was barely a whisper, but he did not look away.

I studied him, my hand drawn to where Utagawa's button hung in my mother's pouch. The path of revenge had nearly dragged me under. But could I forgive him? Could I be forgiven?

It was what Papa had wanted. If I had any hope of being forgiven, I had to be rid of this bag of memories dragging me down. *Anger or trust. Revenge or love.*

I swung my rifle around toward the caves. "Then I will not allow you to go first. A friend does not send a friend into such danger."

Before either man objected, I ran to the openings in the mountain wall, shouting enough to wake a hibernating bear or a nocturnal predator. Fetching several stones, I threw them into the mouth of the caverns, listening with satisfaction as they clattered in the darkness.

Without turning, I knew the men had caught up to me.

"Only you would have thought of that." Ryan had tried for humor, but fear draped heavily over the edges.

I dipped my head. "It is unwise to stick your head in a tiger's den. I have hunted in these mountains far too long to be stupid." I smiled to take the edge off my words. His fear was the same as my own—losing the one we loved again. It was the reason I'd gone back to tell him about the Japanese preparing an ambush.

Utagawa clicked on his flashlight and poked his head into each smooth opening. "This one"—he pointed to the first—"is small. We'd all fit but be close enough to keep warm."

Ryan crawled in, his voice echoing out the entrance. "And it doesn't seem to have been occupied recently."

I dipped my head through the entrance and confirmed there was no scat on the floor, bones, or other signs of predators. The ceiling was so low that Utagawa's head brushed against it. Ryan did not even try to stand and collapsed instead on a wide ledge that appeared dry, despite water dripping through a small crack in the ceiling.

"I don't suppose we could find some tinder dry enough for a fire?" I knew the risk of a fire, but my body craved the warmth. "It would probably vent through the crack and disperse the smoke enough." I deferred to Ryan but couldn't keep the pleading from my request any more than I could stop my teeth from chattering.

"I think I saw some brush and small branches in one of the other caves." Utagawa shrugged at Ryan, who sighed and clicked on his own flashlight.

"Go get what you can find. We need to dry out."

Utagawa hefted his flashlight. "I'll see if I can find some vegetables or fruit too."

I offered my rifle to Utagawa. "Be safe." My voice cracked under the strain.

Utagawa hesitated, hope lighting his face. Flames burned in my chest and I flinched away. I was trying, and that would have to be enough for both of us for now.

"All is well, Moran Kai. All is well." He bowed low once before limping out of the cave.

≈

"Are you going to be okay?" Ryan knew there was no good way to ask the question, but he hoped it would open a door she could walk through all the same.

Kai sank to the ledge and leaned into him, the sinews of her arm tight as she wrapped her arm around his. "I'm so . . . so confused. I just got Papa back." Her breath tickled his arm. "I don't know what to do now. Where will I go once we get to Tagap Ga? The military won't want me. I have no family left. No home." She hiccuped. "You've always been the strong one. I don't know how you do it. How you keep going. How do you not hate God, the Japanese, everything?"

If she only knew. Ryan closed his eyes against the darkness of the cave, of his heart. The anger churning.

Her fingers tangled in his beard, easing him toward her. Under the pressure of her gentle gaze, a tear escaped and dripped onto his lap. Her hand singed his cheek, setting a fire that raced through him. He should leave. John would never have wanted them here alone. But there was an ache in him that echoed in her—something that held him fast, tethered to her touch. When another tear trailed down Ryan's cheek, she swiped it away, the calluses of her thumb gentle on his cheek.

"Is it bad that it makes me feel better to know that you struggle too?" Kai's laugh was fragile with emotion. "It isn't your fault, you know."

Ryan inhaled and opened his eyes. Her lips curved in a conspiratorial grin. "I know. I keep telling myself that. But then something else happens, and I feel like I should have done something different." He was the one responsible, the one in charge, the ranking officer. "One of these days I'll accept that I have no real control, and it'll make my life a whole lot easier." Until then he'd have to find a way to live with the fact that no matter how hard he tried, he might not be able to save anyone, even his Kai.

Cast from the flashlight, angular shadows caressed Kai's sharp cheekbones. Ryan pushed a hand through his hair, and she caught his fingers, imprisoning his hand against his neck.

"I love that you want to protect us. But, Ryan, if you try to save the world, you are going to fall short at some point. You can only do what you can do, and then you have to release the rest. It's not a failure to try, especially in the places others won't."

As his pulse pounded against his fingers, her eyes searched his, the warm amber burning through his reserves.

"If I'd listened, we would be living on the mountain in a little basha, a passel of kids running around. Instead we're here." Cold, hungry, broken, hunted. Evil swirling around them, sucking them in.

"But there are good things," Kai said. "I've always wanted just another minute with Papa, to tell him I loved him. And I got so much more." Kai's fingers played with the pouch around her neck. "I remember little bits and pieces of Papa before Mama died. His pain nearly destroyed him and then me. But before, every morning he'd tell me to greet the waking sun and throw me into the air to catch the shining ball in the sky. It never occurred to me he might drop me. I trusted him then. It never occurred to me that in his desire to do more, to try to earn God's favor, he could be cruel. I liked having the papa of my memories back for a while. To know he loved me, that he regretted leaving, that he regretted being so horrible." Kai's control cracked, her voice breaking against her grief. "I don't remember Mama much anymore. It's like I'm seeing everything through the morning mist. She's lit in this hazy golden light. I can't hear her or see her clearly. I'm going to lose Papa the same way."

Ryan wrapped Kai's hand in his. Her hand was icy, shaking, yet she never complained. She was one of the bravest people he knew. But he would go to his grave knowing he'd failed her. "There isn't anything I can say that will make it better. All the things people told me after Ma and Sarah made it worse. But I am sorry."

"Papa told me I had a choice. Anger or trust. Revenge or love." Amber eyes regarded Ryan through dark lashes, peaceful, decided. "Papa nearly killed himself with grief and anger after Mama died. Maybe I learned that way of living from him. I don't know. But I know I don't want to wait to be free until it's too late to really live. I want what Papa found at the end, and I think that means I choose to trust."

Ryan felt like his training sergeant had just swept his feet out from under him. "But you shouldn't." The admission ripped at his gut. He desperately wanted to let her believe in him, to borrow from her strength of faith, but . . . "I still can't protect you when it really matters." He held up a hand to forestall her objection. "It's my fault that you were . . ." He clenched his jaw against the truth of what happened, his body vibrating with the memory of her screams. "My fault that you were captured. That you were even in a position to be captured. No matter what I do or choose, it seems to be wrong. I want to pretend none of this happened, and I want to destroy the entire Japanese army, all at once. I want to run and I want to fight. And I've no idea what's best anymore."

He leaned his head against the cold rock, praying the coolness would focus his mind into something resembling a logical path forward. But it still ran hot, frantic, out of control, unlovable, unworthy.

"Ryan." She pleaded with him to look at her. When he didn't respond, she nudged him.

His gaze stuck at the sharp bones of her clavicle tracing to the center of her neck. He could not make himself lift his chin, could not see the pity in her expression.

"Yes, we're here in a cave. But think of all the people you saved. Not to mention all the evil you stopped. You earned the title Bear of Burma by tenaciously protecting the innocent people of the mountain like a bear protects her cubs. You stood, made hard choices, fought for good. What more could anyone ask of you?"

His fears crashed into her calm acceptance, shattering against the truth—he could fail and still have done what he was supposed to. Head on her shoulder, Ryan's cries echoed in the cave, gathering momentum, haunting the stones. Releasing them all—Ma, Sarah, little Tu Lum, Trace, John.

"I miss Papa, and I will always miss Aunt Nang Lu and Tu Lum, and I know you will miss Trace, but none of them would want us to stop living, stop fighting for good—right?" Kai bumped him with a shoulder.

Ryan snorted at the irony. "You sound like your father now. The new one, I mean." He bumped her back, hoping to deflect the conversation. He knew she was right. But where did you stand when your entire foundation had been obliterated?

Her lips lifted into a rueful half smile.

He sighed in surrender. "When did the angry little tiger turn into such a wise woman?"

"When you taught me that love was somehow stronger than hate, when you didn't let me go, when you loved me despite my fear . . . You taught me to love." She smoothed a thumb across his cheek.

Goose bumps rippled down his neck, his arms tingling as he scrambled to catch up, his body leaning into her beautifully strong hands.

She'd leaped over the crater and slammed into his thrumming heart. Regardless of his failures, was she saying she loved him too?

She licked her lips, her eyes flicking down, then back up. Heaven help him if he was wrong.

"If we work together," she said, her hand toying with the zinging hair at the nape of his neck, "I'll try."

Ryan's heart stuttered. She wasn't running away anymore. Was it possible she was simply coming to him, to love him? Her golden eyes sparked in the weak beam of light—an answer to the desire he'd held tightly leashed. Reaching out, his knuckles traced from her cheek down her neck, past the triangle at her throat, across her shoulders.

She shivered underneath his touch. Eyelashes splaying on her cheeks as her lips tipped into a shy smile.

Her controlled consent was the permission he longed for, and he eased her into him. His lips brushed her forehead, her cheeks, her mouth. Delicate. Careful. Her body curved into him, her mouth pleading with him, and he warmed in response.

His hands moved to the back of her smooth neck, cupping her head, pressing into her capable arms. His lungs begged for air. He lost all thoughts but the desperation for all of her. Her passion, her strength.

Kai's shaking hands tangled into his shirt and pressed him back, a happy sigh letting him know he'd been right. For once, he'd been right. And yet her hands still shook.

Ryan blanched, understanding that it was fear she struggled to hide. He immediately released her and sat back. After what she'd been through, how could he have been such an idiot to let himself get carried away? Part of him wanted to hunt down the men who had harmed her, but he'd seen what revenge did to a person.

Trust. He had to trust.

Her frown sent a schism of alarm skittering through Ryan. How could such a small woman fill him with such dread?

"You look rather murderous at the moment. I'm not going anywhere. I just . . ." Kai's fingers twisted in her lap.

"You need time. I know." He kissed the tip of her nose, his thumb tracing the cut slicing her cheekbone. "And I'm not angry with *you*."

Kai snuggled under his arm, content. Her hand smoothing up and down his arm sent shots of lightning through his body.

"And you'll be patient with me. Right?"

Not trusting his voice, Ryan nodded his chin against her head so his whiskers rasped in her hair. They made quite a pair. Both warriors in their own right and yet afraid of a kiss and the challenge to trust. He draped a blanket around their shoulders, shielding them from the chill. She hummed and snuggled his other arm around her body, enclosing her frame within the shelter of him.

"We're going to make it, Kai. I'm going to get you to Tagap Ga."

"It's enough that you try." Kai kissed his cheek.

They could rest for a moment, and he would find a way to trust God's promise to work out even this for good. Ryan laid his head on his arm, content as he kept watch.

Just as Ryan's eyes drooped shut, a cuckoo called and Utagawa's flashlight flickered in the entryway.

The Japanese man hesitated a moment before crawling into the cave, his eyes landing on Kai snuggled into Ryan. Ryan smirked at the surprise stretched across the Japanese man's face.

"I couldn't find any berries," Utagawa said. "But I do have the dry wood and tinder. Perhaps you could start the fire while I search a little longer?"

Ryan glanced at Kai and winked, eyebrows wiggling in overdrawn suggestion.

Kai swatted at Ryan and snagged her rifle back from Utagawa. "We can make do with what we have. We wouldn't want you to drown out there."

In moments Ryan had the wood arranged adjacent to the fissure in the ceiling and lifted the flint from his kit. He hated the liability, but Kai's teeth were chattering, and he could feel the chill dulling his own senses. Getting sick wouldn't do anyone any good. He'd have to take the risk.

Ryan struck the steel against the flint, and sparks showered onto the dry grasses. He blew, coaxing it into a modest fire.

A hand on his arm told him Kai was near, and he gathered her in, wrapping a blanket around both of them. They each nibbled an edge off the remaining dried fish before packing the rest away. They'd be hungry, but at least they wouldn't freeze while they slept.

Utagawa was already asleep, sitting upright, and Kai was well on her way as well. Ryan lay next to her, one protective arm flung over her hips. None of them had enough left in them to take watch. They would have to trust that the tiger's attack had run the Japanese far enough away to protect them for the night. And then he had to get them to Tagap Ga. Because Kai needed a place to belong, and he wanted to be that place for her.

≈

I startled awake. *What was that noise?*

A cry, barely a breath, came from outside. I unwound myself from my blanket, grasping for the rifle beneath me. Water dripped steadily from the ceiling, and a frog chirruped happily somewhere near the entrance to our hideaway. Had I really heard men talking? Or was it a creation of my battered mind, dragging my nightmares into reality?

Pebbles cascaded. Closer now.

I nudged Ryan awake. He groaned and rolled into me. I laid a hand on his chest and tapped—short, short, short, long, long, long, short, short, short. S-O-S. His body stiffened under my hand.

A man's voice, for sure this time, speaking in Japanese. They'd found us.

I couldn't breathe. I was suffocating. I could not go back. Would not go back.

Ryan eased from his blankets, pistol in hand, and stretched to wake Utagawa.

But the blankets were empty.

Utagawa was gone.

Chapter Forty-Seven

ANGER BOILED DEEP IN MY gut. We'd trusted Utagawa. Had the man lured them here? But why? Why would he have helped me escape only to recapture me?

And then I realized it could be a trap for Ryan too. The Bear of Burma was an officer in the Allied army. A prize, to be sure.

I would kill Utagawa myself. I jumped to my feet, but Ryan grabbed my arm.

He eased to his feet, keeping a wary eye on the shaft opening. His mouth on my ear, he breathed instructions. "Stand next to the entrance and wait. Let them come to us."

He was right. If we went flying out of the cave, they'd just pick us off one by one. Better to let them come in thinking we were still sleeping.

I tapped his arm once, the army signal for yes, then glided to the far side. I positioned the rifle strap across my body and tugged my knife out of its scabbard. A rifle would be nearly useless at close range. Ryan eased across from me. He would have to let whoever was there into the mine shaft far enough that he wouldn't catch me in the crossfire. I would have to attack first.

Outside there was a smothered gasp.

"Help!"

"Utagawa?" Ryan stepped away from the wall.

No. No. No.

A thud, the sound of wrestling.

Ryan swung around, ready to help his friend, but I shook my head vehemently. "It's a trap!"

He hesitated, weighing. Pounding flesh thudded. My hands tightened on the knife even as I steeled myself against the sounds of pain, against the memory of Utagawa's pleading eyes.

Ryan burst from the cavern, and I pivoted, following. "No!"

But there on the ground was Utagawa grappling with two Japanese soldiers.

The trio spun, fists and feet flying. No matter how Ryan positioned himself, he couldn't get a clear shot. My earlier hesitation might very well cause the death of a man who'd given up everything to help me.

A warrior's cry flew from my mouth, and I leaped onto the back of the nearest attacker, my knife slicing through the man's neck before he could react. The soldier crumpled, and I landed neatly, spinning a fast punch into the nose of the remaining enemy, separating him for Ryan.

Ryan pulled the trigger. The man's body jerked with the impact, collapsing and tumbling down the incline. Blood roared in my ears, and I sucked in air, trying to clear my thoughts, to listen. Were there others?

Utagawa moaned on the ground. Blood oozed from his lips and the ugly slash across his forehead. I sank to the ground and rocked, clutching my red pouch. We had nearly let them kill Utagawa. Utagawa squatted, spitting blood-tinged liquid from his mouth before smiling at us.

"What happened?" Ryan handed Utagawa a handkerchief.

"I heard them and hoped to convince them to move on. But they had been told to watch for a Japanese soldier who'd turned traitor. They did not even ask for my identity before attacking."

Cringing at my handiwork, I sprang to my feet and flew into the darkness of the cavern. If only I had believed his call for help.

"Kai," Utagawa said, sympathy softening the word as he stepped to the entrance. "I saw what they did to you." He stopped inches from me, careful not to touch me.

"And you rescued me."

"Because I regretted what I'd done."

Tu Lum. I sucked in a shaky breath.

"Your subconscious tried to protect you. They did this. Not you. You, Moran Kai, have done nothing today that needs to be forgiven. But because I know you do not believe me, I forgive you."

As if forgiveness were that easy. I knelt, making a pretense of rolling my blanket.

My subconscious—Sharaw—had told me to not trust, to lash out, and I had without thought. All reaction and no thought. I'd questioned Utagawa. After all he'd done, I'd abandoned him, nearly let him be killed. Yet he'd forgiven me. I tightened the coiled blanket, my fingers turning white, the pain harnessing my rampaging anger. If I couldn't forgive him, what made me believe I could be forgiven?

"Did I ever tell you how afraid I am of thunder?" Ryan snuggled a blanket around me.

The scratch of the wool and the sound of his voice reminded me of the basha in Tingrabum. Sitting near him. Finding amusement no matter the circumstances. Building the airstrip for the miraculous evacuation.

"You love the rain," I scoffed. "You always went outside when it stormed. Papa thought you were crazy for it."

Ryan shook his head. "It was my way of convincing myself of how silly my fear was. After Ma and Sarah died in that storm"—his Adam's apple dipped—"I couldn't hear a roll of thunder without going weak in the knees."

Ryan burrowed next to me. Though his leg didn't quite touch mine, I still felt the warmth and electricity crackling between our limbs. My insides quivered in fear and warred with my mind that knew I was safe.

"When I realized why I reacted and then acknowledged the fear along with the fact that I was presently safe, things got better. I don't jump every five seconds during a storm anymore. And I'm beginning to see the good rain brings." His finger tucked a strand of hair behind my ear. "You just have to trust that it will come for you too."

Trust again.

Utagawa handed me a strip of dried meat from his own pack. "What the soldiers did to you, what happened to your father, it will take time to heal."

The rotten smell of fish on my attacker's breath. His rough hands bruising my arms, my neck. The sharp pain of him—

My hand slid to my pouch. Squeezing it tight, the edges of the button bit into my hands. I focused on the pain there, shielding myself from the ache.

"You aren't alone." Ryan folded my hand into his.

Papa had said I wasn't alone either, even if he was gone. Had he meant Ryan? But no, Papa would say it was Karai Kasang.

Ryan gently pried my fingers open. "What's in here anyway?"

I glanced at Utagawa, shrouded in a tattered army blanket. He leaned away, making a noisy show of packing the pallets and erasing signs of our presence. Considerate of my unease.

Shame snaked through me, and I dumped the button and fabric name tag into my hand. Trust. I'd promised to trust Ryan. "It's his." I pointed with my chin to Utagawa.

"You've been carrying this all this time?" Ryan's fingers cradled my own, and I could find no offense in his gentle question.

The fear untangled inside me, his lack of judgment erasing my shame. "Mama always called me her little tiger. That I had gotten all her bravery and Papa's combined." Rubbing my thumb across the button's insignia, I sniffed. "I don't think what I've become is what she meant."

Mama would have been so disappointed. It took bravery to be kind. Courage to be gentle. Strength to restrain. And I'd chosen the wanton anger and revenge of Sharaw instead.

"You did what you could then." He tucked the button back into my pouch. "And now you're choosing differently. That's what you can do now. Just don't let it weigh you down too much. He's changed as much as you."

My eyes followed Ryan's glance. Utagawa threw dirt on the fire to extinguish the coals. He'd sacrificed so much for me. But I could still see him pinning little Tu Lum to the ground, and the anger flared again. *How do I forgive when I can't forget?*

Ryan lowered his eyes, disappointment obvious. "The best we can do now is get to Doc Seagrave's and hope the Japanese scouts don't pick up our trail again. Utagawa needs more medical attention than I can give." Ryan kissed the top of my head.

Utagawa set the packed bags near the cave entrance and poured water onto strips of our cleanest cloth before he handed it to me. "For your knuckles, Moran Kai."

I hadn't even noticed that I'd cracked them open in the fight. Wrapping my knuckles, I bit my lip against the sting, refusing to wallow, like Papa's pigs, in the mess I'd made. Unlike me, the Japanese man cleaned his own cuts with no emotion.

Bruises crowed across his skin, his right eye swollen shut. Twice now he had let me accuse him of being a traitor without reaction. I studied him as he strapped on his pack and rifle. For almost two years I had kept track of every wrong committed against my adopted people, exacting revenge for each unforgivable count. Utagawa simply let the awful things I'd done roll off. And his motivation was more than easing a guilty conscience.

Even while I'd ignored his plea for help, his only worry was for me. Maybe being brave meant something more or different from revenge. Trusting was infinitely harder and more dangerous too. I felt like I ran after morning mist that constantly shifted in front of me, just out of reach.

A trickle of sunlight broadened in the cave mouth. Dawn was near. We needed to move.

We ate a few bites of rations for breakfast and slid our packs onto sore shoulders. Ryan tightened his straps and tiptoed into the slice of light, rifle at the ready. Utagawa grinned at me before following. I hesitated until I heard Ryan's low whistle. All clear.

I ducked out of the cave. The morning air held a chill, and I wished I still had the tiger pelt or at least a dry sweater from the pack the Japanese had taken from me.

Ryan caught my arm and held me gently. My mind calmed.

"We shouldn't be far from the Allied camp." Ryan brushed his hand through my hair, lingering on my cheek. "Can you lead for now so I can help Utagawa? Once we get closer, I'll take point. And keep a sharp eye out for scouts from either side. I trust you to find the way."

He winked at me before slipping his arm under Utagawa's shoulder. But his timely reminder that both sides might view our happy party as the enemy made my hands slick on the rifle stock. Worse, being this close to an offensive meant scouts and lookouts would be trigger-happy maniacs. And since Roi Ji had altered Ryan's fatigues for me, not a single one of us fit the image of the stereotypical American soldier.

Chapter Forty-Eight

WITH THE OTHERS BEHIND ME, I followed a narrow path north. Solid red rock, scattered with stubby trees and boulders, climbed steadily into the sky ahead. Ryan's even steps and Utagawa's limping ones followed behind me in a heartbeat rhythm. My thoughts were as twisted as the pine trees caught in the brutal mountain winds. Around a bend, the track sloped upward, and I fumbled up the crumbling incline, grateful for the dry sunshine. Using the exposed, rotting tree roots to hoist myself over the lip, I reached back and aided Utagawa to the top. His smile warmed me as much as the afternoon sun.

"Rest a minute, Utagawa. I think we're getting close." I turned to help Ryan, then stopped, the sky arresting me.

The mountains, still camouflaged in mist and haunted by storm clouds, were stark against a band of brilliant sun. Rays of light pierced through the haze and darkness. *He marked the horizon, drew a boundary between light and darkness.* I heard Papa paraphrasing Job. *The pillars of heaven tremble and are astonished at his rebuke.* Heaven's enemies would not last. Could I trust that promise?

I felt Mama's hand holding mine, pointing to the sky. *The sky is painted for you, my little tiger. Whenever you see the sky, remember you are loved no matter what and no matter when.*

Ryan hauled himself over the edge, smirking at me. "Did you get lost in the sky again?"

He wrapped a strong arm around my waist. He smelled of smoke and rain.

Ryan squinted at the terrain. "Utagawa," he called to the man trudging ahead. "Let me lead from here."

But Utagawa continued trudging toward a line of trees.

"Utagawa?" Ryan raised his voice.

Why hadn't he waited?

A shot rang out, and I spun, dropping into a shallow crack in the rocky cliff edge, dragging Ryan with me.

A second shot zinged past my head. "Utagawa?"

"Over here." Utagawa's words drew another shot.

I stifled a scream. Ryan held me fast as I clawed at the ground, struggling to get to Utagawa on the edge of the far side of the crevice.

"Let me go. Please, he needs help. I can't let him die. Not yet." Shocked at the pleading in my own voice, I gasped for air. He needed to know I forgave him. I needed him to know. "The crevice isn't deep enough to protect you. I need to go."

Ryan squinted beyond me, assessing the length and depth of the cleft zigzagging through the bedrock. His swallow told me he saw what I'd already seen.

"He'll die if we don't try."

"There are other ways."

"Like what?"

"Don't shoot!" Ryan sneaked his hand above the ledge. A crack made rocks rain on his head.

"Ryan." My hand traced his shoulder. "If we leave him, I will forever wonder if I could have done something. I have to try. Please."

Ryan rolled off me and caressed a hand over my jaw, releasing me. "Be careful, Kailyn."

I crawled on my elbows, hugging the shallow dent in the earth. Rocks dug into my forearms. Tiny pebbles dribbled into my sleeves. I reached Utagawa and grasped his shirt, sliding him toward the edge.

A shot rang out, and Utagawa grunted. With one final tug, I yanked him, and bloody dirt tumbled over the rim. Bile rose in my throat. Utagawa slumped next to me.

"Thank you," he whispered. A stream of blood bubbled from his mouth. His eyes glazed, fixed on the streams of light clawing at the dark horizon. "Thank you." The last word stretched thin as air, evaporating in the daylight.

He was gone. A small smile played on his mouth, and I wiped the dirt from his face.

He'd saved my life, and I hadn't said thank you. It was too late for him to know I wanted to forgive him. Another shot shattered the stones above my head, and I crouched over Utagawa's body, weeping for what should have been. What Utagawa had tried to show me. He would never have been able to go home to Japan, and he'd chosen to trust Karai Kasang anyway. He'd been happy just to give me some kind of peace, a chance to belong.

Yes, Utagawa proved that heaven would eventually win. But was that enough? I was going to die, and Ryan too.

Please. Oh God, please.

"Hold your fire," yelled a man from the tree line. He cursed, shouting the names of his comrades. One by one the rifles stopped until an eerie silence vibrated on the mountains.

Don't move, Ryan. If only I could wing my thoughts to him. Though I couldn't see him, I knew he would do whatever he could to save me . . . including sacrificing himself.

"I'm Captain Ryan McDonough with the OSS," Ryan shouted into the stillness. "Call sign Bear. We're Americans. The man you shot is a friend. We are surrendering peacefully until you can check our credentials. I'm not in uniform."

I squirmed in the pit, coiling and spinning until I could lock eyes with Ryan. But Ryan only shook his head, pulling himself up so slowly I might have imagined it. Once behind a wide tree, he hesitated, sucking in a breath before his shoulders heaved in determination. Arms raised, he pivoted around the tree into the clearing. A shot echoed, and Ryan fell, his ranger hat tumbling from his head, his blond hair shining in the sun.

I screamed, scrabbling through the dirt back to Ryan.

"Hold your fire, you idiot. Hold your fire!" The curses of the other Americans assaulted me, bouncing around the trees in the distance as I fell to Ryan's side. Blood poured from his shoulder.

No.

I dropped my hands to his wound, pressing against the flow. My fingers sticky, stained red, my tears dripping, diluting his blood.

"I love you, Kailyn." Ryan's breath rattled. "Don't lose trust." A breath poured from his mouth, and his eyes drifted closed.

My scream echoed in my head. Running feet. Cacophony of voices. Strangers pushing on Ryan's body. Tearing me away. Their fingers mashed into bruises.

His body lifted, floating. Chatter drifting away. Ghosts blending with the khaki rock, carrying Ryan . . . Utagawa. Silence collapsed in around me. Pulsing fingers of flame reaching, burning, destroying, darkness.

A bird twittered in a broken tree above me. My hands dragged through the blood left on the rock. So much blood.

Papa had said that even if he were gone, I wouldn't be alone.

But I was alone.

Just as the jaiwa had predicted. I was shrouded in the ashes of my life and completely alone. I crumpled, hands pressed against the ground, eyes clenched, desperate to stop the buzzing in my brain.

The cluster of men disappeared into the jungle. Ryan's arm dangling limp seemed to call me to come with him. The sun pressed my shadow into the cold stone, a halo of light eating away at the core of darkness. Hope.

Revenge or love. Anger or trust. I had choices. Didn't I?

I summoned myself to my feet only to have my knees give way. A soldier stood above me, extending his hand. I ignored him, my head dropping to my hands. They were dead. I had no idea where I would go, what I would do. I was no longer Moran Kai, and Sharaw was gone. I did not belong in Kachin territory or American. What now? The question ricocheted in my mind.

What now?

The soldier knelt next to me, his hand on my shoulder. Part of me wanted to sink back into Sharaw, make these men rue the day they'd shot without thinking, without being sure.

"We all know the Bear of Burma." The soldier sighed. "He's a hero to everyone here. They'll all do their best to save him, and Doc Seagrave is a miracle worker."

"A miracle?"

He nodded.

Please.

"If you follow the medics, they'll make sure you're taken care of. Doc says God protects us up here. You won't be alone."

How did he know? I studied the man.

Ryan had been confident things would work out. He'd gotten me to Tagap Ga safely. I realized he'd never promised he would be with me when I arrived, but Utagawa had made me realize that home could be found regardless of where I was or who I was with. I could, like Papa, carry home with me.

I stood, shoulders back. I would choose to trust like Ryan had. The dark-eyed man stood with me as I held my face to the bright, open sky. A long arrow of white clouds stretched across the expanse, pointing toward the path where the soldiers had disappeared. Papa would say the supreme one was drawing an arrow for me to follow. Maybe I should find out.

I took my first steps on my new path. Alone but not alone.

Chapter Forty-Nine

November 1947
Tingrabum

THE MOUNTAIN NOJIE BUM FELL away from under my feet, a sheer drop into the plateau that had once been Tingrabum. Spiraling down into broken rice paddy terraces, the white trail still scarred the green, the rocks too stubborn to give way to the crowding underbrush. Rather like me.

White clouds raced across the sky into the northern peaks, sending gossamer shapes scurrying across the undulating green.

Winter wind lifted my longyi—red with the bright-blue and green pattern Aunt Nang Lu had once called her own. It had been more than five years since we'd stood here last, two years since Japan had surrendered. I hugged my sweater tighter.

I thought I'd lost Ryan in Tagap Ga. I would have if we'd been anywhere but there. Doc Seagrave said the rifle shot to his shoulder had missed most everything critical but had damaged his scapula. Ironically, that shot, instead of killing him, knocked him out of the fighting altogether. It gave him the chance to work at the headquarters, making policy and directing tactics based on what he knew of the jungle and its people. When the treaties were signed, we could have gone to Indiana, but as Ryan said, *What good is winning the war if we can't go back to the place we love and the people who love us?*

He'd been right . . . and Utagawa too. Forgiveness had opened the door for me to walk home—not a place, not even a person. Home was wherever I was at peace, where I could be the person Karai Kasang created me to be.

And so there I stood, looking out over my childhood, a little ache rising in my chest. Though the jungle had crept down Nojie Bum and through most of the village, the stand of bamboo still stood where Ryan had buried Tu Lum and the duwa. But I wasn't here to visit those graves.

I touched Mama's pouch. Papa had given me the pouch as a way to remember Mama. But instead of trusting while life twisted and turned, I had collected memories of all I had lost. The stones weighed heavier and heavier until I thought everything I had lost would drown me. Voices echoed on the trail behind me, and I smiled, knowing that millstones could be cast off and the ashes left by Sharaw could create fertile ground again.

Edging down the trail, I let my hands skip across the soft seed tufts of the grasses.

I remembered walking this trail with Ryan before. I'd thought him so awkward, but he'd loved me. Had never stopped protecting me. I had wasted so much time being angry, pretending I knew best . . . We both had.

Jumping between the terraces, holding my expanding belly, I wove through the dead rice plants, their heads bowed low to the ground. But rice was growing wild even after the fires had scorched the crops. The volunteer sprouts would save money for the village to use the plants that had reseeded themselves.

Every bit was helpful.

We could build the school here at the high point. I wandered to what had been the center of the village and knelt. My fingers dragged in the dirt, almost expecting to find blood. This was where Tu Lum had died. Where Sharaw had been born inside me. The wind stirred my hair, whispering in my ears. I closed my eyes and leaned my face to catch the rays of the sun. Life had driven me to the point where I had nowhere else to go. And when I finally gave in to trust, I found, somehow, that I was not alone.

A tear ran down my cheek and dropped into the dirt, and another chased it. A small monsoon of my own making.

I dug a hole with a stick. Opening my bag, I picked out Utagawa's button and tucked it into the hole, burying it. The last of the broken pieces of before. "Goodbye, my friend."

"It's a good place to leave the past behind and start again." My husband's words were quiet, honoring the silence of this place.

Behind me, the sun lit on Ryan's blond head, his bushy beard.

He held out his hand, and I smiled, letting him help me to my feet. Wrapping my arms around his waist, I leaned into his chest. His heart beat strong and sure against my ear.

In his shadow, our son squatted in the dirt, drawing pictures with his pudgy fingers, waiting patiently for the rest of the village to follow. I knelt and ran my hands through his mass of dark curls, convincing myself he was real. That this was all real.

At the top of the trail, Baw Ni emerged, her smile deepening in wrinkled valleys. My little John jumped to his feet and sprinted up the thin trail before throwing himself into his adopted amoi's arms.

Baw Ni tickled my son's chin and whispered in his ear as he snuggled into her shoulder. We had come full circle, my family adopted into Tingrabum's embrace.

Here we would make our home and rebuild a place of hope. Here I would cut away the last tendrils of anger and bury them alongside the memories, trusting Karai Kasang to make good grow in their place.

Author's Note

THOSE OF YOU WHO KNOW me know that the problem of faith in the face of pain is far from an academic pursuit for me. At the end of my daughter's eighth-grade year, we nearly lost her to an undiagnosed infected appendix, which eventually burst, sending my family into a harrowing life-and-death fight against a septic fungal infection, recurrent bowel obstructions, reactions to medications, and pain even morphine couldn't touch.

My daughter should have died.

Yes, the supreme one protected her from death, but he did not shield us from an exhausting and scary yearlong ordeal that left us both with PTSD. How does one reconcile her pain, my pain, with a loving God? Ultimately it comes down to choosing to trust. I know it sounds simplistic. It isn't. It's a painful choice that requires determination. But it is possible to find faith on the other side of pain.

One of the few books I found helpful during our tenure at the hospital was Laura Story's *When God Doesn't Fix It*. If you are in a place where you're struggling, I highly recommend that book. When you're a bit further in your journey and struggling with trauma reactions, one of the best books I've read is Aundi Kolber's *Try Softer*. And if you'd like to explore how trust, joy, peace, and vulnerability all walk hand in hand, I highly recommend *Daring Greatly* by Brené Brown. I pray this story has at least oriented you toward a God who is big enough and strong enough and who also loves you deeply. May you walk toward his open arms.

I'd also love to hang out with you and chat about books, nature, and finding beauty even when it isn't pretty. You can sign up for my newsletter (and receive a free novella) at my website: www.JanyreTromp.com.

And if you're so inclined, I would love for you to drop a review at your favorite bookseller. Even a sentence or two is a huge help. And if you have a book club, I have resources—including discussion questions, deleted scenes, and an opportunity for me to join you—available on my website, also accessible via the QR code below.

Historical Notes

TINGRABUM IS PURELY MY CREATION, but the events that occurred there are based on stories of other villages in the Hukawng Valley. Catholic and Baptist missionaries were instrumental in helping the hill people prior to WWII and, indeed, recruiting them for service to the Allies and specifically OSS Detachment 101. The Kachin Rangers—often cited as greatly contributing to the initial US Special Forces tactics—were one of the best guerrilla fighting units in modern warfare.

Tagap Ga was the real location of the Allied buildup before the offensive toward the capital of the Kachin state. However, the push I described actually took place a few months earlier and then stalled in southern Hukawng Valley until a second push in the spring of 1944.

Kailyn, her family, and Ryan are all figments of this writer's imagination. There were, however, many brave missionaries who helped in the war efforts. Their stories led me to wonder what would happen to a missionary's daughter under extreme circumstances. Could this child survive the trauma, let alone find her way to hope on the other side?

A set of brothers, who grew up as children of Baptist missionaries in China and north Burma, were instrumental in implementing the rescue operations for Allied airmen. Doc Seagrave also grew up as a missionary child, ran a series of frontline hospitals during WWII, and stayed in Burma after it gained its independence from Britain. Adoniram Judson, the missionary Ryan's mother wanted him to emulate, was a Baptist missionary in the late nineteenth century who served in

Burma, speaking of love and bringing aid to the mountain people. The Kachin people speak of his positive influence with awe to this day.

As for the legend of the sharaw, many of the people groups in the Himalayas have stories of a tiger-man. While the legend told here takes its flavor from stories told by jaiwas, I invented the details.

I also took liberties with some random details in the story. For example, the poison from a upas tree is quite deadly, but the poison degrades quickly and wouldn't have been lethal by the time Kai used it.

If you'd like further information, there are several firsthand accounts of the China-Burma-India theater available. Some of my favorites are *Behind Japanese Lines* by Richard Dunlop, *The Dogs May Bark* by Gertrude Morse, and *American Guerrilla* by Roger Hilsman. Henry Felix Hertz's *Handbook of the Kachin or Chingpaw Language* and missionary Ola Hanson's *The Kachins: Their Customs and Traditions* gave me insight into the Kachin people and their language. I also enjoyed *Tales by Japanese Soldiers* by Kazuo Tamayama, which gave me the much-needed perspective of the Japanese soldier.

While the CBI theater is often called the Forgotten War, I hope this story of forgiveness, trust, and finding your way home will inspire my readers to remember the men and women who worked together in an unforgiving environment.

To those men and women, thank you for your sacrifice.

May we never forget.

Acknowledgments

THANK YOU TO—

Mom for telling me that WWII did, in fact, touch India, which led me to the CBI theater.

My college roommate for letting me come home with her for the summer and introducing me to the Himalayas. I'm still in awe of them.

Ah Roi Marip for helping me with Kachin culture and terminology (any mistakes are purely my own) and Desmond for putting us in contact.

The Michigan Kachin Baptist Church, who welcomed me into their service, spoke of unity, and proved that they truly believe it. I am honored to call you friends.

Tom from Freedom Films Productions and Darcy Briseno for insight into what it's like to be on the mission field.

Terri Nii and her friend for helping me with the Japanese perspective.

My early readers—Rachel Scott McDaniel, Melissa Vigh, and Sarah De Mey—you are my saving graces. Thank you for digging in with me to find the gold.

My agent, Rachel McMillan, and editors—Lindsay Danielson, Rachel Kirsch, Dori Harrell, and Emily Irish—the Kregel sales and marketing team, the myriad of amazing booksellers, and you, my reader, thank you.

And ultimately, thank you to Karai Kasang, who has it all under control.

"A stunner of a debut novel . . . not to be missed."

SARAH SUNDIN, ECPA best-selling and award-winning author
of *Until Leaves Fall in Paris*

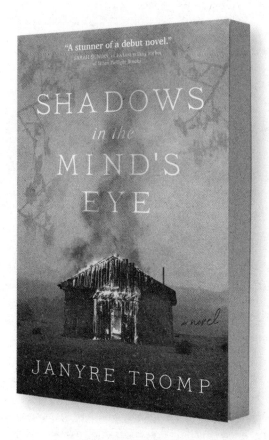

"With alternating points of view, Tromp weaves a complex histori-
cal tale incorporating love, suspense, hurt, and healing—all the ele-
ments that keep the pages turning."

—JULIE CANTRELL, *New York Times* and *USA Today*
best-selling author of *Perennials*